SOVEREIGNS

Sovereigns of Bright and Shadow Book Three

C. E. Page

A catalogue record for this work is available from the National Library of Australia

Cover by: Joolz & Jarling – Julie Nicholls & Uwe Jarling
Map by: Fictive Designs
Formatting by: Enchanted Castle Press
Edited by: Creating Ink – Anna Bishop

Author website: www.cepageauthor.com

V3 071221

SOVEREIGNS

SOVEREIGNS OF BRIGHT & SHADOW

BOOK THREE

C. E. PAGE

ENCHANTED CASTLE
— PRESS —

Content / Trigger Warning

Please be aware that there are scenes within this book that some readers may find confronting. Including torture and violence.

Sexual violence is also discussed but does not occur on the page.

These scenes fall primarily within chapters twenty-three, twenty-four, and twenty-eight.

Reader discretion is advised.

OSMAR
THE ASH WILDS
THE BRIGHT STRAIT
MEDDAR
DENDARA
MAELSTROM
PRAHMA
DALTHERA
THE CITY OF STARS
THE FATHOMS
HEDAR
THE SHADOW TRENCH
THE LAKE OF TEARS
MOTHER'S DEEP
TIKUT
GESAR

HARTSWOOD
DEL HAROL
LITTLE BROOK
MERSTON
WARREN'S GROTTO
DUNHOLD
FORT BRAEMAR
THE FENLANDS
HILLSIDE
KILTON
SWINTON
LONE OAK
FENGATE
LOCH BASTIEN
THE CROSSROADS
NEW BRENNA
KALHANNA
BELHAREN

To Mum and Dad,
For putting up with the near incessant ramblings of your weirdest (and favourite*) daughter for the past three and a half decades.

* You can admit it. I won't tell Megan.

CHAPTER ONE

MARGOT

Firelight reflected in a sunset-coloured slant across the page, clashing with the soft green tones of Margot's mage light. The entry she was reading was tucked away in the very back of Nea's journal, but it hadn't been written in the necromancer's hand. The letters were precise, with very little flourish, the loops and tails tight. Tobias had penned this section.

I am sorry, Nea. You deserved better. It started.

Margot traced her fingers over the page, blinking back the tears that threatened. She'd read the passage that followed enough times that she didn't need to see the words to know what they said.

We all did. There was a blank space before the next paragraph started, as though Tobias wanted to separate the apology from what came after.

If the world survives Evard's wrath, then things need to change. We as mages need to change. It should not be so easy for greedy men to exploit the loopholes left behind by long-dead theorists and fanatics. For fools to threaten the fabric that holds the world together in such a way that the known realms could be destroyed on a simple whim.

A line has been crossed. One that we cannot hope to come back from unscathed. Nea ~~thinks~~ hopes that there is some salvation, and I know she will hunt to the ends of the known realms to find it. I, as she often tells me, have become much more pessimistic. We cannot prevent what is to come. We can only fight to ensure there is some semblance of this world left for the survivors.

Tobias had always been logical and realistic, but he was never prone to pessimism. What had changed? Had he known something Nea hadn't? Margot shook her head. So many good mages and wardens had been lost at Kalhanna, and for what? A tyrant's need for more power. How many more people would they lose before the end? And was Tobias right—was this something they could never truly recover from? Regardless, she did agree with his sentiment about the need for change.

With a sniff, she closed the journal, and her attention moved to Emil, who was watching her as he stirred the coals of their fire with a long stick.

"Nea and Molly will be fine you know? They're both more than capable of looking after themselves." He pulled the end of the stick out of the fire and gave it a flick to douse the flame that shrouded the tip. "Actually, if they can get over their differences and work together, they'll be quite a force to be reckoned with I imagine." He traced a pattern in the air with the glowing end of the stick before poking it back into the coals.

"I wasn't really thinking about either of them this time. But thanks for bringing them back to the forefront of my mind."

"Oh?" The light from the fire made his amber eyes shine. "I'm sorry. I assumed ..."

"It's fine." She chewed the edge of her thumbnail. "Tobias seemed to think that there would be no stopping Evard. That we would just need to pick up the pieces when he was done and hope there was something of our world left."

"The tear in the sky above Kalhanna is evidence that he wasn't entirely wrong," Penny said as she leant back on her hand, her dark eyes glinting almost mischievously. Beside her sat the saffron-coated terrier, Wade. He lifted his head and scented the breeze before letting out a low growl.

"Company," Penny said quietly, the seductive kiss of her keen rolling across Margot's neck as she shared something unspoken with the dog. Penny's mind magic had certainly made it easier to communicate with the man trapped under all that fur.

"What sort of company?" Mateus asked, his starlight silver hair appeared almost the same buttery tone as Molly's in the firelight.

Penny's keen shifted. "What in the realms is a devourer?"

Wade growled again, hackles rising along his spine and his tail standing tall.

"A devourer? They only exist in the Between," Mateus said, his keen testing the air in a cool rush as he stood.

Emil tossed his stick into the flames and shared a look with the other warden, Dale. They both rose as well, hands edging towards their swords.

A twig snapped, and Margot spun to face the sound.

From the shadows stepped a pale girl with a sleek sheet of ink-coloured hair. Her eyes, painted ochre by the firelight, were normally silver–blue. Amelia. She had traded her filthy nightgown for a pair of form-fitting dark pants and a silk shirt the same deep vermillion she had painted her lips. "I should be insulted. How could anyone, but especially one of the Mother's brightest, confuse *me* with one of those filthy bottom feeders." That red-painted mouth pulled into a smile that showed her impossibly white teeth as her gaze dropped to Wade. "Then again, you can't be all that bright, given your current predicament."

The anchor on Margot's palm burned. It didn't like Amelia. It wanted her gone—it wanted her *dead.* "Ready to face your reckoning, betrayer?" Margot didn't know where the words came from, and they leapt from her mouth with a venom she hadn't known she was capable of.

Amelia's head tilted, her arrogant smile faltering at one corner. "You've found yourself a new host it would seem."

"*Ally.* I am not a parasite like you," Margot hissed.

Amelia gave a haughty snort. "Of course *you* would make that distinction. You always were so high and mighty. I have no quarrel with you."

"Then leave," Mateus said, placing his hand on Margot's shoulder. His keen radiated in cool tendrils down Margot's arm, soothing the anchor.

Amelia fixed her pale eyes on Mateus. "You cannot banish me, necromancer." She licked her lips as she studied the small group. "But I will leave. I merely felt an old acquaintance"—her gaze settled on the anchor mark—"and I wanted to make sure she was still sufficiently *shackled.*" With a last sinister curve of her mouth, she stepped back into the shadows and was gone.

"Who was that?" Mateus asked.

"*What* was that?" Dale added, his keen touching Margot and briefly numbing her connection to the source.

"Amelia," Margot responded, rubbing the silver whorl at the centre of her palm. "She's—I don't know exactly. You can ask Niall all about her when we get to Del Harol." The anchor vibrated under her skin. It—*she* knew all about Amelia, including how to destroy her, and would gladly help.

Penny's keen tickled across the back of Margot's skull. "I thought for a moment you might have been possessed," she said.

Mateus shook his head. "It's not a possession. Whatever spirit is contained in that anchor, it spoke true when it told Amelia that it wasn't a parasite. It's more like ... two souls *sharing* one body rather than competing for control of it. Amelia, on the other hand ..."

Wade growled.

"Yes, exactly," Emil said as though he had understood the dog.

Mateus levelled his calculating hazel stare on Wade. "Why did you call her a devourer?"

"She feels like the same dark, twisting magic that they do. But that is also how the Usurper's magic feels at times," Penny said, her keen stirring as she mind-linked with the dog again.

"And the Usurper. He's the one pulling all the strings? The false Shadow Man?" Emil asked.

"Arf!" Wade barked.

Penny nodded, and a quiver went through the anchor. The spirit contained there hated the Usurper perhaps more than it did Amelia. The girl was a product of what she had been made, a tool that had been cast aside when she was found unsatisfactory. The Usurper, however ... he was a grasping brat who needed to be put back in his place. Something shifted under the anger. The hatred was tangled with something else ... admiration? No, that particular feeling was older. This was different—fear. The spirit feared the Usurper, or rather what he would do if he succeeded.

"I'll take it," Emil said, breaking through Margot's thoughts.

"You'll take what?" Margot asked, shaking her head to clear it.

"First watch. Just in case Amelia decides to come back."

"The coward won't visit again tonight," the spirit said before calming to a gentle hum under Margot's skin again.

Penny studied Margot's face with a frown but said nothing as she turned to settle down on her bedroll.

Margot tucked Nea's journal away then lay on her side watching the dwindling flames flickering over the coals of their fire. Amelia's visit had left tension coiled under her skin, but whether it was her own agitation or the anchor's, she couldn't tell. Either way, the tightness was making sleep slow to take her.

Amelia didn't visit again in the several days it took them to reach Del Harol. The college, though bursting at the seams with all manner of mage, warden, and refugee, appeared otherwise unaffected by the turmoil that was gripping the south in the wake of the tear in the barrier. Emil and Dale branched off to find Emil's father, Commander Godfrey, and the rest of the wardens, while Margot and the others headed to High Mage, Niall's study.

When Margot knocked, it was not Niall who answered but Nonna. There were new lines around Nonna's mouth and a dullness to her dark violet gaze. An ache rolled through the anchor mark. The weight of the spirit's sorrow brought heat to the back of Margot's eyes.

"Has something happened?" she asked as Nonna stood back and gestured for them to enter.

"The grove was destroyed." A vaguely familiar voice sounded from the direction of Niall's daybed. A quick glance told her the voice belonged to Garret's grandmother, Camille. She looked almost as worn down as Nonna.

"Who would do such a thing?" Penny asked.

"Kieran," Camille responded dryly.

"Kieran? But he's a Hartswood necromancer. Surely even he wouldn't stoop to something so vile." Penny dropped onto the daybed beside Camille.

"How did he get past the lock-stone? I thought it would prevent anyone with ill intent from entering the estate," Mateus said.

Nonna settled a heavy look on him and then shifted it to Margot. "He *sundered* the lock-stone ... disconnected it from the source."

"How? It would take more than one mage? And powerful mages at that ... Is this Kieran someone like Nea? Is there another divine-blooded soul running amuck in Beldaren that we were not aware of?" Mateus's attempt at humour was shut down by Nonna's glare.

Margot had rarely been on the receiving end of the older woman's true ire, but she had witnessed it often enough that she had to fight back an involuntary wince.

"Kieran is a fool who has blindly sold his soul for a mere taste of power. If I were Nea, I would have done more than give him corruption." Nonna stormed to Niall's desk and sat heavily in the chair.

"Nea *gave* him corruption?" Mateus's eyebrows rose. "That's impossible."

"Improbable," Margot said automatically. "Amelia can infect others. She is responsible for Nea's case, and we know that someone—most likely Evard—found a way to seed corruption in the body by anointing weapons with it."

"But corruption is not a physical thing like a common disease or poison. It's magical in origin."

"It takes a little bit to get used to the idea, but Margot is right," Penny said. "My question would be, how can Nea infect others? And what effect did the anchor have on that ability when it healed her?"

Nonna stood so fast, the chair behind her teetered a moment. "Warren's anchor? Please tell me that none of you let that crazy old bastard put the sodden thing inside you?"

The anchor gave a little jolt as though offended. Margot pressed her lips together and closed her fist. Nonna's gaze zeroed in on her at the same time Penny shot her a look that was full of the sly smugness that had always been infuriating.

"Do you have any idea what you have done?" The glare Nonna had given Mateus was pale in comparison to the one she now wore, and Margot was surprised that steam wasn't coming out of her ears.

"It—*she* wants to help. And she healed Nea's corruption like it was nothing."

Nonna's mouth twisted in a way that was so like Nea. "*She?*"

"Yes, the spirit inside the anchor."

"She's told you who she is then?" Nonna's tone was tight, her dark violet eyes flashing with contempt.

"*Abigail,*" Camille reprimanded softly.

"You knew it wasn't a real anchor? We asked you for the truth, and you still kept half of it from us." A quiver of rage flared up the back of Margot's neck.

"There was no way to be certain," Camille said. "However, there was a chance that it was a spirit-powered anchor. And it appears that was indeed the case."

"You could have warned us," Penny said. "If you had, Margot might have stopped to think before she let Warren attach it to her."

Margot settled her hands on her hips. "Knowing the truth wouldn't have changed my decision, Pen." A warm flicker ran through the anchor mark.

Penny drew a deep breath. "You—"

"Do you know the identity of the spirit?" Mateus asked, cutting her off.

"No," Nonna said. "It could be anyone ... It might not even be human."

"Whoever *she* is, she doesn't like Amelia."

"She doesn't like Amelia? But she has to be from well before Amelia's time." Camille scratched behind Wade's ears as he settled between her and Penny on the daybed.

"I would hazard a guess to say she doesn't like the soul that resides inside Amelia, rather than the actual girl herself," Mateus mused as he studied the items on one of Niall's shelves. "Apart from the resistance to being banished, Amelia seems to be an almost textbook case of possession."

"At first glance it is an easy assumption to make, but Amelia is much more complex than that. She cannot be simply destroyed," Nonna said.

"Who reanimated her?"

"Her mother."

"Her *mother*?" Mateus's cheeks puffed out as Nonna nodded to confirm. "But that's—"

"Before you get the wrong idea, it wasn't done out of some emotionally blinded fit of grief at the girl's passing. Amelia was an experiment almost from the day she was born. We found out too late to prevent it, and binding her to the south wing at Braemar was a last resort. One that nearly cost both Niall and Warren their lives."

Wade growled.

"What sort of experiment? She wasn't part of Evard's *breeding program,* was she?" Penny asked.

A dark anger flashed in Camille's gaze, and her lip curled in a way that reminded Margot of Garret. "No. She came before those atrocities."

"How did Evard get away with it for so long?" Margot asked. It was clear from Nea's recount that Evard's experiments had gone on for the better part of a decade. If mages like Nonna, Niall, and Camille had been aware of it, why didn't they do anything about it?

"There was no real evidence that led back to Evard. And we could never get definitive answers from the mages involved. In fact, several of them took their own lives rather than be questioned."

"So was Evard responsible for Amelia?"

"No. The mage we *believe* assisted Amelia's mother in her experiments became Evard's arcane advisor," Nonna answered.

"Where is this mage now?" Mateus asked.

"Dead. At least we believe so."

"You don't know?" Penny stood, disturbing Wade, who let out a huff.

Camille shook her head. "Almost thirty years ago, an earthquake levelled the section of catacombs that housed his laboratory." There was an odd glint in her eyes as she said it, and Margot wondered if the earthquake had been her doing. She was a stone mage, after all. "He has not been seen since."

"What sort of mage was he?" Margot asked.

"He was originally a healer. But he believed that mages should not be limited to a single discipline of magic simply because they were born with a specific keen. He was not the first to entertain such a philosophy, but he *was* the first to manage altering himself. He became what we would consider a creationist, but in the process, he exposed himself to the Shadow," Nonna replied.

"A *Shadow-touched* creationist?" The jar Mateus had been examining shattered against the floor, scattering the dark seeds it contained.

Wade's hackles rose as he growled.

"He was possessed then?" Mateus asked as he carefully picked up the larger shards of glass and placed them on the desk.

Nonna's mouth tightened at one corner. "You know that being Shadow-touched and possessed are not the same thing ... Nea would be classed as Shadow-touched."

"Was this mage a child of Shadow like Nea then? Or divine blooded in some other way?" Penny asked.

Nonna and Camille both shook their heads.

"He was not born to the Shadow; he was tainted by it. Whether he openly embraced it or simply became its puppet, we do not know," Nonna said. "He was not corrupted though," she added as Margot opened her mouth to ask.

"Puppet or not, his influence was the start of Evard's madness," Camille said.

Margot let out a long sigh and rubbed her hands over her face. "The deeper we dig, the more confusing this becomes. Is Niall here?"

"No, he has gone to Kalhanna with the others to see about sealing the tear."

"Then that is where we need to go," Margot said, starting for the door.

"Wait," Penny said, stalling Margot. "Is there anything else we *should* know about this mage or his experiments?"

Nonna rubbed her fingers over her chin and shared a look with Camille. "Only that his name was Ambrose, and he was originally from Merston."

CHAPTER TWO

GARRET

Garret pressed his hand to his side as his horse kept a steady pace along the road. Margot's corruption treatment only took the edge off the clawing itch, and whilst it softened the insistent voice at the back of his mind, it also dulled his keen-sense. It wasn't completely dormant like it had been in the Between, but it was numbed enough to bother him. He wasn't sure what was worse, the corruption, his diminished keen-sense, or the nagging concern for Nea and Molly. Perhaps they were all feeding off each other.

Beside him, Leith had been unusually stoic, his mouth tight and his gaze set on the road ahead. Garret wondered if it was the weight of what they were riding towards or something else. Most likely it was a combination of the two and that something else was a trouble-attracting necromancer with deep violet eyes.

It had been clear from the time Nea was in Evard's prison that Leith still deeply cared for her. It was something they probably should discuss to clear the air rather than let it become a problem later. The death ward complicated things. Whatever feelings had been developing for Nea before the ward—and Garret would be a fool not to admit that there were strong feelings there—they had increased tenfold after they stepped out of the labyrinth. Then there was the matter of Evard being Garret's father. He still hadn't told Leith, and in truth it was a harder subject to broach than Nea. Did it matter? He let out a sigh and twisted in his saddle to study the force marching behind them.

"You're worried," Leith said.

"Of course I'm worried. We're riding towards a massive tear in the barrier that we have to figure out how to close, Leon is still on the loose with the soul of a god now trapped under his skin, and Kieran—"

"I meant about Nea."

"Well, yes ... and Molly too. There is no way to know if they survived the explosion or if Leon has taken them prisoner."

"I'm not blind, and I believe I know you both well enough to see the signs."

So they were going to have this conversation now then? "If you want me to step aside, I—"

Leith held up a hand. "She never really loved me, you know. Not the way I love her, and I know she hasn't forgiven me for my actions before the purge ... She may never forgive me for that."

Garret had walked through Nea's memories and felt the emotions attached to them. She might not have loved Leith the way he wanted her to, but she had cared deeply for him and, beneath the pain over Kalhanna, he suspected she still did.

"I just wanted you to know that I know there is no future for Nea and I—not the one I envisioned anyway." Leith rubbed the back of his neck. "Cat can be selfish, but I did love her too. Just not as much as I should have. I was so busy holding onto the hope that Nea would come back and everything would return to the way it was before ... I let them both down, and neither of them deserved that."

"Catriona might be spiteful, but I never thought she was truly cruel. And she did stand up to Leon and Kieran in the end. She might still come around."

"If they allowed her to survive after that betrayal," Leith said, his tone laced with bitterness.

"You do have a point there." Leon was definitely someone who held a grudge, and it wasn't hard to imagine him killing Catriona out of spite.

They were quiet for a while when Leith suddenly said, "Do you know I thought Nea was a pirate when I first met her?"

"A pirate?"

"It was back when she was spending time sailing about with Wren on that ship of hers. I was lucky that Nea was in Dalthera that day. They might call it the City of Stars, but they are only referring to everything above the Bright Market." Leith shook his head and played with his horse's mane. "I liked to frequent this tavern in the docks district. It was seedy and rough, and no one there really knew who I was. But that day I'd gotten into some trouble with this merchant prince ... Vince, I think his name was. He had me cornered down some alley, and two of his henchmen were giving me the beating of my life. Then Nea just appeared and put Vince on his arse. He scurried off with his tail between his legs, and Nea ..." He shook his head. "I lost my heart that day, and I didn't even care. I told her she had a pretty name. The women I was used to would simply take the compliment, but not Nea. Something flashed in those strange eyes of hers, and she said, 'If you say for a pretty girl, I will give you the same treatment I just gave Vince.' She was just so brazen and carefree and had no idea who she was talking to; so different to the ladies from court, almost *wild*."

Garret rubbed his fingers over the scar on his lip. "When I first met her, she scolded me for my lack of manners. And despite knowing that I was on orders to take her to Evard, she helped me with Declan's death. She didn't have to. Any other mage in her position would have made a run for it. But she was defiant and prickly, yet soft and willing to help. I was intrigued. I'd heard so much about her from Margot, Emil, and Evard that I thought I knew what to expect. I couldn't have been more wrong."

Leith gave a small laugh and shook his head.

"There's something else we should talk about that is not related to Nea," Garret said.

"Oh?"

"I have recently learned that I was not told the truth about who my father was."

"Some days I wish that was the case for me. Not that Father had much of a hand in my upbringing, but—"

"Evard is my father," Garret said, cutting Leith off.

"Evard? As in my father, Evard?"

"Yes."

Leith worried his lip, his brow furrowing. "But then that makes you—"

"Nothing. I'm an illegitimate heir at best. I have no claim to your throne, nor do I want it. I just thought you should know."

"I was going to say it makes you my brother," Leith said with a chuckle.

Garret toyed with his scar. "It does."

"I always wanted a sibling; I was hoping for a little sister who I could have doted on, but I guess it could be worse." He grinned. "And that explains why everyone was so confused about Henry."

Garret frowned. "Confused about Henry?"

"Yes. Everyone kept saying he looked like you, but if we're half-brothers then it makes more sense. Now that I know, I am not sure why I never noticed the similarities. We both have father's eyes."

Nea had said the similarities in Leith and Garret's eyes were one of the things that made her suspect that Evard was his father, and Henry did have the same deep silver gaze as Leith.

"Does Nea know?"

"Yes. She suspected it, nearly from the moment we met."

"She suspected it?"

Garret shrugged. "She's annoyingly observant at times, and she has spent a great deal of time with both yourself and Evard. If anyone was going to make the connection, it would be her."

Leith fixed him with a shrewd look. "You love her, don't you?"

"I respect her and care for her deeply, but not everyone is as unashamedly romantic as you."

"That's Garret speak for yes," Declan said from behind them.

Of course, he was listening.

"Is that the tear?" Leith asked. His gaze locked onto a flashing patch of sky in the distance.

They were still at least half a day from Kalhanna, but already the air was charged with the magic leaching from the Between. To Garret, whose keen was blocked by the mage bane in Margot's corruption treatment, it felt strangely muffled. But there was no mistaking the everchanging, fluidic nature of it or the general sense of uneasiness. The mages and other wardens present had all started fidgeting as though uncomfortable or unable to sit still.

"Yes, that's the tear. We should probably find a place to make camp and send a smaller group to investigate the college."

Leith gave a signal and slowed his horse.

"Why are we stopping?" Trenton asked as he joined them.

During his time as warden commander, Garret hadn't had much to do with Trenton. Though they had travelled in similar circles, especially once the soldier had been promoted to Leith's personal guard. He was a good man with a seemingly intelligent head on his shoulders and had taken command of Leith's remaining men after the attack at Hartswood.

"Garret thinks we should make camp and send a smaller group out to investigate the college," Leith responded.

Trenton's deep brown gaze settled on Garret, and he gave a nod. "That's a sound plan. The way the mages are talking, I don't like the idea of riding in there blind."

"Who is going on to the college with us?" Declan asked.

"We'll take Zephyr and Harvey."

"We're coming too," Niall said, indicating himself and Aveline as they passed Declan on his way to get the others.

"Alright. The rest of you can find a spot to make camp," Garret said as he touched his horse's sides and guided it away from the larger group to wait for the others.

Barbs stirred under his skin, and he fought the urge to rub at them. Margot's treatment was effective, but it only lasted so long before another application was needed. It seemed too soon for another dose. He hoped it was the proximity of the tear that was affecting the corruption and not that it was growing immune to the treatment. If his corruption was starting to play up, then Nea's must have just about consumed her. Unless she had put the bind-shackles back on. She would have, wouldn't she? But what if infecting Kieran had been the opening it needed to completely dissolve her defences?

His jaw tightened, as did his grip on the reins. The death ward had always thrummed with the soothing cool of Nea's keen. Now the corruption was starting to drown out even that. But was it his corruption suffocating the sensation or hers?

A hand on his arm startled him, and he turned to catch Aveline's crisp green gaze studying him.

"Garret ..." Her brow furrowed, and her mouth twitched at the corner like it always did when she was concerned.

He drew a long breath. "I'm fine."

"If the corruption is getting worse, we can get you a pair of bind-shackles," she said.

"It's not more than I can endure at the moment."

Her fingers tightened on his arm, and he wished he'd chosen to phrase that another way.

"Hector used to say—"

"I know. I'm sorry. I didn't mean it like that." He rubbed a hand over his face. "The corruption isn't my main concern at present."

"Ah ..." She let go of his arm and gave him a motherly smile. "I'd like to tell you she'll be fine, but we both know that would be a lie. She seems resilient though."

He nodded then turned his attention to Declan, Zephyr, Harvey, and—"Bran? What are you doing? You should stay here with Leith."

"You might need a necromancer. Especially if any of those reanimations are still kicking around."

"It's too—"

"Nea would let me come."

"She's not here right now, and if she were, she would tell you it's too dangerous."

"Bran is not wrong. A necromancer would be helpful if any of Kieran's reanimations survived. His knowledge of the barrier could also be invaluable," Declan said, and Bran beamed at him.

"What do you think, Niall?" Garret asked.

Niall sucked his lip under his teeth as he studied Bran. "Necromancers are certainly more sensitive to fluctuations in the source regarding the barrier, and he has a solid understanding of the Between, at least in a metaphysical sense. Perhaps more so than other necromancers given that Nea had a strong influence on his early learning."

Garret ran a hand through his hair. "Fine, you can come." He turned back to the others. "Let's not delay any longer. But be on your guard. There is no telling what we will find at the college."

The closer they got to Kalhanna, the more chaotic the source became. It surged in waves of wild magic, making the others, including Harvey, wince with each change. Garret was thankful that his keen-sense was dulled by Margot's treatment and he didn't have to feel the full brunt of it. Even with the treatment, it was enough to set his teeth on edge and make his stomach churn.

"Why can I feel that?" Harvey asked, earning him a curious look from both Declan and Niall.

"You're sensitive to it given the nature of your birth. However, I would wager that even a true keen-less would feel the magic in the air. It is saturating everything, and there is no telling what sort of effect it will have on anyone, or thing, that encounters it for any great length of time," Niall said. "Best that we figure out how to close that tear promptly."

"Mother's tits, what is that?" Declan exclaimed, pointing to a large shape at the edge of the courtyard.

"Language," Aveline reprimanded.

"Apologies, Mother," he muttered.

"I wouldn't mind knowing what that thing is either though," Bran said, his words muffled as he covered his nose and mouth with his hand. "It feels *wrong*."

Not only did the creature feel wrong—it looked wrong. It was a conglomeration made from the fused flesh of half a dozen bodies. At least. Broken limbs jutted at all angles from the lumpy grey skin that covered the monstrosity. It slowly turned towards them, purple flames glowing in the place of eyes and a wide frog-like mouth opening to show mismatched teeth made of jagged bone.

"It's an abomination," Zephyr whispered. "The leaching source perverted the lingering keen clinging to the reanimations."

"So, it's like a golem?" Declan asked.

"We can discuss it after we destroy it," Harvey said, his fingers wrapping around the hilt of his sword.

"And how exactly do we do that?" Declan asked.

"By severing the magic holding it together," Bran replied as he took a step forward.

The creature zeroed in on the movement and let out a bellow before charging. Garret pushed Bran out of the way, and it hit him, knocking the wind from him and sending spots across his vision. Bone talons raked down his arm and tore at the armour over his stomach. Up close, the smell was a dizzying combination of decaying flesh and brackish water. He twisted in its grip, pulling his head back from the gnashing teeth.

Tendrils of lilac magic gripped the creature, and it dropped Garret with a hoarse scream before lunging towards Bran again. The boy dodged out of the way as the creature was shrouded in lightning. It thrashed on the spot, sending chunks of rotten, grey flesh flying.

Azure flames rushed over its form, adding the scent of burning flesh and bone to the air. The abomination let out a long, grating howl, and pounding footsteps filled the air as another of the creatures came running towards them. Garret charged forward, swinging his sword and cleaving into the flesh of the newcomer. Harvey appeared at the creature's other side—a clean blow severing one of the protruding limbs.

Ice flared along Garret's spine as Nea's keen stirred under the ward mark. His instinct was telling him to suppress it, but the corruption lifted, gripping the rising magic and whipping it into a frenzy under his skin. He had to let it out. Focusing on the creature before him, he could see the threads of purple magic holding it together. His keen grabbed hold of those threads and tore them free. The creature dropped, collapsing into a pile of broken, partially decayed bodies. Nea's keen still charged about under his skin, drowning everything else out. He dropped his sword and fell to his knees, his head in his hands as the corruption screeched along his veins and burrowed into the back of his mind.

Something cold closed around his wrist, and the corruption howled in protest. He looked up. Declan held out a second rose-gold shackle. Garret gave him one short nod and held his other arm out. The second the shackle closed, the corruption was silenced. He swallowed and sat heavily on his heels.

"You alright?" Declan asked. There was a slight quaver to his voice, and concern swam in the depths of his eyes.

Garret gave him a slow nod. "What happened?"

"You used necromancy to destroy the abomination, but it allowed the corruption to take hold. You're lucky Niall thought to bring a set of shackles." The mage swallowed and sat back on his heels. "You had me worried there for a moment, old boy."

"What about the second creature?"

"Bran took care of it."

"Is anyone hurt?" He stood gingerly. His ribs ached, and there was a set of long tears in the sleeve of his jacket. Blood dripped over his fingers from the wounds.

"Only a few minor injuries," Zephyr said. "Would you like me to take a look at that?"

Garret shook his head. "It will keep for the moment."

"Well, that was certainly a welcoming party," Niall said as he joined them. "It appears at first glance that the college wards are keeping the tear somewhat contained."

"That doesn't mean things can't pass through." Bran piped up. "It's like it is a door with a loose latch. It does the job well enough, but every so often there is a strong push that causes it to spring open, and that allows beings from the Between to enter our realm."

"Beings?" Garret asked.

"Devourers and the like, mostly," Zephyr said. "There are quite a few bodies. But the magic of the tear seems to be distorting them as they come through, so whether they perished in the crossing or shortly after arriving here is anyone's guess."

"Can the tear be closed?"

Bran started to shake his head but then nodded. "In theory, but it's not going to be easy."

"Perhaps we can discuss this back at camp. We shouldn't linger here this close to the tear," Aveline said, rubbing her arms.

"Quite right," Niall agreed.

As the others started towards their horses, Garret stopped and studied the tear. Shadows squirmed in the multicoloured clouds within. He no longer felt the wild magic radiating from it, but something on the other side still called to him. How close had he come to succumbing to that incessant voice? He drew a shaking breath and studied the shackles around his wrists. Nea believed he wouldn't give in, but he'd been blindsided, and it had overtaken him before he had a chance to fight back. One tiny mistake and the corruption had nearly won. A hand touched his shoulder, and he turned to meet Harvey's steel-blue gaze.

"Are you alright, Garret?"

"I'm fine." He swallowed.

Harvey's cheek concaved as though he was biting the inside of it as his gaze dropped to Garret's hands.

Garret clenched his fists to stop his fingers shaking. "Let's catch up to the others." He was halfway to the gate before Harvey caught up to him.

The look on Harvey's face suggested he wanted to press the issue further, but he licked his lip and said nothing, for which Garret was thankful. He needed time to process what had happened—what was happening. He tightened his grip on the reins. What he really needed was well beyond his reach and quite possibly in mortal peril herself.

CHAPTER THREE

NEA

The breeze was laced with salt and the distinct tang of an approaching storm. Spray misted the air as the ship carved a path through the waves, which were growing choppier the closer they got to the squall. The charged atmosphere brought a tightness to Nea's limbs that made it nearly impossible for her to sit still. Storms had always stirred an uneasy tension; like they clashed with her keen and set every part of her on edge. She clenched her fists as she drew a breath then released both with a soft sigh as she turned her attention to the distant clouds.

The stormfront was the deep grey of damp ash, every so often lit from within by a shimmer of pearlescent green. They were too far south for the maelstrom, and these clouds did not exhibit the same tumultuous nature.

Beside her, Rourke placed his front paws on the side rail and lifted his tusked muzzle to inhale the breeze. He let out a soft, pleased-sounding grunt, and his tongue lolled out as his lips pulled back into what could only be described as a grin.

It was surreal to see the warrior in this form that appeared as some combination of boar and dog. The russet guard hairs that spread from his spine over his dark sides mimicked the patterns of Rourke's swirling tattoos. And there was no mistaking the deep intelligence in his rust-coloured eyes.

"Not worried about the storm then?" Nea asked him, and he grunted in response as his paws met the deck once more.

"Never seen a storm like that," Rufus, The Azure Queen's boatswain, said as he joined Nea at the rail and studied the blooming clouds with a frown. "My bones don't like it."

"It won't touch us," Dara said, sliding in on Nea's other side. Her dark ringlets bounced with the breeze as she settled her pale eyes on the clouds and inhaled deeply, her fingers tightening on the rail. "But I really wish it would; it sings such a beautiful song. Not like the maelstrom. The maelstrom is all screeches and clangs, no melody."

Rourke gave a soft bark as though he agreed with the girl.

Last time Nea had been on the Queen, Dara had been around the age Henry was now, which would make her eight or nine. The sole survivor of a shipwreck, the girl was keen-touched in some way. Most would say she was a seer, but her keen was too different; almost like she had been touched by the Between itself. Her Faridean heritage made Nea believe she was most likely what the Faridean referred to as a dream singer. The fact that she experienced the keen of others as sound and not a physical sensation was another indicator, though most Faridean mages exhibited the same auditory keen-sense.

"I don't care what tune it's singing. It can stay well over there," Rufus said, pushing off the rail. "We should keep an eye on it anyway." He stalked off, and Nea turned to Dara.

The girl had her head tilted. Her pale green eyes, which gave an uncanniness to her darker Faridean features, narrowed as she studied Nea. "Your song has *changed* ... I didn't know songs could do that. It is almost sad but speaks of hope, and there is another sound melded into it, one with a steady thrum ..." She closed her eyes and softly hummed. "I like the new sound." Opening her eyes, she gave Nea a wide smile before wandering off again.

"And here I thought mages couldn't get any weirder," Molly said as she joined Nea.

"Dara is keen-touched, but not many would class her as a true mage," Nea responded automatically.

"Right. We must categorise the weird into a hierarchy. My keen is purer than your keen or some other pretentious nonsense," Molly said as she scratched behind Rourke's ears.

"It doesn't have anything to do with purity. It's based on how an individual interacts with the source ... and it's only vaguely pretentious." She grinned.

"If that was a joke, it was terrible."

Nea laughed.

"Should we be worried about that?" Molly indicated the storm.

"Dara seems to think it won't hit us," Nea answered, letting her keen out and testing the air. She expected the corruption to stir along with her keen, but whatever Margot had done had transformed it—stripping away the Usurper's influence and leaving only raw power in its wake. Power that was now an integral part of Nea's soul. "It feels a little like the maelstrom, but I don't think it's as dangerous. The clouds certainly appear more stable. I don't fancy testing that theory though as it's definitely magical in origin, and that makes it extremely unpredictable."

Silence stretched between them, bringing an awkwardness that clashed with the charged air of the storm.

"Thank you for saving me," Molly suddenly blurted out. "I should have thanked you sooner, but—"

"You don't need to thank me."

"You endangered yourself when you didn't have to; you could have gone through the portal with Garret. He probably would have preferred that. I imagine he's in quite a mood at the moment." She shook her head and smiled.

"Most likely. But I wouldn't have gone with Garret anyway—when I realised that the barrier would tear, regardless of what we did, I knew I couldn't."

"Why?"

"I need to go to Quel'sapar to find some answers, and Leith needs Garret's counsel. Not only that, but my father is the best person to help Garret learn how to control his brightling keen. Whether Garret wants to use that part of himself or not, he needs to learn how to control it." She studied her fingers.

"Did Garret really tie his soul to yours?"

Nea bit the inside of her cheek. "Yes, the bloody fool that he is."

Molly chuckled. "You're not happy about it? He saved your life if Declan is to be believed."

"He did save my life, and I am not ungrateful, but it's ... complicated. I'm complicated, and Garret deserves better."

"I don't know about that."

Nea blinked at her.

"As an outside observer, I would say that you're exactly what Garret needed and vice versa. You're both stubborn and *complicated* ... but in almost complimentary ways. I think you make each other better people."

Nea opened her mouth, but Molly held up a finger to stop her.

"And you are both clearly attracted to each other in a more than *general acquaintances* kind of way ... more than that, you obviously care about each other."

"Are you feeling alright?" Nea gave her a wry smile.

Molly sighed. "I'm being nice again, aren't I? I'll ruin my reputation if I keep it up." She returned Nea's grin. "But no, I am just starting to realise you're maybe not quite as bad as I originally thought."

"I probably wouldn't have liked myself much either if I were you."

"Can you go back to being a haughty pain in the arse? This"—she gestured at Nea's entire body—"just isn't working for me."

Nea laughed. "I wouldn't say I was haughty. I believe you're the one who had already formed an opinion of me, well before we actually met, and you were determined not to change your mind."

"You didn't do yourself any favours though."

Nea shrugged. "I've told you before that I am well aware of my shortcomings. I don't need everyone to like me or even agree with me."

Molly scrunched up her nose. "I think that's my problem. I wanted to hate you. Margot was a mess for so long after Kalhanna; if you had just let her know you were alright, it would have saved her so much pain. I thought you were a coward. You stirred up all this trouble with Evard, forced a schism in the warden order, and hurt those closest to you. And then just disappeared like it all meant nothing."

Nea opened her mouth to speak, but Molly lifted a hand to stop her.

"Then you reappeared, and you refused to talk about what had happened. You did stupid things like visiting Amelia in the middle of the night and letting yourself get kidnapped by Leon. But then you stabbed Evard in front of his entire court, and I don't care how mad that made Garret because damn if I wouldn't have done the same. Slowly, bit by bit, I was starting to respect you even if I didn't trust you. I'm still not sure I do trust you, but you've earned every inch of that respect. So, I guess that's something."

Nea rolled her lip between her teeth, searching for the right words. "Molly—"

"No, just leave it at that. I've bared my soul enough for the both of us for a while."

"Thank you for coming with me when you could have just made your way back to Del Harol with Margot and the others."

Molly gripped the rail and let out a small huff. "No, I couldn't have. I promised Garret if we got split up, I would keep an eye on you, and I don't break my promises."

"I am perfectly capable of taking care of myself."

"I'm sure you are, but I don't blame Garret for worrying. I don't think I have ever seen him as angry as he was when Leon took you from Fort Braemar. I thought it was in response to being outplayed by Leon, of all people, but then we got you back and he was still different. It could have been a result of his entire life being upended ... but no. I think when you came along something inside him shifted."

"Most likely it was his brightling keen recognising something in mine. Blood calls to blood. It is what my father was hoping to avoid. He knew that the blocks that he put on our keens would erode if we were exposed to each other."

"Emil owes me three crowns! I told him it was magical and not romantic." She gave Nea a wide smile. "Why did Niall block your keens though?"

"To try and prevent Evard from using either of us to sunder the barrier and throw the world into chaos."

"Well, that worked like a charm, didn't it?" Molly's tone was so dry that Nea couldn't hold in her laugh, and Rourke let out a snort that sounded amused.

"Some events cannot be avoided no matter how hard we try to prevent them," Nea said. "But we can come back from this. Last time the barrier was torn, Port Brenna was destroyed, so we're already doing better than the mages back then. All major cities are still standing, and the residual wards around Kalhanna seem to have restricted the bulk of the blast. Hopefully, they can contain most of the beings that emerge from the Between also."

"That's a very Declan thing to say. 'Oh, don't worry so much, Molly. The explosion was much smaller than I was expecting, and look we still have all our limbs.'" She mimicked Declan's tone of voice beautifully and ended with a lopsided grin.

"I'm just saying it could have gone far worse than it did."

"I know." Molly leant on the rail and studied the brooding clouds. "Do you know how far we are from Quel'sapar?"

"It's hard to say. The entrance is enchanted and moves around on a whim ... but I feel that we are near. The air is changing, and it isn't just the storm, it's—"

"Playful. Like the grove at Hartswood."

"Similar." Nea studied her.

"Don't look at me like I'm a puzzle to solve. The grove is—was ... powerful. Margot said the ground itself was soaked with magic and that allowed me to feel something—even as a keen-less."

Nea nodded and let out a sigh. The destruction of the grove had left raw scars across her soul much like those left in the wake of Kalhanna. But unlike Kalhanna, the grove would recover in time.

"Will Agatha and the other spirits be alright?"

"Yes, their energy cannot be destroyed, only changed. When this is all over, and there is time to tend the grove, they will come back. But it will be a long process. The lock-stone, however ... Its destruction will leave Hartswood vulnerable. Lock-stones are not simple magic, and I am not sure even my father could create a new one."

The silence that fell between them again was not quite as uncomfortable as before.

Nea studied her hands before turning her attention back to the storm. Unease crawled down her spine and settled in an itch under the ward mark. Garret's keen burned along the lines of the eight-pointed star, flaring bright. The scratching compulsion of corruption tore into Nea's mind, and Leon's sneer flashed across her vision. Tendrils of dread closed around her throat, and she gripped the rail. What was going on? Her attention dropped to the grey marks on her arm. They were still the swirling silver cloud patterns they had been since Margot had used the anchor on them. It was not her corruption; it was Garret's. She drew a gasping breath as the sensation suddenly stopped.

This was worse than the corruption. Why couldn't she feel Garret? They had been connected by the ward for weeks now, and his keen had been a constant thrum under her skin. If she couldn't feel it, what did that mean? He couldn't be dead. The ward would have taken her life as well. Wouldn't it? Her lungs ached as though starved of air, and her vision started to draw in at the sides as she drew a series of too-fast breaths.

"Nea?" Molly's fingers closed on Nea's arm at the same time Rourke pressed against her leg with a whine. "Mother's tits, your skin is like ice."

"What's going on?" Wren appeared.

Their voices grew muffled as Nea's blood pounded in her ears. Screams tore across the back of her mind, smoke and blood clouded her senses, ash coated her tongue—

Slap.

A hot sting blossomed across her cheek.

She blinked at Molly, who pointed to Wren.

"You were panicking and not responding."

"So, you slapped me?" She was so shocked, she could have laughed.

"It worked, didn't it?"

Nea covered her mouth with her hand and drew a shuddering breath. Rourke was still pressed against her leg, a vibration going through his ribs as he let out a low growl.

"What happened?" Molly asked.

"I don't know." She shook her head. "It was corruption, but it wasn't mine. It was Garret's, and now ... Molly, now I can't *feel* him." She pressed her fingers to the ward mark.

"What do you mean you can't feel him? Is he—he's not—"

"I don't know!"

"Okay. I'd tell you to calm down, but you never take that well. So stop and think," Wren said.

Stop and think. Pressing her lip between her teeth, she massaged her fingers into the fur at Rourke's scruff. The action seemed to calm him as well as her. She could just create a portal and check on Garret. But what if Leon had him and they both got trapped? No, she had to find the thrones before Leon did, especially if he had Garret. A portal was too risky. She drew a long breath and let it out slowly. A quiver stirred in the ward mark, subtle but there, a mere echo of what it had been before but unmistakably Garret's keen. "You're right. I need to focus on what is important, and that is finding the thrones. Garret will be fine. I was just overwhelmed for a moment."

"But—"

"I can still feel him. The connection is just fainter than before," Nea said, cutting Molly off.

She drew another centring breath and turned her attention to the storm once more. As Dara had said, it appeared to be skirting around them. More importantly, a magnetic pull was building ahead of the ship, charging the air in a different way to the storm. It was the twisting sensation of deep-rooted secrets.

A line of light shot out from the centre of the siren figurehead. It collided with an invisible wall, sending ripples of sea-foam-coloured magic through the air, and an island appeared, surrounded by towering crags of rock. The Queen slid gracefully through the gaps between the monoliths until it reached the small bay just beyond.

A slapdash dock edged one side of the cove and just beyond that was a cluttered run of buildings, all seeming to lean on each other as they stretched back towards a grey cliff-face. Rickety stairs, a combination of wood and stone, zig-zagged to the glittering palace above.

"Vince has certainly made some changes," Nea muttered as she studied the elaborate building.

"What did you say?" Molly asked.

"Oh, nothing important." She thrust an arm towards the town. "Welcome to Quel'sapar."

CHAPTER FOUR

HARVEY

There hadn't been much time to debrief after they returned from the college. Instead, they had thrown themselves into helping the others set up camp in the fields that surrounded the old farmstead Leith had commandeered as a temporary base of operations. The next morning, Leith called a meeting in the barn, which he had set up as a war room of sorts, and they had been discussing their best course of action for the better part of two hours.

"Are the creatures coming through a threat?" Leith rested his palms on the table in front of him and levelled his gaze on Garret.

"It doesn't appear so at this stage. Anything that may have survived crossing the tear is no longer in the vicinity of the college," he replied.

"What about the abominations you encountered?"

Garret touched his fingers to one of the shackles around his wrists. Since rescuing Nora and Henry from Kieran, Garret had been different, more withdrawn, easier to anger—both symptoms of his corruption that he had been managing with Margot's treatment. Yesterday, however, whether it was exposure to the tear or something else, the treatment had stopped working and the corruption had nearly consumed him. If Declan hadn't been so fast with the shackles ... Harvey glanced at the storm mage. He was studying Garret, his mouth an uncharacteristically tight line.

"They didn't come through the tear itself. They were created when the wild magic leaching from the Between warped the lingering threads of Kieran's necromancy," Zephyr said.

"Could more be created?"

A look of mortification crossed Zephyr's face.

"I think Leith means, is there enough lingering magic in the air to create more organically, not can we create more ourselves," Garret said, and Leith nodded.

"Exactly that. From your reports, I would not fancy encountering something of that nature, and I would like to be prepared should that be a risk."

"Without spending more time at the college, I couldn't say for certain," Zephyr said.

"Then—someone should—"

"That is inadvisable," Niall said from the side of the room, cutting off Leith's response. He was leaning against the wall, a book propped open on his palm, violet gaze watching the proceedings with mild curiosity.

"The magic is leaching in waves and the results of each wave are unpredictable. We cannot be certain what effect prolonged exposure to the tear will have on the keen of mages or wardens. In fact, it may even *alter* keen-less," Declan elaborated.

"So how can we discover how to close it if we can't study it?" Leith searched each face in turn.

"I think we're going to need Nea," Bran said from his seat next to Aveline.

Leith's brow furrowed. "Nea is—"

"Currently beyond our reach," Declan said quickly. "But surely there are other necromancers who have the same understanding of the Between that she does. After all, interacting with the Between is what your lot do. What about Abigail?" He turned to Bran.

"Maybe, but Nea's relationship to the Between is different to the rest of us," the boy replied.

"Warren's insight would be beneficial, however, getting him here will likely be a challenge. Years living in solitude have only increased his surliness," Niall said.

"I doubt that is possible," Aveline chuckled.

"Do we have any other options?" Leith asked.

They all shared a look.

"What if we send word to Loch Bastien or Merston? Perhaps there is an expert we are overlooking." Leith's rising frustration was evident in his tone.

Aveline made a noise, and the prince's attention snapped to her. "Sophia has thrown her lot in with Evard. Those left at the college will be completely under his heel. Or rather Leon and Kieran's heels now, I guess ... And Merston has been locked down for the past two years. No one gets in ... or out."

"We should still send an envoy. Do you know the reasoning behind this lockdown?"

Niall and Aveline both shook their heads. "High Mage Juliana has always been flighty. Most likely it was a simple knee-jerk reaction to Evard's purging of Kalhanna ... There has been no indication that it is anything more sinister," Niall said.

Leith gave a short nod, his attention falling on Garret. "You've been unusually quiet, Garret. Your thoughts?"

The warden didn't respond. He was staring at the tabletop in front of him, his fingers clenched white-knuckle tight on the edge and his jaw working.

"Garret?"

His head snapped up, and he blinked at Leith. "Sorry?"

"I asked for your opinion on sending an envoy to Merston."

Garret ran a hand through his hair and blew out a breath. "I'm sorry. I was a million miles away."

"More like focused completely inward," Declan whispered to Harvey.

"Do you think it is a good idea though?" Leith prompted.

"Perhaps we can make a decision on the matter after a short break." Niall pushed off the wall. "Garret, a word." He didn't wait for Leith's response, just swept from the room waving for Garret to follow.

"I guess we'll continue this later then." Leith sighed and lifted a hand towards the door, dismissing them. "Declan and Harvey, if you wouldn't mind staying back a moment."

As Aveline, Bran, and Zephyr left, Leith settled his grey gaze on Harvey before switching his attention to Declan. "What is going on with Garret?"

They shared a look.

"The pair of you have to have noticed how he's been of late. It's worse since yesterday."

Declan ran his fingers along his lip. "Margot's treatment contains mage bane, which means it has a numbing effect on his keen. It would be similar to one of your senses suddenly failing you. More than that though, prolonged use of mage bane can have extreme consequences for keen-folk."

"Is that why he has resorted to the bind-shackles? Surely, if he is no longer using the treatment, the side effects of the mage bane would be gone."

Declan's mouth pulled into a tight line.

"He lost control of it yesterday," Harvey said. "Garret likes being in control and—correct me if I am wrong, Declan—when corruption takes over, it erodes personal agency entirely."

"Exactly. I wasn't certain the bind-shackles would be enough to bring him back to himself. But they did manage to stabilise the corruption, and I imagine after a few days of brooding he'll return to his usual self." His smile was tight, like he was trying to convince himself as much as Leith.

"Let's hope you are right." Leith frowned and gestured towards the door.

A shadow slipped past the outside of the tent. Footsteps silent, someone sneaking through the camp and not simply going out to relieve themselves. Harvey sat and studied the bedrolls around him. Garret's was empty. Ever since they had reached Kalhanna, the warden had been unfocused, bothered by matters he refused to share. It wasn't completely unlike him to be creeping about in the middle of the night, but something was definitely off about his behaviour.

Careful not to wake the others, Harvey crept out into the dark camp. A shadowy figure was heading into the trees. It was too small to be Garret, but there was something familiar about the way it slid through the night. *Amelia?*

The shadow stopped just at the edge of his vision and glanced back over her shoulder. She beckoned him with one pale hand.

Following Amelia into the dark woods would be a colossal mistake.

A voice drifted from the dark trees behind the girl. It was a deep rumble that Harvey recognised instantly as Garret. *Bright damn it.* He took a step forward, and Amelia cocked her head before slipping between the trunks and out of sight. Harvey followed her. He had to be absolutely insane, but something was calling him out into the woods—the same curiosity that had dragged him down to the south wing at Braemar.

The shadows under the trees were so thick that when he glanced over his shoulder after several metres, he couldn't see the camp at all. He swallowed and pressed forward, pulled along by that invisible thread. Stepping around a tree trunk, he came nose to nose with—

"Mother's grief, Garret!" Harvey staggered back a step. It was both amazing and infuriating how stealthy Garret could be, given his size.

"Were you following me?" He looked completely run down. There were dark circles beneath his eyes and a tightness to his jaw.

"No, I was following Amelia."

"Amelia?" Garret folded his arms over his chest. The shackles glinted softly in the moonlight.

"I did come out here to find you, but she was lurking by the edge of the forest, then she ..." He might have been concerned about Garret's mental state, but following Amelia into the woods hadn't been his brightest moment either.

"So, you thought you'd follow her."

Harvey rubbed the back of his neck. "When you say it like that it sounds insane. But something was—calling me."

Garret toyed with the scar above his lip. "Calling you?"

"Not with words but a feeling, like I needed to—"

"Well, hello there."

They both turned at the voice. A woman, or rather the spectre of one, was leaning against the trunk of a tree behind them. She wore a gown of silver silk, her translucent form flickering as though it could disappear at any moment. A ball of lilac light burst to life beside her, casting a delicate sheen across her dark hair as she moved away from the tree and walked in a slow circle around them.

"I should be offended that you mistook me for that abhorrent snake," she said lightly as her eyes, which were a soft rose-gold, locked on Harvey.

"Who are you?" Garret asked.

She shrugged. "A figment ... a memory. I will get stronger the more the healer uses her newfound gift, and your proximity to my birthplace allows me to appear as thus." She flicked her fingers towards herself. "But I doubt I will ever see physical form again."

"The healer?" Harvey asked at the same time Garret enquired,

"Why are you here?"

Her gaze flicked from Garret to Harvey and then back again. "I have a warning—a pertinent one given your current predicament.

The *filth* who stole my father's mantle seeks to erode the threads binding you and the Shadow's new daughter. The longer you are afflicted by his influence, the more likely he is to win. The vessel that contains him may have slowed him down, but he is an eel who excels at finding loopholes." She lifted a hand as though she would touch Garret, but he took a step back.

"But Leon is keen-less. That's why Nea trapped the Usurper in his body. To prevent him from accessing magic. Isn't it?" Harvey directed the question at Garret, who gave a nod.

"The bully king was also keen-less, but the *Usurper's* influence still caused him to wreak havoc and misery as he set in motion the final stages of the eons-long machinations that have brought us to this moment." Her lips parted in an almost predatory smile. "And the Usurper did not wear his skin as he does this Leon's."

"You said you came to warn us, but we already know, and the corruption is no longer a threat." Garret indicated the bind-shackles.

"Interesting that you choose to lie to yourself. You are a brightling. Sovereign blood runs through your veins as it does your Shadow-touched counterpart. The rules of this world do not govern either of you, which you should have realised by now."

Garret's jaw tightened as though he was grinding his teeth.

The woman had a point. Ever since they had returned from Kalhanna, Garret had been troubled despite the bind-shackles. Harvey wasn't sure exactly how it worked, but he knew that the shackles were supposed to help, and in Garret's case they didn't seem to be.

"He has already invaded your dreams, hasn't he?" The woman's smile was triumphant as Garret looked away.

"The healer is coming, and she can help you as she did the one who is sister but not by blood. I do not know that she can cure you entirely, but she can strengthen your defences. However, if you let the healer alter your curse, it will change her keen irrevocably. She will accept her fate. For her sole purpose is to help and heal, as mine once was. But it is not a change to take lightly. The Shadow will own her soul, and only he can free her again."

"Which Shadow?"

"The rightful one." The moment the last word left her lips, she disappeared.

Harvey shook his head. "The healer she was referring to has to be Margot, right? She is the only healer I know who has what would be referred to as *a sister who is not by blood*. And was she implying that Margot could heal your corruption?"

Garret drew a long breath. "Maybe ... We should get back to camp. We can discuss it with Declan and the others in the morning." He started to move away.

"Garret, wait."

He stopped but didn't turn back to face Harvey.

"How bad is it?"

A jolt ran across Garret's shoulders before he slowly turned and shrugged. "It's—"

"Be honest." Harvey folded his arms.

"It's ... *bad*."

"So, whoever that was, she was right? I thought those shackles were supposed to stop the corruption from affecting you."

"They prevent it from having access to my keen ... But the corruption is still present, constantly whispering at the back of my mind, grating fingers teasing out every fear. Stirring up anger, and I ... I'm drowning in it." He rubbed his hands over his face. "I cannot even escape it in my sleep. As soon as I close my eyes, I see Leon sneering back at me." He swallowed.

Harvey didn't know what to say. Garret always had such good control of his emotions, but then he had seen corrupted mages. The ones they couldn't help fast enough, they seemed to lose all humanity.

"I can't go on like this, Harvey."

Harvey let out a heavy breath. "Have you told Declan?"

Garret shook his head. "I thought I could deal with it ... *endure* it as long as I had to ... but he should know. If that spectre or whatever she was is right and the Usurper wins ... If I lose control and he takes over then—" He grabbed Harvey's shoulders and looked him in the eye. "You need to end it. If I lose myself, you need to kill me."

Harvey opened his mouth to respond but closed it again. Garret wasn't one for dramatics. If he was concerned that he could lose himself to the corruption, then it was a very real possibility. He nodded. "If the shackles fail and the corruption takes over, I will do as you ask."

Garret's posture softened, and his grip on Harvey loosened. "Thank you."

❧

"And it wasn't Amelia? You're absolutely certain?" Declan's breakfast sat abandoned as he paced, firing questions at Harvey about the events of the night before.

"Sit and eat while we wait for Garret," Zephyr said before her honey-coloured gaze fell on Harvey, and she gave him a small smile. "Harvey has already confirmed that it wasn't Amelia."

Declan scooped up his plate and deposited himself onto the log beside Harvey with a huff.

"This woman implied that the corruption could be healed?" Zephyr asked, tracing her finger around the rim of her cup.

"Yes, and we believe the healer she was referring to is Margot."

"The one who created the cure?"

"She just finished what I had started," Declan said through a mouthful of his breakfast.

Zephyr rolled her eyes at him. "This Margot is a healer. But your healers can only mend wounds of the flesh, not mental or spiritual wounds. Is that correct?"

"Yes," both Harvey and Declan responded.

"Curious then that the spectre in the woods suggested Margot would be able to heal corruption ... Unless she meant through the use of her serum."

"She didn't name Margot, but she said she had healed 'the one who is sister but not by blood,' and we assumed that the sister she referred to was Nea," Harvey said.

Janey joined them, giving Harvey a smile as she sat next to Zephyr. The two women could not be more different. Zephyr was tall and slender, her sleek, ink-black hair shone with highlights of blue when the sun hit it. Janey was a good head shorter, her features softer, and her chestnut hair lit with fiery hues of copper and scarlet. At a distance, her eyes appeared a similar green to Declan's, but up close they had flecks of gold at their centre.

"You still with us, Harvey?" Declan's mouth pulled into that distinctive off-kilter grin.

Harvey was saved any further ribbing as Garret approached looking like he hadn't gotten any sleep. "Leith wants you all in the barn as soon as you're done with breakfast."

Janey stood and her hands flashed. *"Are you alright?"*

Garret ran his finger along his lip and gave a short nod.

The corners of Janey's mouth pulled in, and she settled her hands on her hips.

"I'm fine, Janey. I have to go and find Bran and Aveline." He turned on his heel and strode away.

Janey shook her head. *"Stubborn arse."* She signed.

Harvey chuckled. "You know what he's like, Janey. There's probably only one person in the world who can help when he's in this mood."

Declan snorted. "She's not available right now. He just needs to have a good yell at someone. Any takers?"

"Let him stew. I am sure he'll come around when he's good and ready," Zephyr said as she stood. "Come on. We probably shouldn't keep Leith waiting."

When they entered the barn, Niall, Leith, and Trenton were already there. Aveline and Bran arrived shortly after with Garret.

"Yesterday we concluded that sending an envoy to Merston is a good idea and also sending someone to retrieve Warren." Leith rested his hands on the table in front of him. "So, who are we going to send?"

"I'm the only one here who knows how to reach Warren," Niall said.

"Then you will go retrieve him, though you should probably take a few others with you. What about Merston?" Leith settled his grey gaze on Garret.

"You're best to send a mage or a warden or both. I doubt the college will open to a keen-less. But I would be cautious who you pick. Someone who already has an association with the college or better yet, High Mage Julianna, would be ideal." Garret seemed more focused than the day before, which was a good sign. But it hadn't escaped Harvey's notice that every so often he would press his arm against his side. The movement was surreptitious, and those who didn't know the warden probably wouldn't notice it.

"As High Mage of your own college, I guess that makes you a good option," Leith said to Niall. "Or perhaps you, Aveline?"

"Niall can hardly go to Merston if he is going to collect Warren," Declan said.

"And I'm not the best choice either," Aveline answered. "Last time I saw Julianna, we didn't exactly part on good terms."

"Then we are back at square one."

"Aren't Jasper and Haley from Merston originally?" Harvey asked.

"Originally, yes, but like all healers before the purge, Jasper was sent to Kalhanna for training. He's a good candidate, but sending him leaves us without a healer," Garret replied.

Zephyr held her hand up. "Are you forgetting I can heal?"

"Of course, sorry, Zephyr. We can ask Jasper. Haley has gone—" Garret was cut off by a commotion outside.

A yellow dog came barrelling through the barn door, barking happily. He darted through Declan's legs and leapt onto Zephyr's lap, wiggling as he tried to lick her face.

"Okay, okay. Calm down." She laughed. "Yes, I am sure I can fix this ... as soon as I figure out what *this* is."

The terrier gave her face another lick then flicked his gaze from Declan to Garret to Harvey and then everyone else. His eyes were strangely multifaceted and didn't seem to have just one colour but the whole spectrum. There was a ring of darker yellow fur around one of them.

"Wade?" Declan and Garret said together.

"What in the realms happened to you?" Declan asked, and the dog barked.

"Apparently it happened when he came through the tear," Penny said as she entered the barn followed by Margot, Emil, and a necromancer who Harvey didn't recognise. "So, what have we missed?"

"We were just figuring out who to send to Merston and who was going to retrieve Warren," Leith said.

"Why Merston?" Penny asked.

"To see if there is someone there who might know how we can approach closing the tear, but also to warn them about the current state of things."

"Julianna isn't going to let just anyone in. Even before the lockdown, she was picky about who could enter the college." Penny twisted a coil of her chestnut hair around her finger.

"We were considering sending Jasper," Garret said.

Penny's dark gaze flicked from Leith to Garret. "I can get into Merston. Julianna and I have an *understanding*."

"But you also know how to get to Warren," Niall said.

"Yes, and now so do Margot and Emil." She gave the other mind mage a sly smile.

"And who is the necromancer?" Garret asked.

The man in question was standing just inside the door. His silver hair contrasted against his deep bronze skin, and there was a certain mirth in his hazel gaze as he settled it on Garret. "Arcanius Mateus of the Dalthera Arcanarium at your service. You must be Nea's warden."

Harvey bit down on his remark at Mateus's comment and cast a sideways glance at Declan, who was sporting a wide smirk.

"I'm Garret, and this is ..." He held his hand out, and the others all introduced themselves.

Mateus's gaze settled on Janey, who gave him a small smile and wave.

"That's Janey," Harvey said for her.

Mateus cocked his head to the side as his gaze slid over the jagged scar at Janey's throat. But his features did not show the usual pity or revulsion, merely a mild curiosity. "A pleasure to meet you all."

"And why are you wearing bind-shackles?" Margot asked Garret.

"We can discuss that later."

Margot's mouth tightened at the finality in his tone, but she said nothing.

"Penny can go to Merston. But it would be a good idea to send someone with her. Any takers?" Leith drew their attention back to the matter at hand.

"I'll go with her," Emil said.

"I think Harvey should go as well," Niall said.

"Why me?"

"I have a hunch that you will find answers to some questions that have plagued you since Hartswood," the mage replied.

"Right ... Well, if I am not needed here, then I don't see why not." He directed at Garret and Leith.

They shared a look, and Leith shrugged. "I'm fine with it. Now we just need to settle on who will go retrieve Warren." His gaze shifted to Margot and then Niall. "Any volunteers?"

"I can go see him. I doubt we will get him to come here though, so it might be better to just arm me with questions and hope he deigns to answer them."

"The fen is dangerous, Margot. You shouldn't go alone," Penny said.

"You know what Warren is like about company. It will be easier dealing with him if it is just me."

"What if another necromancer went?" Bran asked. "Wouldn't Warren be more accepting of his own kind?"

"Warren is not accepting of anyone," Niall said dryly. "However, it might not hurt to send a necromancer. If Warren proves too stubborn to come himself then a fellow necromancer has the best hope of understanding any knowledge the old bastard decides to share."

"Personally, I wouldn't mind meeting this Warren," Declan said.

"Excellent." Leith rubbed his hands together. "I am glad that is finally settled. Now the rest of us will focus on fortifying this camp and assessing what can be done about the things coming from the tear. For now, however, I would call this meeting adjourned. Garret, there are a few other matters I wish to discuss."

As they excited the barn, Harvey darted around Declan, who was introducing Zephyr to Margot and the others, and caught up with Janey. He tapped her shoulder, and she turned to him with a wide smile.

"You need to keep an eye on Garret."

Her smile faltered, and she pursed her lips.

"The corruption is hitting him harder than he's letting on."

She rolled her eyes and opened her hands in front of her.

"I know it's obvious, but last night ... last night he asked me to end his life if the corruption took over." He licked his lip. "I've never seen him like that."

The fire in her green eyes softened, and she brushed her fingers against his arm before giving it a squeeze as she rose on her toes and lightly kissed his cheek. *"Don't worry about Garret. Just be careful. You might not like what you learn,"* she signed as she pulled away.

She was referring to the answers Niall said might be at Merston. It had taken Harvey weeks to come to terms with the knowledge that he was not keen-less but the result of Evard's experiments to breed a new type of mage. Niall said his keen had been locked away, but by who and why? Were those the answers he would find at Merston ...? Or could his father have been a mage from the college? If he was and he was still alive, maybe he could shed some light on Evard's experiments, and maybe he would know who had locked away Harvey's keen. The thought was both exciting and nerve-wracking.

"I promise I will try," he said as he slid an arm around her waist and touched a delicate kiss to her lips.

CHAPTER FIVE

MARGOT

The mist that clung in milky swathes across the ground stirred around Margot's legs as she wandered the field. Wade trotted beside her, his golden fur a muted greyish-tan in the predawn light. The anchor whispered in the back of her mind, leading her away from the camp. Any sane person would probably ignore the compulsion, but the anchor had become such an intrinsic part of her that it was like she was following her own instinct. Not 'the whims of a parasitic entity', as Penny seemed to believe. As though Penny had any right to judge Margot for her choice. After all, she had let Nea put that brightling soul inside her. Margot's relationship with the anchor was no different. She let out a huff, the winter air turning her breath into a plume of white.

A shadow lurked ahead. Tall, broad, and coming towards her with a familiar stride. His head snapped up, and his mouth pulled into a frown as his grey gaze settled on her.

"What are you doing wandering about this early, Margot?"

"I could ask you the same question. Harvey told me you haven't been sleeping well."

Wade did a slow circle around Garret's legs then sat in the dewy grass, his head tilted as he watched the pair of them.

Garret rubbed the scar on his top lip as he regarded the dog before his attention returned to Margot. "There is no need for concern. I'm just a little unsettled. It will pass once we have a way to deal with the tear."

Margot shook her head. "I know you better than that. Is it the shackles?"

"They are not helping, but honestly, Margot, you don't need to worry about me. I have it under control."

She didn't believe him for a second. "Why won't you let me try and heal it like I did Nea's?"

"It's an unnecessary risk at this stage. I am managing it just fine."

"But you're not. You might be able to lie to yourself about it, but the rest of us can see straight through you, Garret. You need to let me help you."

"Not at the cost of your own keen."

"That is my decision to make. You—"

"And this is mine!"

She drew a sharp breath at his tone.

They studied each other for a while before Garret said quietly, "I'm sorry."

"You are putting yourself through unnecessary torment." She placed a hand on his arm.

"I can endure it." His jaw worked like he was pressing his back teeth together.

"But you don't have to. I can heal you—I know I can."

"And you are certain that healing Nea didn't change your keen?"

She chewed her thumbnail. It had changed her keen, but she wasn't convinced that it was a negative change. "Yes, it did change my keen."

He opened his mouth to speak, but she lifted a hand to stop him.

"Not in a bad way though, and honestly if changing my keen allows me to actually heal corruption then I will pay that price. We still don't have a proper cure for corruption. What if this is it? What if *I* am it?" The anchor sung under her skin. "What if this is my—" *Destiny?* Could she believe in destiny? She gave a short laugh and shook her head before meeting his cool, grey gaze. "What if changing my keen to cure corruption is my *destiny?*" There, she had said it.

"Since when do you believe in destiny?"

She grabbed his hands and gave them a squeeze. "I don't know. But I feel it at my very centre, that this is something I have to do, and I will pay whatever price I have to. You and Nea throw yourselves into danger and uncertainty time and time again, so you have no place lecturing me about taking risks. And quite frankly, it is time you both stood aside and let others carry some of the burden. Please let me try to heal your corruption."

Wade gave a small yipping bark, and Garret let a breath out as he extracted his hands from Margot's grip. Something was warring deep inside him. She could see it in the tilt of his mouth and the darkness in his eyes as he studied her face.

"You can't be the only one to make sacrifices to save others. That is how you end up like Nea." She sniffed and took a step back.

Garret refused to meet her eye.

"Don't make me watch another of my dearest friends destroy their humanity in the name of protecting me." She turned on her heel.

"Margot, wait."

She stopped and looked back over her shoulder.

"You're right. I should at least let you try. But if anything bad starts to happen, we stop immediately."

"Okay." She gave a nod, a small smile smoothing the tightness of her mouth. "We should get Niall and Declan. They are both experienced with unpredictable magic."

"I'll do it. We'll meet up in the barn shortly."

Niall and Declan weren't the only ones in the barn when Margot arrived. Mateus, Zephyr, and Aveline were there as well, all sitting on one of the benches at the side of the room. The door opened, and Ryan and Jasper walked in. It had taken Ryan a long time to recover from the burns he had received in the fight at Fort Braemar. The left side of his face and neck still bore the scars. His arm and torso had fared better as they had been protected by the enchanted lining of his warden leathers. But there was a webbing of scars between the fingers of his left hand where the skin had fused in the healing process. Margot had never witnessed someone with such extensive burning live to tell the tale, let alone heal well enough for their life to go mostly back to normal.

"You wanted to see me?" Ryan asked Garret after casting a quick glance at those present.

Garret nodded. "We need a warden in case something goes awry. If the corruption takes over or something happens to Margot's keen, you need to be ready to suppress it."

Ryan gave a nod, and he and Jasper joined the others at the side of the room.

Niall came forward with the key to the bind-shackles. "You are both certain you want to do this?" He met Garret's eye then Margot's.

They nodded.

Even though everyone's concern was understandable, it was starting to irritate Margot. She knew what was at stake, probably more than any of them realised. The anchor quivered under her skin, soothing her rising ire. The spirit told her she would be alright but that there was still a need for caution. Garret's corruption wouldn't be like Nea's.

As a daughter of Shadow, Nea's relationship with the corruption had been different. They hadn't healed it, rather they had helped Nea access it, and her own keen had transformed it. Margot hadn't told the others this yet. She probably should have, but she knew deep in her core that healing corruption was what she was meant to do. And it wasn't just the anchor's influence—it was her own purpose. She was as sure of that as her love for Molly. If the others knew the truth about what happened with Nea then they might not let her attempt to heal Garret.

"Ready, Margot?" Niall asked, breaking through her thoughts.

"Yes."

Niall touched the key to Garret's shackles, and they fell away. The high mage collected them and took a step back as Garret gritted his teeth and collapsed into a chair.

Margot placed her hands on his shoulders and let her keen out. The anchor stirred to life, coiling with her keen and twisting it as it searched for the corruption. Her vision blurred for a moment and nails raked across the inside of her skull. Then she was falling into a tangled mass of vines. Something was just ahead of her: a golden light flickering as it fought the vines strangling it. She pushed into the brightness and let her keen empower it.

The vines recoiled as the golden light enveloped her—

Something hard jolted against her back.

Shaking fingers pressed to her neck.

"Margot?" That was Declan's voice. "She's not responding."

"Move," Jasper said.

Warmth flooded her veins, healing keen, like her own. But no, her own keen felt foreign now. "I can't find anything wrong ..." Jasper muttered. "Margot?" He patted her cheeks gently.

Her eyes felt gritty, but she forced them open. Jasper's hazel gaze met hers, and his lower jaw dropped before snapping into a frown. "Are you ... what do you feel?"

Margot shook her head. What *did* she feel? Heavy and cold, but something was burning, consuming her keen. It started in her core and ran out in prickling rivers under every inch of her skin. She studied the backs of her hands and tried to call on her keen to summon a mage light. The orb burst into life, but it was not soft green it had always been. It was silver with shimmers of green and lilac twisting through it. She swallowed.

"Margot?" Niall crouched in front of her. "Oh my, they have changed," he said as his violet gaze met hers. "Can you speak?"

Margot nodded. Of course, she could speak. Why were they acting like something was wrong; she felt fine. She felt better than fine. She glanced at the others. Garret was standing back, his arms folded and his jaw working. Declan rubbing his hands together, his face white. The others all wore similar expressions except Zephyr, who had her head tilted, a sparkle of keen interest in her honey-gold eyes.

"So that is where you ended up then," Zephyr said.

"Where who ended up?" Margot asked. The anchor tingled, bringing a warm smile to her lips.

Both Jasper and Niall let out a heavy breath.

"Who are you talking to?" Declan asked.

"Zephyr," Margot replied.

Declan flicked a look between them.

"Oh, you didn't say it out loud?"

The other woman shook her head. "I thought it might help break through your shock. How do you feel?"

"Different but not necessarily bad. Did it work?" She studied Garret.

"Not entirely. But it is subdued enough that my suppression can control it again," he said tightly. "I am still not convinced it was worth the risk."

"I'm fine."

"You might want to take a look in the mirror. Your keen isn't the only thing that changed," Declan said, his tone light but the humour not quite reaching his eyes.

"What do you mean?"

Niall's keen tickled across the back of her neck, and an image of herself flashed across her mind. There was a streak of black in her golden ringlets that originated from just above her right temple, and her eyes, which should have been warm brown, were a soft pink.

"Oh. That will certainly take some getting used to."

Niall gave a nod. "The eye colour seems to be slowly reverting back to your natural brown, which would suggest it is a temporary result of using your keen. Historically not unheard of, though I can't remember exactly which scholar referenced the phenomenon. However, there is no telling if it could become permanent through prolonged use of this new keen. I would suggest you put a hold on any further testing for now."

Margot bit down on her reply and sighed. "Alright." Her altered keen was prickling under her skin. It could sense the seed of corruption still lurking inside Garret, though his warden suppression had risen and stopped the taint from progressing ... for now. Who knew how long it would be before it took over again. They should just let her heal it and be done with it.

"Now that we have that out of the way, perhaps it is a good time to gather our things and go get Warren," Declan said, flicking a look in Garret's direction.

Garret nodded. "The sooner you get him the better. We have to get that tear closed as quickly as we can." He turned his attention to Jasper. "I'm going to need more of the corruption treatment. I can only suppress it for so long."

"I'll see what we have on hand. There should be another jar or two," Jasper said.

"Good, good. It also might not hurt to send a bird to Del Harol and request more," Niall mused. "Not just for Garret. Exposure to the tear will put the rest of the keen-folk here at an increased risk of corruption."

"Then should I stay and someone else go after Warren? That way I can heal any—"

"It is too risky for you to attempt healing it until we understand this new keen of yours more." Declan cut Margot off.

She folded her arms.

"Don't give me that look. Healing Garret was—"

"Taxing, yes. But maybe it had something to do with him being a brightling. And when did *you* start being cautious about experimenting with new forms of magic?"

Declan's mouth pulled into an uncharacteristically tight line. "When it got me killed."

Everyone looked away from the pair of them, except Mateus who leant forward, avid curiosity sparkling in his eyes as the cool kiss of his keen washed over them.

Jasper muttered something about checking supplies and left with Ryan in tow.

"Leith wanted to see us when we were done here." Aveline slid her hand around the crook of Niall's elbow and dragged him out the door.

Zephyr licked her lip. "I'll go let Bran know he needs to be ready to leave for Fengate shortly." She followed the others.

"I'm sorry, Declan." Margot swallowed. "I didn't think. I just—"

"I got lucky. But I also learned some magics are not worth the price." Something flashed behind his eyes, too fast for her to properly identify. Fear, or perhaps remorse. But with a tilt of his chin it was gone, and he was turning to give Mateus his signature off-kilter grin. "Does the term deathwalker ring a bell?"

Mateus's eyes widened. "I have questions."

Declan laughed. "I bet you do, and I am happy to answer them if you answer some of mine. But they may have to wait until I return from the fens."

"Deal," Mateus said and shook Declan's hand before they both left.

Margot turned to Garret.

"I'll be fine," he said as he started towards the door. "I can control it now." Then he was gone.

That's what it wants you to think. The anchor spirit whispered, and the mark on Margot's palm throbbed in time with the words.

CHAPTER SIX

NEA

Quel'sapar might be the haunt of rogues, pirates, and other dubious members of society, but it was still a city just like any other. A small city that clung to a tiny, enchanted island that shifted about on a whim and could only be reached by an equally enchanted ship; but still a city. It didn't have distinct districts based on class, like New Brenna with its Dust Town and upper market, rather it was one long kind of ... slum that zig-zagged up the cliff face with Vince's palatial mansion perched on top. In the early morning, with a thin mist clinging to the seaside edge of the street and golden sunlight just starting to glitter off the edges of the buildings, it was almost beautiful. A pig dressed in silk. Or maybe a wolf dressed in wool was the more appropriate analogy.

Nea lithely dodged around a red-faced woman carrying an overladen basket of laundry and murmured a quick apology that was met with a stern glare and a grunt. Turning back to the street, she adjusted the hood that hid her hair and counted the buildings. There seemed to be more than last time she had been here. She was sure the rickety pawn shop with the red door had been the end of the row, but now there was another slapdash building with a green door and a slanted sign that read: *Apotikary*. Shaking her head at the misspelling, she glanced to the end of street where Rourke sat in the sand waiting for her. He tilted his head as she approached.

"I was sure the path started somewhere along here," she said to herself as much as him.

Garret's keen fluttered under the ward mark, and she touched her fingers to it. During their time in the Between, she had started to get used to the feeling of his keen tangled with hers. But now his keen was faint and buried deep with the seething wrongness of corruption tainting it. So those moments when it drifted to the surface were a troubling mixture of comfort and anxiety that threatened to dredge up the memories of the purge.

Biting her lip, she lifted her hand. It wouldn't hurt to just check on him, would it? She didn't even have to step through the portal. She could just use it like a window to see where he was. Her keen built behind her navel and lilac flickered over her fingers.

Rourke made a sound—not a growl as such but a warning, and she snapped her fingers over her palm and dropped her arm.

"I need to focus." She rubbed her hands over her face. "I know."

"Talking to yourself again, are you?" Molly jogged up to her. "You could have woken me."

"I tried. You said, 'Mother's tits, Nea, it's too early for that,' and rolled over. And I wasn't talking to myself—this time, I was talking to Rourke."

"You said you were just going for a walk. It didn't look like you were taking a *walk* just now."

Nea toyed with her lip.

"Were you going to check on Garret? Why didn't you?"

"It's dangerous. If Leon has him, there is a chance he could capture us both. If Garret is too close to the tear, then there is a chance that the magic could cause another catastrophe. Portals briefly destabilise the barrier and in turn the source. If I create one too close to the tear, there is no telling what it could do."

"It's always dramatics with you mages," Molly muttered.

"And anyway, Garret is a distraction. I need to focus on finding the old Shadow temple."

Molly's cheek bulged like she was probing it with her tongue. "Bull ... shit," she said, dragging the word out with a grin.

"I'm sorry?"

"Garret *is* a distraction. But are you distracted because you are worried about him? Or are you distracted because you're worried that you're worried about him?"

Nea blinked at her.

"You want to know your biggest fault? It's not that you're impulsive and stubborn. It's that you can't decide if you want to be governed by your head or your heart. From what everyone says, your emotions run deep. So deep that your father said they effect the source itself. And that explains why other mages and wardens wince when you get angry. It would also suggest that you are led by your heart, but then that big brain of yours gets in the way and you overthink things and trip over yourself. You're doing it right now. It's alright to be worried about Garret." She glanced out at the ocean and then back at Nea. "You're allowed to feel the good things just as much as the bad. So, yes, Garret is a distraction, but he's a good one, and being worried about him doesn't mean you are losing focus it just means you're human."

"It's not—"

"How about we keep moving before I decide to slap some sense into you? I've seen Wren do it, so I know it works." There was a sparkle of mischief in her eyes. "You said you're looking for a temple. Where do we start?"

"The path that leads to the temple started right around here, but everything has become so overgrown." She indicated the lush greenery that edged the sand.

Molly cast a look over the beach and then back at the buildings. She mouthed 'apotikary' and gave a snort. "What exactly are we looking for?"

"There used to be a statue of a dog that marked the beginning of the path."

"If you have been there before, can't you just"—she flicked her hands in front of her—"*poof* us in there?"

Nea bit back a laugh. "I could if I remembered what the inside of the temple looked like, but I have only been in there once before and I was too"—a rush of heat ran up the sides of her neck—"distracted to pay any real attention to my surroundings."

"Distracted?"

"That's not important." She stepped around Rourke and headed towards the overgrowth, trying not to think of the last time she had been on this beach: silver moonlight playing over the waves, chill water splashing around her legs as Leith chased her through the shallows. They'd stumbled across the sand, and that was when Nea had noticed the dog statue sitting proud in its little shroud of vines at the edge of an old, well-worn path. "I think it was around about here. I recognise that twisted tree."

She crouched and brushed the sand away from the base of the tree to reveal the slab of stone beneath it. Molly joined her as she traced her fingers along the score marks that marred the grey surface. "Someone took the trail marker."

"Why?"

Nea shrugged and sat back on her heels with a sigh. "I don't know, but at least we found the trail. Come on." She stood and brushed her hands on her pants.

The undergrowth had reclaimed the path, making the going hard. Vines grabbed at their ankles, clothes, and hair and left stinging scratches on Nea's cheeks. The sun was getting higher and the air becoming more humid, but she fought the urge to roll her sleeves up. When Nea had been here with Leith, the trail hadn't exactly been well maintained but it was still clear enough to follow—the undergrowth kept back, and the fallen trees pushed off to the sides. Now only the odd grey stone peeking through the scrub told her they were still heading the right way.

"Oh, wow. I wish Margot was here to see this," Molly said as they rounded a bend.

Sunlight glittered off the waves lapping at the edges of the plinths of stone that guarded the harbour below. Beyond those silent grey sentinels, the ocean extended to the horizon in a fathomless deep blue.

"Leith liked the view as well," Nea said without thinking.

"That explains why you were too *distracted* to pay attention to the temple," Molly said with a grin.

Nea chewed her lip.

"You know, I never understood how the pair of you worked. You're both more attractive than should be allowed, so I get it from a physical sense, but he's so carefree. Well, he was before the world went to shit. And you're so ..." She gestured at Nea as though not sure how exactly to describe her.

"I wasn't always." She studied the horizon. "We were both young idiots. He was trying to run away from his responsibilities, and I needed a little bit of fun. A break from expectations, and just one part of my life that was ... easy."

Molly nodded as though she understood. "If Evard hadn't ... if you didn't disappear."

"I doubt it would have changed much; we were always on borrowed time."

"But what about Henry?"

A smile curved the corner of Nea's mouth. "Maybe ... but by that stage Leith and I wanted—needed different things."

Molly gave another nod then turned her attention back to the path. "We should probably keep moving. Is it much farther?"

Nea shook her head. "It should be just around the next bend."

The entrance to the temple was marked by a bower of roses carved around the mouth of a small cave. Nea summoned a mage light as they approached the entryway, and it bobbed ahead of them as they ducked into the tunnel. They had to crouch for several metres before the passage opened out into a large, circular cavern. Lilac-tinted-light danced over the space, highlighting the gouges in the rock where a statue of the Shadow Man had stood. Nea walked forward and ran her hand along the edge of the stone slab that had once been an altar on which offerings had been laid.

"Everything is gone," she whispered as she examined the empty shelves at the back of the room. Books and other small items littered the ground as though cast aside when they were found wanting. The Shadow Man was not revered in the same manner as the Bright Mother, but he still had his following, especially amongst the types who frequented Quel'sapar. Who would have the audacity to enter the temple and desecrate it in such a manner? *Vince.* But why?

She rested her hands on the edge of the altar again. The swirling marks on her right arm shone purple, and something tugged at her core. Rourke nudged her thigh and put his paws on the edge of the stone slab. What if she fed it her magic? She examined the crescent moon at her palm and then pressed her hand against the centre of the stone and let her keen rush out. The stone was covered in small freckles of milky quartz, and they all lit up with a glimmer of lilac magic, twinkling like a field of stars in a dark sky.

"What did you just do?" Molly asked.

"She reawakened the magic of the temple," a familiar voice said, and Nea looked up.

The Shadow Man was standing where the statue had once been. He was nothing more than a flickering spectre, his dark grey hair brushing his shoulders and his violet eyes sparkling with mischief.

"Is that the Shadow Man?" Molly asked.

Nea gave a nod.

"So, he can tell you where to find the thrones, right?"

The Shadow man chuckled. "Of course not. Even if I did know where they could be found, it would be too easy to just tell you."

"Right, because gods, like mages, need to overcomplicate everything."

"No, because if you are just handed all the answers then what is the point?"

Molly opened her mouth to argue, but Nea placed a hand on her shoulder. "Is there anything you *can* tell us?"

The Shadow Man drew a long breath and frowned. "There was a book once that may have helped, and a key stone that would unlock the way once the seeker found the right path." He lifted a hand and pointed towards one of the frescoes on the wall. It was faded, the paint chipped away in places, but if you tilted your head, it almost looked like a tower. "I imagine the one that ransacked this shrine has them."

Garret's keen suddenly overwhelmed Nea, surging under her skin in a white heat that sent spots dancing across her vision as a bitter taste coated the inside of her mouth. It only lasted a few seconds, then the sensations died down and his keen was once more thrumming through the death ward as it had done before—clear and steady with just an edge of corruption.

The Shadow Man twisted his mouth as he studied her. "The Usurper has his hooks in your brightling. If I were you, I would seek to rectify that as soon as possible."

"How?"

His mouth tightened, and he rubbed his fingers along his forehead. "You are smart enough to figure that out on your own." He started to fade. "It would appear our time is up. I am sure you are aware of what will happen if you fail, but just in case—" He disappeared before he could finish the sentence.

"Well, that was helpful." Molly asked, "What was that warning about Garret? Should you make a portal and check on him?"

Nea shook her head. She desperately wanted to check on Garret, but there was still too much risk there. However, there was one way she might be able to do it without risking a portal. "We need to get back to the Queen."

Nea sat on the edge of the bed in the captain's quarters of The Azure Queen. Dara hovered nearby, twisting her fingers together, and Molly stood by the door holding a steaming cup.

"Nea, I don't know about this," Dara said.

"All you need to do is wait until I am asleep and then link our songs together. I should be able to do the rest."

"But I don't know Garret's song."

"You do. That thrum that you said has blended with my song, that is Garret. You heard him through the death ward." She pointed to the orange star on the inside of her wrist. "I just want you to try, Dara. Please?"

The girl nodded. "Alright."

Nea held out her hand for the cup, and as Molly passed it to her, the scent of the sleeping brew made her eyes heavy. She took a numbing mouthful and winced at the bitter undertone before downing the rest in one go.

Her eyes were already sliding shut as she lay back. Dara's fingers touched her temples and a song built inside her mind. A smooth melancholic melody, it reached a deafening volume then the deep vibrating echo of drum joined it. Nea drew a halting breath, and the darkness flickered before peeling back to reveal what appeared to be the interior of a barn. Garret sat in front of her, head in his hands and the table before him strewn with papers and a large map.

CHAPTER SEVEN

GARRET

"Any word from the capital?" Trenton asked as he joined Leith and Garret in the barn.

"Reanimations prowl the streets and Dust Town has been deserted. Upper market and the temple district haven't fared much better, and the temple itself has been locked down," Garret replied, handing Haley's report to the soldier. "They have taken refuge in the safe house on the south side, but as far as they can tell, Leon and Kieran have either barricaded themselves and their men inside the palace or they have left the capital completely."

"Should we send another small group to help Haley and the others?" Leith asked.

"It's not the worst idea," Trenton said.

Garret shook his head. "It would be better if we could get someone inside the palace. We need to locate Leon and Kieran, Leon in particular. We can't risk losing him while the Usurper is still inhabiting his body."

"Who would we send though? If they are discovered, I doubt Leon would hesitate to have them killed. Assuming he is the one calling the shots now given Kieran's case of corruption." Trenton had a point.

They needed someone who would go unnoticed, who was familiar with the inside of the palace. Garret rubbed the scar above his lip. "Janey."

"Who?"

"Janey," he repeated. "She knows the inside of the palace, including the hidden passageways, like the back of her hand. That knowledge will allow her to move about unnoticed, and she is more than capable of defending herself if needed."

Leith nodded. "And she's in good with the servants."

"If any of them are still alive," Trenton muttered.

Garret started for the door. "I'll ask her now."

"If you wanted to send an escort with her, I have a couple of soldiers who would be suitable. Once they get Janey to the palace, they can meet up with the others in the safe house." Trenton said behind him.

"Alright. If Janey agrees then they can all leave at first light, but you'll need someone who can understand her sign language," Garret said before heading out to find Janey.

He found her with Zephyr and Mateus. The necromancer's attention moved to Garret before either of the women noticed him. His hazel eyes narrowed as the cool touch of his keen smoothed down Garret's spine. The sensation brought Nea to the front of his mind, but Mateus's keen, whilst being similar to Nea's, was not the same. They were two keens cut from the same cloth but sewn together in completely different fashions. A smile tugged at his mouth. Wade would enjoy that analogy.

"Faring better now?" Mateus asked, causing both Zephyr and Janey to look in Garret's direction.

The necromancer was, of course, referring to the corruption, which wasn't gone but had been brought back under the control of Garret's suppression by Margot. Controlling it was taxing, and Garret had taken to using Margot's treatment once more, which took the edge off his keen-sense but kept the braying voice mostly at bay. He just wished it could keep Leon from his dreams. "Much, thank you."

Mateus rubbed his fingers along his lip and gave a short nod.

"We were just trying to figure out how to fix Wade," Zephyr said brightly. "If we were back in the Between, I could switch his body back no problem. Maybe exposing him to the tear again might help."

Garret shook his head. "Until we have a better understanding—"

"I know. No prolonged exposure to it and no messing around or experimenting." She cocked her head to the side, and her keen pressed against his mind. "You're not just 'doing the rounds' though, are you?"

"No, I'm not. I was looking for Janey actually."

The woman in question gave him a wide grin and tapped the centre of her chest.

"Yes. We need someone to infiltrate the palace, and because you know the secret passageways, we came to the conclusion that you would be best suited to the task. It is dangerous, and you certainly don't have to agree to—"

She held up both hands to stop him and then nodded.

"You'll do it?"

Janey nodded again.

Garret was not sure if he was relieved or not. He didn't like sending Janey into danger, and if Harvey were around then he would be sure to put up an argument. For which Garret wouldn't blame him; it had been obvious for a long time that the soldier had a sweet spot for Janey. But she was more than capable of taking care of herself. "Thank you. We are just working out the particulars now." He indicated the barn.

Janey gave Mateus and Zephyr a wave, her smile faltering briefly as the other woman lurched forward and gave her a hug.

"Be careful, Janey," Zephyr said.

"I might not be a healer, but make sure you're getting enough rest," Mateus said to Garret quietly as Janey started towards the barn. "I know you think you have it under control, but I am also sure you know it needs only the tiniest of openings to take over." He then turned to Zephyr with a warm smile. "Niall said he brought a bunch of books with him that might help us understand this tear. Shall we go and see if one might shed some light on what to do with Wade?"

Zephyr cast a look at Garret before answering Mateus's question. "I've already been through most of them but certainly, lead the way." She touched Garret's arm and gave it a small squeeze before following the necromancer towards Niall and Aveline's tent.

The touch had been enough for her keen to flood his body for a moment. As it receded again, the corruption stirred, but Garret's suppression rose and quelled it in an instant as though Zephyr's keen had lent strength to Garret's own. It wasn't something he was unfamiliar with. He and Nea seemed to be able to share keen easily, as if it had always been something they could do. That was a result of the death ward, he was sure. Like Nea, however, Zephyr wasn't a normal mage. She was Nundle, an intrinsic race of the Between. Perhaps that was why she could so easily lend him her keen. The brightling part of him had risen almost as quickly as the corruption when Zephyr's keen had invaded his body. It yearned to understand it, to learn its inner workings and wield it as it had Nea's necromancy and Declan's storm magic. Garret wasn't sure he wanted that. Zephyr's keen was different and ever changing, much like the fabric of the Between itself.

Garret rubbed his hands over his face and blinked at the map laid out on the table. The others had all turned in for the night, but he couldn't risk sleep. The corruption had been edging into his dreams more and more each night, and he wasn't ready to face Leon's silent presence just yet.

Arrogant laughter flickered at the back of his mind, and he reached for the jar of Margot's ointment. The laughter died down as he rubbed a smear over the mark on his side. The hand-sized, web-like stain was a deep grey, almost the same shade as Nea's hair. Before Margot had healed him, it had been jet-black and covered his side nearly all the way from his hip to his armpit.

He drew a long breath and resealed the jar before falling into a chair. Normally, this was about the time he would go for a walk to clear his head, but his thoughts had become groggy, and his limbs weighed down. His body craved sleep.

The ward mark on his wrist rippled with an achingly familiar cold keen. Peppermint clouded his senses, and he inhaled deeply.

"Garret?" Her voice was soft, concerned, and he could see the small pinch between her brows, the sheen of unfathomable sadness in her eyes at the back of his mind. "Garret, look at me."

He opened his eyes and turned in his chair. Nea was beside him, her violet gaze glittering in the lamplight as she studied his features before taking a step closer. The movement and the scratching itch of corruption under his skin brought the scenes from the labyrinth in the Between to the forefront of his mind.

He fought the urge to pull back. This wasn't that cruel spectre pretending to be Nea; it was the real Nea. His Nea. "Are you really here? How are you here?"

"Physically? No. We are both dreaming. It's a long story, and one I will gladly share when we are not so pressed for time." She frowned, her keen brushing him as she stepped between him and the table.

Her fingers traced lightly over his temples and then laced into his hair, their cool tips rubbing small circles across the sides of his skull that sent a tingle of relief down his spine. The coolness of her keen soothed the edges of the corruption, and he let out a groan, closing his eyes and resting his cheek against her chest. The steady beat of her heart thumped against his ear as she held him, her keen bolstering his own and giving him back control.

Almost too soon, she pulled away, her eyes glassy as they searched his. "You don't have to *endure* this. Margot can heal you."

"She tried already, but it's too risky. The price for fixing this is permanently changing her keen ... I can't ask that—"

"If Margot knows the price and is willing to pay, then you need to let her ... Please?"

He studied her face and took hold of her hands. "I have it—"

"Don't be stubborn. I've sacrificed a lot to save this world. Don't make the same mistakes I did ... Please don't make me do this alone."

"She has so much faith in you. It is going to be delightful watching you crush it. We cannot wait for the day you accept your fate and betray her trust. We've seen what she can become, what she will become, and you will be the catalyst."

Garret pressed his teeth together and smothered the rising voice with his suppression.

Nea's keen washed over him again, and the grey marks on her right arm lit up violet for a moment. He twisted her arm, studying the swirling patterns then traced the crescent moon at her palm.

Her mouth twitched at the corner. "Margot transformed it, or she unlocked it so my own keen could. I think I started the process when I infected Kieran," she said.

"Is it healed?"

She shook her head. "It's part of me. I guess you could say it is healed in that I am the one in control now, not it. It's part of my birthright, which makes sense given that I possess the literal blood of the Shadow."

"It seems to be quelling the corruption in me. Could it heal it?"

She opened her mouth to respond then closed it again. "Perhaps, but not through the dream-link. There is only so much I can manipulate here." She leant forward and pressed her lips to the edge of his jaw. "We don't have much longer. Dara is inexperienced, and I don't want to overtax her. I just wanted to check on you."

He turned his head and caught her lips with his. "I'm glad you did," he whispered as he pulled back.

"I wish I could stay a little longer," she said, one corner of her mouth pulling into a smile as she bit her lip.

Garret rested his hands on her hips as he stood. "I do, too, but you really should be getting back." He dropped another kiss to her mouth, and she pressed against him, her fingers winding into his hair.

Guiding her backwards, he reached out and swept the maps, books, and empty cups that littered the table aside before lifting her onto the edge.

Her legs wrapped around him, pinning their bodies together as her fingers slipped under the hem of his shirt, lifting it—

"My, my. I am loathe to interrupt this little fantasy, but the night is quickly escaping us."

Nea froze at the sound of Leon's voice. "What is he doing here?" she hissed under her breath.

"Now, now, Nea, be a good little girl and run along."

Nea's keen spiked, and her brow furrowed. Her grip on Garret tensed as the air around them grew bitterly cold. "I'm sorry. I can't fight him here." Then she disappeared.

Garret locked eyes with Leon's arrogant gaze.

"Don't look at me like that. I couldn't let Nea dominate your time. Not when she was managing to undo all my careful handy work." His fingers lightly brushed his cheek where Nea had burned him with the branding iron Kieran had been going to use on Nora. The flesh was dark and puckered and had not healed well at all. "If it weren't for that damned ward you share, the corruption would have won me your loyalty by now. The longer you stay apart, the harder it will be for her to bring you back. And I am going to make sure she cannot visit you here again." He leapt forward, and Garret dodged out of the way only to slam into someone behind him. Hands closed around his arms as a foot wound between his ankles, and he was slammed forward against the table. The sensation of cold sludge oozed down his spine.

"His suppression," Kieran hissed right beside his ear. "We will not succeed as long as it perseveres. Nea and the healer have given it the upper hand."

"A small detail. One that, given time, can be manipulated in our favour," an oily voice said.

Garret tried to turn to see who had spoken, but Kieran held him firmly in place.

"Oh, do hurry up and get it over with." That voice he knew—sweet and cloying and just a little bit unhinged: Amelia.

"You never were very patient, my dear," the oily voice said.

"One of the many things I learned in my prison was patience, *Father*," Amelia said as she stepped into view. "I simply do not wish to see poor Garret suffer any more than is necessary." She traced cold fingers down his cheek before cupping it and leaning close. "The offer I presented before is always open," she whispered before stepping back.

Leon took her place and grabbed hold of Garret's shirt, hoisting it up to reveal the corruption mark.

Amelia's cold hand traced over the mark, and as her other hand encircled the wrist that held the death ward, an acrid taste coated the back of Garret's tongue and the ward mark burned with cold. Nea's keen flared in icy spikes under his skin, fighting back as a greasy darkness attempted to smother it. Amelia grunted, and her keen pushed down harder, then a drop of blood landed on the table beside Garret's cheek. Nea's keen flared again, a panicked flurry trying desperately to hold its ground. Amelia's hands trembled, and she started to sag beside Garret, then with a final burst of her keen, Nea's lost the fight and was snuffed out.

"I didn't expect her keen to be so strong." Amelia panted as she staggered backwards.

"You did well," the oily voice said. "With that block, it will be nearly impossible for her keen to influence his corruption."

"Perfect." Leon bent so his face was level with Garret's. "I do so enjoy a little torture, and when you give in to that corruption, I am going to make sure you're the one who makes that precious little necromancer of yours scream."

"Warden Commander!" A small hand shook his arm, and Garret vaulted awake.

His chair crashed to the ground as he staggered out of it, retreating until his back slammed against the wall of the barn.

The bird tucked under the messenger boy's arm gave a disgruntled trill as its master blinked at Garret.

"Sorry to startle you, sir."

Garret swallowed. The mark on his wrist was still burning, and the corruption crawled under his skin. There was no sign that Nea, Leon, or anyone else had been in the room.

The boy cleared his throat. "I've got a message for you." He prompted.

"Right, sorry." Garret rubbed his hands over his face. "Here." He pulled a few coins out of his pocket and passed them to the boy, who handed him a piece of folded parchment.

"Pleasure as always, Commander." The boy tipped his hat and then left.

Garret glanced down at the letter; his name was written on the front in a delicate looping style that slanted to the right. *Nea.* He straightened the overturned chair and pulled his jacket on before rubbing his thumb over the seal of the letter. He tapped it against the centre of his palm. As much as he wanted to read it now, it could wait. He needed to catch Janey before she left. He tucked the letter away in the inside pocket of his jacket and drew in a deep breath in an effort to scatter the lingering claws of the dream. It had seemed so real. His keen built under his skin, searching for something that was now missing, a part of itself that had been locked away somewhere deep. But what? He circled his fingers around the ward mark. Nea's keen stirred in an icy flutter, much fainter than ever before but still there.

He stepped out into the cool morning air and scanned the campsite. Janey was standing with Leith, Trenton, and a small group of soldiers. She tilted her head as Garret approached, her brow furrowing as her keen rolled in warm fingers across his shoulders. Her mouth worked into a tight line, and she lifted her hands as though about to sign.

"Ah, there you are, Garret." Leith said. "Shadow's teeth, you look awful! Did you get any sleep last night?"

Garret glanced down at the rumpled shirt under his open jacket and ran a hand through his hair. "I got enough."

Leith frowned. "You're sure? Maybe Jasper could make you a—"

"I'm fine, and I came to tell you I am going with Janey."

"Absolutely not. I need you here. We're expecting more wardens any day now, and you need to be here to organise them."

Trenton cleared his throat. "We'll just give you both a minute." He led his men a short distance away.

Janey settled her hands on her hips but otherwise didn't move.

"Ryan can handle the wardens, and you have Niall and Aveline here as well. I have to go to the capital. I need to see for myself what Leon is up to." If Leon was going to keep interrupting his sleep, then he might as well take the fight to him.

Janey shook her head.

"We don't even know if Leon is at the capital," Leith said. "This is not like you, Garret. The corruption—"

"Is under control again."

Leith's jaw worked, and he rubbed his forehead.

"I'll only be gone long enough to see what Leon's up to, then I will be straight back. Niall and the others won't be doing anything about the tear until Margot returns with Warren anyway."

"I don't like this ... Janey, what do you think?" Leith turned to the mage.

She let out a huff and gestured between them then shrugged.

"How do I know you'll keep your word and come back straight away? What if Leon is there? What's to stop you from—"

"I'm not an idiot, Leith."

"I never said you were, but you haven't been yourself of late."

Garret opened his mouth, but Janey put her hand on his arm.

"*It might help.*" She signed.

Leith frowned then looked to Garret. "Care to interpret that?"

"She said it might help me."

The prince looked from Janey to Garret and then back again. "Alright. But if Leon isn't there, don't go chasing him. If he *is* there, don't do anything rash. Just gather what information you can and then return immediately."

Garret clapped him on the shoulder. "You have my word that I will."

CHAPTER EIGHT

NEA

Nea nearly collided with Dara as she sat bolt upright. Icy fingers had tightened around her heart and throat, making every breath agony. Garret's keen was a hot pulse beneath the skin of her wrist, the ward mark glowing vibrant orange as dark webs appeared around its edges. Keen that belonged to neither her nor Garret coursed through her. Clenching her fists, she fought against the foreign magic. She couldn't let it win, not when it was seeking to smoother the connection caused by the death ward. The ward grew so hot that the skin of her arm started to blister then it—stopped.

The heat receded at an alarming pace, the numbing throb of Garret's warden keen painfully absent. Nea tasted blood. She'd bitten the inside of her cheek. Drawing a halting breath, she pressed her fingers to her mouth.

"What happened?" Molly appeared in front of her, cornflower-blue eyes wide. Her fingers encircled Nea's wrist, inflaming the burned skin, and Nea let out a hiss of pain.

"Sorry, what did I—Mother's tits, are those burns?" Molly asked as she examined the blistered skin around the ward mark. "Go get Wren," she said to Dara, who hovered behind her.

The girl gave a nod and hurried away.

"Leon was there," Nea whispered.

"Leon?!" Molly released her arm.

"I don't know how, but he was there, and he—" She probed the ragged flesh inside her cheek with her tongue. "He banished me from the dream, but he did something else after that ... something to the ward."

"Can you still feel Garret?"

Nea focused on the ward. Garret's keen wasn't completely gone, but it was deeper down, hidden behind something that hadn't been there before. "I think somehow Leon put a block on it."

"That's impossible. He's keen-less."

"Improbable not impossible. I think I have made a huge mistake. I—" She was interrupted by the arrival of Wren.

Behind the captain was a thin-faced woman with dark skin and eyes the same amber shade as Emil's.

"Dara said you needed a healer. This is Arlie." Wren indicated the woman, who dipped her head in greeting.

"Show me." Arlie's voice was soft and lilting.

Nea held her arm out, and Molly stepped back.

"How did this injury occur?" The skin between Arlie's brows pinched as she swept a look around the room.

"The burns are magical in origin," Nea replied.

"Ah." The healer gave a nod and knelt beside Nea before taking the arm in her warm hands. She rolled Nea's wrist examining the mark from all sides. "This is an unusual tattoo."

Nea bit her lip. "It's not a tattoo."

Arlie's amber gaze met her own.

"It's a ward mark," she added.

"Strange." Arlie's keen rolled in warm fingers over Nea's skin, bringing the sensation of sinking into a hot bath. "It does not feel like any oathing I have ever encountered."

Nea fought the urge to pull her arm back. "Are you going to heal me?"

A smile curved the other woman's mouth. "I am." Her keen grew warmer, and a soft green smoke twisted over the burns.

The skin of Nea's wrist began to itch and sting. The irritation grew almost unbearable before Arlie's keen pulled away, leaving newly healed skin in its wake.

"Thank you," Nea said with a relieved sigh.

"You're welcome." The healer dipped her head then turned to Wren and lifted her hand.

Wren held out a few coins but didn't release them into the woman's palm. "Do you still sell information?"

Arlie inhaled slowly; her gaze locked on the coins. "Is that really why you called me here?"

"Yes."

"The price has gone up recently."

"I thought you might say that. What is the going rate these days then?"

"Passage off this Bright forsaken island."

"Passage to where?" Wren's mouth tightened, but she dropped the coins into the woman's hand.

A strange smile curled across Arlie's lips as her fingers closed over the payment. "I don't care where. Most captains who dock here will not risk raising Vince's ire by granting passage to the likes of me. You, however, have shown no issue in the past with insulting him, and so you are my best option."

"Why would granting you passage piss off Vince?" Molly asked.

"Because I am his property," Arlie replied, brushing her hair aside to show the small insignia tattooed on the sensitive skin behind her ear.

Molly shared a glance with Nea, who shrugged. "Vince believes property is an indication of stature. The more you own, the more power you have. That extends to his harem." She studied the woman. "If you are a member of Vince's harem, why are you down here healing people? I thought those tattoos prevented insubordination."

"They protect Vince from harm. I certainly couldn't raise my hand against him. And they prevent us from leaving the city. Leaving the Palace is not exactly forbidden, but even if it were, there are so many of us that he finds it hard to keep track."

"If you can't leave the city, how can Wren grant you passage?" Molly asked.

"We simply need the tattooist to change the mark."

"That's not an easy ask," Nea said, flicking a look at Wren.

"We are a little short on time, Arlie," the captain said.

Arlie's amber gaze narrowed as she studied the three of them. "My guess is you want to get into the palace. I can get you in, but only if you help me with the tattooist first. Your best chance to get in unnoticed is two days from now anyway. Vince will be throwing a party to impress a Faridean merchant captain."

It was a decent chance. Vince would be preoccupied with the captain, and he wouldn't notice a couple of extra women wandering around the palace. "Excellent. That's how we are getting in."

"Like fuck we are!" Molly exclaimed. "I am not joining some pleasure party just so you can—"

"We are not joining a *pleasure party*. We are using the guise of being members of Vince's harem to sneak into his palace. With Vince distracted by his company, we can move through the palace fairly unnoticed. Giving us time to find out where he hid the things he stole from the shrine."

"Except that the minute anyone sees that"—Wren pointed to Nea's hair—"they will know you are not who you say you are. I doubt very much that Vince has a necromancer in his stable."

"Gross," Molly muttered, scrunching her nose up.

"We can dye it. The trickier part is going to be getting our hands on some appropriate attire and then getting in without causing too much fuss."

"I can help with both. Provided of course you help me with the tattooist, and I am granted the passage I seek," Arlie said to Wren.

"You are welcome on the Queen. I could certainly use a healer on my crew, unless of course you'd rather we dropped you somewhere?"

"We can discuss the particulars later. Now." Her amber gaze settled on Nea. "I will return tomorrow evening, and you and I will pay the tattooist a little visit."

Nea gave a nod. "Alright, is there anything we can do in the meantime to prepare for sneaking into the palace?"

Arlie shook her head. "I shall make some arrangements. Until tomorrow." She backed out the door.

"Are we seriously pretending to join a harem? I don't know whether I am impressed or disgusted." Molly sat heavily on the bed.

"You can be both." Nea grinned and ducked as Molly tossed the pillow at her.

"Are you sure you want to do it this way, Nea? Dealing with the tattooist is not going to be easy," Wren said.

"I know, but Arlie needs our help as much as we need hers."

Donnic, the tattooist, was difficult, but Nea had dealt with him before, so she knew what to expect. She was more worried about Leon's presence in Garret's dream. What if he had altered Garret's corruption or done damage to the death ward? And how had he managed it? Had the Usurper figured out a loophole to being trapped in a keen-less body? Or had he found assistance from another mage? Nea wasn't aware of anyone powerful enough to send Leon directly into a dream like that.

She couldn't dwell on it now. Helping Arlie and then getting in and out of Vince's palace in one piece required her complete focus. Once that was over, she could worry about Leon and Garret.

"I still don't like it." Molly was saying. "But I'm too tired to argue about it at the moment."

"If you don't want to come with me, Molly, it's alright. I can do this alone."

Molly's eyes narrowed as she studied Nea. "Oh no. You get up to far too much trouble when left to your own devices. We'll sort out this tattooist, and then I'll crash Vince's party with you. But I'm not going to enjoy it."

The next evening, Arlie arrived at the Queen dressed in a set of dark-coloured clothes, her features hidden under the large cowl of her capelet.

"Do you know where the tattooist currently resides?" Nea asked.

"The same place he always has," Arlie replied.

"Perfect." With a grin Nea, finished braiding her hair and secured it.

"Nea, are you absolutely sure about this?" Wren asked.

"She can handle Donnic, lass," Gendry said, dropping a kiss to the top of Wren's head. "Here, just in case." He held a sheathed knife out to Nea.

The roses carved on the ebony grip made her mouth grow dry. "Where did you get that?"

"Found it in the market. Thought of you as soon as I saw it." He gave the knife a small shake.

The moment Nea's fingers closed around it, a jolt of cold magic ran up her arm and settled at her core. She had given this very blade to Garret and hadn't seen it since. How it had ended up here on Quel'sapar was beyond her. *Home.* A voice cooed against her ear. She could worry about the implications of the blade showing up and the voice that accompanied it later. Right now, Gendry was watching her waiting for—"Thank you, Gen." She forced a smile as she hid the blade away in her satchel.

"Ready?" Molly asked.

Nea gave a nod. "Let's get this done, then we can work on our plan to get into the palace."

"Oh, I almost forgot." Arlie handed a wrapped bundle to Wren. "Here, we'll need these tomorrow. They should fit alright with minor alterations, and they won't be missed."

Wren opened the bundle to reveal a mass of coloured silk and gossamer lace. "I'll put them somewhere safe. Now off you go and be careful. I know you've dealt with Donnic before, Nea, but he's a wily old arsehole."

"That's my favourite kind of target," Molly quipped, tapping her crossbow lightly against her leg.

"You won't need to shoot him, Molly. He and I have an *understanding*."

"When you say things like that, I can't decide if I want to know more or if I'm too scared to ask."

Donnic lived at the far end of the docks in a small shack that looked like it had seen better days. A soft glow flickered from the windows, and as they neared, a wail of sound filled the air followed by a thud. The door flew open, and a half-dressed sailor staggered out, the inflamed lines of a fresh tattoo marking his chest. He blinked at the three women in front of him.

"Don't go in there. He's a Bright damned butcher." He gestured at the unfinished tattoo.

"Fuck off, you gutless prick, and stop driving my customers— fuck." Donnic had appeared in the doorway, and the moment his sharp gaze landed on Nea, the colour drained from his face. "I thought we had an agreement."

Nea started towards the stairs, but the sailor grabbed her arm. "It's not worth it. He'll just take your money and—"

"Get out of here before I let the wee lass with the crossbow shoot you in the arse," the tattooist bellowed.

The sailor dropped his hold on Nea and darted off, falling over his own feet in his haste to get away.

"Now what the fuck are you doing on my doorstep with one of Vince's favourites in tow?" Donnic levelled his gaze on Nea. His keen coiled out in a warm crackle, bringing the sensation of unexplored potential. It was the same feeling Greffon and Wade's keen evoked.

"You are going to undo her binding ward."

"I most certainly am not. Do you know what Vince did to me last time you pulled this little stunt? He hung me in the Bright forsaken gullet for two days."

"Do you know what I will do to you if you don't?" She lifted her hand; flickers of lilac magic danced over her fingers and highlighted the crescent at her palm.

His eyes widened, and he took a step towards her. "Where did you get that inkwork?"

Nea examined the swirling patterns that covered her hand. "It's an evolved version of corruption."

"Doesn't *feel* like corruption. It's like him." He strode to the carving of a large hound beside his door and pressed his hand against it. "I always knew there was more to you." He studied his fingers splayed against the Shadow hound before looking back at Nea. "I can't help you with her." He thrust his chin at Arlie. "Vince will have my head this time."

"Is there a way we could take Vince out?" Molly asked. "I mean, he sounds like a real arse. I'm fairly certain he won't be missed."

"Taking him out will create a power struggle, and there are individuals waiting in the wings who are worse than old Vince," the tattooist said. "Though." He rubbed his chin and studied Nea. "She's getting out on the Queen, isn't she? If Wren will grant me passage to Mother's Deep, I'll help you."

"You want to leave Quel'sapar?" Nea asked.

Donnic folded his arms.

"Fine. Molly, do you mind running back and checking with Wren?"

"I'm not an errand girl." But she was already heading away as she said it.

"Mind if we come inside?" Nea asked.

He held the door open and gestured for them to enter. Arlie gave him a tiny nod as she passed, but he stopped Nea, his fingers encircling her left wrist, right over the death ward. His keen stirred in a flickering warmth, and her eyes met his.

She pressed her lips together and tilted her head in Arlie's direction.

"We'll talk after." He released her, and she took up a seat on the bench along the wall. "Drink?"

"No thank you," Nea replied, and Arlie shook her head at the dark bottle he was holding out.

"Suit yourselves."

A short while later, someone banged on the door, and the tattooist opened it to reveal a breathless Molly. "Wren said she can take you to Mother's Deep, but any funny business and she'll have your balls."

"That sounds about right," the tattooist said with a grin. "Alright, Arlie, get over here." He indicated an ink-stained chair beside his worktable.

Molly settled in Arlie's vacated seat on the bench beside Nea. "When this is done, I need you to take Arlie back to the Queen. She'll be groggy and disorientated."

"I told you—"

"I know you're not an errand girl, Molly. But Donnic and I have other matters to discuss, and I would rather have that talk away from prying ears." She tapped her left wrist.

"Oh." Molly licked her lip. "You'll tell me, right? If anything has happened to Garret?"

"Of course."

"Good." She rested her head against the wall and her gaze flicked along the bottles of ink and herbs that lined the shelf above a scarred table.

The tattooist's keen rose in a warm flicker as he lifted a strange device above Arlie's exposed neck. He brought it down, and she flinched as the needle protruding from the base pricked her skin. "You have to hold still."

Arlie mumbled something, and he gave her shoulder a pat.

"That's right."

Molly glanced at Nea, and she shrugged.

The sensation of the tattooist's keen changed as he dropped the needle three more times. He took a bottle of ink from the shelf and smeared some on his fingertips. The ink glowed with the iridescent hue of oil on water, and he pressed his fingers to the mark on Arlie's neck, smoothing the ink over it and mixing it with the blood that was welling from the needle wounds. The tattoo shimmered, and Arlie hissed as the image changed from Vince's crest to the shape of a flying bird.

"Is it done?" Arlie slurred and slumped sideways.

Donnic straightened her again and nodded to Molly. "She needs to sleep it off. Breaking the ward messes with normal folk, but keen-touched have a rougher time with it. Tell Wren I'll be at the Queen by noon tomorrow, and I'll have a few boxes of cargo."

Molly pressed her lips together and stood. She slid her arm around Arlie's waist and helped her to her feet before guiding her across the room to the door. "I'll be waiting up," she said to Nea and then disappeared into the night.

Donnic held the dark bottle towards Nea, and she took it this time. She gave it a sniff. The liquor within was strangely floral.

"It's something the Farideans are experimenting with. Doesn't taste as bad as it smells."

Nea took a mouthful and choked it down with a cough before handing the bottle back. "It's got a decent burn."

"A burn like that will put hairs on your chest my pa used to say." Donnic chuckled and took a long swing. "Now this ward on your arm." He smacked his lips together. "It's not like anything I've felt before, and wards are my business."

She licked her lips, mostly to chase the numbness from the alcohol away. Donnic might be a wily arsehole as Wren put it, but he was also someone who lived to a code—a highly contradictory and convoluted personal code, but in essence he was honourable enough. "I trust that I have your discretion?"

He studied her. "I'm a man of my word, aren't I? And even if I weren't, I would be a fool to betray your trust given your little gift for severing souls."

The corner of Nea's mouth quirked.

"Why you haven't used that power to take control of everything from here to the Isles I'll never know. Must be made of purer stuff than the rest of us." He ran his tongue along his teeth and swallowed another mouthful before offering the bottle to Nea again.

She grimaced and shook her head. "It's a death ward."

The bottle paused on its way to Donnic's mouth, and he stared blankly at her before slowly setting it down. "And how did you come by that? There's no mage alive who possesses the knowledge or the skill to craft a ward like that."

"It's a long story. But something has happened to the ward." She rolled her sleeve back and held her wrist out to him.

His fingertip traced the lines of the mark, leaving a ticklish path across her skin. "Where's the bearer of the other half?"

"I think he was heading to Kalhanna."

"That's where it came from then?"

"No, it was—"

"Not the ward. The shockwave. Never felt anything like it before. Every keen-touched in the city was affected while it passed over. What happened?"

"The barrier tore."

"The. Barrier. Tore," he repeated slowly. "How the fuck does something like that happen?"

"That is *definitely* a long story." She held her hand out, and he handed her the bottle. The second mouthful made her teeth ache.

"Do you know anything about death wards? I know they can't be destroyed but can they be manipulated?"

Donnic moved to a shelf of books and ran his finger along the spines. He pulled one out and flicked through it before shoving it back and then repeated the process several more times before grunting and lobbing a tome towards Nea.

She caught it and read the title. *Forbidden Wards and Banished Magics.*

"That's the only copy I know of that survived the sinking of Port Brenna. Has a whole chapter on death wards. Did you know they only worked successfully when the parties involved were both divine blooded?" He settled into his chair. "That explains an awful lot about *you* then, doesn't it? Gives a whole new meaning to that inkwork on your right arm as well ... I'd say." He probed the corner of his mouth with his tongue as he leant back and folded his arms. "Deera solvec."

Nea met his gaze.

"I'm right, aren't I?"

She gave a nod and flipped through the chapter.

"And that would make your other half what? A brightling? Hasn't been one of them in several centuries. Show me that mark again." He held his hand out, and when Nea placed her wrist on it, he rolled it around to examine the mark from all angles. "Hmmm ..."

"Hmmm?"

"To answer your question, no they can't be broken, and they can't be easily manipulated either. Someone has gone to great lengths to separate the pair of you. See, unlike an oathing, the shared keen of a death ward allows the bearers to bolster each other's magic in ways that are simply not possible by other means." He rubbed his forehead.

"That is why it was relatively easy to soothe the symptoms of Garret's corruption through the dream-link," Nea mused.

"Fuck me, this situation just keeps getting more insane." Donnic shook his head. "But, yes, exactly. Whoever meddled with the ward wanted to separate you enough that that they could—"

"Give the corruption the upper hand, which would allow them to completely erode Garret's defences and take over." She bolted to her feet.

"Whoa, calm down. It will take them a while, given that they can't sever the connection entirely, just smoother it. This Garret will still be getting enough of your keen to give him a fighting chance, but the longer you are apart, the fainter that connection will become."

Nea flopped onto the chair again. "Is there anything you can do to fix it?"

Donnic shook his head. "Not without you both present, but I probably won't need to. As soon as you come back into contact, the wards should right themselves."

She rubbed her hands over her face. At least she knew what had to be done. Crash Vince's party, find out if he had the book and the key and secure them if he did, and then return to Garret before Leon caused any irreparable damage. "Give me that bottle." She ignored the burn as she took another mouthful. Tomorrow evening couldn't come fast enough.

CHAPTER NINE

HARVEY

"... so how many—"

"Seven," Penny said, cutting Emil off.

"Come on, Pen. Plucking the answer out of my head is cheating," Emil responded.

"No, it's called *you should shield your thoughts better*," the mage said, a feline grin smoothing across her lips.

Harvey laughed. "She's got you there."

Over the days they had been travelling, the three of them had settled into an easy comradery. Not that Harvey was surprised. He had always enjoyed Emil's company. The warden wasn't nearly as serious as Garret could be at times, and that light-hearted nature meant many people underestimated him.

Penny, however, had been a near-complete unknown to Harvey. They had become acquainted during the couple of months they spent at Del Harol, but her haughty exterior seemed to hide unfathomable depths and made it hard to get to know her. Over the last few days, Harvey had found she had a tendency to be brutally honest, and she wasn't one to suffer fools. She also seemed to possess a wicked, and almost inappropriate, sense of humour.

They had skirted around the capital, which added an extra day to their journey. But it had been the safer option, given they didn't know what state the city was in. Things were not good if the groups of refugees fleeing inland were anything to go by. Most people gave the three of them a wide berth, but they had heard rumours of not just mages but also wardens and keen-less turning mad with corruption and the dead walking the streets.

"The Crossroads is just ahead. We can stop there for a spell and see if there is anything on the rumour mill," Emil said.

"Do you think that is wise?" Penny asked.

"Maybe not, but we need to get a better idea of what's going on. We'll be passing Loch Bastien in the next day or two, so it wouldn't hurt to find out what we might expect as we near the college."

"But we're not going anywhere near Loch Bastien," Harvey said.

"True, but it won't hurt to get an idea of what is going on if we can, and I am sure Garret and Leith will appreciate the intel."

Harvey nodded. "I guess that's a good point."

"I'm not sure what *intel* we will find. We haven't seen anyone on the road this side of the capital … But my feet are aching, and I could use a hearty meal and a stiff drink," Penny said.

"So, we're stopping then?" Emil asked.

"Looks like it," Harvey replied.

They passed a road branching off. The slanted signpost read Lone Oak, and below that Kilton, then as they rounded the bend, the Crossroads came into view. It was a large complex. The main tavern was surrounded by multiple buildings ranging in size from a large stable and bathhouse to smaller single-room cabins that could be hired for the night. There were also rooms for rent in the tavern itself and a long, communal bunkhouse.

The Crossroads had been established back in the days when Port Brenna was the capital. It was a major stop on the coastal road that spanned from Port Agatha in the east to Fengate in the west before branching to the then capital in the south. It was still a thriving community of its own. Even today when the road between Port Agatha and the new capital wasn't quite as far.

Harvey sucked a breath through his teeth, and beside him Emil swore.

"Are those bodies?" Penny asked, her dark gaze sweeping over the shapes slumped in the middle of the road.

"Yeah," Harvey said, drawing his sword and starting forward.

Emil did likewise. "Feel that, Pen?" he whispered.

"Corruption," she confirmed softly.

Harvey scanned the buildings, looking for any sign of life. As he neared the pile of bodies in the middle of the road, they moved, limbs jolting and cracking as they pulled themselves to their feet. Reanimations. Harvey had fought them at Hartswood and again at Kalhanna. They were practically unstoppable unless you did enough damage to the body.

He swung his sword and cleaved the arm off the one closest. It hissed and swiped at him with its other arm as he leapt backwards.

"We won't be able to stop them all," Penny said as she brandished a hay fork.

"Oi!" Emil yelled, and a stone hit the head of one of the undead closing in on Penny. It swung to face the warden and started towards him. He charged forward and with a clean strike took its head off. "They may be like the wraiths at Holbrook. If we can get through them, we might find safety at the other end of town."

"I doubt that. The wraiths are only contained by—get off me." Penny let out a squeal and drove the hay fork into the chest of one of the reanimations that had grabbed hold of her. "The ward." She gritted through her teeth as she shoved it away. "These ones are different."

"Emil might be right. I don't know much about reanimations, but the ones Kieran had—" Harvey sliced through two more reanimations, who staggered backwards. "—at Kalhanna were like puppets."

"Exactly," Emil said, kicking one in the chest and stabbing another. "They aren't free thinking. The necromancer who raises them needs to assign them to a task."

"So just run for it?" Having lost her weapon, Penny shielded herself behind Emil and Harvey.

"Yes. On the count of three." Emil lunged forward. "One."

Harvey pushed another back with a slice that opened a dark gash on its chest. "Two."

"Three!" they said together as they charged forward.

Penny went flying past them, dodging around grasping hands and barging her shoulder into one of the reanimations, with enough force to send it staggering.

Once all three of them had made it beyond the last building, the reanimations crumbled back into lifeless lumps on the ground.

"Do you think they were Kieran's work or someone else's?" Emil asked, trying to flick the stagnant blood from the blade of his sword.

"They would have to be Kieran's, surely," Penny said with a shiver as she glanced back at the bodies lying in the road.

"The reanimations at Kalhanna were different, but if Kieran has been experimenting with—" Harvey couldn't finish that sentence. He understood why most necromancers had a rule about creating them. Just the thought of someone defiling the dead like that ... But why were these reanimations here? They acted almost like—guard dogs. "What do you think they were guarding though?"

They both studied him.

"I certainly don't want to go back and find out," Penny said.

"There are too many to fight all at once ..." Emil clucked his tongue as he studied the street. "If we could get them rounded up into one of the buildings—"

"And how exactly are we going to *round them up*?" Penny's mouth twisted into a tight line as she folded her arms.

Both Penny and Emil had valid points. The reanimations wouldn't be a problem if they had Janey; her fire magic worked fantastically against them. Trapping them in one of the buildings wasn't the worst idea Emil had ever had, but it wasn't going to be easy. "We need bait," Harvey said.

"What sort of—oh no. I am not going back in there, and I am certainly not letting either of you use me as bait."

"I'll be the bait. You two just be ready to run in and trap them," Emil said.

"We should just leave it."

"Come on, Pen. It's not like you to shy away from a challenge. Here, I am sure you know enough not to hurt yourself with this." Emil handed Penny his sword.

She took it gingerly, eyeing the congealed blood on the blade and then the reanimations.

"Alright. Harvey, you ready?"

Harvey started to nod and then stopped. "There's a lot of them. What if we can't get them all in one go?"

"Then we'll just have to trap them in multiple groups." He gave Harvey a grin that wasn't quite full of its usual mirth before heading back towards the bodies.

"Emil, wait," Penny said, her knuckles growing white around the hilt of the sword.

He turned and cocked one eyebrow.

She licked her lips. "Be careful."

"Oh, Pen, you do care." He chuckled and then gave her a salute before turning around again. "Might want to stop strangling that sword though," he said over his shoulder as he walked towards the tavern.

Penny glanced sideways at Harvey, who couldn't quite contain his smirk. After lifting the sword again, she gave the tip a shake in his direction. "Not a word," she muttered.

Harvey held his hands up in mock surrender, his grin widening. "I know when to keep my opinions to myself. I'm not Declan."

As Emil neared the bodies, they rose one by one and started towards him. He walked a slow circle around them and then edged towards the larger bunkhouse. One of the reanimations charged, and Penny gasped, but Emil reached the door and pushed it open. He disappeared inside, and the reanimations followed him.

"Wait here," Harvey said to Penny and rushed down the road.

Most of the reanimations had followed Emil into the building, but it occurred to Harvey that they hadn't exactly thought this plan through enough. They didn't know how many entrances the building had or how they were supposed to get the doors to stay shut. What if there was only one door? How would Emil get out?

He was distracted by a reanimation coming from the side.

"Get the door!" Emil yelled as Harvey drove his sword forward through the reanimation's chest.

"Other doors?"

"Locked," Emil said as he dove forward and slammed the door shut. "We need to jam this one somehow—shit! Move, Harvey."

A wagon containing two barrels rushed towards them. They both dove out of the way as it slammed into the door of the cabin. The barrels shattered, and the scent of strong liquor filled the air, turning Harvey's stomach to water. Seconds later, a flaming bottle smashed against the broken wood and fire licked over the spilled alcohol with a growing hiss.

Emil and Harvey backed away.

"Just die!" Penny growled, and Harvey turned as she drove Emil's sword through the stomach of one of the remaining reanimations.

"Decapitation is the most effective method, Pen."

"Yes, thank you, Emil. I am aware." She wrenched the sword free with a stumbling step backwards. The reanimation followed her. With a yell, she swung the sword and it embedded in the side of the reanimation's head. It staggered sideways as she pulled the blade free.

Harvey stepped forward and delivered a clean blow, severing the head completely.

"Here." Penny held the sword out to Emil.

He took it and stared down the street. Smoke was starting to cloud the air, bringing with it the distinct scent of burning flesh. "How did you manage the wagon?"

Penny shrugged. "I'm not some wilting flower, you know? I just kicked out the stops and gave it a shove in the right direction. We should have a look inside the tavern."

Harvey nodded. "I'll go first, just in case." He edged towards the building and pushed the door open. There was no one inside.

As he stepped into the room, a ball of pale pink mage light flickered to life, casting long shadows across the walls and glinting off the blade that was embedded in the wood of the bar top.

The knife was pinning a large piece of parchment in place. Ink and blood were splattered on the page, and the bottom corner was torn off completely. Only one sentence was legible: *Ambrose is at Merston.*

"Do you think this note is what those reanimations were guarding?" Emil asked.

"Who is Ambrose?" Harvey asked as Penny said,

"No, I think that was." Her mage light drifted over a hunched pile of blankets that seemed to be chained to the floor.

The pile shifted, and both Harvey and Emil raised their swords.

"Ambrose ..." the pile croaked. "... is a gutless traitor." The blanket fell back to reveal Evard's cold, grey stare. His cheeks were sunken in, and his skin was sallow under the grime.

Harvey swallowed and shared a glance with Emil and Penny.

"Ah, Penelope." Evard squinted as the light shifted over his face. "I would have loved adding you to my collection. You and Nea and Margot, each delightful for different reasons. Each powerful beyond the norm. Perfect specimens." Evard lifted his arm, his long fingers reaching towards Penny. The blanket slipped to reveal a large stain of dried blood on the front of his shirt. He moved as far forward as the chain would allow, favouring his right leg as he did so. "Nothing to say to your wretch of a king, who has been left here to rot by those that once professed undying loyalty."

"You—"

"I don't want your pity!" Evard roared.

Penny licked her lips. "What should we do?" she whispered, not taking her eyes off Evard.

"Is there anything we can do?" Emil asked.

"We can't leave him here. That's an awful way to die, even for the likes of him," Harvey said.

"Oh, what shall we do with the monster who once was king? Leave him here to starve as those who came before did? Don't find that idea palatable, do you? It would be what he deserves ... but kinder to end it quickly. A simple snap of the neck—clean yet unsatisfying." Evard smacked his lips together. "And yet, if we leave him alive, we can torture him for information."

"We're not all that into torture," Emil said.

"Not all that into torture?" Evard gave a simpering laugh. "You have not lived until you've smelt the fear of your prey, felt the fight slowly drain out of the ones who refuse to submit. Like Nea, she was hard to break. Even after I forced her to the very edge of her own humanity, she had the audacity to keep fighting me. But inch by inch, I was wearing her down. Then that *bastard* had to snatch her away. The ungrateful whelp. If I had known what he was—Ah ha, I see what you are doing, keep me talking and the truth will out itself. Clever, but I know your game now."

"Game?" Harvey asked Emil, who shrugged.

"Wait, I knew your mother." Evard's grey gaze narrowed as he studied Harvey. "She was one of the last before the *accident*. Ambrose favoured her. Most of them were a means to an end, but a rare few like ... Elise, that was the name."

"Shut up," Harvey growled.

"Struck a nerve." Evard ran his tongue along his teeth. "Ambrose cast her aside when you were found unsuitable. A folly. He should have killed you both. I would have. But whatever happened to her?"

Harvey bit the inside of his cheek. He wasn't going to give Evard the satisfaction of an answer.

"Did she take her own life? Many of those who survived the experiments did."

"Okay, I have heard enough of this." Emil frowned. "Should we just kill him and be done with it?"

Penny scrunched her nose up. "It would be kinder than he deserves. I can put a compulsion on him to make him stop talking. Perhaps we should take him back to Garret and Leith?"

"We still need to go to Merston," Harvey said.

"If Ambrose is there, is that wise?" Emil enquired. "Maybe it's better if we head back to the others, given this new information."

"If we could send a message to Garret ... but where would we find a messenger?" Penny mused.

"Penny, did you?" Harvey asked, pointing to Evard. A blank look had stolen across his features, and he appeared to be staring at something on the far wall.

She nodded. "I was sick of hearing him talk."

"We could take him back to the capital. Didn't Haley and Sonia head there after we got to Kalhanna? We can leave him with them or see if there is a messenger who can get a bird to Garret or Leith," Emil said. "I wish we knew more about Ambrose."

Harvey didn't know that he wanted to learn more about Ambrose. But he had a suspicion that Niall had known he would be at Merston, or at least that Harvey would find out about him there. He gave a nod. Taking Evard back to the capital was the better course of action for now. "Sounds like a plan. Penny?"

"I certainly don't want to drag him all the way to Merston with us. Back to the capital it is."

CHAPTER TEN

MARGOT

Sunlight sparkled over the fenlands as their borrowed horses picked a path along the disused north road. Last time Margot had been here, she had admired the haunting beauty of the marsh, but now all she could think about were the wraiths waiting at the ruined town of Holbrook. Her fingers tightened their grip on the reins with each splash, and she scanned the waters between the cheery lilies, investigating every ripple.

"Are you alright, Margot? You seem a little on edge," Declan asked.

"We're getting close to Holbrook," she replied, not taking her eyes off a large set of ripples to her left.

"That's where you encountered the wraiths?"

She gave a nod. "They came upon us without warning. We're lucky we didn't lose Penny."

"I can't feel anything undead out there at the moment," Bran offered with a warm smile. "I imagine I would be able to sense these wraiths like any other reanimation."

"See, there's nothing to worry about."

"Perhaps." She studied the trees ahead. "The wraiths didn't attack until we reached those trees. We need to be on our guard, and when the first reanimation shows itself, spur your horses. Don't stop until you're beyond the ward in the middle of the tree at the other end of the town."

"If there is a ward around the town, wouldn't we feel it when we cross it on this side?" Declan asked.

"I don't know. None of us noticed it last time."

"We'll be careful, Margot," Bran said.

Margot's horse pivoted his ears as they passed the first of the trees. He gave a snort and tossed his head.

Bran's keen stirred in a cold ripple, and he rubbed his temples. "I think I found the wraiths." The colour drained from his face. "Go."

Margot didn't need telling twice. She planted her heels into the sides of her horse, and it surged forward. Grey blurs stirred in the water, but she kept her eyes ahead as the signpost for Holbrook came into view and beyond it the mouldering buildings. Her horse shied as something came barrelling from the left.

Storm magic crackled, and the creature was shrouded in lightning, but it barely slowed.

Margot's horse reared, and she clung to its neck, her teeth sinking cruelly into her lip as she bit back a scream. The horse dropped its front hooves and wheeled around, but the gaunt bodies had closed in, blocking the way out.

Purple magic shrouded the wraiths and turned the air in Margot's lungs to ice.

"I can't destroy them," Bran yelled, and the heads of the wraiths twisted in his direction. They were moving slower now as though Bran's magic was weighing them down. "Go, Margot!"

An opening had appeared in front of her horse, and it charged forward at Bran's shout. Claws caught Margot's leg, and she was dragged sideways. She kicked at her attacker, her heel colliding with soft flesh.

"Go, go." She urged the horse, and it gave a terrified whinny as it trampled the body in front of it.

They passed through the tree, the sticky pull of the ward nearly dragging her from the saddle. When they emerged on the other side, the horse pranced and spun, nostrils flaring, until Margot's murmurs and pats managed to calm it down. It was still tense beneath her, its ears flicking in every direction as it tossed its head and snorted.

"Where's Bran?" Declan asked, and Margot stared at the gap in the giant tree, cold dread coiling in her stomach.

Something crashed through the forest to their right, and Margot's horse shied, nearly unseating her again.

"I'm here," Bran panted. His snow-white hair was full of leaves and sticks, and there was a tacky smear of mud on his cheek. His horse was flicking its head in agitation, but that was probably to do with the thin branch caught in its bridle and the oozing gash that marked the animal's shoulder. "Both in one piece?" His hands trembled as he pulled his horse's head around to untangle the branch.

Margot glanced down at the torn leg of her pants. The skin beneath was thankfully unharmed. "I'm shaken but otherwise alright."

"Completely unscathed," Declan said, his green gaze studying the air at the centre of the tree as the white shapes of the wraiths retreated. "I would like to know what sort of enchantment allows them to linger like that. Do you think they are animated all the time or are they stationary until something triggers their activation? Like how you can program a golem. What if they are not reanimations at all but rather some kind of flesh golem like the abominations around the tear?"

"I bet Nea could tell you. She knows heaps about wraiths," Bran said, his voice was thin and shaky. "But right now, how about we focus on getting to Warren? I don't want to linger this close to Holbrook." He looked peaky, and his keen flickered between soothing cool and stabbing ice.

"You overextended yourself," Margot said, trying to keep the reprimand out of her voice.

"It will be fine once I've had a rest and something to eat."

"Bran—"

"I don't need a lecture, Margot! I know the danger, but there was no other choice. Those things would have killed you," he snapped in a fashion that reminded her of Nea.

It wasn't really a surprise. Unlike most necromancers, who could trace their heritage back at least ten generations, Bran was an orphan. Given that he had been only two or three when he had been left at the base of the lock-stone outside Hartswood, and no one knew where he had come from, Nonna had raised him. Though orphan or not, she ended up raising most of the children who came to Hartswood, Margot and Emil included.

Now that she thought of it, a lot of the children from Hartswood had sad histories. Emil's mother had run off with some noble from Osmar, leaving an infant Emil in Godfrey's care. Margot's parents had both been taken by a plague when she was eight and Ivan twelve, but they had been sent to Hartswood long before that as their parents had spent most of the year on the road. Nea's mother had disowned her because she was a deathborn, or maybe it was guilt over taking part in Ambrose's experiments. Would Nea have been born a normal necromancer if Sophia hadn't had anything to do with Ambrose?

"Which way?" Declan asked, cutting through Margot's thoughts.

"We follow the path through the woods until we come to a boulder that looks like a rabbit," she replied.

Declan gave a nod and clucked his tongue as he tapped his horse's sides and guided it away from Holbrook.

"Okay, there's the bunny rock. Now what?" Bran asked. His voice wasn't as shaky as it had been, but the longer they had ridden, the more slumped his shoulders had become.

They had stopped for a rest and for Margot to heal the cut on his horse's shoulder. During that break, he had let her check him over to confirm that he had not been wounded by the wraiths. Everything seemed fine, but his keen should have started to recover by now.

"One of us needs to feed it some of our magic—not you," Margot said with a sharp look in Bran's direction.

"I'll do it." Declan slipped from the saddle and placed his hand on the rock.

Static prickled through the air, making Margot's hair stand on end, and a silver-blue shimmer rippled over the surface of the boulder. After a moment, the door in the cliff grated open, and they rode through.

Warren was waiting for them, crossbow raised.

"It's Margot," she said, lifting her hands.

"What are you doing back here?" He lowered the crossbow a fraction.

"Niall sent us; he wants to know if you can help us with the tear."

The old necromancer drew a long breath. "Fine, get inside. The boy needs assistance. Took on the wraiths again, did you?"

Did they really have another option?

Margot slid off her horse, and Declan held out his hand for the reins. "Go with Bran. I'll see to the horses and be right in."

She gave him a nod and started after Warren.

"I'm fine. There's no need to fuss," Bran muttered but handed his reins to Declan and joined Margot.

Inside the cottage, Warren made Bran sit on the bed while he rummaged around in his bottles and jars. He grabbed a cup and tossed a handful of dried herbs into it before dousing them with hot water from the pot by the fire.

Margot scrunched her nose at the smell. She couldn't recognise any of the herbs.

"Now where did I put—ah ha, there you are." He pulled a small wooden box off the shelf and took a pinch of the silvery powder inside and deposited it into the cup before licking the residue from his fingers. "Hmmm, gone a bit stale, but it'll do." He stirred the powder into the liquid and then handed the tea to Bran. "The whole lot. It'll have you back on your feet before you know it. Risky to use that much keen in a place like that. Barrier's normally thin there, but with the instability caused by the tear ..." He shook his head.

"Shadow's teeth! That's bloody awful." Bran coughed but threw back the rest of the tea without complaint. "I didn't have a choice. But why couldn't I sever the reanimation threads? I thought wraiths were just another type of reanimation." He smacked his lips together and placed the cup aside.

"What did I miss?" Declan asked as he came through the door.

"Nothing yet," Margot replied.

"Good, good." Declan rubbed his hands together and sat on the bed beside Bran.

Warren's blue gaze didn't leave the young necromancer. "They aren't 'just another type of reanimation'. They are complex and not anchored to the mage who originally created them."

"Are they more like golems than reanimations?" Declan asked, leaning forward.

"That would be a crude way to put it." Warren's mouth tightened at the corner. "Their creation does share similar magic with golem creation, but that is where the similarities end."

"Except that, like golems, wraiths can be programmed for a purpose?"

"Declan, we don't have time to be discussing this," Margot said, folding her arms. "Will you come back to Kalhanna with us?" she asked Warren.

"No."

"No? but—"

"I can't help you with the tear more than any other necromancer can."

Margot collapsed against the table. "So, we wasted our time coming here."

"I wouldn't say—"

"Bright damnit!" She slammed her fists down on the tabletop. "I am sick of taking a step only to be knocked back several feet. I could have been back there keeping an eye on Garret—I *should* have been! Not trapsing across the Bright forsaken marshes, chasing a fucking dead end—again." The anchor gave a jolt in response to her anger.

Warren's mouth worked as he stared at her. "Has the brightling been ... compromised?"

"If by compromised you mean corrupted, then yes," Declan replied.

"And Nea?" There was a frailty to Warren's voice. "The journal?"

Of course, last time Margot had been here the lock on the journal that was connected to Nea's lifeforce had opened, leading them all to believe the worst. There hadn't been time to get an explanation about that from Nea when Margot had encountered her on the beach.

"She's alive and well. I didn't get a chance to ask her about the journal, but I did heal her corruption, or rather this did." Margot stroked the anchor mark.

Warren's shoulders relaxed.

"Did you know what she really was?" Declan asked.

The older mage's eyes narrowed, and his keen stirred in an icy flurry. "I knew what she was. The others were harder to convince, and I don't think they ever truly believed it, even after she and the brightling were exposed to each other."

"Hang on. What are we talking about?" Bran asked. Some of the colour had returned to his cheeks.

"Nea," Declan replied.

"I know we're talking about Nea, but what do you mean by what she really is?"

Warren pulled back the sleeve of his shirt and showed the flower-shaped birthmark to Bran.

"But that's a—no ... really? So, you're a deathborn, and Nea is as well? Honestly, that explains a lot." He leant against the wall.

"She's not just a deathborn though," Declan said. "She's a deera solvec."

"Wait, was that the old tongue?" Bran sat forward again. "Deera solvec ..." he muttered and tapped his chin. "A daughter of Shadow? Shadow's teeth! And Garret is a brightling. Then are they some sort of soul-matched pair?"

"Soul matches are complete myth. There's no such thing as souls destined to be together in a romantic sense. Nea and Garret, however, are two sides of one coin," Warren said.

"But isn't that just splitting hairs?" Declan asked with a grin. "It was obvious to everyone but themselves that there was something between them."

"Yes. A *shared destiny*. That is not the same thing as romantic entanglement."

"Oh, there has been *entanglement* alright." Declan's grin became wolfish.

Warren let out a huff and rolled his eyes.

"Declan," Margot reprimanded.

"I'm just saying that they are perfect for each other, and I knew that from the second I laid eyes on Nea. My first thought was, damn, why did I have to get myself killed before I met her? And the second was, Garret has no hope."

"That's why you feel so strange. What are you then, some kind of spirit? You seem corporeal, and if you were a spirit, Margot shouldn't be able to see you unless the anchor—"

"He's a deathwalker!" Bran said, jumping to his feet. "It's so amaz—whoa." He grabbed his head and flopped back onto the bed. "I think I got up way too fast."

"A deathwalker? Been an eon or two since one of those popped up. How did you manage that?"

Declan gave a small shrug. "I am not exactly sure. I was messing around with a theory, and then I—" He ran his tongue along his teeth, suddenly fascinated with the shelf on the other wall. "Died." The word had weight. The same kind of weight Kalhanna did when Nea said it. "Then Nea came along and did a re-enactment, and I got stuck between worlds. Nea was the only one who could see me for the longest time, even when she was wearing bind-shackles."

Warren nodded his head slowly. "How did you die?"

Declan paled, and his hand went to his throat. "Is that really relevant?"

"If Nea put you back in your own body then it is. Where is the scar of your death wound?"

"This isn't my original ... body." He rubbed his forehead, his mouth twisting. "That's buried at Little Brook. When Nea and Garret went into the Between, I had corporeal form there and I kept it when we came back to this realm. I can't explain how it works because I don't understand it myself." It was strange to see Declan so uncomfortable about seemingly impossible magic. He would normally be pacing about, talking fast, and jumping from one conclusion to the next before anyone had a chance to catch up. But then this magic was linked inexplicably to his death. Of course that would rattle even the likes of Declan. Margot was surprised she hadn't considered that before. It was probably callous, but she had just assumed that Declan would take it in his stride the way he did everything else.

"Fascinating." This was the most animated she had seen Warren. He seemed genuinely interested in Declan's predicament. "Do you know if the repository at Kalhanna is still intact?" he asked as his dark blue gaze swept to Margot.

She shook her head. "It was, last time I was there, but that was in the immediate aftermath of the purge. I don't know if the tear has affected it."

"I don't think it would have. There was minimal damage done to the ruins," Bran said. "Why?"

"There was a text sequestered there that featured deathwalkers. It is a handbook of reanimation and soul magic. Most necromancers have never laid eyes on it as the theories and magics contained within were deemed *unsavoury*. I believe Abigail and I are the only ones alive aware of its existence."

"Why would it be at Kalhanna and not Hartswood?" Bran asked.

"To make it harder for necromancers to stumble upon, I imagine," Declan said. "If someone like Kieran were to get his hands on such a book ..."

"Right." Bran's brow furrowed.

"I think I will come with you to Kalhanna," Warren said. "But we're not going back through Holbrook."

"Are you saying we didn't have to face the wraiths?" Margot settled her hands on her hips.

"Of course not. They make good guard dogs though." Warren busied himself chucking a few things into a bag. "Well, there's no sense in lingering here. Let's get a move on while we still have enough daylight to find the path."

CHAPTER ELEVEN

GARRET

The farms that edged the eastern side of the capital had been laid to waste. Buildings burned and livestock slaughtered or left to fend for themselves as winter settled its grip on the world. The people were gone. The living, anyway. Reanimations roamed the ruined farmsteads. They didn't seem driven by any real purpose. They had been simply left behind by Kieran, cast aside like broken tools.

"This is …" Micha, one of the guards Trenton had sent with them, shook his head. "If this is the true face of magic, then maybe we're better off without it."

Janey made a noise that sounded a lot like contempt. If she still had full use of her voice, Garret was certain she would be giving Micha an earful.

The soldier was not the only one who had been vocal lately about the distrust of mages and the need for change. Garret couldn't really blame keen-less for having that view. In his time as commander, he had dealt with many highly dangerous mages. Those that either drew too much power and became corrupted or those that had no moral obligations to hold them back to begin with. But you didn't need magic to be dangerous and wreak havoc. He had seen atrocities done at the hands of plenty of keen-less as well. Still, the seething discontent was the type that could easily spark into a war. That had been Evard's plan to begin with, hadn't it? Turn the general populace against mages, and while everyone was distracted, breach the barrier and free the Usurper.

He drew a long breath, and Janey touched his elbow, worry swimming in her green gaze.

"I'm fine." He had never been a liar, not directly anyway. Omission was not the same as an outright lie after all. But that lie, the same one Nea used as a shield, became easier every time he said it.

The tightening of Janey's mouth and the flash in her eyes told him she didn't buy it. She could be infuriatingly perceptive, which wasn't surprising given she had spent more than a decade having to communicate without words.

Garret sighed and rubbed the scar above his lip. "I have to be, Janey. If I admit the truth, even for a moment ..."

She gave his arm a squeeze.

"You need to see this, Commander," Micha called from ahead.

The title didn't feel like it fit right anymore. He and the warden commander were two very different people. Too much had changed, or maybe that role had just been armour, like Nea's lie about being fine, and he had simply outgrown it.

"What is it?" He caught up with Micha, who was standing on the threshold of a house. The broken door hung at an angle on its bottom hinge. The top hinge had been torn clean out of the frame.

The soldier stepped aside, and there huddled in the corner of what had been the kitchen, her sapphire-blue eyes bright beneath the lank strands of her ink-black hair, was Catriona. She straightened when she saw Garret, her cracked lips shifting into the barest hint of a smile. Her cheeks were sunken, and her skin had a greyish pallor that couldn't be entirely attributed to the dirt and grime.

She stood slowly, her torn dress hanging off her thin frame. "Well, isn't this a surprise?" Her voice held none of its usual velvet tone.

"Leon let you live?"

"He left me to *rot*." She coughed and lifted the back of her hand to her mouth. The rose-gold shackle that encircled it caught the light.

Garret turned to Micha. "Take her—"

Janey tapped him on the shoulder, cutting him off. "*She needs help now.*"

"Your order, Commander?"

"Make sure any reanimations in the immediate area are dealt with and set a watch. Once Janey has taken care of Catriona's urgent needs, you and the rest of the guard will escort her back to the camp."

The soldier looked like he might protest but after a moment, gave a nod and moved to do Garret's bidding.

"Alright, Janey, what do you need?"

"*Water and soap.*" She signed then cast an eye over Catriona, who was watching them both with a guarded expression. "*Clothes and simple food. Soup.*"

"I'll see what I can do."

A short while later, Janey helped Catriona bathe. They had managed to find a few items of clothing in the house—a pair of pants that had obviously belonged to the farmer and had to be tied at the waist with a length of rope to prevent them falling. The blouse was also a few sizes too big, but Janey had taken her sewing kit and made a few quick alterations, so it didn't gape too much at the neck and wrists. To ward off the creeping cold, Catriona had a tattered old blanket wrapped around her shoulders. She was on her second bowl of broth now, Janey watching her like a hawk ready to swoop in if she started to eat too quickly.

"Should we wait until morning to move her?" Micha asked as he joined Garret.

Garret scanned the darkening clouds. "Might be best. We can all sleep in the house tonight."

"Do you want us to return once we've taken her back?"

"No, Janey and I will be fine on our own. And by the time you make it back to join us, we will likely be ready to return to the camp ourselves."

Micha sucked his lip between his teeth then released it again. "Could the others take her back, and I continue on with you?"

Garret studied him a moment then looked to where the rest of Trenton's men were sitting.

"You know she and Leon were rutting like a pair of rabbits?" One of them said, taking no care to lower his voice. "Do you really think she can be trusted? What if he ordered her to stay behind, so we would take her in and she could bring us down from the inside?"

The muscle in Garret's jaw tightened and he stood. "That's not really Leon's style and take a good look at her." He thrust his hand in Catriona's direction. "She was shackled and left for dead. If we hadn't found her when we did, she wouldn't have lasted much longer." The corruption was latching onto Garret's annoyance, whipping it into a fury. He gritted his teeth and forced it back down, but it was still there, scurrying through the back of his mind ready to pounce when his guard dropped again.

"She's a mind mage. You know they can—"

"Her powers are bound. She cannot use them, and unless someone finds the key to that particular pair of shackles, she will be permanently that way." Not an exact truth. Garret could unlock them if he wanted to, the way he had done Nea's. Even if he did want to, Catriona was too weak right now to even attempt it. The strain that unlocking them without the key took on the body of the mage involved would kill her.

"I still don't think it is wise to—"

"That's enough. Trenton put Garret in charge, so we follow his orders," Micha said.

"He can't be trusted either. How long was he Evard's right-hand man? And everyone knows he's corrupted. It's only a matter of time before he goes batshit crazy and attempts to kill the lot of us."

"Leith and Trenton both—"

"Leave it," Garret growled, cutting Micha off. "You will escort her back to Leith, and you'll not lay a single finger on her. Despite her recent actions, she is still his wife and therefore your future queen, and you will treat her with the respect she is entitled until the prince himself tells you otherwise." He clenched his fists as the itch of corruption prickled across the back of his neck. Nea's keen under the ward mark was a fluttering panic as though it was trying desperately to sooth the growing taint.

The soldier stood, his hand twitching towards his sword.

"Don't be an idiot. Sit down," Micha said, but the guard ignored him, dark eyes locked on Garret.

The other men didn't move; their gazes were trained on their comrade as though waiting for his signal.

"If you follow through with this, you are betraying an order from your commanding officer, and you are all aware that Trenton does not suffer fools," Micha said, and the men seemed to relax. All except the one standing. He gripped the hilt of his sword and took a step forward.

A ball of flame hit the ground right in front of the soldier's boots, and he stopped short, his ire turning on Janey. Flames were flickering over her fingertips, and she cocked her head as though challenging the soldier.

"Everyone just needs to calm down," Catriona said, her voice still frail and scratchy.

"We don't take orders from whores. Leith will see you—"

Garret landed a punch against the soldier's jaw. The corruption rolled happily at his centre as he shook the ache of the blow from his hand. With a pained snarl, the guard drew his sword.

Janey started to summon her power again, but Garret shot her a look and shook his head. This was his fight.

The soldier charged, sword raised. Garret dodged out of the way and drew his own sword. His keen was stirring under his skin, surging between crisp necromancy and crackling storm magic. His blade met a blow from his opponent's. The grate of metal and reverberation down his arm stilled the corruption for a moment as instinct took over. He couldn't let that brightling part of his keen out again. Last time he had, it had let the corruption take over entirely. Distracted, he barely managed to dodge a blow from the soldier's sword. The blade tugged through the thigh of his pants. He pressed forward, ignoring the burning of his keen. The soldier staggered backwards, blocking each of Garret's blows with a grunt. He was favouring his shoulder. An old injury? Garret backed off, and the soldier took the opening. Their swords met again, but this time Garret drove his weight into the blow. His opponent staggered back with a wince.

"Yield," Garret said.

The soldier shook his head.

"That shoulder will lose you this fight."

With another wince, the soldier threw his sword down. "End it then. Show them your true colours."

"I'm not in the business of killing." The corruption brayed at back of his mind demanding blood, and he sheathed his sword. "Micha. Keep an eye on him around Catriona." He started away, the corruption prickling.

"Wait, where are you going?" Micha caught up to him.

"I can't stay here."

Janey appeared beside Micha, her hands on her hips.

"Janey—"

She made a cutting motion with her hand.

"It's too dangerous. That soldier was right about me."

She shook her head and signed. *"I'm coming. Just wait while I get my things."*

Garret turned back to Micha. "Leave for the camp at first light. If anything happens to Catriona before you get her to Leith—"

"She'll be safe. I'll make sure of it."

If things were bleak outside the capital, they were far worse inside it. Dust Town was a ruin of burned houses and broken bodies. Rats and dogs prowled the streets, fighting over the spoils. The smell was vile; smoke, burned flesh, and refuse. And beneath it all, lingering death.

As they passed the burned husk of Margot's old clinic, Garret could feel eyes on him and the soft pressure of a warden's keen-sense. He shared a look with Janey. She gave a small nod, indicating she had felt something too. They both scanned the surrounding buildings, Janey's keen building in a warm rush. The brightling part of him reached towards the feeling of her keen, desperate to learn how it worked. Garret pushed the feeling back down and the corruption along with it. He couldn't afford the risk of letting that part of himself out, no matter how curious his keen was.

Janey peered into the darkened doorway of a nearby building. Her keen increased from a steady warmth to a wild rush of heat down Garret's spine as she retreated from the threshold.

Something stirred in the murky interior of the building. There was a thump and a curse then a pair of large eyes in a wide freckled face peered around the door frame. Janey immediately relaxed, her keen dying to a flickering ember. She edged forward and crouched to the child's height, but he shook his head and backed into the dark. Janey threw a glance over her shoulder at Garret and then tilted her head towards the door.

With a sigh, Garret crouched beside her. "It's alright," he said softly. "We won't hurt you."

There was a scuffle inside then four small forms crept out of the darkness. They looked almost as bad as Catriona had, covered in ash and grime, clothes torn, and wounds left untended. The boy who had originally approached the door looked to be the oldest. There were two other boys and a small girl; her hair was a matted tangle of creamy gold stained with blood.

"I'm Garret, and this is Janey," he said.

"You're mages. Mama told me not to trust mages," the eldest boy said.

"Janey is a mage, but I'm not. I'm a warden." Garret kept his voice level and soothing as he let his keen-sense out. The boy had the numb sensation of a warden, but the girl had the soft smoothness of water magic. Her blue eyes widened as her keen stirred in response to Garret.

"You don't feel right," the boy said.

The corruption. Garret inhaled slowly. "I'm not like other wardens, but I promise we won't hurt you. Where are your parents?"

"Dead," said one of the other boys. He had a hollow-eyed look about him.

The girl shook her head vigorously.

"Are you all related?"

"No. They're brothers." The first boy pointed to the other two. "Lily is from the upper market; she doesn't know what happened to her parents. Mine were dragged off by the guards."

Garret traced his fingers along his lip. "Do the rest of you have names?"

Lily gave him a small smile.

"Kevin." He indicated himself. "And that's Colm and Cyril."

Janey straightened from her crouch, and Garret followed suit. *"They can't stay here."* She signed.

He nodded.

"What's she doing with her hands?" Kevin backed up, raising his arm to protect the other children.

Janey lifted both her hands in front of her and shook her head.

"Janey can't talk like you and I can, so she needs to use her hands to speak," Garret explained.

"And you can understand her?"

"Yes."

The children all crept forward again. "What did she say?" Colm, the hollow-eyed boy asked.

"She said you can't stay here, and she is right. We can take you to the temple—"

"Not the temple. Too many of the dead people that way," Kevin said.

"Dead people?"

"The ones the necromancer brought back to life, but they're not like they were before they died."

"Reanimations." Garret shared a look with Janey. "We can take you to a safe house, and someone there might be able to get you out of the city. You can join the refugees heading inland."

Lily shook her head again.

"Her parents told her to stay. She won't leave. It was hard enough to get her to come back here with us, but the *reanimations*." Kevin said the word slowly, eyes intent on Garret's as though he were asking for confirmation.

Garret gave a nod.

"They would have killed her if we left her where we found her," Kevin finished.

"If you come with us, we might be able to find out what happened to your parents," Garret said to the girl. "I can't promise we will find them, but we'll do what we can."

Lily looked from Garret to Janey, then she edged towards the fire mage and held her hand out. Janey took hold of the girl's fingers and gave them a squeeze.

"You'll go with Janey?" Garret asked.

The girl dipped her head and gripped Janey's hand tighter.

"Alright. The safe house isn't too far but stay close and be quiet." Garret led them through the ruin of Dust Town and into the south side.

The safe house itself had survived mostly unscathed, though the entire south side appeared to have fared better than other parts of the city as well. It seemed like an eon since Garret had been here. Last time had been just after they rescued Nea and Margot from Evard. Not even an entire year and yet so much had happened.

The warehouse was empty but there were signs of life. Haley's favourite grey woollen shawl was tossed over the back of a chair. A few mugs sat on the table along with a small pile of dice. The large orange cat curled up on one of the pallet beds at the other end of the room lifted its head and blinked in Garret's direction then promptly returned to its nap. Emil would be pleased the cat had survived at least; the other warden had a soft spot for felines.

"It's safe," Garret called over his shoulder, and Janey and the children came in. "I'll see what sort of rations the others have left."

While Garret organised something for the children to eat, Janey bustled around them like a mother hen, making them wash and finding them blankets and dry clothes. There weren't many options available, but she made do, and soon each child was sitting on a bed with a bowl of stew in their lap and a borrowed oversized shirt on their back.

Janey and Garret were just settling down themselves when a sound outside caught Garret's attention. He stood slowly and pressed a finger to his lips as he edged towards the door.

It slammed open and a body came flying at him. The smaller frame hit his, sending them both staggering. Garret tucked his toes between his attacker's ankles. She stumbled and grabbed him, dragging him down with her and twisting so he landed on his back beneath her. A gleaming knife was pressed to the side of his throat.

"Garret!" Haley sheathed the knife and brushed her chin-length brown hair behind her ear as she got off him. "What are you doing here?" she asked, holding out a hand to help him to his feet.

"I came to see if Leon and Kieran were still in the palace."

"Leon and Kieran? No, they haven't been back since just after the tear." Her bright hazel gaze swept the room, passing over Janey and falling on the children. Kevin stood in front of the others, his fists raised. "Strange crew you've got with you this time. Sorry I attacked you. You don't exactly *feel* like you used to."

"Right ..." Between the corruption and the awakening of his brightling keen, it was no surprise her keen-sense hadn't recognised him. "We can discuss that later. Where are the others?" he asked as Haley brushed past him to investigate the pot of stew by the fire.

"Sonia and Callie should be back soon; they were helping a group of refugees get out. They were the last ones stranded outside the upper market. Grace is helping at the temple. The wards are keeping the reanimations at bay for now, but it means that most of those left in the upper market have congregated there and the sisters are run off their feet." She helped herself to a bowl and sat next to Janey. "Where did you find the kids?" she asked through a mouthful.

"Dust Town, near Margot's old clinic."

Haley blinked. "We swept that area several times; there were no survivors."

"We only started hiding there yesterday after the dead—reanimations found our other place," Kevin said. He had settled on the bed next to Lily again.

"Have you been into the palace?" Garret asked.

She shook her head. "That's where most of the reanimations came from. We thought it best to help those we could rather than risk our necks trying to hack through the undead."

"You did the right thing. I'm going to investigate the palace though."

Janey stood and tapped the centre of her chest.

"It's best if you stay here."

She shook her head.

There would be no arguing with her. She might not be able to verbally spar with him, but she was as stubborn as an ox when she wanted to be.

"Fine."

"What about us?" Kevin asked.

"Haley can take care of you. When we get back, we will see about taking you to the temple."

"Babysitting?" Haley scrunched her nose at Garret.

"It's still only early. We'll be back by full dark."

"And if you're not?"

If they weren't? Garret cast a look at Janey, who shrugged. "If we're not, then round up the others and leave for the camp outside Kalhanna tomorrow morning."

CHAPTER TWELVE

HARVEY

The capital was nearly devoid of life from the east dock through to the south side. It was eerie to walk through areas that were once bustling but now lay silent. Vermin crawled through piles of debris, scattered furniture, and overturned carts in the lower market. Dark pools shone here and there where the winter rain hadn't quite managed to wash the stains of blood from the street.

Evard tutted as he stumbled along beside Harvey. Penny had lifted her compulsion, concerned that if she left it longer, what was left of his mind would become completely addled. Not that he wouldn't deserve such a fate, but as Penny had pointed out, there could be something that still lingered in that sordid mind that might help them in the fight against Leon and Kieran.

"This wasn't my vision," Evard said, lifting his bound hands and rubbing them along his jaw.

He'd been unexpectedly compliant even without Penny's mind magic influencing him, as though he had accepted his defeat. That in itself made Harvey wary. Evard's moods had always been mercurial, his whims unpredictable.

"If he kills everyone, who will be left to rule over?"

Behind Harvey, Emil clucked his tongue. "You're worried about people's lives now? That didn't seem to matter when you were throwing down orders to purge—"

Penny made a shushing noise.

"Those mages were an obstacle. Nea had soured their minds against me, driven them into a panic over stories of chaos and darkness and the end of the world. My aim wasn't to end the world; it was to carve it anew. She could have claimed her slice of immortality right alongside me; been queen of the new world, but instead she let her morals cloud her judgment. Her power is a gift. One with which she could shake the very fabric of existence, and what does she do with it? Nothing! She is as ungrateful as the rest of you."

"Penny, can you shut him up again?" Emil asked.

"No, Emil, you set him off this time—you can deal with the consequences."

The door to the safe house just ahead of them opened and two figures stepped out onto the street. Garret and—

"Janey? What are you doing here? You're supposed to be back at Kalhanna," Harvey said.

Janey's attention snapped to him, but so did Garret's, his grey eyes darkening as they fell on Evard.

"You were supposed to be going to Merston. What are you doing here and with him?"

"Is that any way to greet your—" Evard's words were cut off as he went sprawling into the street.

"Penny?" Harvey asked over his shoulder.

She shook her head and pointed to Emil, who shrugged.

"Take him inside," Harvey said.

Emil hauled Evard to his feet then shunted him into the safe house.

"We found him at the Crossroads, chained up and left for dead, guarded by some new kind of reanimation," Harvey said.

"Why bring him back here?" Garret asked.

"We thought you and Leith might like to question him, see if you can glean anything from his ramblings. His mind is—"

"Broken," Penny said. "He was always verbose about his cruelty, but he was sharp and clever, not bitter and rambling. It seemed barbaric to leave him as we found him."

Garret rubbed a hand through his hair. He looked rougher than usual, much like he had done in those weeks after Declan's death, with dark circles under his eyes and longer-than-normal scruff on his chin.

"Then have Sonia and Haley take him back to Leith and head to Merston."

"About that. We learned that someone called Ambrose is at Merston. He is the one who started the—" Harvey pressed his lips together. What would you call it?

"He is responsible for Evard's *experiments*," Penny said, her mouth twisting as though she had tasted something particularly sour.

Garret's jaw worked.

"It is also apparently where Leon and Kieran were heading."

"Merston?"

Harvey nodded. "We weren't sure whether you would still want us to go there, and we couldn't send a bird because there were no messengers to be found between here and the Crossroads."

"That does change things." Garret pressed his fingers to the bridge of his nose.

Janey placed her hand gently on his arm, a frown wrinkling her brow as she studied his face.

"I'm fine."

"You're not. Do you have shackles?" Penny asked.

Was it the corruption? Sometimes not having keen-sense was a burden, then Harvey remembered that he probably did have keen-sense, just it was locked away because he was a *failed experiment*. He bit the inside of his cheek.

"Your concern is noted, Penny. But I can control it for now." Garret was saying.

Penny folded her arms, her dark eyes narrowing. It was a look that Harvey had seen her give Emil once or twice. "Fine. Make yourself a martyr; it's not me who your stubborn idiocrasy is going to hurt in the end." She brushed past Garret.

Janey licked her lip and met Harvey's eye.

"Where were you pair off to anyway?" Harvey asked.

"The palace," Garret said tightly.

"I could come with you if you need an extra set of hands or eyes." Janey nodded.

Garret drew a long breath and toyed with his scar. After a moment, he said, "Alright. But when we are done, the pair of you"— he indicated Janey and Harvey—"and everyone else inside the safe house are heading back to Leith."

Harvey wasn't about to argue with Garret, at least not right at this moment. But he hadn't missed the fact that Garret excluded himself. He shared a look with Janey. What was the warden up to?

Upper market was just as silent as lower market, but the streets were cleaner, the buildings almost untouched. It was simply as though everyone had just got up one morning and not returned. Except for the reanimations. Once again, they seemed different to the ones Harvey had encountered before. They wandered mindlessly through the streets, drawn to sound, and would attack if they encountered anything living. This made them easy enough to avoid.

Garret skirted the temple where those who hadn't fled the city were holed up under the protection of the temple wards and the care of the priestesses of the Bright. It seemed he wanted to avoid people as much as the reanimations. Not unusual for Garret, but Harvey thought he would have at least liked to check in there and see what was going on. Instead, he kept heading towards the palace, creeping along the outer wall until they reached the old servants' entrance that they had escaped through the day they had rescued Margot and Nea from Evard.

There were no signs of life inside the palace. Bodies of servants and courtiers lay crumpled in the hallways. Garret and Janey kept sharing looks, and they both appeared tenser than normal. Harvey wondered if it was something their keen-sense was picking up. He had managed to feel things before, like Janey's keen and that of Nea's son, Henry. Maybe it was like a muscle that grew stronger as you worked it, developing a memory until one day it was simply second nature. If it was then maybe Harvey could—but did he really want to? Keen-sense seemed useful, but what if learning to use it unlocked the rest of his keen? He rubbed the back of his neck and feeling eyes on him, glanced sideways.

Janey was watching him, her head tilted. "*Can you feel it?*" She signed.

He shook his head.

Her eyes narrowed. "*Have you tried?*"

"I'm worried if I try things will change." He signed back.

The corner of Janey's mouth twitched, and she threw a look in Garret's direction. The warden was opening a door into a side room just ahead of them. Turning back to Harvey, she took hold of his hand. Her fingers grew warm against his as a small jolt ran up his arm and woodsmoke tickled the back of his throat.

Janey released her grip. "*Sorry. Too much?*"

Harvey studied his fingers. "Was that your keen?"

She opened her palms in front of her and nodded, then she shook her head.

"Yes, and no?" Small flickers of warmth were still twitching along his fingers. "Did the block on my keen do something?"

"*I don't know.*" She signed then glanced down the hall.

He followed her line of sight. "Where's Garret?"

They hurried to the room the warden had been investigating, shoulders bumping as they reached the door.

"Isn't this Leith's room?" Harvey whispered to Janey as he took in the green drapes around the large bed. Garret was over by the dresser, a hairbrush in his hand, his thumb running over the bristles as he examined the other items in the open drawer.

Harvey went to enter the room, but Janey caught his elbow. "*Give him a minute.*" She signed.

Garret must have sensed them because at that moment he turned. He held the hairbrush out to Janey; she moved forward and took it gently.

As she stepped back, turning the brush in her fingers, Harvey studied it. Roses had been carved into the dark wood of the handle. Though most of the paint had worn off, it still clung in patches of pale pink and green. "That doesn't look like it belonged to Leith."

"Because it's Nea's," Garret said with a sigh.

"Oh? *Oh* ... and Leith kept it?" Harvey looked down at his hand as Janey pressed the brush into it.

"*Try.*" She signed when he took it from her.

Harvey focused on the brush, running his thumb along the bristles as Garret had done; the flickering warmth of Janey's keen had finally left his fingertips, but now it was replaced with a bone-numbing chill. Henry's keen had been cool, but this was different. This was the deep breath stealing cold of winter.

"You've figured out how to use your keen-sense?" Garret asked.

"Sort of. It seems to take a lot of focus or ..." He could feel something—deeper in the palace, a seething oily feeling that brought bile to the back of his throat. "What is *that*?"

"Corruption," Garret said. "And not the normal kind."

Harvey held the brush out to Garret.

His fingers twitched towards it, but he closed his fist and lowered it, his other hand coming to grip the section of wrist the purple rose of his death ward marked. "Give it to Janey. Would you please pass it on to Nea when she returns?" he asked the mage.

Janey's eyes narrowed as she studied Garret, but she gave a single nod and took the brush from Harvey then slipped it into her bag.

"I am guessing that corruption wasn't present before," Harvey said.

Both Janey and Garret shook their heads.

"*What were you doing in here?*" Janey signed.

Garret cast a glance around the room. "I'm not sure. I felt ..." His gaze flicked to Janey's bag. "Nea's keen seems to soothe the corruption, even in its residual form," he said softly as he moved to close the drawer.

Something stopped it, and Garret reached inside, giving the drawer a wiggle as he tugged on whatever was blocking it. He pulled out a battered looking journal.

"What's that?" Harvey asked.

"It was Nea's too," Garret said as he slid the drawer shut with one hand and flipped the journal open with the other. He thumbed through the pages. "It just appears to be random notes ... We should check Evard's study." He snapped the journal shut and made for the door.

Janey nearly had to jog to keep up with Garret's clipped pace as he left Leith's room and headed down the hall. She was frowning so hard at the warden's back that Harvey was surprised he hadn't combusted on the spot. Something was definitely up with Garret, and Harvey was starting to wonder if it was more than the corruption that was driving the change.

As they entered Evard's study, Garret headed straight for the bookcase. He ran his fingertips along the spines on the middle shelf and then pulled several free before feeling around in the cavity he had created. There was a click, and a section of wall grated open to reveal a narrow gap just big enough for a person to squeeze through.

Janey edged towards the opening.

"Did you know this one was here?" Garret asked her, and she shook her head, her nose scrunching, most likely at the smell that was wafting out of the opening. Stagnant air, mould, and something that Harvey had smelt before but couldn't quite place. "Would you mind, Janey?" Garret indicated the stairs that descended into darkness.

The air around Harvey grew warm then a small ball of amber light crackled into life beside Janey. She guided it into the opening. The light shone off the thin threads of the spiderwebs that clung to the walls and ceiling and revealed dark patches of grime on the stairs that looked in some part like blood stains.

Garret went first, sideways and ducking his head to fit through the opening. Janey had no trouble, but even though Harvey wasn't as broad or tall as Garret, he still had to half crouch and shimmy along until they reached the first landing.

That seething oily feeling grew stronger the deeper they went, until they emerged into what could only be called a torture chamber. Tiny cells lined one wall, and the middle of the room held several tables with cracked leather cuffs attached to them. There was another table against the far wall with dust-shrouded tools laid out on it and next to that a cabinet containing an assortment of jars, bottles, and books.

As Janey's mage light bobbed beside them, it cast a warm orange glow on the scene. Had Harvey's mother been in one of those cells? Strapped to one of those— He raked his fingers over the back of his neck, and the world blurred around him as he moved from the chamber into the next one.

Even in dim light coming from the previous room it was clear this one was better appointed. There were two cells, one on each side of the space, and these held proper beds and basic furnishings. The feeling of corruption was stronger in here, radiating out from a broken section of wall directly across from him. He edged towards it; the light didn't reach into the corridor beyond. But marks remarkably similar to those that had contained Amelia glimmered faintly in the gloom. They seemed to surround an open doorway at the other end of the short hall. Something moved in the shadows there beyond the door frame.

Harvey cast a glance over his shoulder at Janey and Garret as they entered the second room and moved towards him. When he turned back to the other door, a sickly green mage light flickered to life and a man stepped out of the shadows. His sandy hair was matted and lank. His good eye, painted a strange teal colour by the mage light, glittered with a sharp sort of madness. There was a dark webbing of veins over his left cheek, and the sclera of that eye was completely black. He ran his tongue along his cracked lips.

"Hello, brother, welcome home."

CHAPTER THIRTEEN

NEA

The dark paste Molly had covered Nea's hair with had begun to itch, and she fought the urge to rake her fingers across her scalp. It shouldn't be too much longer; at least she hoped. The deep earthy scent of the herbs brought hazy memories to the surface of her mind. They weren't all-consuming like those moments she was dragged back to the purge, but that didn't mean they weren't painful.

When she closed her eyes, she could almost hear Tobias muttering under his breath as he made notes in his journal, trying to perfect an ointment for an ailment that Nea couldn't quite remember.

"Those herbs should have done their work now," Molly said, breaking through the memory.

Nea followed her outside and leant over the railing of the ship as Molly dosed her head with warm water and then scrubbed it with a soap that smelt like Osmarian jasmine. Dark foam dripped off the end of her hair as Molly rinsed the soap away then threw a drying cloth at her.

The now coal-black lengths of her hair were coiling into neat curls as they dried. She shifted them over her shoulder and leant against the side rail of the ship, tilting her face towards the midday sun. She'd spent a year and a half of her life on this ship with Wren and

Gendry, and sitting here now, the sun drying her hair and a plate of exotic fruits on her lap, she almost missed it. Maybe when all this was over and they had a chance to catch their breath, she'd disappear over the horizon with the Queen for a while. But then what of Henry? He'd spent more time than he should have without his mother, and could she leave Margot behind again? Or, she pressed her fingers to the ward mark, Garret? They had to survive what was to come before she needed to worry about that.

Gendry settled beside her and gave her a grin as he stole a piece of starfruit from her plate. "You sure about this?"

"About sneaking into Vince's palace of carnal delights and possibly stealing some of his most prized possessions out from under his nose?" She shrugged. "It'll be just like old times."

"But you and Molly are going in alone, and you have no idea where he keeps the book or the keystone or if he even has them."

"He probably just tossed them into the back corner of his vault."

"Given they are connected to the Shadow Man, I doubt that." He took another slice of fruit.

"If he's so enamoured with the Shadow, why desecrate the shrine?"

Gendry shrugged. "Because he's a selfish prick. He moved the important parts into his estate, and those who seek the Shadow's counsel can pay a tithe for the privilege. Don't underestimate Vince. It's been a long time since the pair of you went toe to toe."

"I'll be fine. Is the ship ready to leave tonight?" The plan was to have the Queen leave as soon as Molly and Nea departed for Vince's party. Nea would create a portal to get herself and Molly back to the ship once they had secured the book and the key. That was if Vince actually had them. If he didn't? Well, she'd just have to cross that bridge when they got to it.

He nodded. "As soon as Donnic gets here, we can leave whenever we need to. And speak of the Shadow."

Donnic had just appeared at the top of the gangplank, a crate in his arms. "I have a few more back on the dock," he said as Rufus took the crate from him.

"Of course, you do," the boatswain muttered and nodded his head to a couple of crew members nearby. They hurried down the gangplank to fetch the other crates as Donnic gave Nea and Gendry a wave.

"I had better go and find Molly, so we can get ready." She stood and started to move away.

"Nea."

She stopped and turned back to him. "You know you're as good as family to Wren and I. When you're finished saving the realms, you and yours will always be welcome on the Queen."

"I know." She gave him a small smile. "And I am grateful for that." There were a few pieces of fruit still on the plate—she held it out.

Gendry took it with a grin.

"What is this bullshit?" Molly tugged at the translucent fabric covering her midsection.

Nea bit back a smile as she secured the buttons at her wrists. The sleeves of her top were not only long but opaque enough to mask the death ward and the swirling grey Shadow marks. They couldn't hide the patterns over the back of her hand or the crescent moon on her palm. She'd just have to try to avoid bringing attention to it.

Unlike Molly's outfit, which was shades of blue, had short cap sleeves, and a criss-cross bodice that became a thin sheet of translucent silk over her stomach, Nea's stopped just below her bust line, leaving her midsection completely bare. It was a combination of deep greens with piping in a golden yellow. Evard's colours. The thought brought a sour taste to her mouth that drove her smile away.

"Well, you both certainly look like you belong at Vince's party," Arlie said as she joined them. She was still pale, and her keen wasn't the steady warmth it had been, but some of the colour was slowly returning to her cheeks. Given time, she would be back to her usual self. "Here, let me help you with your hair." She held out a brush and a set of hair pins.

Arlie braided the sides of Molly's hair back and joined the braids in a high pony. The creamy ends danced against her shoulder blades. She sectioned Nea's hair in a similar way but laced golden ribbons into the braids and left the bulk of it tumbling down her back in a mass of dark, wavy curls.

"I'd say you're both ready," Arlie said as she collapsed onto a crate. "I'm alright." She waved away their concern. "Just overextended myself a bit. Now do you remember the way to get in?"

Nea nodded. "We sneak around to the west side servants' entrance and the cook will be waiting for us. Are you sure she can be trusted?"

Arlie gave a small nod.

"Ready then?" Nea asked Molly.

"Ready? Yes. Hap—"

"I get it, Molly. You'll be back in your comfy clothes and shooting fools with your crossbow before you know it. Speaking of which ..."

"I know I need to leave it behind, but you can portal back to the Queen when we are done, right?"

Nea drew a breath. "How many times—"

"Right?"

"Yes, I should be able to *portal* back here when we are done." She gave her satchel a pat. It would be staying behind with Molly's crossbow. The knife Gendry had given her was secured to the side of her thigh and reachable through a slit she had made in the loose-fitting pants. Molly had made similar alterations to her outfit.

"Good. Then let's get this over with." Molly placed her crossbow with Nea's satchel, and they headed for the door.

It didn't take them long to reach the west side of Vince's palace, and as Arlie had promised, the cook was waiting for them. She cleaned her hands on her apron as she ushered them inside. "Give me your cloaks. The festivities have already started. Vince is currently in the north garden pavilion."

They slipped their cloaks off and handed them to her.

"Do you know where he keeps his Shadow shrine?" Nea asked.

"In the main hall."

"Fuck," Molly muttered. "We're not going to get in there unnoticed."

"We'll just have to be careful," Nea said. "Come on. We at least need to check it out. Just act like you belong here and try not to bring too much attention to yourself." She stepped out of the kitchen with her head held high and then sauntered down the hall emphasising the roll of her hips. She felt like an absolute idiot but hoped she at least looked the part.

They entered the main hall. Tables covered in platters of food and jugs of drink had been set at one side of the room. Various lounges and piles of pillows were positioned across the middle of the empty space. Nea wasn't surprised about the display of decadence or the feeling that the whole event could dissolve into an orgy. Vince had never been one for subtlety. In a way, it reminded her of the Usurper's estate and his masquerade. If Vince was as enamoured with the Shadow as he seemed, then perhaps there was something more to that similarity.

"What will this shrine look like?" Molly asked, her arm brushing against Nea's as she edged closer to avoid a serving girl who was making a show of coyly avoiding the advances of a man dressed in a gaudy orange vest.

"Like that, I imagine," Nea said, lifting her hand to indicate the large alcove set into the end of the room behind what looked like a throne carved out of obsidian.

The statue of the Shadow man that had once sat in the centre of the shrine took pride of place on the large slab behind the throne. All around the statue were lit candles and offerings, from dried roses and dark shining stones to smooth ivory bones and glittering daggers.

"No sign of a book or a key—get your hand off me." Molly whirled around.

The hand in question belonged to a tall man with a wide, gleaming grin. The sides of his head were shaved to reveal tattoos in a pattern of waves that stood out against the bronze tone of his skin. He didn't look Faridean, but he didn't look quite Osmarian either. His eyes, a darker shade of golden-brown, were not on Molly but on Nea as he toyed with the gold earring hanging from one of his ears. A cloying soft-fingered keen tickled across her scalp, and she immediately slammed her mental walls up.

"So, what are we stealing?" he asked in a voice that was deep and smooth and unmistakably Faridean.

"Who are you?" Molly asked.

"I'm a shadow in the night. Who are you?"

"Cut the bullshit," Molly said with an eye-roll.

"What makes you think we are here to steal something?" Nea asked.

"Like knows like." He edged closer. "Neither of you are Vince's girls. Blondie, here, moves too much like a soldier, and if Vince *owned* something as unique as you, he'd never stop crowing about it." With another smug grin, he folded his arms.

"If it's that obvious, why haven't you revealed us to Vince?"

"If I did that, Blondie, I'd just draw unwanted attention to myself. But we can work together. Vince has something I want, and I imagine it's the same for you. So, I'll ask again, what are we stealing?"

"What are you stealing?" Nea threw back at him in a whisper, glancing around to make sure no one was listening.

The man moved forward and pressed his palm against the statue. "A necklace, large green stone inlaid with robrillium on a robrillium chain. It's a family heirloom that I would like returned. Now your turn."

"A book."

He let out a low, rumbling laugh. "A book? I didn't know Vince could read." After a moment, he held his hand out. "Varlan."

Nea chewed her lip as she studied his hand. "Nea." She gave the offered hand a shake.

"Vince has mentioned you before. Gave him quite a bit of trouble a few years back, didn't you?"

She shrugged. "This is Molly." The other woman fixed her with a glare. "Any idea where Vince might keep his more treasured possessions?"

"Not in his vault. I already tried there. Bunch of junk. *Valuable junk.* But nothing magical and certainly no books."

"What about his private chambers?" Molly asked.

Varlan shrugged. "Might be worth checking out. Going to have to make it look like we're heading off to find a secluded space for something more *private* though." He tilted his head to indicate the party behind them.

"Not going to—"

"The estate does have a library. Or it did," Nea said over Molly's retort. "We could try there first."

"Still have to get away from the main party without causing suspicion."

Molly let out a groan.

"Come on," Varlan said in a louder voice. "Let's find us somewhere to get better acquainted." He slid an arm around each of their waists and guided them towards a side door. As he did, the main doors opened, and Vince appeared.

Nea ducked her head. "That's Vince," she hissed at Molly.

"Do you think he noticed?" Molly asked as they slipped into the hallway and Varlan released them.

"I don't know. We should hurry," Nea said, heading towards the door that used to lead to the library. As she reached for the handle, the moon on her palm lit up, and she closed her fingers, drawing her hand back. "The door's warded."

"What sort of ward?" Varlan asked.

"The sort that will either trigger an alarm or make you lose your fingers," Nea answered.

"So, I guess that's where he keeps the good stuff then," Molly said. "Can you disarm it? Is that something that can be done with wards."

"Maybe if I had a few hours and knew the exact purpose of the ward. Or if I was ..." She touched her fingers to her wrist. "Garret," she whispered.

"Did something happen?" Molly's voice was tight.

Nea shook her head. "No, but if I could use his keen, I could unlock the ward without triggering it ... At least I think so."

"We are wasting time," Varlan said, throwing a glance back the way they had come.

Nea licked her lip. Garret's keen was faint and buried deep, but if she could bring it back to the surface, she might be able to navigate the barrier that had formed and locked it away. Numbness stirred at her core then faded. She drew a deep breath and tried again. Pain edged up the sides of her neck and into her jaw. She stumbled into the wall and gripped her head. It shouldn't be this hard.

"Nea?" Molly's gaze met hers.

"I can't bring his keen to the surface."

"Could you make a portal to get us in there?" Molly asked softly, flicking a look in Varlan's direction.

She had been inside Vince's library once before, but she wasn't sure she remembered enough of the details to accurately picture the space and anchor the portal. Maybe she didn't need to. Placing her hand against the wall just beside the warded door, she let her keen out. Shimmers of lilac magic rippled over the wall. She focused on her desire to move forward through the wood and stone into the room beyond. Then an oval opened in front of her, showing the library on the other side. It flickered, unstable without a proper anchor.

"Quick," she urged Molly and Varlan.

Molly leapt through without a second thought, but Varlan gave Nea an appraising look before he stepped through.

Nea followed them, and the portal snapped shut the second her feet met the floor on the other side.

"That's a handy little trick. You could make quite the name for yourself in my line of work," Varlan said as he summoned a pale pink mage light and scanned the room around them.

Molly had her fingers pressed to her temples, her skin looking peaky in the watery moonlight coming in the high windows. "It never gets better," she muttered.

Nea studied the room. Where should they start? There appeared to be nothing out of the ordinary here. But Varlan was moving towards a marble bust of Vince. He ran his fingers around the bottom of the statue, and then there was a soft click. A shelf to Nea's left shuddered backwards to reveal a narrow staircase descending into the dark.

"You found that awfully quickly," Molly said, her eyes narrowed as she studied him.

Varlan shrugged. "I'd be a poor thief if I didn't know a thing or two about my mark. Shall we?" He indicated the stairs.

"You first," Molly said.

He shrugged again and moved down the first few steps, his mage light casting long shadows into the dark.

Molly flicked a look at Nea before following him.

The stairs led them into a vault-like chamber. An assortment of relics sat on the small pedestals that lined one wall. Varlan rubbed his hands together and strode to the one at the end. He lifted a glittering robrillium chain. The heavy green stone hanging from it caught the light from the pink orb floating beside him. The robrillium inlays in the stone glowed with an oily luminance before he slipped it away in the inner pocket of his jacket.

"Which of these do you think is the key?" Molly asked Nea as she studied the various items in the room.

Nea let her keen out. It tugged her towards a shelf in the far corner that held a plain looking wooden chest with bands of robrillium around it. As her fingertips met the lid, a shock ran through them—not enough to hurt but enough to set her teeth on edge. Inside on the padded base was an age-worn book that looked like it would crumble to dust if she touched it.

"Hello, Nea," a distinctly Osmarian voice said behind her.

She thought it had been too easy. Slowly, she turned. Vince was standing at the entryway to the room flanked by several guards. At least one of them was a warden.

"When I heard you were sniffing around town, I wondered how long it would be before we crossed paths." He folded his arms behind his back and rocked on his heels, the gilt stitching on his sapphire-blue coat catching the light. "It appears you have once again stolen one of my most prized possessions, and as Donnic appears to be no longer in that hovel of his, I have no one to punish." He snorted a laugh. "Except you, of course. You see, I learn from mistakes." He indicated one of the wardens. "You will not slip through my clutches so easily this time."

Varlan cleared his throat. "Am I free to go?"

Vince's gaze slid to him, and he laughed again. "Of course, once you return what is mine."

"You promised it in payment," Varlan growled, folding his arms over his chest.

"Of all people, Varlan, you should know how honour works among thieves."

Varlan swore under his breath.

Molly chose that moment to spring from behind one of the pedestals. She landed on the closest guard, knocking him off balance and sending him staggering into Vince.

Vince growled as he stumbled backwards, the movement gapping the front of his shirt to reveal an oval of quartz spotted stone, like a tiny piece of the altar from the Shadow temple, hanging around his neck. Familiar magic rippled over the stone.

"Molly, the key is around his neck," Nea called and grabbed a golden idol off the shelf beside her. She pelted it at the head of the closest guard, and he knocked it aside before charging at her.

Her keen surged under her skin, and she opened her fingers in front of her, a shimmering portal springing to life between her and the guard. He went barrelling through the portal, and she snapped it shut. To her right, Varlan had one of the wardens baled up against the wall, a numb bubble of suppression around them.

Molly was a blur, dodging the remaining warden guard. Nea summoned her keen again, but the warden slammed his suppression down on her as he shoved Molly aside, sending her crashing into Vince. Nea didn't see what happened next as the warden grabbed her, his fingers digging into her arms as he pinned her against the wall. She thrashed in his grasp, but her arms were clamped against her sides. Her fingers snagged in the slit at her thigh, the cool hilt of the blade hidden there whispering against their tips. She closed her fingers around it as she smashed her head forward. The warden dodged the headbutt, but his grip on her loosened just enough. She pulled the knife free and stabbed it into this thigh. He grunted, and his grip loosened further. She drove her shoulder into his sternum, the buckles on the front of his leather armour sending a sharp jolt of pain down her arm. She gritted her teeth and forced him back as she swung the knife again.

A loud thud sounded, and he crumpled before her. Varlan stood behind him, hilt of a sword raised. "Don't like killing if I can avoid it," he said. "Now might be a good time to get us out of here.

Molly was still grappling with Vince, but footsteps were pounding down the stairs. Nea grabbed the small chest containing the book and summoned another portal. "We have to go now!" she yelled as Varlan disappeared through the shimmering doorway.

Shoving Vince into a pedestal, Molly spun and raced towards Nea, knocking relics and their stands into his path as he pursued her across the room. The second Molly entered the portal, Nea leapt after her.

As her feet hit the deck of the Queen, she slammed the doorway shut. Spots danced in front of her eyes as she teetered onto her hands and knees, the chest containing the book thudding onto the deck beside her.

"Nea?" Molly's worried face swam across her vision.

"Move." Arlie took Molly's place.

"I'm fine," Nea said faintly. "I just overextended my keen." Creating portals had been getting easier, especially if she was only traveling short distances and not crossing the barrier. It shouldn't have drained her the way it had. She pressed her fingers to her left wrist. If cutting her keen off from Garret's had limited how much of the source she could channel, then they were in big trouble. She needed her keen to be fully functioning now more than ever. Forcing a smile, she shot a look at Molly. "Did you manage to get the key?"

Molly held up the glittering stone on its broken chain. "Yep. And you got the book?"

Nea patted the chest beside her. "It's pretty fragile. I hope I'll be able to read it without destroying it." She ran her hand through her hair. "We'll have to wait a little longer before I can create another portal."

Rourke nudged Nea's elbow with his nose and let out a soft whine.

"I'll be alright. I just need to rest," she said, smoothing her hand over his ears before looking up at the others around them.

Wren, Arlie, and the twins, Pippa and Kiki, were a short distance away. They all looked almost as tired as Nea felt. Donnic and Gendry stood farther down the deck talking in hushed tones. The tattooist was frowning and rubbing at his forehead as though fending off a headache. Dara approached the two men. Her steps faltered, and Gendry caught her before she fell.

"What's got into all the mages?" Molly asked.

"Something has happened to the source," Varlan's deep voice said to Nea's left. He sat with his back resting against the side rail of the ship, his eyes closed.

Nea brought her keen-sense to the surface. It wasn't quick and effortless as it should have been but sluggish and weak, the effort required to access it bringing a dull ache to her temples. He was right; the source felt different, thin and fading like it was draining from the air around them. A result of the tear? Surely it shouldn't feel this way this far from Kalhanna? No, it wasn't fading. It was draining away—a body of water pulling back with the tide. But it was receding too far and fast. What would happen when the tide came back in? She tilted her head back to study the sky above them. It was shimmering with magic, a brighter patch like a seam forming directly above. "Wren, we need to move the ship now!" She vaulted to her feet. Too fast—her head swam, and she gripped it.

"I don't think I can summon enough wind to move us."

The air was growing prickly, tightening as the seam in the sky above grew brighter.

"What the fuck is that?" Molly asked, and Rourke growled as he pressed against Nea's leg.

"It's another tear. That's where the source is going."

"Is it going to explode like the last one?" Molly asked.

Nea nodded. "It's not as big as the one above Kalhanna, but the source isn't as thin here, and if we stay directly underneath it ..."

"Shit. Shit, shit, shit!"

"Yep." Nea studied the mages present. "Kiki and Pippa, do you think you can lend Wren some of your keen?"

The twins nodded. "Of course," they said as one.

"Not all of it. Just enough that she can get the ship moving."

"I can, too."

"No, Arlie, we are going to need a functioning healer regardless of whether this plan works or not."

"What can I do?" Donnic asked.

"I'm going to need a boost as well," she replied, and Donnic nodded. Nea then shot a look at Varlan. "I consider letting me borrow a small bit of your keen fair enough payback for that stunt you pulled with Vince."

A smooth smile rolled across Varlan's lips. "I like a woman who's not afraid to take command, and if lending you a bit of keen will save all our arses, then who am I to say no?"

"What about the rest of us?" Gendry asked.

"Once the Queen starts moving, just try to keep her steady." A small hand touched her wrist, and she glanced down to meet Dara's pale gaze. "You should go inside, Dara."

The girl shook her head. "I can help." Her brow furrowed, and she squeezed her eyes shut "The song is changing. It's loud and screeching. But I can help." She opened her eyes.

"There is something you can do." Nea took hold of the girl's hand. "When the screeching stops, squeeze my fingers."

Dara nodded and shifted her feet, standing straighter as her face turned towards the shimmering patch of sky.

"Everyone ready?"

A chorus of positive responses came down the deck, and beside her Donnic rested a hand on her shoulder.

"Wait for it ..."

Dara's fingers tightened on Nea's.

The world held its breath.

A ripping sound started as the shimmering patch of sky grew brighter.

"Now!"

The wind howled, and the ship gave a jolting lurch that nearly threw Nea from her feet, but Donnic stopped her from falling. Varlan touched her other shoulder, and both his and Donnic's keen sung along her veins, prickling the hairs on the back of her neck. It wasn't like sharing keen with Garret. That was smooth and easy, like the keen belonged to her as much as him. This time the foreign keen surged about, trying to find its way back home. But she latched onto it, forcing it to meld with her own.

Her teeth ached and the sky roared as the tearing sound increased. She lifted her hand and an oval of shimmering purple light formed in front of the ship, but it wasn't big enough. She fed it more magic, tasting blood as her teeth sunk into the side of her cheek. The ship lurched forward again, and her knees buckled.

A pale sky appeared above her flecked with dark spots. Faces swam across her vision, and a large hand pressed to her cheek. Then she was falling.

Not again.

CHAPTER FOURTEEN

Harvey

"No love for your long-lost brother?" the man on the other side of the rune marks asked in a voice that was almost as oily as the twisting mass in Harvey's gut.

Harvey shook his head. And the man tilted his chin, his good eye flicking to study Janey and then Garret.

"Ah yes, the *chosen* one. Such a waste. If only Father had known about you, he could have sculpted you right. Made you unstoppable. Instead, you are a shallow reflection of what you should be." He inhaled slowly. "And you feel like *her*. The one they all wanted. A little legitimate Shadow blood, and suddenly everyone loses their heads. She's an ungrateful little bitch who is more trouble than she's worth."

"What are you?" Harvey asked.

The man chuckled. "I'm a failed experiment, just like our dear sister. You've met her, haven't you? She's much prettier than me. But then, Father was not as cruel with her, didn't demand as much *sacrifice*."

Janey's fingers laced with Harvey's, and she gave his hand a tug, drawing him back from the doorway. He turned to her, and she let his hand go to sign. "*We shouldn't stay here.*"

"But ..." He cast a glance over his shoulder at the man in the doorway.

"Janey is right," Garret said. He had his arms folded over his chest and his jaw was tight like he was grinding his teeth.

"You should listen to your friends. There is nothing here but discarded sons and dusty memories." He backed away into the darkness. "But if it is answers you seek, you should find Father. I am certain he would love to be reacquainted, especially given his oversight regarding your keen."

"What oversight?" Harvey started towards the rune-marked doorway, but Janey caught his arm, pulling him up short. "What about my keen?"

A sniggering laughter came from the darkness. "You'll find out in due time, I am sure. If you see Amelia, please give her my regards."

Harvey let Janey drag him away. She released her grip on him only when they were halfway across the torture chamber and Garret stumbled, his hands gripping his head. She hurried to check on the warden, but jolted to a stop, her green eyes widening as she turned to Harvey.

"Janey? What's going on?"

She shook her head and pressed a hand over her mouth as she swooned sideways. Harvey rushed forward and caught her before she hit the ground.

"Janey." He gave her limp form a small shake and turned to Garret, who was sitting with his head tilted against the wall. The colour had drained from his skin, and he seemed to be having a hard time keeping his eyes open. "Garret, what's happening?"

"It's the source. Something ... something is affecting it."

"Is it the tear?" Harvey tightened his grip on Janey.

"I don't know," Garret responded weakly. "It's like all magic is being drawn out of the world."

"That pretentious prick of a necromancer finally did something right," the oily voice of the man behind the rune marks said right beside Harvey.

Harvey shied away from him, reinforcing his grip on Janey.

"Oh, come now. I am not about to harm my baby brother, even if you are the reason Father sent Mother away. The brightling, however—" He took a step towards Garret, and the air grew icy.

Garret pushed himself to his feet but still leant heavily on the wall. The air around him seemed to shimmer with violet light.

"Ah, yes, I forgot that little detail. Are you sure you want to do that? It's all the corruption needs to take over. *Death spoils all it touches*, after all."

Garret swallowed.

The air around Harvey seemed to tremble, then a shudder rolled over him. It was like an earthquake but the ground remained steadfast. The air was quaking, or was it the source? Janey twitched in Harvey's arms. She grabbed his wrist, and a surge of heat tore through him—something shifted inside and then the heat went charging back into her. Harvey let her go, and she gained her feet as nimble as a cat as the air around her erupted into flames.

"Oh, the little one has *teeth*." The man grinned. "I'll happily dance with you, sweetheart."

The flames around Janey leapt forward, shrouding the man, but he twisted his hand through them, and they flickered before seeming to absorb into his open palm.

"What's this? You've never seen a mage who could absorb the keen of another have—" He jolted as the tip of a sword burst from his chest. With a sadistic grin, he turned and punched Garret. "Nice try, but you can't kill me that easily."

Garret staggered backwards, that purple light shrouding him again, but he seemed to be warring with himself. It was clear his head was not in this fight.

Harvey pushed Janey behind him and drew his own sword.

"What are you going to do, hmm? You could never match me, even before Father *broke* you."

Something inside Harvey was calling out. A flicker of purple and red ran over his fingers, and his instinct took over. The world blurred around him until his fingers met the chest of the other man. How had he crossed the room so quickly? He didn't have time to process the thought as his hand broke through the skin of the man's chest. Harvey wrenched his arm back, freeing his bloodstained fingers—the heart clutched in them gave a feeble throb, bringing a bitter lump to the back of his throat. The man blinked as a dribble of red ran down his chin, then he collapsed onto the floor.

Harvey met Garret's eye; the warden looked as shocked as he felt. The heart was still heavy in his palm, blood oozing between his fingers. He released it, and it rolled onto the lifeless body with a meaty plop. "What just happened?"

Janey took a step towards him, but he lifted his hands and retreated from her.

"I—" The world blurred around him again, and he found himself standing outside the palace entryway. Bile coated the back of his tongue, and the lump in his throat shifted as a cold sweat broke over his shoulders.

A short while later, he leant against the cool stones of the wall. Warm fingers brushed his hair from his forehead, and he opened his eyes to find Janey studying his face. The concern that shone in her green gaze was warring with curiosity. She should have been repulsed. She shouldn't be looking at him with that soft smile, not when she had just watched him rip his own brother's heart from his chest. Blood still stained his fingers, itching as it dried.

"Do you want to talk?"

He shook his head. "No, I want to forget what happened down there. I don't want this power, whatever it is. I want to go back to being keen-less. I can't—" The world around him seemed to shudder with each rise in his emotions.

Janey traced her fingers along her lip as she studied him, the movement not quite hiding her frown. *"We need to get you to Niall."* She signed.

Harvey glanced over her shoulder. He wanted Garret's opinion on what had happened. The warden was nowhere in sight. "Where's Garret?"

Janey pressed her lips together and shrugged.

"Is he still ... down there?"

She shook her head and grabbed his hands, not bothered by the tacky blood that marred his fingers and drew him to his feet.

"You shouldn't have left Garret ... the corruption."

"*You needed me more. He'll be okay. The corruption hasn't won yet.*"

"But—"

She grabbed hold of his hands again and squeezed them, her eyes imploring him to trust her.

"Alright. We should head back to the safe house and get the others."

Janey nodded and let go of one of his hands, the other she gave a small tug as she started walking towards the gate.

Harvey cast a look back over his shoulder. They really shouldn't leave Garret behind. But the warden had been up to something, and if he had used the chaos to slip away, they had no hope of finding him until he wanted to be found. Hopefully, the corruption hadn't completely overtaken him.

"Where's Garret?" Emil asked as he opened the door to the safe house.

"We lost him in the castle."

Janey shook her head. "*Not lost. He has something he needs to do.*"

"In the state he is in it's almost the same thing," Harvey replied.

She settled her hands on her hips.

"What happened to *you*?" Penny asked as she shoved Emil out of the way.

"I'd rather not talk about it."

Janey lifted her hands as though about to sign, but Harvey gently pushed them down.

"I need time to process it before everyone starts poking and prodding me." He let Janey's hands go and stepped between Penny and Emil. A smooth pressure rolled over the back of his neck, like fingers easing out a knotted muscle.

"Leave it, Pen," Emil said, and the sensation stopped.

Inside the safe house, four children were settled on a single pallet bed by the far wall. Three appeared to be asleep, but the fourth was studying Harvey, her large blue eyes blinking owlishly. Haley sat beside the pallet bed, a steaming cup in her hand and an empty plate balanced on one knee.

"What now?" Emil asked. "Should we go after Garret?"

"There is nothing any of us can do for him, especially if his corruption has taken over, which is extremely likely," Penny said as she settled herself at the table in the centre of the room.

Janey shook her head. "*He's still fighting.*"

That soft pressure rolled across Harvey's neck again, bringing a cloying taste to the back of his mouth. Was that someone's keen? It wasn't Haley or Emil. He didn't think wardens would feel like that, and Janey's keen was a soothing warmth—except when she had attacked the corrupted mage, then it had been a wild all-consuming heat. Penny then.

"We felt it, too," Penny was saying. "It was like the source was completely blocked."

"No, Pen, it was like it was draining away," Emil said, picking up the ginger cat and scratching behind his ears. "It stabilised again pretty quickly though. We need to mention it to Niall when we get back. In case it is a result of the tear. If it can alter the source this far from Kalhanna ..."

"My br—that *thing* said the necromancer had finally done something right. I guess he meant Kieran," Harvey said, meeting Janey's eye.

"What thing?" Emil asked.

"He was like Amelia but different, and he did something to Janey's magic. Was he a warden?"

She shook her head. "*He absorbed my keen.*" She signed, and that cloying sensation started again.

"Can you still summon flame?" Penny asked.

Janey held her palm out. A spark flickered across her skin as a series of warm prickles ran up Harvey's spine. The flame grew until an orb of fire floated in the air above her fingers. She closed them, and the fireball disappeared, leaving a small coil of smoke behind.

"If he's like Amelia, where is he now?" Emil asked.

Janey shot a look in Harvey's direction.

"Dead," he said, rubbing at the dried blood on his fingers.

"You're sure? Amelia—"

"He's dead! We need to get ourselves organised and leave for Leith's camp first thing tomorrow. There is nothing left in this city for us."

Penny's keen touched the back of his neck again, but Emil lifted a hand in her direction and shook his head.

CHAPTER FIFTEEN

MARGOT

"I thought it would be bigger," Warren said as he studied the shimmering tear in the distance.

"It's big enough," Declan said dryly. "Niall thinks the wards around the college have it contained, but who knows how long that will last."

A shudder went through the source, and the colours in the torn patch of sky changed, flickering between saffron and violet before settling again to an iridescent oily sheen.

Bran rubbed the side of his jaw. "I wish it wouldn't do that."

"It pulses like that often?" Warren asked.

"Not often, though it seems to be doing it more frequently. Sets your teeth on edge, doesn't it?" Declan said with a grin.

The anchor mark twinged, sending a vibration through Margot's body that left a weight in the pit of her stomach. That hadn't been an ordinary shockwave. Something big was coming. "We should—"

The world around them gave a violent lurch as the tear flickered again. This time the colours slammed against the edge of the college wards in a spray like waves hitting an outcrop.

The anchor ached, and Margot lifted her hand to study the shimmers of green, lilac, and silver roving over her fingers. Another shudder rocked the world accompanied by a tearing sound. The horses tossed their heads and pranced about. Margot gripped the mane of hers as it reared back, nearly unseating her.

"Shoosh, it's okay." She crooned and stroked its neck, but it was too panicked to respond. A second shockwave sent it wheeling around, and Margot hit the ground with a bone-shaking jolt.

"You alright?" Declan helped her to her feet.

She nodded. "We can't stay out here," she yelled above the unnatural wind that had whipped up.

A wave of colour splashed against the invisible wards around the college again, and the air around them stilled as a crack seemed to form, allowing the multihued magic to leach out in a slow trickle. The source around Margot quivered, and nausea rolled through her stomach as her legs weakened.

"The source ..." Bran rasped as he fell to his knees beside her. "Why does it feel like that?"

"The tear is draining it away," Warren said, his voice an age-soaked croak.

There was an ear-splitting boom, and Margot threw her hand up, the anchor draining the last of her strength as the wards around the college succumbed and a dome of glittering silver light erupted around the four of them.

"Margot?" Bran's voice enquired.

She opened her eyes to find him sitting on his heels next to her. "What happened to the tear?"

"It expanded past the wards, but it seems to have stabilised itself again," Declan said.

"Is everyone alright?"

"We'll recover. Lucky you had that anchor or who knows what that blast could have done to our keen," Warren said.

Margot studied her fingers as she sat. "What did it do?"

"I'm not certain, but I would say it created some kind of ward," Declan replied, his hand held out as though he wanted to inspect the anchor.

She placed her hand on his, and he traced his fingers over the mark on her palm. A silver-blue spark tickled her skin, and he released her.

"Do you feel alright? Your eyes have gone pink again."

"I feel …" How did she feel? Right before the blast, it was like all the keen had left her body, and she could have crumbled away to dust at the slightest breeze, but now she felt—"Fine. Great, actually."

"Do you think the tear can displace things?" Bran asked.

"Displace things?"

"Yeah, like that." He was pointing at something offshore.

Margot followed the line of his finger to the large ship that had appeared in the water. She knew that ship, from the sleek lines of the siren figurehead to the curve of the dark wood that made the side rails. The Azure Queen.

She ran down the slope to the beach, the salt brush snagging around her ankles and the sand shifting under her boots, making the way treacherous. She stumbled as she broke onto the harder sand at the tideline and waved her hands above her head. Hopefully, Rufus had his spyglass out and was checking the shore. The others joined her as a rowboat was lowered over the side.

As the boat entered the shallows, Molly vaulted out and splashed towards her. She threw her arms around Margot and buried her face in the side of her neck.

Margot pressed a kiss to her temple. "I missed you so much."

Molly mumbled something in response and then pulled back and grabbed Margot's cheeks as she pressed their lips together in a feverish kiss.

Declan cleared his throat, and Molly released Margot.

Her cornflower-blue eyes widened slightly as she stepped back. "What is that?" Her fingers brushed the black streak in Margot's hair. "And what the fuck happened to your eyes?"

Bran chuckled.

Margot shrugged. "It's a long story. Why are you dressed like you joined some kind of … harem?"

"Because we did," Nea said. Her skin was looking paler than ever, and she was leaning heavily on a large man Margot didn't recognise. His keen radiated in playful flurries that promised great potential. It reminded her of Arcanius Greffon's. This man's dark hair was trimmed short, and intricate tattoos covered his bare forearms. Some of them seemed to gleam with magic, a lot like the ward marks Nea and Garret shared.

"You joined a harem?" Declan asked, his eyebrow hitching upwards.

"We did *not* join a harem. We crashed a party." Molly rolled her eyes. "Thank you, Nea. Now I will never hear the end of it."

"You're welcome." Nea gave her small smile that shifted almost instantly into a frown. "We need to get to the college and do something about that tear. Another has formed outside Quel'sapar. The damage has made the source unstable, and if—"

"You're going straight to a warm bed to rest," Margot said. "I doubt tall, dark, and tattooed here wants to lug your sorry arse about the place."

Declan let out a bark of laughter.

"Donnic," the man supporting Nea said.

"And they are?" Declan's gaze swept over Nea's shoulder to the flame-haired pirate, Wren, and her partner, Gendry. The large dog with tusks that had come through the tear with Wade was stalking along beside them. Rourke? Was that the name?

"That is Wren and Gendry," Nea replied.

"Is that dog Rourke? Did the magic of the tear affect him like it did Wade?" Declan asked.

Nea gave a nod then winced and pressed the heal of her palm to her forehead. "You might be right about that rest, Margot. Is the camp far?"

"Too far for you to go on foot. We can—"

Rourke gave a savage growl, cutting her off.

"What in the stars is that?" Wren asked, pointing over Margot's shoulder.

Margot turned. A massive creature was hulking down the slope towards the beach. A conglomeration of limbs protruded from its lumpy body—bodies? What in the Bright's name? It looked like a pile of corpses had stood up and morphed themselves into a vague resemblance of a sentry golem. Though not all the bodies appeared human, and there were two more of the creatures ambling along behind it.

Bran let out a groan. "Not these guys again."

"They shouldn't be a problem now that we know how to destroy them. Off you trot," Declan said, waving Bran towards the creatures.

"Absolutely not. His keen is still unstable after the last lot of reanimations we tangled with. If necromancy is required to destroy them then—"

"I'll handle it." Nea stepped away from Donnic.

"You're worse off than me," Bran chided. "You can't even stand straight."

Nea straightened her shoulders but swayed, and Donnic caught her as she stumbled.

"Good thing we have a backup, backup necromancer." Declan chuckled. "Warren, I shall keep them distracted if you want to do the honours." He stepped forward, silver-blue sparks dancing across his fingertips.

There was a familiar click, and a glowing crossbow bolt struck the closest construct right between its flickering purple eyes. The shot tore through the thing's skull, leaving a gaping hole in its wake as it thudded into the neck of the one behind. Neither construct faltered. They actually picked up pace.

"Nice bow. But enchanted or not, a crossbow bolt isn't going to drop the likes of these," Warren said as he stepped forward, the air frosting around him as ribbons of violet twisted over the backs of his hands.

"Okay, but what about them?" Molly indicated the dark creatures that looked like elongated skeletons with too many teeth and lashing red tongues.

"Yes, it should work on those."

"Aim for the heart, Molly," Nea said.

The creatures charged. Lightning flashed on both sides, static lifting Margot's hair as Declan and Wren unleashed their storm magic. Molly sent bolts flying in quick succession as Gendry drew his sword and Rourke dashed into the fray, teeth bared and growling.

"Here." Donnic pushed Nea towards Bran as he started forward.

Black blood splattered against the sand, and lilac magic flashed. It didn't take long, and the creatures had all been dealt with. Then the tear pulsed again, and the bodies started rolling together. Another construct rose to its feet. This one bigger than the others had been. It let out a roar that stank of rotting fleshing and backhanded Warren as he started to pull his power. Nea lifted her hand, the grey marks shimmering as she sent a bolt of purple magic towards it. She made a grabbing motion and snatched her fist back towards herself. Bran lost his grip on her, and they both fell to the ground.

"Nea?" Bran shook her. "Margot!" There was an edge of panic in his voice.

Margot checked Nea's pulse. It was still there, but beneath the erratic fluttering of Nea's keen, Garret's suppression surged. The anchor shuddered under Margot's skin. Something was very wrong. This wasn't how a death ward was supposed to work at all.

"Let me see." Donnic crouched beside her and grabbed Nea's arm. He rolled back her sleeve and pressed his hand over the orange eight-pointed star. His keen stirred, and his jaw worked, then he drew a breath and sat back on his heels.

"You know a bit about death wards then?" Warren asked, peering over Donnic's shoulder.

Donnic shook his head. "Wards yes, death wards specifically ... no. I just stabilised what I could, but without the other ward present, there is little else I can do."

The anchor throbbed under Margot's skin. They were running out of time. If they lost Nea they—a jolt ran from the tips of her fingers up her arm. "*Lose the Shadow and you will lose the Bright,*" the spirit whispered across her mind.

Declan was staring at Nea, his mouth twisted and his cheeks pale. "We had best be getting her back to Garret. That ward connects them in such a way that whatever this is may be having a negative effect on him also ... Unless ..." He licked his lip. "Unless Nea's predicament is a direct result of Garret's corruption."

Bitterness coated the back of Margot's tongue. The joy of seeing Molly and Nea again had been replaced with a deep dread, but whether it was her own or the anchor's, she wasn't sure.

Niall ran his fingers over Nea's brow, his keen a soothing roll down Margot's spine. He puffed his cheeks as he looked up and met Aveline's gaze then Margot's and shook his head. "I do not know what is wrong."

"Perhaps it is simply exhaustion?" Jasper said and held his hands up in surrender when they all turned to him. "I mean, it is clear that Nea's connection to the source is very different from your standard mage, and that was before she and Garret went all—" He rubbed his hands together and ended by locking his fingers to form a cage. "—with their keens. It only stands to reason that the tear would affect her differently than the rest of us."

Aveline walked over and gave Niall's arm a squeeze. "Jasper is right. You said Nea's keen was showing all the standard signs of overexertion before she fell into this sleep, Margot?"

Margot nodded and flicked a look in Warren's direction. The old man was by the door, arms folded as he watched them.

"Nea will be fine. We have more pressing issues to attend to," he said.

"Garret did mention she had fallen into a sleep like this before. Maybe we should just let it run its course," Jasper offered.

"Well one of you has some intelligence at least. And where is this Garret, hmm?" Warren's blue gaze zeroed in on Niall.

The mind mage pressed his lips together.

"He went to see how things are going in the capital. He should be back soon," Aveline answered.

The door banged open, and Leith came striding in with Ryan on his heels. Both were splattered in black blood similar to that from the creatures at the beach. Leith stopped short when his grey gaze fell on Nea's prone form. The corner of his mouth tightened, and his brow furrowed. "Is she?"

"She'll be fine," Warren said. "What's the news from the college?"

"The creatures seem to be emerging with each pulse, so we get a breather between waves," Ryan replied. "And the tear itself appears to be calming down again, giving us a longer break between pulses. But with full dark approaching, we need to reinforce the night watch. If we don't stay on top of the creatures emerging, we will find ourselves quickly overrun."

"Then we should—" A commotion outside cut Niall off.

A guard Margot vaguely recognised marched into the room; behind him, a woman in a set of ill-fitting, obviously borrowed clothes. Sections of her dark hair hung around her face in limp clumps. There was a sallowness to her features that hadn't been there before, but there was no mistaking the ferocity in her sapphire gaze. Catriona.

Leith licked his lip as he looked from Nea's body to his wife. "Cat?" He approached her slowly and lifted his arms. "Are you hurt?"

Her nostrils flared as she settled her gaze on him. "No more than I deserve." There was a weariness beneath the velvet tones of her voice.

"We should give you a moment," Aveline said. "Jasper, would you please help me move Nea to the infirmary tent?"

Jasper scooped Nea up then he and Aveline left.

"Come on Warren, I will fill you and Declan in on the developments we've made in researching ways to deal with the tear," Niall said, waving Warren after him. "You should come, too, Margot."

"Catriona will need to see Jasper or myself once you are done here," Margot said to Leith before she followed Niall.

C H A P T E R S I X T E E N

GARRET

Magic that felt like a perverted form of Nea's twisted through the air. It wasn't the necromancy that now stirred under Garret's skin. No, this was different. It was like the soothing warmth of healing keen mixed with the snapping cold summoned when Nea grabbed someone's soul. Hot. Cold. Hot. Cold. And it was coming from Harvey.

He moved in a blur across the room, red magic laced with violet twisting in ribbons over his skin, then he was pulling his bloodied hand back from the chest of the corrupted mage, the still-pumping heart clutched in his fingers.

A tremor ran through him as he met Garret's eye, the heart rolling from his fingertips and onto the chest of the body at his feet.

"What just happened?"

Janey took a step towards him, but he threw his hands up, cheek concaving as though he was biting the inside of it.

"I—" Red-purple magic twisted over his skin, then he was gone. Not the way Nea disappeared when she used a portal. No, this was like the world was folding around him, or perhaps he was moving faster than everything else. Like the way a bee's wings vibrated to keep it airborne.

Janey started after him but stopped and turned back to Garret, a question in her eyes.

"Go. I'll be fine."

She hesitated a moment longer then nodded and signed. *"Do what you need to, but don't be reckless. I have faith in you."* Then she disappeared up the stairs.

Garret stared at the body; crawling magic still clung to it. A corrupted form of necromancy? The man had been a mage, but Garret hadn't been able to pinpoint what kind. It was like his body held more than one kind of keen. And the way he had absorbed Janey's magic ... He shook his head. His brightling keen had a similar effect, absorbing and learning the way a keen worked before being able to reproduce it. But this was different again. This mage's keen had not held that same desire to learn. It had been a ravenous urge to consume and destroy.

He toyed with his scar as he glanced the way Janey had gone. She had faith in him. Nea had told him something similar when they were trapped in the Between. She believed in his better nature, believed he wouldn't allow himself to succumb to the corruption. When the source had faded, he'd had a few moments of blissful clarity with no voice braying in the back of his mind. It was enough to harden his resolve.

He took the journal he had found in Leith's drawer out and ran his fingers over the cover. Nea's keen shifted across the leather in cool swirls. It had been her keen that had drawn him to the room in the first place. Just the briefest touch of the keen still clinging to her hairbrush had stilled the corruption as though it reawakened that part of him Amelia had stolen.

He let the journal fall open. More than half the pages were blank. Was that intentional? Was it like Samson's journal and there were words hidden there that the naked eye couldn't see? He didn't think so. More likely Nea had started the journal just before she had fled to Kalhanna. He thumbed through the pages until an entry caught his attention. A word written halfway down the page had been underlined and the question mark beside it traced over several times: *Ambrose?*

That was the name of the mage Harvey had said was at Merston, the one helping Evard try to breed the ultimate mage. He scanned the paragraphs that followed, but there was nothing else there that could help him.

A groan caught his attention, and he studied the body.

The fingers twitched, and the corrupted mage slowly sat. "Well, now, that is an interesting development." He probed the closing wound in his chest. The heart was still lying on the ground beside him. "Very interesting."

Garret's keen shifted, drawing the attention of the other mage. He lifted his hand as he had seen Nea do, and lilac magic shrouded the man. He could feel the edges of the man's soul. It had been broken and cobbled back together, more than once. Instinct guided him to grab hold of the threads, to sunder them and send the soul back where it belonged.

The man lifted his hand as well—that ravenous keen building, draining Garret's away. He had to fight back, had to draw more power. Pain sliced through his mind, the corruption rising the longer he drew on his keen. He reached for his suppression, but something was wrong. It was unresponsive like it had been in the Between. If he didn't act now, either the mage or the corruption would win.

He closed his fist, his keen latching onto those strings holding the corrupted mage together. He yanked at them, and his vision swam. The pain in his skull increased, but he pulled again, the coppery scent of blood filling his senses as something warm trickled over his lip.

"Yes," the corrupted mage hissed. "Give them exactly what they want." His cackling laugh ended in a wet gurgle as Garret yanked at the threads holding him together once more, and they tore.

Garret could taste blood now, not just smell it. A wild itch inflamed his side from the base of his ribs to his collarbone. He fell to his knees and gripped his head, trying to sort his own thoughts from those of the corruption. Someone was calling him, a familiar voice that brought soothing fingers to his brow. He opened his eyes, but she wasn't there. She couldn't be. The death ward burned with cold, then the world flipped, and everything went dark.

Something cool and wet pressed against his cheek and rubbed across his forehead. A voice murmured, and a drawer scraped shut. He willed his eyes to open, his limbs to move, but his body was too heavy. The cool damp crossed his forehead again.

"It's a lost cause," a man said. "Even if he wakes, the corruption is too advanced. We'll just have to put him out of his misery anyway."

Garret didn't recognise the voice, but he wanted to respond. To tell them that the corruption was satiated for now; that it wasn't scratching at the edge of his resolve, plying him with promises of ultimate power.

"You just worry about the reanimations. I will handle the commander," another voice said, this one female.

"And drive yourself to exhaustion in the process. You can't suppress it forever."

That explained the lack of corruption. Were they both wardens then?

"I know what I am doing." The woman pressed the damp cloth to Garret's cheek again, and his body finally responded.

He caught her hand and opened his eyes. The woman gave a small yelp, her blue-green gaze widening as she extracted her fingers from Garret's. He sat and tried to stand, only to slam against the floor as his legs came out from under him.

"Easy now," the woman said.

Garret tried to stand again; his limbs protested as though they were moving through thick mud.

"Help me with him, would you?"

The man grabbed hold of Garret's shirt then hauled him to his feet and pushed him back onto the bed. Garret struggled as he was pinned down, instinct telling him to fight. The surging prickle of storm magic built under his skin, searching for an opening in the woman's suppression.

"Calm down. We're just trying to help." There was a sternness beneath her tone now, and Garret stopped struggling to get a good look at her.

She was built a lot like Molly and Nea, both in height and curves. Her grey hair was several shades lighter than Nea's, but she was definitely a warden and not a necromancer. Or was she? She was the one suppressing him, but her suppression didn't feel quite right. He flicked a look to the man. His dark hair, light brown skin, and the lines of his features placed him as Osmarian, but he didn't have the typical accent.

"Let him go, Hugh," the woman said.

The man released Garret and moved to the cabinet by the door, folding his arms as he leant against it. "I'm watching you, Commander. Try anything at all, and I won't hesitate to put you in the ground."

"*Hugh*," the woman reprimanded and then turned her attention back to Garret. "It's alright. We're friends."

"I don't know either of you," Garret said, resting his back against the wall.

The woman smiled brightly, and her eyes flashed indigo before returning to blue–green. "I'm Gwyn, and this is Hugh."

"And where am I?"

She looked at her fingers, the movement reminding him of Nea. "In the catacombs under the city. That's where a lot of us ended up after Ambrose disappeared."

"Ambrose?" Garret straightened. "Then are you like that—"

"None of us are like Jackson," Hugh growled.

"We are the results of Ambrose's efforts, however," Gwyn said.

"How many of you are there?"

"Three left. Evard had us hunted down when he realised we had survived."

Hugh made a noise of contempt, his dark eyes stormy as he levelled them on Garret. "You're responsible for a few of those exterminations, *Commander*."

"I only ever *exterminated* a target when I was given no other choice," Garret said.

"And what of the ones who didn't fight back? The ones you dragged here and presented to your king? They were killed all the same simply because they were loose ends and not his precious deathborn."

"Hugh, that's enough," Gwyn said.

"You deserve that corruption."

Garret pushed himself to his feet.

"Oh, for the love of Bright. Sit down, Commander. And you"—she rounded on Hugh—"go and see if Sam needs help."

"But—"

"Now, Hugh!"

Hugh shot a dark look at Garret. "If you do anything to her, Shadow help me, I will make you pay." He left the room.

"Right, well. Now that unpleasantness is out of the way. How are you feeling? I tried to get a restorative in you, but I don't know how much you actually swallowed."

"Why are you helping me?"

Her eyes changed colour again as she studied him. "Why not? You needed help. I wasn't going to just leave you in that"—a shudder went through her—"place."

"But Hugh—"

"Can be an arse." She pressed her fingers to her forehead, and the suppression field around Garret quivered. "But I don't think you're a bad man ... despite the rumours."

"Rumours?"

She gave a sad sort of smile. "You're not popular amongst those of us living outside the colleges. It's not your fault. Even before the purge at Kalhanna, Evard was painting non-college mages in a grim light. Then his own arcane advisor turned a whole college against him and, well, the target on our backs got significantly bigger." The suppression field flickered again.

"You can drop that suppression. I have the corruption under control for the moment. And, honestly, I'm not in any state to pose a real threat to you."

The moment she dropped the suppression, the corruption stirred. He gritted his teeth against it. His own suppression should have stirred to calm it, but it was worryingly absent.

"What's she like?"

"Who?"

She held up Nea's journal, the one he had taken from Leith's room. "Nea. When Ambrose found out she had survived, he became obsessed with her."

Garret drew a deep breath. "Infuriating," he answered with a small smile. "Brilliant and brave and kind. She—" He touched his fingers to the ward on his wrist. Nea's keen was there, cool and soothing, forcing the corruption to back down.

Gwyn's eyes shifted to indigo and back again, a knowing smile just barely curving the corners of her mouth. "Hold onto that feeling. It will help you fight the corruption."

"What do you mean when he found out she had survived?"

"I was too young to really remember Sophia, but I know she was heavily pregnant when she left. And she never returned, not like some of the others. She told Ambrose the child had died and that she was done with helping him." She moved to the cabinet and pulled out a bundle of letters, shuffling through them until she found one in particular and handed it to Garret.

Ambrose,

I am writing to inform you that I lost the child. Your meddling has cost me everything, and I can no longer have any part in your endeavours. I did not reveal the true nature of your experiments to the Council of Sages and nor do I intend to. But should you contact me again, I will not hesitate to reveal your every sordid secret.

Good luck playing god.

Regards,

Sophia.

"Why lie? Sophia had no love for Nea—that is clear enough."

"I don't know," Gwyn said, taking the letter from him and placing it neatly with the others before closing the cabinet and resting her forehead against the door. "It was maybe two years later that the section of catacombs Ambrose had been keeping us in collapsed. Most of us made it out, but Ambrose wasn't the same after that and he had lost Evard's support, so we went into hiding. True hiding, in the mountains around Merston. When Ambrose found out about Nea though, he would disappear for weeks on end. One time we followed him and saw him watching her. We didn't know who she was, but he was obsessed. That's when he started pushing Jackson harder." She turned back to face him. "He kept muttering about merging the keen of the deera solvec with Jackson's. He wasn't a brightling, but he was close enough that their keens would be compatible."

"Merging their keen?" Garret pressed his fingers to the ward.

Gwyn's mouth twisted. "Yes. He seemed to think it would give him exactly what he wanted. Then Nea disappeared."

"After Kalhanna—"

"No, this was at least a decade before the purge. She had been spending her time between Del Harol and Kalhanna for most of her life, and then she was just—gone. Not even Keegan could find her with his magic."

"Her father sent her to Osmar."

"Osmar." Her voice had taken on a dreamy tone. "I would love to see it one day. Maybe if Ambrose fails in destroying the world ... But anyway ... Keegan still should have been able to find her."

"What happened after Nea disappeared?"

"Ambrose was furious. He changed tactics with Jackson, started giving him these tonics and teas. He'd beat him for hours on end, bringing him to the edge of death only to carve runes into his skin and revive him again. Then he would force him to overextend his keen time and time again." She licked her lip, her eyes changing colour as they met his. "Then Nea came back and Evard figured out what she was. I am sure you know everything that comes after her introduction into Evard's court."

"But where does Kieran come into it?"

"Evard no longer trusted Ambrose. He needed someone else who could pull the strings for him. Kieran was perfect, until Ambrose got inside his head and convinced him he could claim the power for himself. It was Ambrose who taught him how to create the new reanimations."

Garret rubbed his hands over his face. Nea should be hearing this or Declan, they could surely use this information better than he could. "You're not loyal to Ambrose?"

She shook her head. "We weren't *special* like Jackson, but we were helpful enough until Evard started hunting us down. Then we were a liability, so Ambrose abandoned us and without him we scattered to the winds. Sam, Hugh, and I always stayed close to each other, and we were aware of where the others were, but one by one they were being picked off."

"I'm sorry."

She shrugged. "It's not your fault. Ambrose broke many of the others. We were toys to him. Experiments—a means to an end, easily cast aside when we were found wanting."

"Thank you for helping me, Gwyn."

She waved his thanks away with a smile. "You should get some rest before you move on." She started for the door. "If you are going after Ambrose, be careful. He gave up his humanity a long time ago."

CHAPTER SEVENTEEN

NEA

The savage thirst tearing at Nea's throat must have been what had woken her. She sat slowly, blinking in the darkness, her body heavy and numb like it had been when she wore the shackles. Her gaze dropped to her wrists, but the rose-gold bands were not there. What was this then? It felt like—

"Garret," she whispered, twisting to look around the room she was in. It appeared to be some kind of infirmary. Pallet beds lined the sides of the room, several held sleeping patients. The astringent herbal notes of tonics and balms scented the air.

Where? Memories stirred. The new tear forming outside Quel'sapar, most likely due to the nature of the magic that shrouded the island. Her keen draining away and the desperate effort to form a portal big enough for the Queen to pass through. The last thing that came to mind was meeting Margot and the others on the beach below Kalhanna—that explained the infirmary she was in. But where was the infirmary located?

The ground was cold against her bare feet, and she pulled the thin blanket off the bed behind her, wrapping it around her shoulders as she crept towards the door. Outside the sky was a sea of stars, the gibbous moon casting a milky-grey light across the tops of the tents.

Nea's breath clouded the air, and she pulled the blanket tighter around her shoulders as she shivered.

A shadow moved beside her, and the warm weight of Rourke's large form pressed against her leg. He gave a low rumble, not a growl or a whine, but something like a question. She shook her head and started towards the barn a short distance away. Light spilled through the open door in a warm glow, and murmured voices carried across the otherwise silent campsite.

She stopped in the middle of the open doorway; Zephyr sat on a chair, her knees tucked up under her chin as Declan paced in front of the large table. Nea had seen that same table through the dream-link with Garret. Mateus sat opposite Zephyr, several books open around him. Wade was lying beside his chair. The dog's ears flicked in Nea's direction, and he lifted his head to look at her, his tail wagging.

"What are you doing out of bed?"

Nea jumped as Margot's voice sounded behind her. "I'm fine."

Margot's hands settled on her hips.

"Okay, so I am not *fine*. But I am well enough, and we don't have time for me to be lying about convalescing."

"You completely depleted your keen. I am surprised you are mobile at all. The damage it should have done to your organs—any normal mage would be on death's door right now."

"I am not a normal mage," Nea said with a tired sigh. Now more than ever she really wished she had just been born a normal necromancer, then saving the known realms might be someone else's problem.

"Which is why you should be resting. We don't know how depleting your keen has affected you."

Nea rubbed a hand through her hair. "All it seems to have done is swapped my keen for Garret's."

"Swapped your keen? Like what was happening in the Between?" Declan asked, and Nea turned to face him.

"No, not exactly. More like his keen is suppressing mine, and I can't turn it off."

"Could Donnic stabilising the ward have something to do with it?"

"Donnic stabilised the ward?"

Declan nodded.

"You should sit down, Nea," Zephyr said, pulling out a chair. "I'll go make us some tea."

Nea flicked a look at Margot, and the healer waved her towards the chair. "I know there's no way I will get you back in bed now," she said and turned on her heel.

"Where are you going?"

"To get your boots and something warmer for you to put on. Even if you're too stubborn to take yourself back to bed, I'll not have you catch your death of cold on my watch."

Nea folded herself into the chair and tucked the blanket around her. She was still wearing the disguise she used to sneak into Vince's palace. The thin material and exposed midriff might have been fine in the balmy atmosphere of Quel'sapar, but here in Beldaren it was about as effective as wearing her underwear.

"Do you know what Donnic did?" Nea asked Declan as Rourke settled on the floor beside Wade.

Declan shook his head. "I'm not even sure Donnic knows what he did exactly. But he probably saved your life."

"Is he here now or did he stay with Wren?"

"He's here. But he probably regrets it with how much Warren and your father have been picking his brain about wards."

"And you haven't been?"

He gave her a lopsided grin. "I can't get a word in edgewise."

"Certainly not from lack of trying." Mateus chuckled.

Zephyr returned and placed a cup of tea in front of Nea. The steam rising in a thin coil carried the scent of mint and the underlying notes of liquorice root. "From memory you prefer mint?"

Nea gave a nod and took a tentative sip of the tea. The sweetness of the liquorice was perfectly balanced with the peppermint.

Margot returned and held up the blanket while Nea changed into a pair of pants and a linen shirt under a woollen tunic. She slipped her feet into her boots and fastened a heavy shawl around her shoulders before settling back down to her tea. "What is the news from the college? Have you made any progress with the tear?"

Declan shook his head.

"Any time we manage to start sealing it, it sends out another pulse and all our good work is undone. Not to mention there have been some negative side effects amongst some of the mages and wardens who were too close during one of the pulses," Mateus said. He lifted his cup to take a sip and paused. "It seems like we need to fully seal it in one go, but that would take an army of necromancers."

"Which is why Niall is looking at our options to ward it instead of close it," Zephyr said. "Though the sooner you and Garret go after those thrones, the better. Did you find what you need?"

"I think I have, but I didn't get a chance to read it with the tear widening so fast." She cradled her mug, the warmth radiating out into her hands and settling at her core.

"You mean this?" Declan placed the small wooden chest Nea had taken from Vince's vault on the table.

"Have you read it yet?"

"Read what? We can't get the bloody thing open."

Nea placed her cup on the table as she stood. "You can't open it? It opened fine before." She placed her hands on the top of the chest and quickly withdrew them as a static jolt stung her palms.

"See." Declan folded his arms.

"That didn't happen before." She studied her hands and then brushed her fingers over the death ward. Only Garret's keen stirred under her skin as though her own had gone completely dormant. Was it possible that mages who managed to survive completely exhausting their keen became keen-less? Is that what had happened here? Nea's keen was gone and only Garret's remained. Did that mean the piece of her keen locked into Garret's half of the ward was gone too?

"Nea?" Declan shook her shoulder, and she met his forest-toned gaze. There was something there that hadn't been before. Was it sorrow or regret? Something had definitely quelled his usual infectious mirth.

"I'm fine." She collapsed into the chair. "I think it needs my keen to open, but it's gone."

"Your keen will come back. You just need to rest," Margot said.

Nea shook her head. "I'm not so sure it will this time."

The cool touch of Mateus's necromancy smoothed down her spine. "There's something there under all the *warden*. It's faint but still there."

"What if you try feeding her Shadow mark, Margot?" Zephyr asked.

"What do you mean? My keen or ..." Margot lifted her hand and studied her palm.

"Exactly." Zephyr sat forward. "The spirit that powers that anchor is of the Shadow blood. It might be able to bolster the Shadow blood in Nea."

Maybe it wasn't Nea's keen specifically that could open the chest but rather Shadow keen. "Have you tried opening the chest, Margot?" she asked before taking a sip of her tea.

"No. After Declan, Mateus, and Bran all tried a few times it was clear there was no point."

"You think the chest will open to those with Shadow-blooded keen?" Mateus asked. "That's an intricate and rather specific ward."

"Which means someone thought whatever it was hiding was profoundly important." Declan chimed in, his fingers twitching towards the top of the chest.

"It's been opened before because Vince had the keystone," Nea said.

"The keystone? That hunk of rock Molly has around her neck?"

Nea nodded. "There is an impression on the inside of the chest where it had obviously been sitting. Margot, why don't you try opening the chest now?"

"Or I could try Zephyr's idea and see if the anchor can bolster your Shadow blood."

"Alright, we can try that first." Nea stood and held up her right palm. The cloud-like patterns that swirled up her arm were mostly hidden by the sleeve of her shirt, but those across the back of her hand were a deep grey.

Margot placed her silver-marked palm against Nea's. Magic that was some combination of Margot's healing keen and the coolness of necromancy stirred along Nea's veins. The marks on the back of her hand glowed a soft lilac as Margot's eyes shifted from their usual whiskey brown to a soft rosy pink. A sharp pain scraped up the back of Nea's neck and settled in her jaw. She shut her eyes in an effort to stave off the threatening headache. An image flashed across the back of her eyelids: a woman with long dark hair and pink eyes. The lines of her features were familiar, but Nea couldn't exactly put her finger on why. Then the image was scattered by a flash of scarlet. And Declan was helping her to her feet.

Mateus was guiding Margot into a chair. She ran her hand through her hair, her fingers unusually pale against the black streak that had appeared when she had healed Garret's corruption.

"Any change?" Declan asked, a quiver running through his hands where they gripped her arms.

Nea turned her attention inward. Her keen-sense felt a little more stable, but it was still muted. Normally, with him this close, the static prickle of his storm magic would be slightly uncomfortable, but it was a faint flicker. Her own keen was still completely blanketed by the heavy numbness of Garret's suppression. She shook her head. "Are you alright, Margot?"

"Just a headache, but it will pass." She gave Nea a shaky smile. "It was worth a try."

Nea wasn't so sure. The anchor spirit had definitely been a powerful mage in her time, and the way she seemed to completely overtake Margot when the healer engaged the anchor mark was worrying. If the spirit decided she wanted to be the one in control all the time, none of them would be able to stop her without harming Margot in the process.

"Should we see if Margot can open the chest now?" Mateus asked.

"I don't know if that is wise. I don't think Margot should use the anchor," Nea replied.

"Now you sound like Garret." Margot stood and settled her hands on her hips.

"The spirit—"

"Doesn't mean any harm. If she wanted to possess me, she has had months to do so."

Nea bit down on her retort and then with a huff said, "Just be careful."

"I have been." Margot stepped up to the table. "Alright." She lowered her hands towards the lid of the chest then hesitated and drew a breath before gripping it and pulling. A flicker of lilac-toned silver ran over the chest, and it clicked open.

"What's inside?" Declan and Mateus both asked. Each of them leaning forward to get a better look.

Margot met Nea's eye. "It looks too fragile to touch, but you are right. There is an impression that looks like it would fit the stone Molly has."

Nea stood and reached into the chest. She gently lifted the book out and placed it on the table. There were no etchings on the cover that indicated what the book might be called, but it had the same eerie keen as the *Book of Souls* clinging to it. Nea had only touched that book a handful of times. The secrets it held ...

Evard stood across from her, hand outstretched. "Give me the book."

Nea held the tome tight against her chest as she glanced towards the door. Could she make it before he grabbed her?

"You're not a fool. You know you won't make it to that door." His tone was steady, but beneath it was that cold edge that warned her he was losing his temper. Something he did more often of late. "Give. Me. The. BOOK!"

The shout sent a tremor through her. Warmth from the fire cracking in the hearth behind her flooded her spine, and she was hit with the realisation of what had to be done. "You want the book?" She tilted it towards him; his fingers lifted. With a deep breath to steady her resolve, she flung the book into the flames.

A hand touched her shoulder. "Are you alright, my lovely? You went inward for a moment there."

She shook her head to scatter the remnants of the memory and glanced at the four faces all staring at her. "I'm fine." The aged cover was rough under her fingers. Through the heaviness of Garret's keen, the magic clinging to the book felt almost hollow—weary after years of waiting to fulfil the purpose for which it had been created. Very gently, she slid her fingers along the edge of the cover and opened it. But as she moved to turn the pages, the book shuddered and collapsed into a pile of dust, a small plume of it clouding the air.

"I'm surprised it didn't do that the second you lifted it out of the chest," Mateus said. "What now? If we were back at the Arcanarium, Greffon could probably reconstruct it."

"I doubt he could." Nea stirred her fingers through the dust pile left by the book. That eerie, hair-prickling keen was still clinging to it. "Bright damn it!" She slammed her hands down, sending the dust into the air around her.

"Nea!" Margot reprimanded.

But Nea was focused on the dust floating around her. She reached for her keen to form a mage light but only the numbing warmth of suppression rose. But she had seen it there in the swirling dust motes—a tiny clue that was reinforced by the fresco of the tower in the Shadow temple. She pushed away from the table and headed for the door.

"Nea, where are you going?" Margot called.

"I need to find Molly," she answered over her shoulder.

"It's the middle of the night. Surely this can wait until morning." Margot caught up with her.

"No, it can't, because I need to leave for Loch Bastien right away."

"Loch Bastien?" Margot stopped, but Nea kept striding towards the run of tents. "Wait." Margot caught her arm, and she turned back to face her. Declan, Zephyr, and Mateus were all standing just outside the door of the barn watching them. "I know you are impulsive, but just stop and think for a minute. It is the middle of the night, and you are still recovering from exhausting your keen, which is still missing, I might add. What did you see in there? What triggered this sudden desire to get to Loch Bastien?"

"The dust from the book formed a symbol I have seen before. I didn't think anything of it at the time, given I was running from Leon. And in Quel'sapar, the Shadow Man showed me a tower." Her heart pounded. "I *know* Loch Bastien is where I need to start looking for the thrones."

"Oh, you *know*. Right, well, off you trot and wake Molly in the middle of the night, so you can run off on your own again and pursue a hunch without letting any of us know what is actually going on." Margot made a shooing motion. "I guess I'll see you in three years. If the world survives that long."

A tremor ran through Nea, and she licked her lip. "Margot, that's not fair. This is nothing like before."

"Really? Because from where I am standing it feels exactly the same. You keeping all the information to yourself before disappearing to fix things without letting anyone help you."

"I let you all help and look what happened. Garret got corrupted, you ended up with a soul we know nothing about implanted in your body, Bran nearly died—"

"People will get hurt whether you let them help or not."

"She's right," Declan said, an uncanny seriousness to his tone.

Nea glanced his way and drew a slow breath. "We don't have time to wait; I need to find those thrones."

"But can you use them without your keen? Or Garret?"

He had a point.

"We can discuss it further in the morning. If whatever Donnic did is responsible for your missing keen, maybe he can fix it before you go running off into danger," Mateus said. "There's no sense in waking the whole camp now just to buy yourself a handful of hours. If Donnic can fix your keen, then it will actually save you time because you can just create a portal to get yourself over to Loch Bastien in an instant."

Nea rubbed her hand through her hair. Mateus was right. She would be better off with her keen functioning properly again. "Alright." She let Margot herd her back to the infirmary tent.

Dawn had barely begun to light the sky when Nea emerged from the infirmary. A group of soldiers and wardens stood at the edge of camp; the change in watch taking place as the night guard filled in the day guard before heading for bed. Leith sat by the central fire, stirring the glowing coals with a long stick. He looked up as Nea neared, and she gave him a small smile and wave.

"Can't sleep either?" she asked as she sat across from him and pulled her shawl tighter around her shoulders.

He gave a grunt that could have been a sound of amusement. "Even when I can I seem to be dreaming about tactics and guard rosters. Tea?" He indicated the pot hanging by the edge of the flames, and she gave a nod.

"I'll make it; you never let it steep long enough." She checked the water level in the pot and nudged it closer to the flames before grabbing a pair of cups.

Feeling Leith's gaze on her, she looked up. Those grey eyes were so like Garret's, especially now that his light-heartedness had been dampened. Leith's mouth was thinner and his nose sharper. He certainly resembled their father much more than Garret did, but there were other similarities in their features too. His lips twitched as she studied him.

"What happened to your hair?" he asked as he passed her a jar of dried herbal mixture.

"I had to dye it so I could sneak into one of Vince's parties unnoticed." She added the dark mix to the cups before carefully pouring the freshly boiled water in. A smoky scent filled the air, reminding her of Gendry. "Since when do you drink Faridean black?" she asked as she passed it to him.

"It's Cat's favourite," he said, staring into the liquid in his cup as though it held all the answers in the world.

They sat in silence for a while as the camp started to come to life around them. It wasn't an easy silence like it would be with Garret, but it never had been. Leith was too full of life and seemed to possess a need to be in constant motion, and sometimes it had been hard to keep up. Fun and freeing certainly, but never completely comfortable. They had been dancers on the borrowed time of a single song.

"Nea," he said suddenly, drawing her out of her reverie. Her gaze met his, and he rubbed his fingers along his brow. She had never seen him look quite so unsure of himself. "I'm sorry."

"It's al—"

"I loved you so much. I still do ... Maybe not in the all-consuming way I did before, but that feeling is still there."

"Leith." She shook her head.

"I'm not saying I want things to go back to the way they were before. I know there is something between you and Garret, and I have Cat to think about. But I needed you to know ..." He drew a long breath and then let it out again in a rush. "I never meant to choose my father over you, but you had already made up your mind and weren't listening to reason. I know why *now*. I keep thinking if you had just told me the truth back then—but you did. I was just too stubborn to actually listen."

Nea chewed her lip. "I didn't exactly make it easy. I also didn't expect to survive once I started actively defying Evard. I'm sorry too." She downed the last of her tea. "I did love you; I know I told you that I didn't, but I did. And I would be a liar if I didn't admit a part of me still does, but it's different now."

They shared a smile.

"Good morning," Declan said as he joined them. He held up a folded piece of parchment. "Emil and the others are on their way back. There was some complication involving reanimations on the way to Merston."

"Merston?" Nea flicked a look between Declan and Leith.

"We were looking for mages to help us with the tear," Leith answered. "Any word from Garret?" he asked Declan.

The storm mage shook his head, a frown furrowing his brow. "I don't expect we will get word from him any time soon. It seems that they have lost track of him in the city. Emil said that Harvey went with Garret and Janey into the palace, and they got separated. He's vague on the details, but it's clear that they haven't seen Garret since."

Nea pressed her fingers to the ward mark, but since the warden keen had taken over it had been silent.

"Do they think his corruption ..." Leith glanced at Nea.

"Emil didn't say."

"Didn't Margot stabilise his corruption?" Nea placed her cup carefully on the ground beside her, trying to ignore the tremble in her fingers.

"She did. At least, she gave him back control of it—"

"You can't control corruption!" She flew to her feet. "You know that, Declan. How could you let him go—"

"I wasn't here when he left," Declan said gently.

She turned to Leith. "You let him go, knowing how dangerous and unstable corrupted mages are?"

"He didn't give me much choice, and he's a warden not a mage. His suppression was keeping it—"

"Warden or mage, it doesn't matter! Corruption edges into the very back of your mind and will not let you be until you comply to its wishes. Why did he go to the capital?" She wasn't sure she wanted the answer. She could still see the gloating malice in Leon's gaze. If the Usurper had figured out a way to manipulate the source through Leon's body despite him being keen-less ...

"He wanted to see if Leon and Kieran were still at the capital. He promised me he would come straight back."

Nea rubbed her hands over her face and let out a huff. She should have used a portal to check on him after she realised Leon was showing up in his dreams. "I have to go after him."

"What about Loch Bastien? I think finding the thrones is more important than running around chasing after Garret at this point," Declan said, checking the water in the pot.

"Leon was showing up in his dreams. Did he tell you that?"

Declan swore under his breath. "No, he didn't tell me." He rubbed his forehead and shook his head. "The Bright damned idiot."

"Good morning," Bran said as he joined them. "What's got your drawers in a twist?" He directed at Declan.

"Apparently, I made a mistake letting Garret go to the capital," Leith answered.

Bran shrugged. "Maybe, but Garret's more than capable of taking care of himself."

"And it's not like he gave you much choice," Zephyr added, stifling a yawn as she approached. "He'll be fine though. The link to Nea's keen through the ward was keeping the corruption somewhat stabilised. As long as he hasn't engaged the brightling part of his keen and channelled the source, he should still have some modicum of control."

"We can't know that. Not without—" Nea pressed her fingers to the ward mark, hoping that this time she would feel something. Nothing stirred beneath the ward, bringing a rush of hot-cold prickles up the back of her neck. Normally the source would be responding to her rising emotions, but it was as silent and numb as the warden keen now weighing down her core. "I need to go after him."

"But the thrones—"

"You can go ahead to Loch Bastien and start looking while I detour to the capital," she said, cutting Declan off. "You have a better chance of getting around Sophia anyway."

"Doubtful. Last she heard, I was dead. Suddenly turning up at the college alive and well is certain to raise her suspicions. And even if it didn't, I wouldn't know where to start looking."

"The hidden portal chamber. I don't think it was sealed just to hide the portal."

"I don't remember there being all that much in that room, except the portal itself."

"Maybe you're right." Nea chewed her lip. "We do have very little to go on ... Essentially we are just stabbing around in a dark room, hoping that the answer might fall into our laps ... But then, I thought you *loved* a good challenge."

"Don't fall for it," Bran muttered.

But Declan's mouth pulled into his usual lopsided grin. "You have me there, my lovely. I do enjoy a good challenge."

Leith cleared his throat. "Perhaps we should call a meeting and discuss this properly. I don't want anyone else going running off before we consider all the implications of them doing so." He stood and brushed his palms on the front of his pants.

Nea didn't want to wait around for a meeting. She wanted to get to the capital to find Garret, so they could go back to finding the thrones. But Leith was right; they did need to consider the implications of what happened next. Nea knew deep down Garret would fight the corruption until his dying breath. But if Leon had managed to get inside his dreams with the Usurper's help, then that left him vulnerable to a completely different threat. If Leon could reach inside his dreams, the next step was shifting the Usurper directly into Garret's body, and if that happened ... If Garret's soul lost that fight ... they were doomed whether they found the thrones or not.

CHAPTER EIGHTEEN

HARVEY

Evard hummed to himself as he limped along in front of Harvey and Janey. He hadn't said much since they'd left the city except to remark on the weather or complain about the food. It was strange to see him reduced to this shell of a person, fluctuating between bitter spite and imbecilic rambling. The Evard Harvey knew had been cruel and calculating despite being prone to outbursts of temper.

Penny and Emil were in front of Evard, snatches of their conversation drifting back every so often as one of them half-turned to flick a look in Harvey's direction. Janey and Garret were still the only ones who knew the truth about what had happened in that chamber beneath the castle. Harvey glanced down at his fingers. His chest tightened, and he swallowed.

A hand touched his arm, and he met Janey's gaze. She worried her lip between her teeth in a way that was almost Nea-like before giving him the barest of smiles. *"It doesn't change anything."*

Except it changed everything. Harvey didn't know how he had done it. One second he had been standing on one side of the room, a tugging sensation building behind his navel, and the next his fingers were closing around the beating heart of ... his brother. It couldn't be true. There was no way Harvey was related to that thing. There was only Harvey and Lorrie. His mother had given no indication she had ever had another child.

Janey's fingers brushed his arm again, giving it a small squeeze and pulling him to a stop as her other hand touched his chin, drawing his gaze back to her. A sheen of concern glittered in her eyes, highlighting the golden flecks that ringed her pupils.

He reached towards her waist, but clenched his fists and shook his head as he took a step back from her. "You shouldn't trust me. I could hurt you." He lifted his hands, and a flicker of purple-red light trembled over his fingertips. "I don't know how I did it, and if it happened again ... if I ... I'd never be able to forgive myself."

She frowned and settled her hands on her hips but didn't try to touch him again. Good. She needed to stay away.

"What was that?" Penny asked, and Harvey looked up. She and the others had stopped and were watching his exchange with Janey with differing levels of curiosity.

"Nothing," Harvey said with a quick look at Janey.

"*You need to tell them the truth.*" She signed, her movements sharper than usual.

"You know keeping secrets is how all this mess started in the first place," Emil said. "If Nea had just told us everything in the beginning, we would have been done and dusted with all this four years ago and the world *probably* wouldn't be exploding around us now."

"Probably?" Penny asked, one dark brow arching.

Emil shrugged. "No one knows what sort of mess Declan might get himself into, and Evard can't be the only arsehole who wanted to watch the world burn."

"I didn't want to watch it burn; I wanted to claim immortality and rule it for all eternity." He frowned and rubbed his brow. "That is what I was promised."

Janey made a face and rolled her hand in front of her chest, opening it towards Emil and Penny.

Harvey shook his head, and the air around them gave a small shudder.

"The only other mage whose emotions affect the source like that is Nea," Emil said quietly.

Penny scrunched her nose up as she studied Harvey. "And it makes sense, given her heritage. Even without the added boost of the Shadow blood, she's from a long line of powerful rule-bending mages."

But Harvey was not. His mother wasn't even technically a real mage. Nea had called her a seer. But his—Ambrose was a complete unknown, and it was clear that he had done something to Harvey when he was an infant. The source trembled again, and Harvey clenched his jaw. He needed to get this under control before something—

The world blurred at the edges, that pulling sensation behind his navel dragging him forward, then a weight pressed down on him, and the sensation was replaced with a warm numbness that spread from his core to the tips of his toes. He turned. The others were still standing in the middle of the road, almost fifty meters away.

Emil started towards Harvey. "Well, that explains why you're such a pain in the arse to spar against. I thought you were just fast, but all this time you had magical assistance." He grinned.

"How did you—?"

"Warden, remember? You almost got out of range before I could slam the suppression down. I've never seen anything like that before. Declan and Nea are going to lose their heads over this. Niall, too, I expect." Emil reached him and gave him a clap on the shoulder. "Why hide it? I don't see how—"

"Moving fast isn't all I can do. I ..." He met Emil's amber gaze. "... pulled my brother's heart out of his chest and killed him."

Emil blinked but didn't lift his hand from Harvey's shoulder. Instead, he gave it a squeeze. "I can see why you're so rattled by it."

"You're not disgusted or frightened I might do it to you, too? I don't know how to control it. It just happened, like moving fast. I have no idea how to turn it on and off."

The warden gave a snort. "I grew up at Hartswood with Nea; weird, magical shit doesn't bother me in the slightest." He glanced back at Janey, Penny, and Evard, who were slowly approaching. "A bit of advice that Nea should have listened to; don't push everyone one away because you're worried they might get hurt. We're all capable of making up our minds about the risks we are willing to take." He let go of Harvey's shoulder and gave the two mages a wide grin. "How about you girls take the lead for a while? If we keep up this pace, we should make it to the camp before lunch tomorrow." With a wink, he nudged Evard forward before falling into step beside Harvey. He seemed to respect Harvey's need for silence, and once again Harvey was struck by how easy it was to underestimate Emil. He seemed flippant and unfocused at times, but it was clear he paid much more attention than people gave him credit for.

The camp was a bustle of activity when they arrived the next day. Mages and wardens, armed to the teeth, were heading off in groups towards the college—members of Leith's guard and what looked like a local militia amongst them. They navigated their way to the barn and knocked before entering to find Nea, Declan, Leith, Niall, Margot, and Trenton standing around the central table.

"Ah, *Nea*," Evard said with a slow exhale, drawing the attention of everyone in the room. "You and I could have done great things, my dear. Instead, you chose to fight me every step of the way, and what price did that impertinence cost you?" He stepped forward, hand lifting towards her. "Given the circumstances we now find ourselves in, despite your best efforts, was it worth it?"

Nea stood straighter, her violet eyes darkening as she settled them on Evard. "I should ask you the same question." Her gaze shifted to Emil. "What is he doing here?"

"We found him left for dead at the Crossroads. It seemed cruel to leave him like that, and Penny thought he might be useful. He's a bit addled, but he still has some moments of clarity." He cracked his knuckles. "Mind you, he has yet to say anything worth repeating."

"Trenton, take him and have him put under close watch. We can question him when we are done here," Leith said, not sparing his father another glance. "I need a full report of what happened in the capital." He settled his grey gaze on Harvey before flicking it to Janey.

Janey lifted her hands, but Harvey shook his head. "I can do it."

He recounted what they had discovered at the Crossroads, Emil and Penny piping in to answer questions or add details. Then he told them about the chamber they had found under the palace, but he paused when he got to the part about the corrupted mage. He licked his lip and met Janey's eye.

She nodded and gave him a reassuring smile.

"There was a doorway that had marks around it like the south wing at Fort Braemar. A man was imprisoned there. He was some kind of mage—I don't know what type." He looked at Janey, and she gave a shrug and shake of her head. "And he was corrupted. We were leaving when both Garret and Janey just seemed to collapse. Garret said something was happening to the source."

"You felt the aftershock of the tear breaking the Kalhanna wards all the way to the capital?" Declan asked.

"Is that what that was?" Emil asked, but Niall and Nea both shushed him.

"What happened once the aftershock had passed?" Nea asked.

"The man was free. He said Kieran had finally done something right then he attacked us. He absorbed Janey's keen and—"

"Absorbed it?" Nea and Declan both asked, sharing a look.

"You're sure he didn't block it?" Declan asked Janey, and she shook her head.

"It wasn't suppression. I could feel my keen dragging towards him." Nea frowned at Janey's hands.

"It wasn't suppression. It was like the mage was pulling her keen towards himself." Harvey interpreted for the necromancer's benefit.

"That doesn't sound like what Garret does, so it's doubtful this mage was another brightling." Nea rolled her lip between her teeth. "Did he give any indication of what he might be?"

"A failed experiment," Harvey replied, and Nea gave a sharp intake of breath.

"We can circle back to this," Leith said. "What happened after this mage absorbed Janey's keen?"

Harvey drew a slow breath and rubbed his fingers over his forehead. "I don't know exactly, but something inside me just shifted and then I was standing in front of him with his heart clutched in my fingers."

Nea blinked at him and opened her mouth to speak.

"I've never heard of a keen that could do that!" Declan exclaimed, cutting her off. "What did it feel like? And when you say you were standing in front of him with his heart in your hand, did you physically remove the heart or summon it clean out of his body? Do you think—"

"Boundaries, Declan," Nea said, her tone tight.

"Right." The storm mage shot Nea a look. "That's supposed to be Garret's line." His lopsided grin pulled into place, and she rolled her eyes in response.

"Well, he's not here right now, so someone has to remind you that there are times when your curiosity might need to come with a little empathy. What happened after that?"

Harvey rubbed the back of his neck again. "I don't know. One minute I'm standing there with a dead body at my feet, and the next I was outside the palace."

"Did you create a portal?"

Janey shook her head and waved her hands around herself.

"It's not a portal. You can still see him to track his movement, but he moves so fast he becomes a blur," Emil said.

"Interesting," Nea, Declan, and Niall all said at once.

Harvey flicked a look around the room. Everyone was studying him like he had grown an extra head.

"Is that when you lost Garret?" Leith asked.

He nodded. "Janey left him to follow after me. He wasn't good. The aftershock had really rattled him, and then during the fight the mage tried to goad him into using his keen, and he struggled to contain it. I guess he didn't want a repeat of what happened when we fought those abominations at Kalhanna. I've never seen him so unfocused in a fight."

"Did he say anything to you, Janey?"

She shook her head and opened her hands in that way she did when she was hunting for words. Then she gave a huff and gestured at Niall and Penny and tapped her head.

Soft fingers caressed the back of Harvey's neck, and that cloying sensation coated his tongue, making him swallow.

"Ah," Niall said softly. "I see."

"You see what? Care to fill those of us who can't read minds in on the details?" Declan quipped.

"Janey left Garret because Harvey presented the greater need of her assistance. There was nothing she could do to ease Garret's suffering except leave him to his own devices, knowing full and well that he was likely going to continue tracking Leon."

Janey rolled her hand in front of her, and Niall gave a nod.

"However, even if she could have stopped Garret from going off on his own, she wouldn't have because this is something he *needs* to do. It is his fight." Janey prompted Niall again, and he let out a sigh. "Yes, I agree."

"Agree with what?" Leith asked.

"That even though Garret might be under the influence of corruption, he is not an idiot and unlikely to do anything too rash."

"I still think I should go after him." Nea folded her arms across her chest, but Harvey didn't miss the slight tremble in her hands.

"I should go as well. You should have let me finish healing him the first time around," Margot said.

"The risks were—"

"Mine to take. We have a perfectly good way to *completely* deal with corruption, and still you refuse to let me even try. Why the fuck bother keeping me around then?"

The room broke into a cacophony of raised voices. They had obviously been arguing about several different things for a while before Harvey and the others arrived.

"Bright Mother's tits, this is ridiculous," Penny said, and a heavy jolt of compulsion thudded over Harvey, rattling the inside of his skull and bringing small spots dancing across his vision. "The lot of you need to calm down and listen to each other," she said when everyone's attention fell on her. "Nea is going to go after Garret whether you want her to or not."

"That's not fair. I ..."

Penny's brows arched as she stared Nea down.

The necromancer scowled. "Fine. I guess I have become somewhat predictable."

Emil's cough failed to hide his laugh.

"I agree that Margot shouldn't be using the anchor at all, but if she is aware of the risk and is willing to take it then really you just need to get out of her way," Penny continued, and Margot gave her a smile.

"What is so important about Loch Bastien?" Emil asked Declan.

"Nea thinks a lead to the location of the thrones can be found there."

"Then that is important, too, but there are reanimations at the Crossroads inn."

"Reanimations?" Nea asked.

"More like those wraiths from Holbrook," Emil replied.

Nea met her father's eye, something unspoken passing between them.

"I'm going after Garret," Nea said.

Janey stepped forward, tapping her own chest.

"Then I'm going, too," Harvey said.

"No, I think you should stay here and work with both Warren and my father. If you don't get even a basic understanding of that keen, it will only make you a liability later," Nea said.

"But you can't understand Janey's sign language."

Nea chewed her lip, and her eyes flicked to Penny. "There's a fairly easy solution to that problem, and we'll need a warden, too, just in case Garret's corruption ...." She swallowed whatever else she had been going to say.

Emil raised his hand. "I'll come."

"I still think I should go with you," Margot said.

"No, you and Molly take Declan and Bran to Loch Bastien and see if you can find that lead on the thrones. The anchor is Shadow-touched, so it should resonate if you are on the right track, and I have a feeling a necromancer will come in handy." Nea licked her lip and met Leith's eye. "Is all that fine with you? You, technically, are the one in charge here." The corner of her mouth curved ever so slightly.

Leith gave an amused-sounding huff. "Would it change your mind if I said no?"

"You already know the answer to that."

Leith laughed. "Indeed. I can't say I'm happy with that plan, but given our options, I can see how it might be the best course of action. We need Garret back. I should have never let him go in the first place."

"The only way to do that would have been to chain him to this barn," Declan said with a grin.

"Once we find Garret, we'll send word if we can and join you at Loch Bastien if you are still there. Though it might be better to arrange another meeting place outside of the college just in case Sophia proves to be an issue." It was highly likely that her mother would choose to be difficult. "We'll discuss our options on the way to the capital."

"That's settled then. We can start working on your keen in the morning, Harvey," Niall said.

Nea was right. The keen made him a liability, but he didn't want to learn how to control it—he just wanted it gone. He'd meet Niall in the morning, but he wouldn't be working on the keen. He'd ask Niall to put the block back on it and, failing that, find himself a pair of bind-shackles and throw away the key.

CHAPTER NINETEEN

GARRET

Nea was laid out on the sun-drenched stones beside him, droplets of water drying on her skin. Several slid across the purple flower-shaped birthmark on her hip as she stretched and propped herself on her elbows. The gentle lapping of the enchanted pool and the soft notes of birdsong the only sounds as her violet eyes found his.

"Feel better now?" she asked, biting her lip in a manner that was very different to the usual way she chewed it when thinking.

"If I said no?"

A warm smile curved her mouth, and she lifted herself towards him, her lips lightly brushing his. "Then I would say you are an appalling liar."

A chill rolled down Garret's spine, and he glanced over Nea's shoulder to the dark figure at the edge of the trees. When he looked back at Nea, her brow was furrowed. Something warm slid over his hands, and he looked down to see her blood pouring over them.

Leon stepped away from the treeline and let out a laugh that silenced the birdsong.

The floor slammed against Garret. He pulled himself into a sitting position and rested his back against the side of the bed with a groan. The room he was in was neat, a large cabinet to one side and a small kitchen across from him. There was also a table in the centre of the room, around which were several chairs.

"Good morning, Commander," a voice said, and Garret tilted his head to find the man from the day before, Hugh, leaning against the wall. "Did you sleep well?" There was something off about the tilt of his mouth and the tone of his voice. But it could have been the dregs of the dream still clinging to Garret's senses.

"I—"

"Oh, you're awake," Gwyn said brightly as she returned. "Legs still not cooperating?" she asked, a curious sparkle in her eyes as they changed colour from blue–green to indigo.

Garret pulled himself to his feet. His limbs were still stiff, but nothing like they had been the day before. "No, I just—"

"Fell out of bed," Hugh said with a small smirk.

"Would you like some breakfast?" Gwyn asked, checking the pot by the fire. "I can fix you some porridge or tea?"

The way she said tea reminded him of Frell, the witch from the Between who had drugged them and tried to rewrite Nea's memories. He shook his head. "No, thank you. I should be moving on. But thank you for helping me yesterday."

Gwyn smiled brightly. "Oh, don't mention it, Commander. But you really shouldn't be heading off with an empty stomach." She gave the pot a stir, and the scent of oats spiced with cinnamon and honey filled the air. "The sun is barely up. I am sure one bowl won't hurt."

He hadn't eaten in a good while, and the smell was making his stomach rumble. One bowl wouldn't hurt, would it? After all, if she meant any harm, she had had ample opportunity while he had been unconscious. "Alright." He took up one of the chairs while Gwyn filled a bowl. She placed it in front of him and handed him a spoon before getting one for herself and Hugh.

"Where are you headed next?" she asked as she dipped her spoon into her porridge and lifted it again to blow gently on the steaming scoop.

Back to Leith's camp at Kalhanna should have been his answer. "I'm not sure ... North maybe."

"North as in Del Harol with the rest of the refugees."

Garret shook his head.

"He's not going to tell you his plans, Gwyn, and I wouldn't either if I were in his position," Hugh said. The blatant animosity from the day before seemed to be gone, but something still lingered there under his tone.

"The only other place that is north that is worth going to is Merston," Gwyn mused. "And I wouldn't be heading there if I were you."

Garret said nothing, just focused on his bowl.

"That's were Ambrose is, and he's surrounded himself with a personal guard of reanimations courtesy of Kieran."

"Why Merston?" Garret asked.

Both Hugh and Gwyn shrugged.

"He's always considered it his birthplace, and he thinks there is forgotten magic in the mountains beyond it. But he has been all over that section of mountains and hasn't found it yet. I think whatever he's looking for is closer to Del Harol, personally." Gwyn's spoon scraped against the side of her bowl. "I'm going to make some tea," she said as she stood. "Are you sure you don't want a cup? It's nothing fancy, just plain old peppermint."

Garret pushed his empty bowl aside and toyed with his scar. The porridge had brought a heavy warmth to his centre that reminded him how tired he was. "Sure, why not?"

Hugh studied Garret then flicked a look at Gwyn. She gave him a sweet smile in return. "You want a cup, too?"

"No, I should go and relieve Sam. I can't say it's been a pleasure, Commander. Good luck with the journey north."

Gwyn shook her head as she placed the steaming cup in front of Garret. "There you go. Why don't you tell me more about Nea?" She settled down with her own tea and rested her chin on her hand.

Garret took a tentative sip from his cup. There was something sweet under the peppermint, something familiar that he couldn't quite place.

"Liquorice root," Gwyn said, startling him. "I like the little bit of sweetness it adds."

"Oh, Nea adds it sometimes too. Though she complains if you add too much because it makes the tea too sweet." He bit back a grin.

"She doesn't like sweet things?" Gwyn asked, leaning forward.

"Not overly. She usually avoids the liquorice in favour of a little chamomile." He took a bigger sip.

"Chamomile puts me straight to sleep."

Garret shook his head, trying to clear the fogginess that had dulled his thoughts. The edges of his vision were starting to blur, and a numbness was creeping up his fingers. He opened his mouth to speak, but his tongue felt too thick. His cheek met the wood of the table. The cup rolled away, its contents darking the wood in a growing puddle.

"It's done then?" Hugh's voice asked.

"Yes ... should ... Leon ..." Gwyn answered. Her words garbled like he was listening to her underwater.

Leon? The edges of his vision were growing dark. He tried to push himself off the table, but his arms weren't responding again. Their voices were flickering in and out.

"... Nea?" Hugh asked.

"She'll come," Gwyn answered, all the warmth gone from her voice. "Especially now we have bait."

Garret stumbled to his feet, his head was swimming, vision blurring and refocusing in a way that turned his stomach to water. A chair came into focus, and he staggered to it, his hands heavy as he reached for the jug sitting in the middle of the table. It wobbled as he knocked it, and cool fingers pressed over his, steadying the jug and bringing a soothing chill to the lines of the ward mark at his wrist. No, she couldn't be here. This is what Leon wanted. His throat tightened, and he only managed to croak out her name. "Nea."

She said something in response. Her voice sounded almost too sweet, the words mumbled by the thick buzzing inside his skull. He had to make her leave, but his body was too heavy, his throat too dry. He slumped forward, the wooden tabletop cold against his cheek as his eyes slid shut again.

Light sent a wash of red against his eyelids, a sharp pain sliced through the fog in his mind, and he rubbed his temples. Tentatively, he opened his eyes. He didn't recognise the room he was in, but he recognised the man sitting at the table: Leon.

"Has it worn off yet?" Leon asked casually. "It's such a simple drug but so effective."

Garret leapt to his feet, ready to charge across the room, but he was pulled up short as a chain tightened and the shackles around his wrists bit into his flesh.

Leon let out an indulgent snigger. "You strode right into my net. I had thought to go after Nea first, but your corruption afforded me an opportunity too perfect to refuse."

Garret pressed his back teeth together and gave the chain another tug.

"I really need to thank Nea when she gets here. Her mistake has granted me a world of untold power." He took a sip from the mug he was holding. "I can't use your corruption to my advantage anymore—not while we need to keep you under the influence of mage bane, but I can manipulate you both in *other* ways."

The door opened, and Gwyn entered carrying a tray. She glanced at Garret, her eyes indigo.

"Gwyn is one of Ambrose's favourite pets," Leon said, beckoning her closer. "Her keen is very curious in that she has the ability to manipulate souls, much like our dear Nea. Unfortunately, Gwyn cannot use her keen to kill." He stood and stroked Gwyn's cheek with the back of his knuckles before taking the tray from her. "Thank you, my dear."

She flicked another look at Garret; her eyes were blue–green again.

Leon ran his fingers over the items on the tray. "Now." He lifted a long thin knife, testing the edge of the blade before placing it down again. "Gwyn, if you would be so kind as to restrain our guest."

A heavy weight pressed down on Garret's soul; he'd felt this before, when Nea had used her keen on him that first night at Fort Braemar. Gwyn's control wasn't nearly as refined as Nea's. He could feel the faults, the edges where his suppression could work into, but it didn't rise. Was the mage bane blocking his warden keen as well as his brightling? No, his suppression had been absent since he had used Nea's keen to kill Jackson.

Leon stood right in front of Garret and held out his hand. "Give me your arm," he demanded.

Garret struggled against the compulsion pushing down on his soul. The mage bane had made his keen sluggish, but it was still there if he could just burn through the last of the drug. Pain was blossoming behind his eyes, spots of red and black dancing as he fought.

Gwyn let out a grunt and pushed down harder, her breath coming out in ragged pants.

His arm jolted upwards, and Leon caught it, tearing back the sleeve to reveal the purple death ward.

"Oh, it is a pretty thing, isn't it?" Sharp pain followed the path of his finger as he traced the lines of the mark. "Now, let's summon Nea, shall we?" He clamped his hand over the mark, and ice flooded Garret's veins.

His keen burned through the last of the mage bane, surging into his body in a manner that made his knees weak. He couldn't falter now. He pressed back against Gwyn's compulsion, and she let out a gasp as she lost her grip on him.

The second he was free, Garret slammed his fist into Leon's gut and kicked his shin.

Leon swore as he stumbled backwards, out of Garret's reach. "I told you to restrain him!" he bellowed at Gwyn.

"I did, but he's too strong. It wouldn't be a problem if you hadn't insisted on letting the drug wear off."

Leon snarled and slapped her. "I don't want excuses. Restrain him now or it will be you I am making scream."

Gwyn swallowed and her keen clamped down on Garret again. But he was ready for her; the familiar crackle of storm magic built under his skin, surging against the compulsion and into Gwyn's body.

"I can't." She gasped, a trickle of blood running from her nose. "My keen isn't strong enough."

"Do not release him again," Leon growled and edged towards Garret.

With a moan, Gwyn lost her hold and slumped to the floor.

Leon wasn't quite in striking distance, but Garret still made a charge at him, tugging violently at the chains. He'd used too much keen to fight off Gwyn, and the corruption was scurrying up his spine.

With an undignified yelp, Leon backed up, nearly tripping over Gwyn's body. "I need a warden now!" Leon bellowed towards the door.

A heavy suppression dropped down on Garret's shoulders as two wardens entered the room.

"Get shackles on him!"

The wardens shared a look and started towards Garret. As soon as they got within striking distance, he lashed out, driving his fist into the jaw of the closest one. Without his full range of movement, he was quickly overpowered—his head slammed against the wall as one of the men restrained him while the other clamped the cold bands of a pair of bind-shackles around his wrists just below the iron of the chains that restrained him. They both gave him a solid punch as they released him and stepped beyond reach once more.

"I'm not done with you," Leon said as backed to the door. "Hugh," he yelled, and the mage appeared.

He took one look at Gwyn's slumped form and advanced on Garret. "I warned you, Commander." He clenched his fist and lifted it.

"She did that to herself under his order," Garret said, jutting his jaw towards Leon, who still lurked in the doorway.

Hugh lowered his hand. The twist of his mouth told Garret he was warring with himself. Maybe that was something Garret could use to his advantage. He just needed to wait for the right moment.

"I'm not going to fight a man in chains. I have more honour than that." He shot a look at the pair of wardens before he bent and checked Gwyn's pulse.

"She just overextended her keen. She'll be fine after she sleeps it off," Garret said, sitting on the bed and rubbing the shackles.

Hugh scooped Gwyn up and gave Garret a nod before leaving.

Leon studied Garret for a few moments before pulling the door shut and snapping the lock.

Garret drew a shuddering breath and wrapped his fingers around the ward-marked wrist. The shackles prevented him from feeling Nea's keen. He hoped they would protect her from whatever torture Leon was intending, but the wards linked them so intimately, she was sure to feel something.

CHAPTER TWENTY

Harvey

The sun was barely up when Harvey met Niall outside the barn the next morning. The mage led him out to the field. There had been a heavy frost overnight, leaving a wicked bite in the air and small patches of white-dusted grass that crunched underfoot.

"Now." Niall turned to him, fingers locked as he stretched his arms. "I am well aware that you would rather I just replace the block on your keen and be done with it. However, given the unique nature of the magic you wield, I am not certain it will be a permanent solution. It would be better for us to get a proper understanding of how your keen works before we go placing blocks or looking at cutting you off from the source indefinitely."

Harvey didn't want to test his keen—he just wanted things to go back to the way they had been before. "With all due respect—"

"You have my solemn vow that I will replace the block, if that is what you wish, once we know *what* we are dealing with."

Harvey rubbed the back of his neck. "Alright, what do I need to do?"

"In order to understand your connection to the source, I need you to access your keen-sense."

"I don't know how to; it just happens on its own."

Niall gave a deep chuckle. "Indeed, it does. That is the nature of innate magical ability. It is as instinctual to our bodies as breathing, and yet we can learn to control it. A keen-sense that is constantly engaged becomes tiring over time. Like a tensed muscle, it will eventually either succumb to fatigue and simply give out or tear under the prolonged strain. But muscles by their very nature can be trained to the point where they develop a memory so deep that they can perform functions without the need for conscious input. Keen-sense is the same, and an understanding of keen-sense is where all mages start their training as it is the ability that most commonly develops first."

"What do you need me to do?"

"Close your eyes."

Harvey did as instructed.

"Innate magic, the kind we are born with, is not governed by our thoughts so much as our feelings. Focus on the world around you. What do you hear?"

He drew a deep breath and listened. All around him the world was coming to life—the birds singing, the camp waking up. Somewhere off in the trees to his right, a fox was barking. "I can hear the world starting to stir, the people back at camp preparing for the day."

"Good. Now what can you feel?"

There was a slight breeze bringing with it a biting cold. "The chill on the air."

"Yes, and?"

"And ..." That was all he could feel. Unless Niall meant his own keen, which was an alluring throb just at the edge of Harvey's senses. "I can feel your keen. It's like Penny's, coercive and full of promises ... cloying and almost sweet."

"Excellent. Now what happens when you turn that focus inward?"

A flash of red and purple, the world vibrating around him. Even with his eyes closed, he could see the outline of Niall's body—the weak points where his keen could break through exposed in red flickers. Farther out, he could feel the churning mass of the tear. It sent an uneasy quiver through his core and turned his stomach in a way that made him thankful he hadn't eaten yet. He drew his focus back to the air around himself, to the source. It was a blanket over everything, one that he could fold and twist. "I can feel the source ... I think."

"What does it feel like?"

"Like a blanket cast over the world and yet completely permeating it. As though the world is woven from it ... or to it?" He opened his eyes and rubbed his temples to stave off the headache that was building.

Niall's keen settled on him, and the mage gave a nod. "Yes, that was the source ... Interesting. It would seem that your keen is rather similar to Nea's in a very rudimentary sense."

At Harvey's puzzled look, he continued.

"It is the way your keen is connected to the source. Nea's is that way because she is divine-blooded, but you are not. The source seems to respond to your emotions as it does Nea's, but the way in which you both channel it and the limitations on what you can do are vastly different. Nea can create portals, which seems to be an extension of her ability as a necromancer to interact with the barrier between worlds. You, however, can't break through the barrier, but you can fold the source around yourself and move at an alarming speed through the physical world." He chewed his lip. "And then there is the ability to kill, which you both seem to possess. Nea, of course, does so by stripping the soul directly from the body. Again, this is linked very much to her necromancy. You, however, pulled someone's heart directly from their chest. I suspect it has something to do with that ability to fold the source."

"But I can't control that—it just happens."

"Each time you have engaged your keen, your emotions have been running high. Magic is a *feeling* thing, and once we understand that we can have better control of it. Use your keen to run to the other end of the field." He indicated the treeline with an open palm.

"I don't—"

"Don't think; just do."

Harvey drew a breath and started to run. The source was still vibrating around him. If he focused on it, he could see the folds developing. A tree loomed before him, and he skidded to a stop. A look over his shoulder told him he had crossed the field. Niall was waving at him to come back.

"Excellent," he said once Harvey reached him. "Do you know how you did it?"

Harvey shrugged. "I just focused on the source. I could see the way it was folding, and I just ..." He opened his hands out the way Janey would when she was hunting for words.

"I think with practice you can certainly learn to control it."

"What about the other part? I don't want to risk killing someone—"

"The man you killed was attacking you and your friends, correct?"

Harvey nodded.

"And your emotions were already high due to the nature of what you had uncovered. You lost control of it because you lost control of your emotions. Control your emotions and you will control the magic. Now that you have lost control once, I doubt very much that you would do so again. The first time is always the worst."

Did young mages lose control with catastrophic results often, or was Niall comparing him to Nea again?

"Could you isolate that part of my keen and turn it off?"

Niall shook his head. "Unfortunately, isolating a specific function of an individual's keen is extremely difficult and not always successful. And now that I have some understanding of your keen, I believe any block placed on it wouldn't be permanent; unless you resorted to long-term mage bane use, which is not advisable given it will present you with a slow, somewhat agonising death. Or bind-shackles might be suitable, given that unlike a normal mage your body is not used to a sustained connection to the source, so any detrimental effect from the shackles will be easier to bear."

Harvey drew a long breath then let it out in a huff.

"Whilst you consider your options, it would be advisable to continue to work on learning control."

It was a lot to consider. He really wished Janey was there to talk it through. Maybe he should keep working with Niall on controlling it and ask her opinion when she returned. It couldn't hurt, really. He studied the trees at the other side of the field. Those few moments when he had been in control of it had felt exhilarating, like something had been missing his entire life and it had finally clicked into place. He gave Niall a nod. "Let's keep working on controlling it for now."

The mage clapped his hands together. "Excellent. Close your eyes again, and let's work on that focus."

It had been several days since Harvey had started training with Niall. They met every morning just before dawn and spent the next few hours working on Harvey's control. It was getting much easier to manipulate the source, and the times when instinct took over and Harvey lost control of his keen were getting fewer and fewer. As an added benefit, the source had stopped being so sensitive to his emotions. Niall said it was something that would never go away entirely, but if he wanted to know how to better deal with that part of his keen then he should talk to Nea when she got back.

"There you are, Harvey," Leith said as he settled down across from him, a bowl balanced on one hand.

"You were looking for me?"

"I hoped to catch you and Niall this morning. I want eyes on the college again. The creatures coming from the tear seemed to have stopped, and I would like to know if something is causing it."

Harvey examined the ragged patch of sky. It pulsed a deep blue this morning, but that would change. The churning clouds contained in the tear never settled on one colour for long.

"I was thinking of sending Zephyr, Mateus, Donnic, Niall, and Warren, but I want someone else to go just in case."

"And you were hoping I would go with them," Harvey said.

Getting closer to the tear again was the last thing he wanted to do. The magic leaching out of the Between seemed to negatively affect anyone who was exposed to it for too long. Mages and wardens especially as they were already source sensitive.

Leith nodded. "And maybe take Micha. The pair of you can make sure the mages don't get too caught up in their theorising and forget that they have limited time at the college." He studied the tear. "If it expands again, we may need to move the camp. I don't want to put anyone at more risk than is absolutely necessary."

"I'll go round up Micha then." He stood and headed towards the field where Trenton was running his men through a few drills.

Once he had collected Micha, they met up with Niall and the others and started the trek to the college.

The closer to the tear they got, the more Harvey's skin crawled. The source around him was vibrating so fast that it felt like he was wrapped too tight in a blanket and couldn't find the opening to free himself.

The other mages were suffering as well. Niall was fidgeting and talking faster than normal as he discussed something with Warren, who was wearing a deep scowl and every so often would rub his forehead. Donnic was quiet, but each time the tear above them pulsed, he would wince and then crack his knuckles. Zephyr stretched her arms out and tugged at the sleeves of her jacket as though it was suddenly too small for her. Wade let out a soft whine and Rourke a rumbling growl as they trotted along beside her.

"Tear really does a number on the mages," Micha said, and Harvey flicked a look his way.

"It makes your bowels feel like they are trying to turn themselves inside out," Mateus muttered as he rubbed his stomach. "You should consider yourself lucky to be keen-less."

"I've never envied those born with magic, even before all this." The soldier gestured at the sky above. "And we shouldn't linger here. I keep feeling things that aren't there touch me."

"I have no intention of lingering," Niall said. "Mateus, if you and Warren would like to begin."

The chill that Harvey now recognised as necromancy filled the air as Mateus and Warren turned their focus to the tear. The sky flickered between purple and green.

"It's no use," Warren said. "For every inch of the barrier we mend, another foot tears. It's almost like it is feeding off our keen. Resetting the college wards might be our best course of action."

"It's too far beyond the wards now," Donnic said.

Micha wandered away to inspect the bodies that littered the courtyard. Harvey didn't blame him for being disinterested. The mages could spend hours debating and still end up with nothing to show for it. They had been trying to seal the tear for weeks and kept coming back to the same conclusion, so Harvey didn't know why they bothered to keep trying.

"What if we reinforced or warded the barrier beyond the edges of the tear?" Zephyr asked. "Of course, we can't reinforce it all in one go because the tear covers too much ground—we'd need a hundred necromancers. But maybe we could reinforce it on one side to prevent it spreading farther inland."

"It could work, but we would still need more necromancers," Mateus said.

"What if we created a lock-stone and anchored the tear to it?" Donnic asked.

"Lock-stones are extremely complicated magic. We would need to find an appropriate anchor point, and then we would need someone like Nea to actually anchor the source to it. No other mages have the intrinsic relationship with the source that she has," Warren replied.

"Zephyr does or—" Niall pointed to Zephyr and then glanced at Harvey.

"I don't doubt that Zephyr does have the ability in her own realm, but the source is different on this side of the barrier. And Harvey has barely gained control of his keen. It would be like tasking a toddler with running a kingdom." Warren folded his arms.

"Warren is correct that my keen functions differently on this side of the barrier. I could certainly try to anchor the source, but I doubt I would be successful. I can't even put Wade and Rourke back in their normal bodies, and polymorphing is much simpler than creating a lock-stone."

"I think we could manage it," Mateus said, rubbing his fingers along his lip. "At least, in theory we can. Between us and the rest of the mages at camp we have enough raw power. We would need to find a suitable point to create the lock-stone, and Zephyr can help Harvey with the actual anchoring. Warren and I can handle the linking of the barrier to the stone, and Donnic can seal it so that it doesn't all come flying apart." They all stared at him. "It doesn't have to be a permanent lock-stone. It just has to hold long enough for Nea and Garret to get their arses to those thrones and fix everything."

"What do you think, Harvey?" Niall asked after a few moments.

Harvey rubbed the back of his neck. "I don't know. Warren is right that I can barely control my keen. I don't have decades of experience like the rest of you, and my proposed role seems fairly crucial."

"Zephyr will be able to guide you—you wouldn't be doing it alone," Mateus said. "And we're not talking about doing it right now. You'll have a day or two to get some practice in while we get everything else in place."

"A day or two?"

Mateus nodded. "It really is our best option."

"Yeah, and if it fails, we'll all likely be dead, so ..." Warren shrugged.

Harvey drew a deep breath; he should have made Niall lock away his keen instead of trying to control it. Now that he had experienced it and learned some control, he wasn't sure he could go back to living without it. The awakening of his keen really had made him feel whole in a way that was nearly impossible to describe. But what Mateus was asking was too much. If something went wrong and it was Harvey's fault ... Still, if they didn't try and the tear continued to expand, the cost would be great. Could Harvey live with himself if he could have prevented the tear from harming more people? Letting the breath out in a huff, he met Mateus's hazel gaze and gave a sharp nod.

CHAPTER TWENTY-ONE

Nea

Nea had known what to expect when they reached the capital, but neither Emil or Harvey's reports had mentioned the pervading sense of dread or the scent of fear and death. The source was agitated—not buckled and weak like it had been at Kalhanna but seething and barbed. The thin threads of necromancy still clinging to the reanimations lying defeated in the streets were laced with a tell-tale wrongness, as though Kieran had created them in a corruption-induced tantrum. These were not the carefully sculpted puppets he had commanded at Kalhanna. Even without full access to her keen, she could tell that undead still roaming the dark parts of the street were mindless automatons of flesh piloted by spirits that had never been human.

She pressed the back of her hand against her mouth and closed her eyes. Infecting Kieran had been a mistake—she had known that almost from the second she had done it, but she could never have imagined it would lead to this.

A hand touched her shoulder, and she opened her eyes to meet Emil's amber gaze. He gave her a hollow smile.

"I'm fine," she whispered.

"None of us have been *fine* for months, Nea," he whispered back. "If you're blaming yourself for this"—he gestured at the destruction around them—"then don't."

She glanced at Penny and Janey, who were carefully picking their way around an overturned cart. "If—"

"It's not your fault," he said sternly and released her shoulder. "Come on. We're almost at the palace."

She looked back the way they had come. Grey bodies were shambling along the street. A cat yowled somewhere towards Dust Town, and as one the reanimations rushed towards the sound. If she had access to her necromancy, she could make short work of them. Chewing her lip, she followed Emil, her focus now inward, trying to shift the heavy suppression that had settled on her core and refused to let go. The suppression was worse than being shackled; at least with bind-shackles the connection to the source was cut off entirely. This was like teasing a starving dog by leaving a hearty meal just beyond its reach.

They crossed the upper market, avoiding the Bright temple and heading straight for the palace.

Inside was different to the city. There were no reanimations here, only bodies slumped where they had fallen and a deep stillness that left fingerprints on the back of your neck. Janey led them to Evard's study, and Nea paused at the door. Last time she had been in this room, she had attacked Evard with a pen knife, giving him the scar that now marred the left side of his face. If she had managed a killing blow, would they still be in this mess they were in now? Kalhanna might still be standing, but Evard had been only one piece of the Usurper's plan.

Something inside the room clicked, and Janey stepped away from the bookcase as it scraped open to reveal a narrow staircase leading downwards. Nea had only been down there once, and the visit had been extremely brief, but it had been long enough to see the atrocities that had been hidden away.

Janey stepped towards the opening.

"I'll go first," Emil said.

He disappeared into the doorway then called back, "A little light might help."

Penny chuckled, and a pale pink mage light bloomed to life beside her. She guided it into the passageway.

"Thanks, Pen."

"You're welcome." She followed him.

Janey went next, leaving Nea alone in the room. She ran her fingers along the edge of the desk. This study held so many memories—some grim, like those last weeks before the purge, and others sweeter. Margot sitting in the chair in the corner, nursing a cup of tea and chatting away about her day. Or Leith coming in to distract her because it was 'high time she had a break.'

"Are you coming, Nea?" Penny's voice called from the dark stairs.

Nea shook her head to scatter the memories that were stirring and headed into the passageway. Penny's mage light cast long shadows back up the stairs, but there was enough of a glow that Nea could carefully navigate her way down, one hand trained on the wall to steady herself.

The stairs opened out into a torture chamber, or at least a room that bore a striking resemblance to one.

"So, this is where Evard's—I can't finish that sentence," Penny said as she studied the tables with their leather straps and the cells that lined the wall. "Do you—actually, no, I definitely don't want to know the answer to that."

"Good call," Emil said, his tone unusually heavy. "Wait, what is that?" He moved towards what looked like a hunk of rotten meat laying on the floor beside a stain that was unmistakably blood. "Oh, that's disgusting ..." He drew his sword and poked the object.

"Don't touch it," Penny reprimanded.

Janey waved her hands to get their attention then signed something.

"No wonder he was freaking out," Emil said.

"What is it?" Nea asked.

"That is the heart that Harvey pulled from the chest of the corrupted mage they found down here," Penny answered.

Janey nodded and signed something again.

"Good point. Where *is* the body?" Emil turned in a slow circle, examining the room. "Can you make the light brighter, Pen?"

Penny's keen shifted, and the light drifted towards the ceiling, growing brighter as it did so. Shadows bounced across the walls, and the light revealed a pair of legs sticking out behind one of the overturned tables near the side of the room.

Nea moved to it. She knew it wouldn't be Garret—the death ward meant that one couldn't die without the other—but the fear that it might be still shifted in her stomach.

The mage had been handsome, and she could definitely see a resemblance to Harvey in the line of his chin and the blond waves that lay in a mass of snarls around his head. Black webs of corruption stained one side of his face and neck before disappearing under his shirt. She crouched and rested her fingertips against his cold cheek.

"Are you going to tell Nea not to touch it?" Emil quipped at Penny. "At least I didn't touch it with my bare hands," he added in a mutter.

Penny said something, but Nea had drowned them out. Her own keen was clinging to the body; Garret must have done this. But then he would have given the corruption all the opening it needed to take over. Her breath hitched as she sucked it over her lip, her chest tightening. The amount of power he would have had to use to kill this mage ... But the residual magic didn't have the signature of Garret's brightling keen; it was purely Nea's. Had he pulled her keen through the death ward to kill this mage? If he had and it happened to be at the same time Nea had overextended her keen, then his suppression overtaking her body made sense. It had simply moved into the void left behind by Nea's keen. Did that mean that her keen wasn't gone but merely housed in Garret's body? Was that possible? If only Declan was around to discuss it.

"Nea?" Emil asked, his tone careful.

"Garret did this," she said looking up at the three concerned faces hovering above her.

Janey shook her head and signed.

Nea didn't need Penny or Emil to translate it this time.

"Harvey would have slowed him down, but I don't think he killed him."

"Did you not see the rotting heart over there?" Emil asked.

"If this mage was like Amelia, then he would have been extremely hard to kill. Amelia is a reanimation, a very sophisticated one, but still a reanimation. If this mage was the same, then the only way to kill him would have been to break the necromancy reanimating him."

"I thought destroying the body killed reanimations."

"Standard reanimations, yes, but not wraiths. Wraiths can keep going despite wounds that would destroy normal reanimations. Whatever Garret did here, it would require him to channel an immense amount of power. So much that he either overextended his keen or succumbed to corruption entirely." Her voice wavered, and she covered her mouth with her palm. No, she couldn't give up hope. Garret would fight the corruption until it killed him. Warm arms slid around her, and Janey's flickering keen rolled down her spine as the other woman's cheek pressed against the back of her shoulder. It was surprisingly soothing.

When the other mage pulled away, she brushed her hair behind her ear and signed something.

"He's stronger than he thinks," Penny said. "And she's not wrong, but everyone has a breaking point. We should see if we can find any signs of where he might have gone."

"I've got a pretty good idea, and I don't think he was alone," Emil said from the other side of the room. He was pointing at something on the ground, and Nea and the other two women joined him. Penny's mage light bobbed over the floor, illuminating a path through the dust—a channel leading into the corridor as though someone had dragged a body away into the darkness.

They followed the drag marks in the dust until they reached a solid wall. Nea pressed her palms against it and gave it a shove, but nothing happened.

Beside her, Emil pushed his shoulder into it and grunted then stepped back with a shake of his head. "There's nowhere else they could have gone," he said.

Janey inspected the stone wall, tapping on seemingly random discoloured stones and running her fingers along groves. After a few minutes, she too gave up.

"Maybe it's not a physical mechanism," Penny said as she examined the wall. "Like the boulder outside Warren's grotto." Her keen slid in seductive fingers across Nea's shoulders, and a shimmer of pink rippled over the wall.

Somewhere, a mechanism clicked, and the door grated open to reveal another passageway—this one ending a short distance away in a fork. The drag marks had stopped just inside the door, the floor here smooth and dust free.

"Which way do you think they went?" Emil asked.

Nea moved to the place the corridor forked and focused on her keen-sense. It was harder to bring it to the surface with the suppression, but she managed to feel a thin thread of magic to the right. It wasn't Garret, but it was almost familiar.

"There's something that way." She indicated the right path.

Janey stopped beside her, and the warm bloom of fire magic radiated out. The other mage gave a nod and met Nea's eye then turned to Emil and signed something.

"There is also something to the left. Should we split up and check both paths?" he translated.

Nea pressed her lip between her teeth as she considered the left path. She was still being pulled to the right, but Janey had a point. "It's not a bad idea. I'll take the right."

Janey pointed to the left and then to Emil.

"I guess I am coming down the right with you," Penny said to Nea before turning to the others. "Be careful."

"We'll meet back here in roughly an hour—better make it two. We don't know how deep these tunnels go," Nea said.

"It's not exactly easy to tell the time down here, Nea," Emil said as Janey signed something.

"The catacombs?" Penny asked.

"That makes sense and means we need to be extra careful. Check every doorway with your keen-sense before going through, and if you come across a chamber that seems to whisper with the voices of the dead, don't enter it."

"Because a room full of dead voices sounds like the sort of thing we would go dashing into? We're not all impulsively curious necromancers, you know?" Emil said with a grin.

Janey rolled her eyes and gave him a shove towards the left path. She summoned an amber-coloured mage light and gave Nea and Penny a wave before heading off after the warden.

"Shall we?" Penny indicated the right tunnel, the orb of pink light already bobbing at the entrance.

They followed along the path, Nea testing the side passages with her keen-sense. Most of them were simply tombs, but others were dusty old storage rooms, the items decayed beyond use.

"You're sure there is something down here?" Penny asked for the third time.

"Yes, I felt *something*."

"Did you actually feel it, or did you just want to feel it? The likelihood that Garret is—"

"It wasn't Garret I felt. There is something here, something calling me ... If I could just get my keen-sense to work right." She let out a huff. Battling the suppression was taxing, and the headache that had been throbbing behind her left eye had started to move into her jaw.

Penny picked a cobweb off her sleeve before meeting Nea's gaze, her dark eyes appearing black in the gloom. "Are you sure it is wise to go running off down here, chasing something in the dark that is *calling* you?"

"Firstly, I didn't go *running* off. Second, no, I don't think it is wise, but nothing I have done for the last five years could be considered wise."

"I would say last decade just to be safe," Penny said with a laugh and gave Nea's shoulder a squeeze. "It's good to see the old you is still in there somewhere." She studied the tunnel ahead of them. "We need to find whatever it is soon, because we're running out of time to get back to the others."

Nea gritted her teeth and let her keen-sense out again. "I don't think it's much farther."

They went back to their companionable silence, but Penny kept throwing glances Nea's way.

"Get it out."

"I'm just curious, which one is better. I mean Leith is—" She made an appreciative sound. "But Garret..." She bit her lip. "Those muscles and all that quiet stoicism. I *do* have a soft spot for the strong, silent types."

"I'm not going to dignify that with an answer. But since you seem to be channelling your fifteen-year-old self, maybe you could tell me what is going on between you and Emil?"

It was hard to make Penny blush, but even under the dim glow from the mage light it was clear her cheeks had coloured. "*Emil?* Bright mother no. There's nothing going on. We're merely flirting with each other the way we always have."

"Ah huh." Nea's chuckle stopped short as her gaze fell on the door ahead. The magic she had been following was clinging to it, but it was the rose and eight-pointed star motif carved at its centre that caught her attention. "I think we found it."

She moved to the door and placed her palm against the motif. Cool magic prickled up her arm, and the door shuddered before crumbling into a pile of splinters at her feet. She waved the small plume of dust away and stepped into the room. There was nothing inside except a stone slab radiating a soft violet glow.

Swallowing, she moved to the edge of the block. A strange script she had never encountered before was carved into its surface around a thin slot that looked like something was supposed to be inserted into it.

"Well, that's not what I was expecting. What do you think goes in there?"

Nea rested her hand against the top of her satchel. "A blade. That's why the magic was so familiar." She retrieved the wrapped knife from her bag, and as the cloth fell away, the roses carved into the hilt glowed violet.

"Maybe we should leave it alone," Penny said with a step back.

"Maybe ..." But Nea needed to know what it would do. "Stand back and be ready to run just in case." She slowly inserted the blade into the slot in the top of the stone. The violet light all rushed into the knife, then it grew too bright and Nea was forced to shield her eyes.

After what felt like an hour but was probably only a few moments, the light receded. The handle of the knife had changed. It looked more like the hilt of a sword, an intricate filigree of rose branches forming a cage-like guard.

"Given that Molly somehow ended up with Melete's bow, do you think that's Xaria's razor?" Penny asked, edging towards it.

Nea swallowed and touched the hilt. "Only one way to find out." She drew the blade from the stone. It was a rapier and much lighter than Nea was expecting. The long dark blade shone with the sheen of oil on water, and the hilt seemed designed to match her hand perfectly. The closest she had ever come to using a sword had been the play fights she, Margot, and Emil had gotten into when they were younger. There was no way she would be able to wield a weapon like this in actual combat. But if her magic never came back, she was going to have to figure out a way to defend herself. No. She was just as likely to stab herself as her enemy. She laid the sword on the stone and retreated a step. "We should go and see if Emil and Janey found anything." She backed towards the door.

"After all of that you're not going to take it?" Penny grabbed the hilt and attempted to lift it. "Shadow's teeth. I guess it's staying there then. Seems like a shame though," she said pointedly.

"I don't know the first thing about using a sword, Penny. If it wants to be used so badly, it will need to find someone else to wield it."

"You've had that knife a very long time though, haven't you? What if it was meant for you?"

Tobias had given it to her for her eighteenth birthday. He said he had found it at the market and it reminded him of her. She had thought it lost when she used it to stab Willem during the purge. But he had carried it for three years before it found its way back to her after he had died attempting to capture Garret's family. Then she had given it to Garret to hold onto, but he'd lost it when they went into the Between, only for Gendry to find it at the market in Quel'sapar. Maybe Penny was right. She edged towards the stone again. "It would be better if it was still a knife."

The sword quivered and in an instant, it became a knife again.

Penny grinned at her. "I'd take it if I were you."

Nea picked it up. "I wonder if it can change at will. It never did before."

"Maybe its keen was exhausted and it needed to be recharged. Ask it to turn back into a sword."

"Can you turn back into a sword?"

The handle grew cool under her fingers, and the blade lengthened until she was once again holding the rapier.

"You should take it."

Nea nodded. Even if she didn't take it now, she had the sense that it would just turn up again. "Alright, but if it stays a sword, I'm going to need a scabbard and decade's worth of swordsmanship lessons."

The blade shrunk back into a dagger again, and she wrapped it in the cloth before tucking it neatly into her satchel. As they stepped into the tunnel, the pile of splinters lifted and formed themselves into the door once more.

&

Emil and Janey were waiting for them when they finally made it back to the forked tunnel.

"Someone has been living down here," Emil said as they approached. He was holding something out.

As they neared and Penny's mage light swooped over the object, Nea's stomach dropped. It was a sheathed sword; she recognised the carvings that covered the leather. Garret always seemed to think better when his hands were moving. Wood carving and sketching were his preferred tools for focus, but she had watched him draw his knife along this scabbard many times. She traced her fingertip over one of the designs that marked the leather—a small star-shaped flower, much like the birthmark on her hip—newer than the other carvings.

"Garret would never leave this behind," Emil said, fingers tightening on the scabbard.

"Where did you find it?" Nea asked.

Janey pointed down the left tunnel and then waved for Nea to follow.

They eventually came to a small cluster of chambers that appeared to be living quarters. Two of the rooms held several beds and a small collection of discarded personal items like old clothes that needed mending. The largest room was a small kitchen with a table surrounded by several chairs at its centre and a pallet bed pushed up against one wall. A collection of cups littered the table.

"It looked like whoever was living here left in a hurry," Emil said.

Nea wandered to the cabinet at the side of the room. Small jars lined the shelves. She opened several and examined the contents. "They appear to be teas and medical supplies, but a couple seem to be missing." She turned.

Penny was by the bench. She held up a jar. "Peppermint, if I am not mistaken. But this one I am not sure of. It looks like chamomile." She passed a second jar to Nea.

She removed the stopper and tipped some of the herb inside onto her hand. The dried petals had once been white but were slightly yellowed with big puffy centres. It did look almost like chamomile, but it was an easy mistake to make and a mostly harmless one. Unless you mixed it with the wrong herb. "It's just feverwort. What's in that other jar?" She tipped the herb back into its jar and brushed the remaining crumbs from her palm.

Penny unstoppered the final container and gave it a sniff only to recoil with a sneeze. "Mage bane."

The jar Nea had been holding shattered as it hit the stone floor.

"Nea?" Emil asked as Janey swooped in to clean up the broken glass and scattered herbs.

"Mage bane and feverwort is Leon's drug of choice. It's what he used when he captured me at Fort Braemar."

"Do you think Leon was here and he drugged Garret?" Emil asked.

Nea shook her head. "I don't know. He probably wasn't here but someone working with him was."

"Or it could just be a coincidence," Penny said, placing the jar of mage bane down and pushing it as far away from herself as she could. "Just because Leon used it on you once doesn't mean he has anything to do with whatever happened here."

The door opened and a man walked in. He was short with choppy blond hair and beetle-black eyes. His mouth opened in a small 'O' as he flicked his gaze over each of them in turn. He slowly started closing the door, but Emil rushed him and yanked it open. The man staggered backwards, tripping over his own feet as he tried to run.

"Up you get now." Emil hoisted him upright and gave him a shove back into the room before closing the door and leaning against it with his arms folded. "Introductions are in order, I believe. I am Emil, and these lovely ladies are Penny, Janey, and Nea." He flicked a finger at each of them. As he got to Nea, the man's eyes widened, and he backed into the far corner.

"I had nothing to do with it," he said, cowering and covering his head. "I wasn't even here."

"He seems terrified of you for some reason," Penny said, her keen rolling along Nea's shoulders. "Oh, I see." She edged towards the man. "Sam, is it?"

He nodded.

"We're not going to hurt you; we are just looking for our friend. A big warden with dark red hair. Have you seen him?"

He nodded again. "Gwyn found him in the catacombs. She was taking care of him."

"What do you mean you had nothing to do with it?" Emil asked, not moving from the doorway. "Nothing to do with what exactly?"

"Taking him to the Master. That was Gwyn, though Hugh went with her like he always does. He's never been able to say no to Gwyn, but I didn't want any part in it anymore."

"Where?" Nea asked, taking a step towards the man. He recoiled and flicked a look between her and Penny. "Where did they take Garret?" she said slowly, trying to keep the rising fear from her voice.

"They are in an old farmstead on the way to Merston. Just this side of Port Agatha."

"Let's go." Nea made for the door, but Emil blocked her path.

"Hang on. How do we know he's telling the truth and he won't just go running ahead to warn Leon?"

Penny's keen rose again. "He's telling the truth, and I doubt he will go running to Leon, but if you wish I can place a simple compulsion on him."

Emil nodded. "Do it, just in case." He moved out of Nea's way as the cloying sensation of Penny's keen deepened.

As Nea stepped out of the room, a wash of salt air hit her along with the sound of water lapping against the shore. The tunnel must lead out to the docks. Janey caught up to her and gave her a small, reassuring smile as she squeezed her arm. They walked slowly down the tunnel, which did in fact emerge from a small warehouse at the very edge of the dock. Penny and Emil joined them, and they turned towards the beach. Nea could only hope that they found Garret before it was too late.

CHAPTER TWENTY-TWO

MARGOT

They travelled in a large group until they reached the outskirts of the capital where they parted ways. Nea, Emil, Penny, and Janey headed into the city, and Margot, Molly, Declan, and Bran continued on, skirting the city proper in favour of navigating the farmland. Penny had promised less reanimations that way. And so far, that had been the case. The few reanimations they had stumbled upon were easily dealt with, especially as they had Molly's enchanted crossbow and Bran's necromancy to aid them.

They could have chosen to avoid the Crossroads but passing through them was the swiftest route to Loch Bastien, and Margot was anxious to get to the college as quickly as possible. Not to mention both Bran and Declan were curious about the wraiths.

The anchor quivered as they neared the inn about the same time the tacky pull of a ward gripped Margot's shoulders.

Static prickled up the back of her neck raising the hairs there as Declan summoned his keen, small arcs of silver-blue dancing over his fingers.

Molly readied her bow and edged closer to Margot, her mouth drawn tight, and her cornflower-blue eyes focused on the road ahead. "If anything moves, make a run for it," she said.

Bran let out a groan and gripped his head. "I don't think I want to know what Kieran did to create these reanimations. The source here is ..."

"Corrupted," Declan said thickly.

"But the source is neutral; it can't be *corrupted*," Bran said with a look in Margot's direction. "Can it?"

Margot shook her head; she didn't think the source could be corrupted as such, but it could be altered and influenced. The source at Kalhanna was still prickly and scarred, changed by the events of the purge. And the fact that it seemed to respond directly to Nea's emotions proved that it could be extremely delicate.

"Penny and Emil said they destroyed most of the wraiths, didn't they?" Molly asked.

"Yes. They burned them in one of the buildings."

"Okay, so that explains why they look like that."

Margot followed the line of Molly's bow, which was pointing to the burned shell of what had been one of the bunkhouses. Charred shapes were pulling themselves out of the ashes, some missing limbs and others with weapons still sticking out of their bodies. There were others as well—these mostly whole and not charred—they were shambling to their feet from the pile in the middle of the road.

"They don't feel quite like the ones at Holbrook. The magic is similar but there is something about it that I can't quite put my finger on," Declan mused.

"Okay, you got a look at them. Now we should run," Molly said.

"That's probably—"

"Go!" Molly let off a bolt. It flew through three of the bodies and exploded in a shower of sparks against the side of the inn.

As one the reanimations charged, the chill of Bran's necromancy clouded the air.

"No, you'll exhaust your keen again. Molly's right—run." Margot spun and ran back towards the place she had felt the ward. It dragged stickily over her skin as Bran and Declan thudded through alongside her.

Molly ran for the ward, the reanimations closing in on her as they moved faster than should have been possible. She was almost to safety when one grabbed her.

"No!" Margot raced forward, arms outstretched. The anchor burned her palm as a bolt of lilac-tinted silver shot out and hit the wraith holding Molly. It twitched and shuddered, dropping her. Margot could feel the intricate strings of necromancy holding it together, anchoring it to the Crossroads and giving it purpose. She focused on those threads, tugging at them, but they were impossible to break. The wraith jerked and snarled. Its body was dead but there was heat at its core, a throbbing heart around which the necromancy was tangled. Margot burrowed her keen into that heart and squeezed. Several of the strings gave way, and she squeezed harder, popping several more. The wraith hissed, and as the final thread gave way, it dropped to the ground.

Molly was back through the ward now, the other wraiths collapsing into silent bodies again. Margot's breath was coming fast and uneven, but she rushed to Molly. "Are you hurt?"

She shook her head. "Just a little shaken."

Margot nodded and threw her arms around Molly's neck, burying her face in her sweet-orange-scented hair. "I thought I was going to lose you."

Molly stroked the back of Margot's head with a shaking hand. "I'm alright." She pulled back and cupped Margot's cheeks, her blue eyes searching Margot's. "See? But your eyes have turned pink again." With a small smile, she pulled Margot's lips to her own.

Margot laced her fingers with Molly's and drew her closer, pressing their bodies together as she deepened the kiss.

After a while, Declan cleared his throat. "We probably should get moving. I would suggest avoiding crossing those wards. That anchor seems to be more than capable of dealing with the wraiths, but I doubt you have the stamina to destroy them all."

Margot gave a nod and let him pull her to her feet. "I don't think I could take on more than one at a time anyway, and we would be overwhelmed quickly."

"Do you know how you did it?" Bran asked.

She shook her head. "It was like I could see the necromancy animating the corpse, but I couldn't break it. Instead, I found the heart and used my healing keen to force a heart attack, which destroyed it and severed the corpse from the necromancy."

"Fascinating," Declan said. "So, was it you or the anchor?"

"Both. I think. The anchor allowed me to see the necromancy, but it was my natural keen that destroyed the wraith."

"I wonder if that is how healing the corruption works as well … The anchor opens up the channel for your keen to follow and then mend." He tugged at his lower lip. "But, of course, if corruption is a form of possession, then it makes sense that necromancy is required to assess the nature of the possession. However, necromancers cannot *heal*. And they cannot drive out the possession because it is not true possession but more like a festering wound. You need both necromancy and healing working in tandem to overcome it! It makes so much sense."

Bran probed his cheek with his tongue and looked from Declan to Margot and then to Molly.

"It's better to just let him ramble," Molly said. "Come on. We're running out of daylight, and I want to be as far from this shithole as possible before nightfall."

By mid-morning the next day, the tower of Loch Bastien came into view. The sky above was heavy and grey with the promise of rain, though given the biting chill in the air it would be more like sleet by the time it fell. Either way, crossing the lake to reach the island wasn't going to be pleasant.

The small run of buildings, including the dock master's house perched on the peer, were eerily silent. Even the scrappy chickens that usually dotted the edges of the road were absent.

"Do you think Bess and Vincent—?" Molly didn't finish the thought, but she didn't need to.

"I hope not," Declan said quietly. "Perhaps they got wind of what was coming and fled to Little Brook. I believe the innkeeper, Gerda, is Bess's sister."

"We should check the shack; the weather might have just driven them inside," Margot said, but there was no smoke rising from the chimney, and Bess always had a pot of soup bubbling away.

"I'll go." Bran strode across the peer, his boots seeming awfully loud on the aged boards. He eased the door open, and a violet orb of light flared to life, casting lilac highlights in his snow-white hair. Then he disappeared into the building only to come out again with a shake of his head. "It looks like they left in a hurry."

"We can't dwell on what might have happened to them; we need to get to the college," Molly said. "We can take one of the boats."

"Has anyone considered what will happen when we get across the lake? Sophia isn't exactly friendly at the best of times," Bran said. "And it's not like we can sneak in unnoticed. As soon as we pass the college wards, they will know we are coming."

"Not to mention as far as Sophia knows, I am supposed to be dead." Declan gave a low chuckle. "That is going to be an interesting conversation ... unless." He ran a hand through his hair. "We could sneak in through the hot springs entrance. Sophia will know someone has crossed the wards, but it will take her a while to realise we are inside the college itself. The chamber Nea thinks we should search is right near the repository, so we might be able to get in and out completely unnoticed."

"Or you and Bran sneak in through the hot springs and Molly and I will deal with Sophia. It's not like the wards register how many people cross them, only that they have been crossed," Margot said.

"That definitely sounds like a better plan." Molly gave a nod. "Come on." She indicated one of the boats secured to the side of the peer.

They almost didn't need Declan's storm magic as a stiff breeze had started to pick up, breaking the surface of the lake into a choppy mess of white-crested waves. When they reached the point where the college wards should have dragged over them, there was no change.

Declan's keen faltered as he shared a look with Margot.

"We should have felt the wards by now, right?" Bran asked, studying the imposing tower waiting just ahead of them.

Margot nodded. "College wards are too powerful to be simply broken. They have to be actively taken down by the current High Mage. Even the wards at Kalhanna held despite the tear."

"But the tear did manage to break them," Molly said.

"Only after weeks of continued assault."

The boat scraped along the side of the dock, and they all climbed out. No one came to greet them, which was not completely unheard of, but it was unusual. They were about halfway up the stairs when the clouds finally let go. Icy rain pelted their backs as they ran for the college doors, which were hanging open and dotted with scorch marks.

Inside, the corridor was stained with blood, more scorch marks, and patches of magical rime. The source was fragile, prickling with the aftermath of whatever had occurred here. Suddenly it buckled and Margot was on her back, Molly shielding her as a bolt of flame exploded against the wall above them.

Declan's keen built, sending a wave of static over Margot seconds before the entire corridor lit up with a silver-blue glow. Someone gave a yelp of pain and rolled out of the shadows from where the fireball had originated.

Molly got to her feet, crossbow trained on the mage. "Try anything else and you'll find a bolt between your eyes. Where is Sophia?"

The mage was only a teenager; he lifted his hands slowly. "Who are you?"

"I believe I asked you a question first."

"Hang on, Molly," Bran said, stepping between her and the young mage. "Hey, we aren't going to hurt you. My name is Bran, and these are my friends, Declan, Molly, and Margot. We were sent to see how things were faring here at the college." He cast a glance around the corridor. "Not great, I guess, going off the state of the source and the lack of perimeter wards. Are you the only one left?"

The mage shook his head. "Warden Commander Leon forced Sophia to drop the wards, then the corrupted attacked and a lot of the older mages were dragged off. Some fought back, and the rest of us hid until he was gone. Please ask your friend to stop pointing that thing at me."

Bran flicked a look at Molly.

She lowered the bow. "Where are the others?"

The boy licked his lip and shot a look at Bran, who gave a nod. "This way." He led them through the college to the library.

A handful of mages, mostly children and teenagers, were clustered around the room. There were also several wardens and senior mages to one side, some sporting hastily patched wounds. They turned, immediately drawing swords and pulling their keen.

Molly lifted her crossbow.

Margot pushed her arm down, forcing her to lower it again, and shook her head.

"Declan? We thought you were dead," one of the mages said.

"Yes, amazing how easily rumours get blown out of proportion, isn't it?" he said tightly. "I have been ... out of action for some time but, as you can see, I'm certainly not dead—much to my mother's relief." He rubbed a hand through his hair. "So what happened here?"

"Leon," said a gruff-looking warden sitting on the edge of one of the tables. "The bastard did something to the High Mage, and next thing we know the wards are down. Then a bunch of corrupted mages and wardens showed up. We were overrun before we knew it. This is all that's left. The rest were either captured or killed in the fight." He pushed off the table and folded his arms. "What are you lot doing here?"

"We're looking for some answers about how to deal with the tear in the barrier that has formed at Kalhanna. That search has led us here," Declan said. "But that can wait. I see that you have wounded who could use the services of a healer, and I am sure you remember Margot." He indicated Margot, who had been hanging back and letting him take the lead.

"Is the infirmary still intact?"

"It is. I can help too." A young girl stepped forward. She was maybe twelve, with a smattering of freckles across her nose and large blue-grey eyes. "I was training under the head healer, but he was taken by Leon."

Margot let her keen-sense inspect the girl. The warm throb of healing magic rose, and she gave a nod. The girl's keen was too immature to be of any real aid, but an extra set of hands never went astray. "Let's go. We'll need to get some water boiling and make sure the space is tidy." She handed her pack off to Bran. "Send in the cases that need urgent attention first. You and Declan can deal with the minor injuries. Molly, can you raid the kitchens and see if we can come up with something decent to eat? A stew and some bread would be ideal."

After so many months cast adrift and chasing down Nea's secrets, it felt good to slide back into the role of healer. It had always been her calling, and the anchor purred in response to that thought as though the spirit shared the same purpose.

Muscles aching and fingers red from scrubbing, Margot finally settled down with the others and a large bowl of soup. She broke her freshly baked roll and dipped it into the broth, savouring the taste as warmth spread through her. Molly might have trained as a soldier, but she was a fantastic cook, able to conjure something delicious and heart-warming from even the most rudimentary ingredients.

"Leon took Sophia," Declan said. dipping a piece of his roll into his soup.

"I had figured that much."

He popped the bread into his mouth and chewed thoughtfully. "It certainly makes our job easier. But what are we going to do with everyone here? Should we send them to Leith? Or on to Del Harol?"

"They can manage on their own here. I imagine that it is about as safe as anywhere else, and they seem to have been coping okay so far."

He nodded. "Seeing the college in this state is ... unsettling. The colleges are supposed to be safe havens, steadfast and enduring. Someone like *Leon* shouldn't be able to wreak havoc on them in this manner."

"Kalhanna." She bit down on the word, but it was out before she could stop it. "Kalhanna proved the colleges aren't as infallible as most of us would believe." She stirred her spoon through the remaining soup in her bowl. "But we can learn from our mistakes, and the colleges can be rebuilt."

"And the lives lost?" There was a sharpness to Declan's tone that had never been there before. Even in times of despair he seemed optimistic and able to bounce back, but something had changed. Of course, it had. He had *died.* It was easy to forget when he was sitting beside her so warm and full of life, joking with Emil or flirting with Molly, but he had been touched by death in a way none of them could ever understand. Except maybe Nea.

"Declan," she said softly. "Do you want to talk about it?"

He stabbed at a piece of carrot in the bottom of his bowl. "I'm fine."

She placed her fingers on his wrist, stilling his movements. "You're not."

"No. You are right. I'm not fine." He shook his head, and when his green eyes met hers, they were full of fire. "I'm angry. Furious. At Evard and Leon, but also at myself. I don't deserve this body. I gave up my life already, chasing down a fairy-tale cure. There was no cure, Margot. Just centuries of machinations from an upstart who believed he is entitled to more power than he was given." He stabbed at the carrot again, his spoon scraping against the bottom of his bowl with a screech that set her teeth on edge.

The anchor grew warm as though the spirit agreed with him. Margot carefully took the bowl and spoon from him and placed them aside. "But we did find a cure in the end."

"You are only one mage, Margot. You cannot hope to heal the dozens who are getting corrupted each day." His keen was prickling around him as he stood. "I need some fresh air."

She watched his back as he strode away, her heart aching.

"I imagine coming back from the dead takes a fair amount of adjustment," Bran said as he took up Declan's seat. "And he hasn't exactly had time to sit and adjust, to consider all the implications. Though I didn't know him before he died, I get the impression that he was always certain of himself, and now that certainty has been unsettled. He has experienced firsthand just how fragile the physical body can be."

"You sound a lot like Nonna."

"Nea, actually. But then again, though she'd hate to admit it, she does sound a lot like Nonna at times." He chuckled. "She asked me to keep an eye on him in case he needs help adjusting. She said a necromancer's specific understanding of death would be useful."

Margot chewed the side of her thumb and studied the doorway Declan had exited through. Hopefully, come morning he would be more focused. She was going to need some of the old Declan to help her figure out whatever it was Nea thought they could find here. The anchor gave a twinge, and she rubbed her palms together.

The sounds of stones grating over each other filled the air as the massive form of the sentry golem tilted its head to study their small group.

"Clearance code," it said in a deep voice that reverberated inside Margot's skull.

"Ah. We don't have one," Margot said. "But we don't wish to enter the repository. We are looking for something else."

The golem shifted, the glowing runes that covered its body changing from rust to lilac and then back again. It held out one massive hand. "You are like her."

"Like who?" Margot asked as she rested her palm against that of the golem, fighting to control the tremble in her fingers.

The anchor grew hot, and the golem inhaled deeply.

"She is inside," the gravelly voice said.

As Margot studied the golem, she could see the threads of necromancy that anchored the soul to the stone. An image flashed across her mind: a hunched old man with a long white beard, each breath bringing him closer to death. A light touch and a lilac-toned silver light, then he was new again, age-weary body replaced with living stone. Were golems just another kind of reanimation then?

"Who was she?" Margot asked.

The golem withdrew its hand and tilted its head. Its face didn't show a change in emotion, but Margot got the sense that a deep sadness had overcome the soul housed within. She glanced back at Declan and the others, who were hovering by the foot of the stairs.

"You don't have to tell me if it's ... painful."

The golem let out a breath that smelt of sulphur and decay. "Hope."

"Hope?" Margot traced the swirl on her palm. "Was that her name?"

Stone grated on stone as the golem tilted its head again, but it didn't answer. Instead, it said, "What do you seek?"

"The thrones of eternity," Declan said, taking a step forward.

The golem growled and tensed.

Declan lifted his hands and took a step back. "I learned my lesson the first time, I assure you."

"Oh, that's right. That's how Garret ended up with that busted lip. You were down here messing with this thing and nearly got the pair of you killed," Molly said.

"I wasn't messing with it. I was trying to understand how it functioned."

"Necromancy and geomancy working in tandem with a healthy dose of runic magic. Not many mages can pull off this sort of thing anymore. It doesn't help that geomancers are one of the rarer types of elemental mage. Camille is the only one I know, and she's ancient," Bran said, taking a step towards the golem. "But you've also got to get a necromancer who's not too squeamish about creating animations."

"Don't you mean reanimations?" Molly asked.

Bran shook his head. "A reanimation is when a soul is put inside a body that was previously living. A golem was never living in the first place, so you can't *re*-animate it."

"*Right.*" Molly puffed her cheeks as she blew out a breath.

"The thrones of eternity," the golem said slowly, each word grating over the last until Margot's skull felt like it might split under the pressure.

"Yes, exactly." Declan stepped forward and rubbed his hands together, all signs of his melancholy from the night before gone.

"They are lost."

"We know that much, but we are trying to find them."

"You will be disappointed." The golem lifted a plate-sized hand and indicated the narrow gap in the wall to their left.

"Thank you," Margot said as Bran was already ducking into the crevice with Declan close on his heels.

"You will need hope," the golem said before settling back into its position in front of the repository doors.

Margot examined the mark on her palm and then the golem before following Molly into the tunnel. Did the golem mean the anchor or actual hope? Margot's faith had been all but destroyed by the events of the last year. She didn't know if she could keep clinging to hope without any proof that it was worth her time.

The crevice wound around until it opened into a large chamber with a decorative arch, much like the one at Del Harol, set into the far wall. Rune marks glimmered faintly around the edges of the relief. They seethed with magic that felt very much like Nea's.

"Aside from the portal, there is nothing here," Bran said, kicking a stone and sending up a flurry of dust. "Maybe Nea meant the repository. But good luck getting past Old Stony without a clearance code."

Molly eyed the portal. "That connects to Del Harol, right?"

"It would connect to any portal that is still standing, but Del Harol is the only one that I know of," Declan said. "And travel by it would be extremely dangerous as the magic that allows it to function is dying."

"What if that's the clue? What if we need to use the portal to reach the thrones?" Bran asked.

"It's plausible." Declan traced his fingers along his lip. "However, I don't think Nea meant the portal. If she did then why not just send us to the one at Del Harol? It is not in as bad a shape as this one, and why risk a run in with Sophia?"

"But what else could it be?" Bran placed his palms against the stones between the arch, and the runes glimmered brighter for a moment.

"What about that?" Molly indicated the ground.

Their footsteps had tracked through the dust, revealing small patches of coloured tiles. Was it a pool of reflection like the one in which the portal archway at Del Harol sat?

"Declan, can you—" Margot flicked her hands in a sweeping motion towards the floor.

A static prickle rolled over her, charging her hair, and then a gust of wind tore through the room, stirring up the dust. She shut her eyes tight and covered her nose and mouth with the edge of her shawl as the dirt and debris scratched over the skin of her cheeks. When the wind died down again, she opened her eyes and brushed the grit from her shoulders.

"Shadow's teeth!" Bran spun in a slow circle, eyes trained on the floor and little avalanches of dust raining down from his hair and clothes.

"Is that a map?" Molly asked, crouching and tracing her finger along a line of faded blue tiles that could have been a river.

Declan stared at the mosaic with something between trepidation and awe. It was a feeling Margot herself had become very accustomed to over the recent months. She chewed her thumb and knelt to brush away a little of the remaining dust in the corner she was standing in. The tiles beneath the dirt formed a purple rose overlaying a yellow eight-pointed star. There was a small divot in the very centre that looked like it might fit—

"Bring the keystone here, Molly."

Molly lifted the chain over her head and placed the stone on Margot's waiting palm. It seemed to radiate the soothing cool of necromancy, but there was something else beneath the cool, something almost unfathomable. Margot carefully pressed the stone into the hole. It lay there silent, the speckles of quartz dotting its surface reflecting Declan's silver-blue mage light.

Feed it. The anchor seemed to vibrate as the spirit's voice echoed across the back of her mind.

Margot swallowed and pressed her palm over the stone, sending her keen into it. The stone clicked under her hand, and glowing lines of yellow and purple magic radiated out from the points of the star. They scrawled across the map as though planning multiple journeys before they faded one by one, until only a single path of light remained. It retracted into one glowing point.

"Is that in the Spine?" Bran asked as he circled the point of light. "Yes, look that has to be Del Harol." He leapt to a point on the map that did indeed look like it could represent Del Harol, then he pointed to another spot farther away, towards the edge of the map. "And that is—"

"Merston," Margot said at the same time he did.

"But there is nothing in those mountains between the two colleges. The area is too treacherous to settle," she added.

"That sounds like the perfect location to hide something you don't want found," Molly said.

"There used to be a temple somewhere along that range." Declan indicated a spot in the mountains between Del Harol and Merston. "Samson believed it to be the start of some kind of pilgrims' path."

"Let's sketch this map down and then get out of here. I don't think we'll find anything else in this ruin," Margot said as she dusted her hands on the front of her pants.

"Way ahead of you," Bran said, holding up his journal.

While Bran took several sketches of the map, Margot wandered around the chamber. She needed to make sure there was nothing they had missed, because Nea was bound to ask—several times at least. There were faded images painted on some of the walls and a pile of rotten wood that looked like it might have been a bookcase at one stage. Otherwise, the chamber was bare. The anchor purred in the back of her mind, giving her the impression that they had found what they came for.

Back upstairs, they decided to stay another night before heading for Camille's homestead to meet up with Nea. It gave Margot another chance to check on the wounded she had tended the day before and try and make sure that they had enough provisions for the coming weeks. She showed the healer's apprentice how to make a few remedies: a salve for scrapes and burns, a tea for headaches, and a steaming mix for common colds. She also gave her a tonic for fevers and one for stomach upsets. It was enough that she could tend any mild ailment that arose until better help arrived. Declan had sent a message to Aveline, outlining the state of the college, and another to Del Harol asking for assistance to be sent if possible.

Working was a balm for her soul, but as soon as she stopped, the dread that had lined her stomach ever since Evard had taken her captive stirred. The golem had said they would be disappointed in their search for the thrones, so what was waiting for them in those mountains if not their salvation?

CHAPTER TWENTY-THREE

NEA

"Nea, you need to slow down," Penny said breathlessly as she caught up. "You are going to run yourself ragged before we get there, and you'll be in no shape to help Garret."

"I'm fine."

"You're not. You've hardly slept or eaten since we left the capital."

"Pen is right. We should try and find a place to camp for the night," Emil said, and Janey nodded. "I know you're worried about Garret—we all are, but racing into Leon's den exhausted and unprepared is beyond foolish."

Nea bit her lip and met his amber gaze. He was right, of course. But icy fingers squeezed her heart and dragged through her stomach every time she thought about facing down Leon. "Alright, we can stop for the night. But we leave at first light."

"Of course," Emil said, leading them into the trees.

A short while later, they had a small camp set up, and Janey was busy throwing together something to eat while Nea fed the infant flames of their fire. The orange tongues licking over the sticks stirred a memory in the back of her mind ...

"I still don't know why Evard is so obsessed with you," Leon said softly as he stroked the bars of her cell with one fingertip. "You're

attractive—I'll give him that. And that defiance ..." He inhaled slowly and then let the breath out with an almost lusty hiss. "Oh, I cannot wait until he lets me get my hands on you. I am going to enjoy breaking your spirit. Will I beat it out of you? I think not. A beating is too simple." His hands wrapped around the bars. "Your kind doesn't respond all that well to brute force, but if I was to violate that perfect form of yours in other ways ..." He pushed away from the bars as footsteps sounded and Victor, the head jailor, came into view.

"What are you doing down here?"

"We were just having a little chat." Leon sneered at Nea and then brushed by the jailor.

Victor pushed a plate through the slot in the bottom of the door. "You need to eat," he muttered as he took the untouched plate from the day before away.

Janey snapped her fingers in front of Nea's face, scattering the memory. She held up a cup, the familiar scent of peppermint rising from it.

"Thank you."

"We should reach the farmstead Sam mentioned by mid-afternoon tomorrow," Emil said as he settled down next to Penny. "We need a plan."

"I'm going to offer myself up as bait and while Leon is distracted, the rest of you are going to sneak in and get Garret out," Nea said, blowing on her tea.

"That is the worst plan I have ever heard of," Penny said.

Janey's brow furrowed and she hastily signed.

"If we fail, Leon will have both you and Garret. And he will torture you," Emil translated.

"I'm counting on it," Nea said. "He'll be so busy with me that getting Garret out will be easy."

"We don't know what sort of numbers he has with him, or if Garret's corruption has taken over completely. It's far too dangerous," Emil said, leaning forward and spilling his tea.

"Not to mention that Leon's idea of torture is beyond vile and cruel," Penny said.

"All torture is vile and cruel, Penny. I can endure it."

"I saw the memory, Nea," Penny snapped. "It's about power for him. You did something that robbed him of his sense of power, and he means to do the same to you in the most brutal fashion."

Nea licked her lip and swallowed. "I know. But he won't do it straight away. He'll want to savour it—he's not Willem."

"What does Willem have to do with it?" Emil asked.

"He—"

"Nothing," Nea snapped, cutting Penny off. "Willem has nothing to do with it."

Janey made a small noise and met Nea's eye.

"I'm fine. It is in the past, and he is in the ground."

Emil glanced from one face to the next, his confusion slowly giving way to realisation and then a fierce anger as he bolted to his feet, knocking over his tea. "That son of a bitch!"

"Sit down, Emil," Penny said, bending to scoop up the cup as it landed against her foot.

"Willem never managed to follow through with it, anyway. It's a bit hard to assault someone with a knife sticking out of your ribs," Nea said tightly. Though there had been others who were not so lucky—Garret's sister, Bridie, for one.

"Regardless, you are not offering yourself as bait to Leon," Emil said darkly. "Not on my watch."

"I—"

"No! Have you taken complete leave of your senses? How can you be so calm about it when you believe he means to—to—" He couldn't finish the sentence. "It's not worth it. It would kill Garret to know you sacrificed yourself like that to save him."

Nea huffed into her tea, swirling the remaining contents before downing them.

"Wait. When he was taking you to Evard, did he? If he did, I'll tear his fucking head off."

She shook her head. "No. And he had ample opportunity, which makes me believe that he likes using the threat of it more than the actual act. He craves that feeling of absolute power over his victims and will do whatever he can to prolong it. And that is why you will have time to get Garret out."

"We'll think of another plan," Emil said as he sat again.

"I—"

"We will think of something else. I'm not letting you go through with this."

Nea folded her arms, and Emil stabbed at the coals of their fire with a stick, sending a flurry of sparks into the air.

Penny's keen brushed against Nea's mind, and her voice followed. *"He's right, you know?"*

"Of course, he is. But don't tell him that. It will go straight to his head," Nea silently replied.

The afternoon shadows were starting to converge into dusk as Nea and Emil crept through the undergrowth towards the farmhouse that Leon had taken over. Several guards stood watch around the space, at least two of them reanimations. There was no sign of Leon or Kieran, but it was clear that something important was kept here. The door opened, and a woman with grey hair stepped out into the courtyard.

"I don't recognise that necromancer. Do you?" Nea whispered.

Emil shook his head.

As though sensing them, the women turned and scanned the treeline. Nea eased back into the shadows and held her breath. After a few moments, the woman looked away again and headed into one of the outbuildings.

Seconds trickled by, and then the door opened again. This time a man Nea also didn't recognise emerged, followed by Kieran. The necromancer looked thinner than he had before, his movements almost erratic as he glanced about and rubbed at the sides of his head. His silver hair was lank, and his clothes tattered and hanging off his body in a dishevelled mess. Given that Kieran had always erred towards vanity, it was almost shocking to see him looking so unkempt. The corruption mark in the shape of Nea's handprint spanned his cheek, but the edges were still neat, as though the corruption hadn't grown. Did it work differently because Nea had infected him and not the Usurper?

"We should return to the others," Emil whispered.

Nea gave a small nod.

"Well?" Penny asked when they stepped from the trees into the small campsite.

"We didn't see Leon, but Kieran is there as well as a few other mages, wardens, and keen-less, some of which are definitely reanimations.

Janey opened her hands in front of her, a question in her eyes.

"We haven't got a plan yet," Nea said. "But if we wait for full dark, there is plenty of cover that will allow us to get quite close to the house itself before we need to expose ourselves."

Emil nodded. "We might even be able to take out a few of the guards silently to make things easier." He picked up a stick and started tracing out a map of the farmstead in the dirt. "This seems to be the main entrance. And we saw a woman go into this building. There is no indication of where they are keeping Garret or if he is even here, but the house makes the most sense."

"We should still check the barn and that other outbuilding," Nea said. "I think it would be best if we split up and come in from different sides. It does not appear to be a large force. I'd say they have just stopped here to wait for something."

Penny gave her a pointed look. "A necromancer who lets herself be governed by her impulsiveness perhaps."

"Which is why I would rather we go with my plan. At least let me draw Leon out, then you can all sweep in while they are distracted."

"We are not reigniting that argument. You were outvoted, Nea. Just let it go." Emil huffed. "I think full dark is too early. If we wait until after midnight, most of the camp should be asleep, and we'll only have the current watch to deal with. We could be in and out without too much fuss if we took that approach."

Nea licked her lip. "Alright. We should try and get some rest then; I don't think a fire is advisable this close to the farmstead."

Janey signed and then pointed into the trees.

"Sure, we can check it out," Emil said.

They followed Janey down a short slope and then across the stream to an outcrop of stone. The space extended back into a small cave that would provide some decent cover.

Penny flicked out her sleeping roll. "I can take first watch if someone wants to relieve me in a couple of hours."

"I'll take it," Emil said. "You can have the second watch."

It was dark when Nea awoke. Emil was sitting just under the opening of the outcrop. He gave her a smile as she approached. "I thought Penny was taking the second watch?"

"Nature calls." She shrugged and stepped neatly around him.

"Do you want me to come with, just in case?"

"I doubt I'll get into trouble in the few minutes it takes me to find a suitable spot and then get back here." She stifled a yawn and headed towards the sounds of the stream.

She had just finished when the branches of a nearby shrub rustled. Bolting upright, she hastily fastened her pants and scanned the dark trees. A deer emerged, its nose flaring as it studied her before picking a path to the water.

Nea swallowed and moved to the edge of the stream herself. She dipped her hands into the frigid water and then splashed some on her face. The deer's head snapped up and it flicked its ear as though listening to the night around them. Nea listened also.

There was no sound, not even the scurry of small creatures in the underbrush. Then with a snort, the deer leapt away into the forest. Nea slowly rose to her feet and turned to head back to the outcrop, but she came face to face with a woman dressed in dark clothing. It was hard to see her features in the gloom, but she thought she resembled the necromancer from Leon's camp.

"I suggest you remain silent," she whispered as her keen pressed down, gripping the edges of Nea's soul and paralysing her.

The keen felt much like Nea's own but tainted by something that was not corruption. Almost like it had been taken apart and cobbled back together.

"Funny, I expected more of a fight from you." The woman stepped close enough that Nea could make out the soft blue-green colour of her eyes. They flashed, darkening to a deep indigo. "Everyone goes on about how special you are. How the Shadow himself chose you, but I can't see how you're all that different to me."

Nea struggled against the pressure of the woman's keen, but with Garret's suppression blocking her, it was like pounding fists against a wall of stone.

The woman's brow furrowed and then she let out a soft laugh. "Ambrose will be disappointed when he learns you have lost your keen." Her magic pressed down harder, and Nea's knees weakened. "Alright, Hugh."

A man stepped from the shadows, the same one who had been with Kieran. He studied Nea with a frown and then moved forward and took hold of her. "I'm sorry," he whispered so softly Nea wouldn't have heard it if his lips hadn't been right beside her ear. Then he scooped her up and settled her over his shoulder as he followed the woman into the dark trees.

When they reached the farmhouse, he deposited her on the ground and hastily tied her hands behind her back. Only once the thin cotton of a gag had been pressed across her mouth and fastened cruelly tight behind her head did the pressure of the woman's keen relent.

"You don't think that's a bit tight, Gwyn?" Hugh asked the woman.

"I don't hear her complaining." There was a smirk in her voice, and Hugh, who was standing in front of Nea, frowned.

Now that Gwyn's magic wasn't pressing down on her, she could feel his keen—soft and warm like Margot's, and at the same time a bright crackle that reminded her of Donnic. He stepped aside, and a tremor ran through her as Leon's gaze settled on her and the familiar lecherous sneer pulled across his features.

"Hello, Nea. I was wondering when you'd join the party."

CHAPTER TWENTY-FOUR

GARRET

A sharp slap against Garret's face wrenched him from sleep. He leapt up, nearly colliding with the person in front of him, only to be stopped short by the chain that anchored him to the wall.

Leon's gloating snigger sounded from the gloom.

Garret had no idea what time it was but going by the darkness and the chill in the air, it wasn't yet dawn.

"Sorry to interrupt what I am sure was a delightful dream," Leon said as he picked something up from the table. The watery moonlight glittered along the edge of a knife. "There has been a development that I thought you needed to be made aware of. After all, I can't torture you into submission if you do not know the stakes." He snapped his fingers, and the door opened.

The glare of a green mage light momentarily blinded him, and he lifted his hand to shield his eyes. Someone entered the room, dragging something heavy. They deposited their burden on the floor at Leon's feet.

Garret blinked, willing the haze to clear from his vision as the dark shape on the floor struggled to their feet.

Leon grabbed the captive and pulled them against his chest, knife flashing in the light as it pressed against the side of their neck.

The spots finally cleared, and Garret's blood turned to ice as Nea's violet gaze met his. The piece of cloth gagging her couldn't hide her split lip or the blossoming bruise that darkened one side of her face. She struggled against Leon's grip, the knife drawing a thin line of red as it edged dangerously close to her throat.

"That's enough of that," Leon growled in her ear, dropping the knife and grabbing hold of her hair, which had been dyed black again. He yanked it hard, and she let out a muffled yelp. "Can't have you prematurely killing yourself before I've had a chance to have some *fun.*"

"Let her go. You have me. You don't need Nea as well."

Leon let out a snort of a laugh and tightened his hold on Nea. "I did tell you once I was going to make you watch as I showed you what a real man does when he is presented with an insolent bitch. Even a will as strong as Nea's can be broken with the right approach." He traced a fingertip along her bruised cheek before gripping her chin savagely and forcing her to meet his eye. "Had you not been so defiant in the past, you might have saved yourself from what is to come." He inhaled sharply and released her. "Hugh, if you would see that Nea is made comfortable."

Hugh stepped into the light and took hold of Nea's arm, guiding her towards the door. She struggled against him, but he whispered something that made her stop. Then he threw a dark look in Leon's direction before leaving the room.

Leon didn't notice the look from Hugh as he had already turned his gloating gaze back to Garret. "Well, Garret, how does that little development make you feel?"

Garret stared at the door; his heart hammering in his chest. He knew exactly what Leon had planned for Nea, and there was no way he could prevent it. Not while he was chained here.

"Not going to answer the question? Can it be that I have defeated you with the simple threat of what I will do to Nea? You could have prevented her suffering. After all, you're the reason she is here."

Leon picked up the discarded knife and whistled as he moved towards the door. "I am disappointed in you, Garret. I expected more of a show, but then we are only just getting started."

Whoosh—crack.

Murmured voices.

Crack.

Garret winced and glared at the opened window. He couldn't see what was going on outside, but he didn't need to see it to know. It had been going on for a while—no sound except for the steady *whoosh-crack* of a thorough whipping.

Crack. This time followed by a grunted whimper.

"There's no sense in holding it in, my dear," Leon's sneering voice said. "Let him hear you scream."

Whoosh—crack.

Garret winced again. "Just give him what he wants. Please, Nea," he whispered.

Crack. Crack. Crack.

More murmured voices.

"Again!" Leon snarled.

"But, sir—" The soldier's words were cut off by the sound of a solid punch.

"You don't stop until I tell you to. Hit. Her. Again."

"Her body can't take much more; she'll pass out if we keep going."

Leon let out a huff. "Get Hugh," he ordered in a tone that was pure ice.

Footsteps pounded as a shadow raced past the window.

"You can end your own agony, my dear," Leon said. "Just one little scream and I will give you a reprieve."

"Go fuck yourself." Nea panted.

Smack! That sounded like a backhanded strike against a cheek.

Garret tugged against the chain, but it held fast.

"My, my, what do we have here?" An oily voice—one Garret recognised from his dream. "Is this any way to treat someone as special as this lovely specimen?"

"We weren't expecting you," Leon said sharply.

"I prefer it when I am unexpected," the oily voice replied. "I am certain the Master would not be impressed with this. Nea is very dear to him. Aren't you, pet?"

Nea muttered something.

"Such profanity." The man made a tutting noise. "Surely Sophia would have taught you better manners ... then again she said something similar to me right before I killed her. I guess the apple doesn't fall all that far from the tree after all."

"The Master has no objections." It sounded like the words were ground out through Leon's teeth.

"Let him speak for himself."

Leon let out a growl, and then something thumped against the side of the house. His fist? "You can't just—" His words were cut off, and then a silkier voice that Garret recognised as the Usurper said, "Have you found the thrones yet, Ambrose?"

"Not yet, but I believe we are close. Julianna has had her mages scouting the range behind Merston. Now that we have both the brightling and the deera solvec in our possession, we shouldn't have any trouble going forward," Ambrose said.

"Have you not noticed that our dear Nea seems to have gotten herself into a rather confounding predicament?" The Usurper's tone became tight.

"Surely you can control Leon, given that you are sharing his body."

"It does not work as seamlessly as that. But I am not talking about Leon's perversions. I am talking about her *keen*."

What about Nea's keen? Garret assumed Leon had drugged her with mage bane or put a pair of bind-shackles on her. He craned his neck, tilting his ear towards the window to hear better.

"A rather disappointing development indeed. But if that is the case then we might as well put her out of her misery."

"Don't be a fool. You kill her and you will kill the brightling as well. Aside from his corruption, his keen remains intact, and his will can be forced."

"Then is that what Leon is attempting here? To use Nea's suffering to force the brightling to do our bidding? Why not just have Gwyn or Amelia control him."

"Amelia has become unpredictable, and Gwyn is nowhere near powerful enough to control him if his powers are unbound. Which they will need to be to claim the thrones."

A shadow passed the window.

"Ambrose, I thought you were still at Merston," Hugh said.

"I shall return there shortly. I simply wanted to see the deera solvec for myself. I must say, I am disappointed. I believe I will leave you to it and check in with Gwyn before I depart. Master." There was a disrespectful note beneath Ambrose's tone. Perhaps Amelia wasn't the only one entertaining thoughts of rebelling against the Usurper.

"Heal her," Leon's voice barked.

"So you can do this all over again?" Hugh replied, an edge to his voice. "It would be better to let her have a proper rest. Magical healing can be taxing and—"

Something crashed against the side of the house, and Hugh let out a pained grunt.

"I did not ask for your opinion. I ordered you to heal her."

"Fine." Hugh's voice was tight.

"You see, Nea, I am not a complete monster," Leon crooned after a few moments.

She murmured something too quiet for Garret to hear.

Smack.

"The sooner you learn the consequences of your insolence, the better for you." The sound of fingers snapping in a hurry up gesture. "Proceed."

Silence fractured by a lilted note of birdsong and a mumbled protest.

"WHIP HER!" Leon roared.

Whoosh—crack.

Garret pressed his face into his hands and sat on the bed. He desperately wanted to block out the sound of the whip cutting into Nea's flesh, but if she could endure the physical torture, then he could endure the mental.

Finally, after what felt like hours, a gasping yelp of pain echoed through the window, followed by a sob. Garret shut his eyes and swallowed the bile that had risen in his throat.

The next blow and the three that followed came with agonised cries, each getting louder than the last.

"That's enough," Leon said, his tone edged with pleasure. "I told you I would break you, my dear, and this … this is just the beginning. Take her to Hugh. Tell him I want her whole again by evening."

The door opened, and Leon strode in, a gloating smile on his face as he marched to the window and snapped it shut. He turned slowly and regarded Garret as he folded his arms over his chest. "I almost thought she wouldn't break. But there you have it. Even the most defiant of souls has a breaking point. By this time tomorrow, she will do anything I ask just to spare herself more suffering. And what about you? If I promise to spare her further torment, will you supplicate yourself before me?"

Garret ground his back teeth together. Yes, he would do anything to stop Leon from continuing to hurt Nea, but Leon enjoyed the feeling of power too much to keep that promise. Nea could endure a little longer, and so could Garret. Just long enough to figure out how to get himself free. If he worked at it, maybe he could loosen the loop that anchored his chains.

"I'll take that as a no." Leon's head tilted. "Or is it a *not yet*? We'll see how you're feeling after tomorrow's demonstration."

Garret didn't sleep much that night. Every time he closed his eyes, he could hear Nea being whipped … could imagine her violet eyes glossy with tears. He was working at the points that anchored his chains to the wall, but they remained steadfast. Still, if he kept at it, then maybe they would loosen just enough.

As birdsong announced the morning, the door opened, and Gwyn came in bearing a tray.

"I'm not hungry," he said by way of greeting. Actually, he was famished, but he wasn't going to eat anything she offered. Not after she had drugged him, and certainly not since she was working with Leon.

She worried her lip and placed the tray neatly on the floor just within his reach then moved to the hearth and lit the fire. "I'm sorry."

"You're sorry?" He folded his arms and sat up straighter. "For what?"

"For … I didn't realise …"

"That Leon is a completely unhinged brute?"

"He's not," she said, turning away from the growing flames to face him again. "The Master's vision for this world will exact a heavy price, but it will be worth it."

"Worth what he is doing to Nea? I doubt she would agree … Do you think because she was the one who the Shadow chose and not you that she is somehow deserving of what Leon has done to her? Of what he intends to do to her?"

She licked her lip, her eyes changing from blue-green to indigo and back again. "She is standing in the way. I would welcome the Master's plan, regardless of the cost."

"Remember those words when Leon turns on you. Because he will. As soon as you are no longer useful, he will cast you aside and then you'll be the one whose screams put that sick smile on his face. If you don't believe me, ask Hugh for his opinion on the matter."

She rested her hand on the door handle. "You should eat something before Leon gets here." And then she was gone again.

Garret examined the contents on the tray. A cup of tea and a bowl of porridge. He scrunched his nose and moved to push it away, but his eyes found the spoon. After dragging the tray closer, he picked the utensil up and tilted it in the light. It wasn't the best weapon, but he could definitely do some damage with it if Leon got close enough. He nudged the tray back out of his reach, the liquid in the cup splashing out.

Leon left him alone for most of the day, which was concerning. Gwyn had been in and out to tend the fire, but she barely spoke to him other than to insist he eat something. He considered asking her about Nea, but he wouldn't give Leon the satisfaction, and he wasn't certain he wanted to know what was happening to her at that moment.

It was well into late afternoon when Leon finally arrived. "Not hungry?" he asked, fingering the branding iron he was carrying as he examined the most recently discarded tray of food. "I can't blame you. The anticipation is enough to drive away even my hunger. I've barely scratched the surface of Nea's resolve. Do you know she had the gall to tell me she would kill me the first chance she got?" He made a tutting noise and shook his head as he moved to the hearth and placed the brand within the flames. "Foolish, really, when I have already proved that I can break her. Of course, I had no choice but to prove it again. She's quite the little wildcat when she's cornered, isn't she?" He touched his fingers to the new scar that intersected his lower lip. It was a jagged tear that had not healed well.

Had Hugh deliberately let it scar or had Nea torn the lip in such a way that even magical healing couldn't prevent the scarring? To cause that kind of damage, she would have had to have bitten him, surely. But for her to bite his lip, he would have been extremely close. The bottom dropped out of Garret's stomach.

"Would you like to know what I have planned or would you rather be surprised? You and Nea are in for quite the experience, and I am certain at least one of you is going to be eating out of the palm of my hand by the time I am done."

"You're sounding a lot like Evard and look how he ended up."

Leon made a rush for him but stopped just out of reach. "Do you know what is worse than a broken spirit?" he hissed. "A *violated* one."

Garret's fingers tightened around the spoon. The second Leon stepped within reach he would drive it into his eye.

"We are ready," Leon called towards the door.

The same wardens who'd helped Leon restrain Garret entered, dragging a struggling Nea. She was wearing an oversized shirt that was stained with patches of blood. A scar twisted across the right side of her face from her ear to just above her lip. It was the deep pink of newly healed skin.

"Ah, Nea, I am so glad you could join us," Leon purred as if they were merely sitting down to tea.

"Like I had a choice in the matter," Nea spat. She refused to meet Garret's eye, instead keeping her gaze firmly locked on Leon.

"Now, now, my dear. And we were starting to get along so well." He lifted his hand to touch her scarred cheek, but she twisted her face away from him. "It was a shame to ruin such a lovely face, but your insolence couldn't go unpunished." Dropping his hand, he moved to the fire and lifted the brand from the flames to show her the glowing end. "Tell me, do you recognise this?"

Last time Garret had seen it, the end had been ignited with violet magic.

"It leaves such a distinct mark." Leon traced his fingers over his own scarred cheek and gave a nod.

One of the wardens slammed Nea's back against the tabletop. She kicked and struggled, but he pressed down harder.

"Don't—"

The second warden slapped her, cutting off her plea, and then ripped her shirt, exposing the pale flesh of her torso, which was littered with purple bruises.

"Now where should I test it? Hmmm?"

Nea shuddered as Leon traced his fingers over her skin.

"Such a pristine landscape. It seems a terrible shame to spoil it." He met Garret's eye with a smirk.

Garret bit the inside of his cheek. He didn't want to give Leon any more ammunition. His grip tightened on the spoon as he put weight on the chains.

"How disappointing. I expected more of a fuss from the pair of you." He pressed the brand into the skin over Nea's ribs, and she bit her lip, muffling her scream.

"Very nice." He heated the iron again. "But what about ..."

This time he held it to her chest, and she couldn't hold the scream in—it ended in a sob and a rasping, "please."

"Oh, Nea, don't tell me a few touches of a brand and that steadfast resolve of yours is gone?" Leon purred. "Come now. I know you better than that."

"Please—" The word dissolved into another scream as he pressed the brand against her skin again.

"Stop," Garret growled as he pulled the chains. "Let her go, and I'll do whatever you ask."

"No!" Nea twisted, trying to look in Garret's direction. "You can't let him—" Her yelp of pain cut through her words as Leon touched the brand against her side with a laugh.

"Oh, now this is more like it."

The chains creaked, and Garret leant against them harder. It was no use—the anchor point on the chain barely moved. He glared at the bands of rose-gold around his wrists. If he focused hard enough, could he make them release? He'd done it before, but he hadn't been the one shackled at the time. If only he had access to his suppression, so he could try. His suppression. Distracted by what Leon was doing to Nea, he hadn't noticed the numbness that had returned to his core. He let it build, forcing it into the shackles and seeking out the magic that gave them purpose. Pain sliced through his wrists, burning pain that made him stop.

Then Nea gasped and sobbed.

He bit down against the pain and drove his suppression into the shackles. The first fell away with a dull clunk, followed closely by the second. Ignoring the pain tearing at his wrists, he threw all his weight against the chains once more. They gave way, and he stumbled to the ground.

Leon let out a yell as Garret tackled him, the branding iron skittering across the floor. Lightning and cold necromancy crackled under his skin, fighting for release, but he pushed it down. He was going to tear Leon apart with his bare hands. Spoon still clutched in his fingers, he drove it towards Leon's face, but the bastard struggled and thrashed, and the spoon left a grating line across his cheek instead of meeting Garret's intended mark.

"Get him off me!" Leon snarled.

Hands grabbed the back of Garret's shirt, attempting to haul him up, but he thrust his elbow backwards and the warden behind him grunted.

Leon's knuckles found Garret's jaw. "Restrain him now!" He panted in a wild panic as Garret grabbed him by the throat and slammed his head against the floor. "You can't kill me. I'm as immortal as Amelia now," he rasped.

The door banged open. "What the fuck is going on in here?" Emil asked. "Garret, where's—Nea!" He rushed around Leon and Garret.

"I'm ... just get Garret," she panted.

Emil grabbed the back of Garret's shirt. "I know he deserves it, but we need to get out of here." He started to drag Garret towards the door.

"Not until I tear his fucking throat out."

"There's no time." Emil gave him another shove towards the door. "Come on. Otherwise Nea suffered for nothing."

Garret swallowed and looked back at Leon's dazed form. "What you did to her is pale in comparison to what is coming for you." He let Emil drag him away.

Outside was utter chaos. The barn was on fire, and guards were running about yelling for buckets. Emil led him to the treeline where Penny was waiting, wringing her hands.

"Where's Nea?" Garret asked.

"With Janey and that Hugh fellow."

"Hugh? He works for Leon."

"Not anymore," Penny said. "He's the one who helped us, and he's tending to Nea's wounds. Did Leon ..." Her eyes widened as she looked from Garret to Emil and back again. "What did he do to her?"

"He tortured her. What do you think he did?" Garret said sharply. Now that the shackles were gone, the corruption was rearing its head, flared on by his fear for Nea and anger at Leon.

"Come on. We need to get out of here before Leon rallies his men and comes after us." Emil waved them on, and Penny took off with a nod.

She led them into the forest, across a small stream, and past an outcrop of rock and didn't stop until they reached a small section of cleared trees a good way from the farmstead.

Janey and Hugh were sitting with Nea in the centre of the clearing. She was already dressed in a change of clothes, her face several shades paler than normal.

"I tried to minimise the scarring."

Nea nodded slowly. "Thank you. I'm sorry I punched you."

Hugh rubbed his jaw and stood. "It's alright. I probably would have punched me too if I had just been through what you have."

"Nea," Garret said softly.

Her gaze snapped to him, and her lower lip wavered as she bit down on it. "I'm ... Hugh healed me." She swallowed and stood.

Garret strode to her and pulled her tight against his chest as he buried his face in her hair. "I'm sorry."

She tensed. "I'll be fine. It's nothing that a little bit of time can't fix." Her attempt at a light tone was ruined by the tremor in her voice. The source around them tightened as her fingers gripped his shirt, and she pressed her face harder against his chest. The tightness released with a shudder as she let out a sob.

"*We should give you some space.*" Janey signed and ushered Hugh away.

Garret smoothed a hand over Nea's hair. His eyes were suddenly stinging, and he rubbed them. "Why did you risk coming after Leon?"

A jolt ran through her, and she pushed away from him, a fire in her violet gaze despite the tears she was swiping away.

"Why did you go after him in the first place? And with a raging case of corruption no less."

"I had it under control."

"That was under *control,* was it? Because the only person in control at that farmstead was Leon." She said his name with a whimper and rubbed her hands over her face.

"Nea ..." He reached for her, but she shied away.

"I can't do this right now. I need some space." She spun on her heels and ran.

"Nea, wait." He started after her, but Janey caught his arm and pulled him up short.

"*I'll go. She needs space and someone who understands what she has been through.*" She gestured to the ragged scar across her throat, her eyes full of meaning.

Garret let out a shuddering breath and nodded.

Janey patted his arm then snapped her fingers at Penny and indicated the swinging branches Nea had disturbed in her mad dash to escape.

 NEA

Branches whipped against her as she ran, loam and moss skidding under her feet. A slope she hadn't anticipated brought her to her hands and knees, nose inches above the chill waters of a woodland stream.

Blood and smoke and ash clouded her senses, and she pressed the back of her hand over her mouth as the screams of the dying overshadowed the subtle sounds of the forest. She dipped her fingers into the frigid water, dirt and blood blooming like oversized flowers across the surface only to be washed away.

"Nea?" A light hand touched her shoulder.

She bolted to her feet, ready to flee.

"It's Penny."

Her breath was coming too fast, her ribs tightening with each gasp. Hot and cold fingers scraped across her shoulders and up the back of her neck.

"You're safe." A touch of magic on her mind, soft and suggestive.

She wasn't safe; her safety had been stolen from her by the bite of braided leather against her back, the cruel kiss of hot metal against her skin, and the—she couldn't hold in the sob. It tore through her, loosening all the terrors and hurts—those that were new and those that had already scarred over. Images from Kalhanna all mixed up with Leon's sneering face and soft promises of relief if she just surrendered. But the relief was only replaced with more pain, more fear—empty promises.

"Make me forget, Pen," she whispered.

"I don't think that is wise."

"I can't keep going like this. I want to forget. I *need* to."

A soft hand touched her arm, and she met Janey's gaze. Janey nodded and gestured to the scar at her throat, then she slowly turned and lifted her shirt. Her back was a patchwork of scars: thin, neat lines, and thicker, ropey slices. Nea clenched her fists and swallowed as Janey lowered her shirt again and turned back to face her.

"I didn't realise."

Janey gave her a sad smile and signed something.

"I was only young," Penny translated. "Time makes it easier."

"It's too much." The source quivered. "I can't."

Janey grabbed hold of her hands and gave them a squeeze then drew her into a hug, rubbing small circles on her back. "You can," she said in that strained voice she used when she absolutely had too. "You're strong."

"Janey's right. You are the strongest person I know," Penny said. "Anyone else would have given up after Kalhanna. Most people probably would have given up before the purge. Don't let Leon win."

A hot tear rolled down her cheek and dripped off her lip. "But he has won already."

"Only if you *let* him."

She met Penny's dark gaze over Janey's shoulder. Penny was right; Leon's goal had been to break her, and if she fell to pieces now then he had won. Every part of her felt fragile, ready to disperse with the first strong breeze like the downy seeds of a dandelion. But she could hold it together to see this through, just like she had been doing since the purge. Once it was all over, then she could breakdown. Garret had told her it was her scars that reminded her she was human, and Leon had just given her a whole heap more. She bit her lip. It would be hard, but she could keep fighting through this. She wasn't going to let Leon win. She would tear his soul out and banish it to the farthest depths of the Between, the Usurper's along with it, but first she needed to find the thrones, and for that she would need—"I have to fix my keen."

"That shouldn't be a problem," Penny said.

"I'm not so sure."

Janey leant back and gestured to the air around her with a grin.

"What Janey means is the source has been responding to you ever since we got you back from Leon. I would hazard a guess that the proximity to Garret has something to do with it; it is his warden keen that is blocking yours, after all."

Garret. She worried her lip. He had been with Leon longer than she had, and he'd been forced to listen and watch as Leon tortured her. It hadn't just been about breaking Nea—it had been about breaking Garret, too, and she had pushed him away when he needed her most. "I'm a selfish idiot," she muttered. "I was so caught up in my own panic that I didn't stop to think about what Garret has been through."

"He'll be fine. I am sure Emil is proving to be a distraction," Penny said. "What would Nonna say? You can't pour from an empty jug. You are in no state to be worrying about fixing Garret right now."

Janey nodded.

"Try accessing your keen," Penny prompted.

Nea turned her attention inward. The numb throb of suppression still blanketed out every other feeling, but there was a chill seeping through at the edges—small cracks that would eventually collapse the dam. She focused on the closest, latching onto that chill like a piece of a soul and giving it an experimental tug.

For a moment, she was hit with an overwhelming assortment of sensations. Penny's mind magic, Janey's fiery keen, the bright burning of Garret under the ward mark. She let out a rough gasp and wrapped her arms around herself.

Janey clapped her hands.

"You almost had it. Try again," Penny said.

With a steadying breath, Nea latched onto that cold sensation again. It was stronger now; a deep, bone-chilling blizzard held back by a tattered curtain. She dug into the tears and ripped them clean open. The force of her keen barrelling back into her body sent her to her knees with a choking cough. She lifted her hand and watched as sparks of lilac danced across her fingertips, then she summoned a mage light. The small purple orb flickered to life and then shifted to green, blue, pink, and red before she closed her fingers over it and snuffed it out. Her keen was back, and it seemed stronger than ever.

"I was starting to think I would never feel that again," she said softly.

Janey studied Nea's fingers, her head tilted. She flicked a look at Penny and signed.

"I don't know, but Nea's keen has always been different." Penny shrugged and turned to Nea. "How do you get the mage light to change colours?" she asked.

"Mage light derives its colour from the way our keen interacts with the source, kind of like sunlight refracted through a prism. With a little bit of effort, we can alter that interaction; not enough to completely alter our keen, but just enough to change the colour of our mage light. My father never showed you?"

Penny shook her head.

An amber light burst to life in front of Janey, and her tongue stuck out of the corner of her mouth as her brow furrowed and her keen grew hot. After a few moments, her keen died down again, the light still glowing a soft orange.

"It takes a bit of practice. Our magic travels along the path with the least resistance. Even a subtle change can be like trying to divert a river one stone at a time." Discussing the mechanics of magic brought a stillness to her mind. It couldn't take away the terror or pain, but it eased it somehow, made it bearable. "We should be getting back to the others."

Emil and Hugh were waiting in the clearing, but Garret was nowhere in sight.

"Where's Garret?" Nea asked, a tremor running through her.

"That way," Emil said, pointing to the right.

"You let him go off on his own?"

"He's not exactly in the best mood—"

"Of course he's not. Leon tortured him!" She took off through the trees. "Garret?"

No answer.

She could barely feel him above her fear that Leon had somehow taken him again. "Garret, please answer me." She caught a flash of movement and changed course.

There he was.

His back was to her, his fists clenched by his sides, the purple lines of the death ward visible through the torn sleeve of his shirt. His keen radiated out in spikes as though he was trying to regain control. Beneath the bright warmth was the seething wrongness of corruption.

"Garret?"

"I know you have faith in me, Nea, but I can't keep fighting it. You put the Usurper inside Leon, which means he cannot be killed by normal means. But if I let it take over, I can use it to destroy them both." His tone was cold steel, his knuckles growing white as he clenched his fists tighter. "The only thing holding it back is the thought that I might disappoint you."

"That can't be the only reason," she said softly. "Garret, look at me."

He shook his head. "I can't."

She moved to his side and gently took hold of his face, turning it to meet hers. His eyes were closed tight, a sheen on his cheeks that could have been the remnants of tears. "Please look at me."

Slowly, he opened his eyes, his frown depending. "I couldn't save you."

"I'm fi—I'm still here. We're both still here, and I have no intention of going anywhere without you again ... I'll be alright." She rubbed her thumbs over his cheeks, dashing away the wetness. "We'll both be."

He lifted his hands as though he wanted to touch her but lowered them again.

"It's alright." She dropped her grip on his face and took hold of his hands, winding his arms behind her waist as she burrowed against him. Her keen was calling to his, seeking to soothe the corruption that was threatening to consume him. His arms tightened around her, and he rested his chin on her shoulder as a tremor went through him.

She ran her keen slowly along the edge of his, finding the point where it tangled with the corruption. The taint reared back as she tried to grab hold of it, but she let her keen surge forward, consuming the darkness and dragging it towards herself.

The tension left Garret the moment the corruption entered Nea's body. She bit her lip hard enough to draw blood as the taint prickled through her veins and roared across her mind, trying to bend her to its will.

"Nea, what are you doing?" Garret started to pull back from her.

"Don't let me go." If he let her go, she would get swept away by the corruption. Her right arm itched, the swirling grey lines shifting between a deep midnight purple and a fathomless black. The itch drew into the centre of her palm, culminating into a wild heat. She let go of Garret and reached for the closest tree. Rough bark rubbed against her skin as she forced the corruption out of her body. A webbing of black fanned over the bark, and the leaves above them shrivelled and darkened. Then with a loud sigh the whole tree collapsed into a pile of blackened ash.

"It's gone." The relief in Garret's tone was palpable, and he gripped her tightly once more. "Are you alright?" Still holding her shoulders, he pulled back far enough to search her face.

"I'll be okay. It took a lot out of me." She pressed her sleeve to her nose to stem the blood. "We should go back to the others and try and put as much distance between us and Leon as we can."

Garret's gaze darkened, and his fingers tensed as they laced with hers, but he said nothing as they walked slowly back to the clearing where the others were waiting.

"Alright, Pen, pay up," Emil said as they emerged from the trees.

Penny rolled her eyes and slapped a coin onto Emil's open palm. "What now?" she asked Nea and Garret.

"We should head to meet Margot and the others," Nea said.

"Do you think they will still be there when we get back?"

"We might even beat them." Nea held out a hand to create a portal.

"Are you sure you've recovered enough to channel the amount of source required for that?" Garret asked, his tone was casual enough, but the fingers laced with Nea's quivered.

"It'll be fine. We're not crossing the barrier." She let her power build at her core then focused on Camille's farmstead. The air in front of her palm shimmered, then an oval sprung open. She drew a steadying breath as the oval flickered, threatening to close. "Go on," she prompted.

Penny, Emil, and Janey leapt through, but Hugh was staring at the portal with his mouth agape.

"Are you coming?"

"No. I'll make my own way." He backed away from the portal.

"Thank you for your help," Nea said then stepped into the glimmering doorway, tugging Garret after her.

The second they emerged, the portal snapped shut and Nea stumbled. Garret caught her and looped his arm around her waist for support.

"No more magic tonight," he said tightly.

"I'm fine."

"You're not. You need to rest."

She reached up and cupped the sides of his face. "I know my limitations better than most."

"And yet you always ignore them."

He had a point. She bit down on her retort.

The door opened, and Bran stuck his head out. "We were wondering when you would get here. I see you found Garret." His smile dropped. "Shadow's teeth, what happened to you?"

"Leon," Emil said, wincing sharply as Penny prodded his side.

"Look out, Bran. Let them in," Margot's voice called.

The kitchen could barely fit them all. "Right, if you are not in need of my urgent attention, I suggest you get out and give me some space. Not you, Molly."

Everyone except Molly, Nea, and Garret left. Garret collapsed into a chair at the table with a heavy sigh.

"I'll make some tea," Molly said.

Margot's keen swelled. It was different now that she shared her body with the anchor, but still at the very core it was the gentle warmth of healing magic. A soft green mist permeated the air around Garret, and the bruises faded, the split in his lip sealing. Once she was done with Garret, she turned her attention to Nea.

"I'm alright, Margot, just worn out."

But Margot ignored her, and the soothing feeling of sliding into a hot bath rolled over her. "What happened to Garret's corruption?" Margot asked as her keen drew away from Nea and she took a cup of tea from Molly.

"I got rid of it," Nea said, inhaling the steam from her own tea with an involuntary sigh.

"You got rid of it?"

"Yes," Nea replied. "Apparently, the anchor spirit isn't the only one capable of healing corruption. It probably has something to do with the Shadow blood."

Margot shifted her gaze to Garret and let a long breath out through her nose. Her lips were pursed in that way that suggested she was about to deal with a particularly stubborn patient. "You two need rest. Do you need me to fix you a sleeping draught instead of the tea?"

Nea shook her head. "That won't be necessary."

"Garret?"

"No, I'll be fine." He stood and took hold of Nea's hand once more. "We'll see you in the morning." He led Nea down the hall to the room at the end.

It was small with minimal personal effects, save for the little collection of carved animals on the windowsill. Garret moved to the table beside the bed and placed his tea down. "I understand if you don't want to share the bed, but I don't think I'll be able to sleep without you close by. I'll take the floor."

"Don't be ridiculous." She placed her cup next to his.

"After what you've been—"

"I'm fine."

"But Leon ..." He didn't quite meet her eye.

Was he worried Leon had raped her? Was that what had been bothering him? Why he seemed so afraid she might break if he touched her?

"He didn't rape me."

A jolt ran through him. "But—"

"He threatened to, but it never came to that. Not after I nearly tore his lip off, anyway." She tried to keep her voice even. Biting Leon had resulted in the scar that now marked her cheek and a beating that probably would have killed her if Hugh hadn't stepped in. "Is that why you've been treating me like I'm fragile, like I'll shatter if you touch me?"

"I thought ... you ..." His jaw tightened, and he swallowed.

"Garret." She lowered herself onto his lap, her knees brushing against the outside of his thighs as she looped her arms around the back of his neck. "I was worried about you. After what Leon put you through, I didn't want to push *you* too far. I would usually tell you

I'm fine, but I am not. And this time I can't hide behind that lie because it's too far from the truth. It's going to take time to heal, but I am not going anywhere. And I'm not going to break if you touch me. You should know by now I'm made of tougher stuff than that." She fought to keep the waver out of her voice, and she hoped he didn't notice the tremble in her fingers as she plied them through his hair.

He let out a soft, slightly bitter chuckle. It was the first sign of humour he'd shown since they escaped Leon's encampment. Slowly, his arms came around her, and he pulled her close, his cheek resting against the centre of her chest as a shudder ran through him.

Nea wasn't sure how long they sat like that, but the prickling rush of pins and needles started in her toes as the noises of the rest of their group out in the kitchen reached them. Voices murmured and footsteps sounded in the hall as the others found rooms for the night. Nea pressed a kiss to Garret's forehead and slid off his lap. She stripped to her underwear and then crawled under the blanket.

Garret pulled his shirt off. Moonlight shone over the silver webbing of corruption scars that reached up his side from his hip to his armpit. He rubbed his hand over them before sliding into the bed beside her. There was barely enough room for the pair of them, but Nea didn't mind as Garret's arms wove around her again and pulled her close. The steady beat of his heart and the gentle stirring of his breath against her hair slowly lulled her. Garret was her safe harbour; she had known that since their time in the Between. He made her feel safe, but more importantly, he made her feel *home* in a way nothing had ever made her feel before.

"Garret?"

"Hmm?" he mumbled sleepily.

"I love you. You know that, right?" she whispered.

He pressed his lips to the back of her head. "I am not sure I deserve it. But I know, and I love you too."

CHAPTER TWENTY-SIX

MARGOT

"We should probably get up. I think I just heard Declan and Bran in the kitchen, and that can't end well," Molly said as she rolled over.

"Or we could just stay here and let the others deal with it," Margot said, roping her arms around Molly's waist.

Molly chuckled and rolled around, so their chests were pressed against each other. "I'm normally the one who argues for a sleep in."

"And I have finally figured out why." Margot touched her lips to the end of Molly's nose then dropped them to her mouth.

Molly was right, of course. They needed to get moving, and not just because Declan and Bran might destroy the kitchen in their efforts to make breakfast. There hadn't been time last night to tell Nea about the map they had found at Loch Bastien. And even if there had been, she wouldn't have burdened her with it. Both Nea and Garret had looked worse than Margot had ever seen them. It was best to let them rest and recover. A decision she was happy with once Penny and Emil had filled her in on what happened, or the details they knew at least. The thought of what Leon may have done to them both made her heart ache. Maybe if she stayed here where the bed was warm and laced with the soft, sweet-orange scent of Molly's favourite soap, they could avoid any more suffering.

"Are you awake, Molly?" Bran asked as he knocked against the door. "I can't remember what you put in those breakfast cakes."

Molly extracted herself from Margot and pressed another kiss to her lips before pulling her shirt on and opening the door. "I'll be out in a minute," she said softly to Bran. "Try not to wake the whole household." She closed the door and found the rest of her clothes. "Meet me in the kitchen when you are ready."

"No point in staying here now," Margot muttered as she tossed the blankets off and gave Molly a grin. "I'll join you shortly."

When Margot emerged from the room, Declan was standing at the end of the hall, his ear pressed against the door Garret and Nea had taken the night before.

"What are you doing?" Margot whispered.

"Garret's usually up before the sun."

"He was dead on his feet last night. I imagine he's catching up on all the sleep he has been avoiding for the last couple of months."

Declan licked his lip as he studied the door. "What if they went running off without us again?" He rested his fingers on the knob.

"I doubt they would have in the state they were both in, and besides, they don't know about the map yet."

"Still can't hurt to check." He pushed the door open slowly and peeked inside.

Margot ducked her head under his arm and had a look herself. The room was bathed in sunlight. Two cups of tea sat on the table beside the bed. Nea was lying facing the door, her braid coiling across the pillow and her dark lashes resting against her cheek. Garret's arm was over her waist, their fingers woven together. "Satisfied?" Margot whispered.

"Spying on Nea and Garret, are we?" Emil asked quietly.

"Alright, you lot, shut that door before you wake them. Nea was always a light sleeper, and I imagine Garret is no different," Penny hissed behind them.

Declan closed the door, and they all crept towards the kitchen. "Anyone else suddenly feel all warm and fuzzy inside? Like that was the most innocent thing you've ever witnessed?"

"What's gotten into Declan?" Bran asked. He was up to his elbows in a bowl of dough.

"Nothing. He just had to check to make sure Nea and Garret didn't run off in the night to take on the Usurper by themselves. They didn't, of course."

"Nea wouldn't go running off on us again." Bran pulled the ball of dough out of the bowl and dropped it onto the floured benchtop. "But Declan is right. They are pretty cute when they're sleeping. Like a savage dog who you know is going to try and tear your arms off when it wakes up but looks so innocent and loveable at rest that you almost want to pat it."

Emil let out a loud laugh. "You owe me by the way, Molly."

She shook her head. "No, actually, you owe me. Nea confirmed that the attraction was initially magical in origin."

"That is clearly not the case now."

"Doesn't matter," Molly said, pinching off a ball of Bran's dough and shaping it.

Janey, who was making the tea, grinned. "*Magic or not, it took them long enough.*" She signed.

"Indeed. Though you are hardly one to talk." Declan chuckled.

"*That was Harvey's doing, not mine.*" Her smile widened. "*It wasn't my fault that he was too blind to read the signs.*"

The kitchen dissolved into laughter once more.

"Okay, calm down, everyone," Penny said with a sobering chuckle. "We don't want to wake them prematurely; they've earned this chance to rest; three times over at least. Now where is this map?"

"In my journal," Bran said, pointing to the open pack on the end of the table.

Margot fished the journal out of the bag and handed it to Penny as Janey prepared cups of tea for everyone and Molly slid a tray into the oven.

A short while later, Nea emerged from the hallway. Declan offered her a cup of tea, and she took it with a sleepy smile of thanks before folding herself into a chair.

"Something smells wonderful," Garret said as he joined them.

Bran grinned and held up the tray he had just pulled from the oven. He placed it on a trivet and carefully removed one of the fruit-spotted buns and popped it on a plate, which he then set in front of Nea with a flourish. "I know it's not Nonna's celebration bread, but it's midwinter, and you know what that means."

Nea's cheeks coloured slightly. "Oh, Bran, you didn't have to go to the trouble."

"It was no trouble; I was hungry and making them anyway, but I just happened to remember what day it was. Happy birthday."

There weren't enough chairs, so Declan and Emil settled on the floor. Penny took the big chair by the fire, and everyone else clustered around the table. The buns were good, though given that Molly had helped Bran make them, Margot wasn't all that surprised. They chatted quietly. Well Declan and Emil chatted, and the rest of them tried to get a word in where they could. It was nice and almost easy to forget the chaos that was tearing the world apart. Chaos that they needed to get back to and figure out how to stop.

Nea and Garret seemed to be of the same mind as Margot as they had their heads bowed in quiet discussion, Nea's tea mostly untouched, which was unusual for her. "So, I was right about the anchor being helpful at Loch Bastien then?" Her violet gaze met Margot's.

"Yes. Stranger still, the sentry golem recognised it."

"Recognised it?" Nea leant forward.

"It told me I was like *her* but then corrected itself and said she was inside me. I think that is easy enough to understand." Margot sipped her tea.

"Interesting. And Amelia recognised the anchor as well, didn't she?"

"Yes."

"I wonder whose spirit it is."

"If Amelia recognised it, then perhaps it is someone who knew Evette," Declan mused.

"Evette? As in Samson's wife?" Margot asked.

"She is possessing Amelia's body," Nea answered. "I'd say Ambrose had someone jam her in there." There was a note of disgust in Nea's tone.

"The anchor spirit feels older than that though." Margot frowned and traced the rim of her cup with her index finger.

"Amelia or rather Evette confirmed it herself, didn't she, when we were in the labyrinth?" Garret asked Nea, and she gave him a nod. "We know that she was corrupted, and that Samson was trying to produce a cure. We also know that Samson himself somehow became corrupted. What if Evette was originally a daughter of Shadow and not a deathborn? Or what if Evette isn't the only soul inhabiting Amelia's body?"

"It's unlike you to provide such an intriguing commentary." Declan grinned.

"It would explain why Amelia can give others corruption. Also, Jackson, the corrupted mage we encountered under the palace," Garret said with a look in Janey's direction. "He felt like his soul had been fractured and cobbled back together, and there were parts of him that didn't feel like they matched the others. If Ambrose has been messing about with pieces of souls, then—"

"That is why Evard wanted the soul piece that was under Kalhanna; the piece I put in Penny. Of course he was collecting powerful souls or fragments of them. But Evard didn't have all the information because he wasn't the one actually in charge. That is why it is so confusing and seems contradictory. If we ignore Evard and look at the Usurper's main goal again—he wanted out of the

Between, but more importantly, he wants to take the power from his parents and become a true god. For that he needs the thrones, and to claim the thrones he needs a consort who has enough divine blood to use them." Nea had leapt to her feet and started pacing. "That is why he's collecting souls. Each one brings him that much closer to what he needs, but not close enough. When the Bright Mother created Garret, she put the last of her power into him, which was more than perhaps any brightling who had come before. The Shadow Man chose me because of my bloodline. My ancestors were Shadow-blooded, and I was a deathborn, which meant I was touched by the Shadow twice over."

"Wouldn't that be thrice once he chose you?" Declan asked.

"Exactly. That is why the Usurper is scared of me. I'm almost as powerful as he is, but with the death ward and the access to Garret's keen as well as my own ..."

"You'd be more powerful."

"That is why he tried to keep Garret and I apart."

"We can't delay then. We need to get to this temple and find those thrones."

Nea shook her head. "We should go back to Kalhanna and regroup. I need to speak with my father, and I want to try to seal the tear before we go after the thrones."

"But won't you be able to seal it once you claim them?"

"Yes, but there is no telling what effect that will have on our world. If we seal it now, we can minimise the damage."

Nea seemed back to her usual self, bouncing from foot to foot and gesturing wildly as she theorised with Declan. But every so often she would go still, and a tremor would run through her hands before she touched her fingers to the scar on her cheek.

"We should get a move on," Nea said, finally picking up her satchel and slinging it over her shoulder.

Everyone else scrambled to gather their things, and soon they were all standing outside. Nea lifted her hand, and her keen built in a cool swirl as a shimmering purple oval opened in front of her. The camp outside Kalhanna was visible in the middle of the void.

"I hate this part," Molly muttered as she eyed the portal, but she was the first one through when Nea gave them the nod, followed by Emil and Penny, then Bran, Janey, and Declan.

"Are you sure you're both okay? If you need to take a few days no one will blame you," Margot said.

Garret rested a hand on Nea's shoulder, his keen rising brightly as though he was lending her strength. They shared a look and a small nod.

"We'll be fine. We can rest once this is done," Nea said with a nod towards the portal. "Through you go. It's not exactly easy to keep this thing open." There was a hint of a smile in her voice—the old Nea who would tease her about taking too long to tie her boots or eat her breakfast, just peeking through.

With a sigh, Margot stepped into the portal, and her stomach dropped. Her limbs felt like they were being stretched and shrunk repeatedly, and then she was both in and out of her body at once. She emerged on the other side and stumbled, but Emil caught her before she hit the ground.

"I'm going to be sick," she muttered, and pressed her fingers over her mouth.

Molly sat on the grass beside her. She looked as peaky as Margot felt, but she managed a small smile. "It never gets better."

"I think I will stick to walking in the future, no matter how long it takes."

"Declan!" Zephyr gave a shout and bounded over. She threw her arms around his neck, and he staggered back a step with a chuckle.

"I missed you too, my dear."

"I see you found Garret." Leith joined them. His gaze landed on Nea, and the colour drained from his face as he lifted his hand as though he was going to touch her. She licked her lip and pressed against Garret. "What happened?" Leith's grey eyes flicked from Nea to Garret and then to the rest of them.

"Leon," Emil growled.

"Where can I find my father?" Nea asked.

"He was in the barn with Mateus, Donnic, and Harvey. They are figuring out the final details for the lock-stone," Leith replied.

"Lock-stone?" Declan and Nea asked together.

"Our intention is to anchor the tear to a lock-stone to prevent it from growing further. We came to the conclusion that it cannot be sealed at this stage, but if we can stall its growth, then that buys us more time to figure it out. Or for Nea and Garret to find the thrones," Zephyr said.

"I'd best go and see how they are doing then." Nea started across the camp.

"Hold up, lovely, I'm coming too." Declan jogged after her.

Leith drew a long breath as he watched Nea go. "How bad was it?"

Garret's jaw worked.

"Bad," Emil said with a cautious glance in Garret's direction. "I wouldn't press her for information about it. At least not yet anyway."

Leith gave a nod and settled his gaze back on Garret. "If you are up to it, we should discuss what has been happening in your absence."

"Lead the way," Garret said.

"Well, I guess the rest of us can just put our feet up for a bit then." Emil grinned, and Janey rolled her eyes.

They were closing in on the end of this nightmare, for better or worse. The anchor quivered under her skin. The end might be in sight, but they still had a long way to go.

CHAPTER TWENTY-SEVEN

HARVEY

Harvey leant against the wall and studied his fingernails. Niall and Mateus both stood at the table, heads bent and matching scowls firmly in place. The apple cake and tea that Aveline had delivered a while ago was mostly untouched, forgotten as they rounded the fifth lap of their circular argument. *Mages.* He shook his head.

Donnic sat on the bench beside him, a journal on his knee in which he was sketching. The page closest to Harvey was covered in portraits of women. One of them, her hand resting on her cocked hip and a long braid over her shoulder, looked remarkably like Molly. Another was pensive, her fingers tracing her lower lip, a collection of escaped curls around her face and a weighty stare that seemed to go right to your soul. There was no mistaking it was Nea. Then there was a short curvy woman dressed like a pirate with a head full of curls, and a pair of twins grinning mischievously up from the page. As though sensing Harvey's gaze, Donnic stopped sketching and met his eye. "Zephyr seems to be taking a while to get back."

"That's probably her now," Harvey said as the door opened. "Maybe she can end this argument."

But it wasn't Zephyr. It was Nea, looking paler than usual with a long scar across her cheek that certainly hadn't been there before.

The haunted look that always seemed to linger behind her eyes now seemed front and centre. Had something happened to Garret? No, Niall and Declan had been fairly certain that with the death ward, if one of them perished, the other would as well. But Garret didn't have to be dead. Had his corruption completely overtaken him?

Harvey slowly stood, and Nea's violet gaze snapped to him. She was usually fairly observant, but this was something else. This was the instinctive movement of someone who expected an attack at any moment. Why was she so on edge?

Declan came through the door, almost colliding with her. He muttered a quick, "Sorry, my lovely," which drew the attention of Niall and Mateus.

"Nea," Niall said, and her gaze shifted to him, her lip quivering. The mind mage's posture changed as he studied his daughter. His shoulders dipped slightly, and he took a step towards her. "What's happened?" His voice was full of deep concern as he lifted his hand towards her marked cheek.

She shied back, her fingertips rising to touch the scar.

Mateus moved to stand with Harvey and Donnic, giving the pair of them space.

Nea tracked his movement before meeting her father's eye again. "I'm ... It's nothing I can't endure."

Harvey hated that expression. The idea that people were not given more to deal with than they could endure. It was utter bullshit and led to needless suffering. "Where's Garret?" he blurted out before he could stop himself.

"He's with Leith and the others," Declan said.

"Perhaps now might be a good time for a break," Donnic said, ushering Mateus towards the door. "Come on. We'll find Zephyr and fill you in on the current plan," he added to Declan, grabbing the storm mage's arm and guiding him after Mateus.

Harvey followed them and pulled the door shut, but not before he heard Niall say, "Now, my girl, tell me what happened." His tone was comforting and came with the cloying swirl of his keen.

"I've never seen her that way," Mateus said, shaking his head. "Do you know what happened?" he asked Declan.

"We don't know all the details and neither of them is ready to share. Which is understandable." There was a strange quality to Declan's voice. It was a tone he often took on when people started discussing his death. He seemed to take most of it in his stride, happy to theorise about the magic involved, but the event had changed him, tainted his previous joyful curiosity. "But knowing Leon ..." Declan continued with a shake of his head.

"Leon tortured them both?" Harvey asked, even though he knew what the answer would be.

Declan nodded, his mouth a grim line.

"What about Garret's corruption?" Mateus asked. Clinical, that was Mateus, like Margot at times—straight to the root of the matter, though not completely uncaring. Just focused.

"Nea healed it."

"Nea? Not Margot?" The necromancer's starlight brows inched towards his hairline. "I thought the anchor—"

"The anchor can heal corruption, but so can Nea, which is not surprising given both Nea and the anchor are Shadow-blooded," Declan said with a touch of his usual lop-sided smile. There he went slipping into the ease of discussing the mechanics of magic. Nea, Harvey had noticed, did that too—focused on the *how* to distract herself from whatever it was that put that haunted look in her eyes. Memories and regret, he supposed. None of them were going to emerge from this unscathed.

Warm fingers slid into Harvey's as an equally warm body pressed against his side, bringing with it the scents of cinnamon and woodsmoke. Janey. A smile tugged at the corners of his mouth. He glanced down at her. The golden flecks at the centre of her green gaze were glittering.

"*I missed you.*" She signed.

"I missed you, too," he said softly, and her smile brightened.

"*Garret needs to talk.*"

"He sent you to tell me that?"

She shook her head. "*Leith did. Not for Garret. He needs you for something. But you should talk to Garret after. He won't admit it, but he needs it.*"

Harvey glanced at Declan, who was gesturing wildly as he discussed something with Mateus and Donnic.

Janey's fingers touched the side of his chin, drawing his focus back to her before she signed, "*I think you need it as much as Garret does.*" She gave him one of her knowing looks. It was easy to forget just how insanely good at reading people she was.

He pressed a kiss to the top of her head, pausing a heartbeat to savour the spicy-smoky scent of her hair before retreating.

Her mouth twisted into a frown, and she settled her hands on her hips in mock agitation.

"What did I do?"

She rolled her eyes and then surged forward, her lips meeting his and setting a wild flame alight at his core as her keen seemed to invade his body. This was nothing like the usual sweet kisses they shared, and Harvey was so stunned, his hands still hung limply at his sides, though they ached to latch onto her and pull her closer. Then her tongue lightly traced his lower lip, and the world melted. Wrapping his arms around her, he tilted her back as he pressed her against his chest. Her fingers found purchase in the curls at the nape of his neck, making him groan. She tasted like she smelt—smoky cinnamon, almost like that tea Margot liked to make at midwinter, the one that warmed you from the tips of your toes to the top of your head. His keen rose, responding to hers, and a jolt ran through the source around them—

Declan let out a loud whistle. "You two need to take that to a tent." His tone implied his roguish grin was firmly in place.

Harvey released his grip on Janey with a reluctant sigh. He'd never had a kiss quite like that before, the way their keens had seemed to mingle bringing new sensations and a depth to the moment. It was heady and all-consuming, and he craved more. "I should probably go check in with Garret and Leith," he said, rubbing the back of his neck.

Janey gave him a warm smile and then made a shooing motion before shifting her attention to Declan and the others.

Stars begun to dot the darkening sky as Harvey wandered along the edge of the forest under the guise of collecting wood for the fire. Really, he just needed to clear his head. Talking with Garret had helped, but it had also churned up a whole lot of questions about Ambrose and the other children from his experiments. Most of them were dead, apparently. Garret had seemed genuinely sorry about that. He didn't like killing. But if those mages had been like Jackson ... That was the corrupted mage's name—his brother's name.

He felt Nea's keen before he saw her, cool and deep—the complete opposite of Janey's. Heat touched the back of his neck at the memory of the kiss. Had that only been a few hours ago? It felt like an eternity. He cleared his throat and settled his gaze on the necromancer. The haunted look was still there, but it was as it had been before—a soft sadness at the edge of her amethyst eyes, not the wide panic of a cornered animal like it had been earlier in the day.

Her mouth twisted as they studied each other, and she touched her fingers to the scar on her cheek. "It is taking some getting used to," she said and gave a bitter snort of a laugh. "Leon did say he was going to '*ruin that pretty face*'. I guess he keeps his promises."

Harvey rubbed the back of his neck, unsure how to respond to that and equally as uncertain as to why she had sought him out. "If it helps, I don't think it has ruined your face." It would be a lie to say Nea wasn't an attractive woman, and the scar hadn't taken away her beauty. If anything, it had added a certain wistful quality to it.

The corner of her mouth quirked. He wasn't sure he would call it a smile. "I've never been all that concerned with my complexion. It's just annoying. The way it pulls sometimes. My face doesn't feel like it belongs to me anymore."

That sentiment he could definitely understand, but it wasn't Harvey's face that felt foreign—it was his whole body. The pricking sensation of his keen rising in response any time a mage or warden accessed their own or the way the source would quiver if he let his emotions get the better of him. How it had jolted when—he cleared his throat again. "Were you looking for me? Or were you also doing a Garret?"

"Doing a Garret?"

"Stomping through the forest to clear your head."

That elicited a small laugh from her. A sound Harvey hadn't heard her make often, and he found himself smiling in response. She had a lovely laugh, bright and clear like his sister Lorie's. He hadn't heard Lorie laugh for the longest time; their mother's death had taken her mirth the way he assumed the purge had taken Nea's. You could see glimpses of what Nea's humour might have been like when she let her guard down, and he hoped it was the same for Lorie. That given time to heal, her laughter and zest for life would return. When all this was over, he would pay her visit, finally meet his niece, who would be three come spring.

"No, I wasn't *doing a Garret*. I was actually looking for you," Nea said, cutting through his thoughts of his sister.

"Well then, what can I do for you?"

The shadows were lengthening around them, and Nea flicked her fingers. A small ball of lilac light bloomed at their tips and then lifted to bob almost merrily above their heads. "Can you create a mage light?" she asked, pointing to the orb.

"Why?"

The right corner of her mouth tightened, and one iron grey brow twitched upward. "I want to get a measure of your keen before we attempt the lock-stone tomorrow."

"A measure of my keen? Your father has already—"

"Humour me?" Her tone was gentle.

"I don't know how to create a mage light."

She blinked at that. "But mage lights are the basics. What has my father been doing with you?"

"Once I learned to use my keen-sense, we skipped basics and landed in the middle of crazy advanced magic that most normal mages couldn't even dream of doing." His tone sounded more bitter than he intended. He was grateful that Niall had been teaching him control, but he wouldn't have minded learning a few basics.

Nea let out a long sigh as though she wasn't surprised in the slightest. "May I?" She lifted her hand towards him.

Harvey touched his palm against hers, and the sensation of her keen deepened, stealing his breath for a moment. His own keen rose, hot and cold all at once, and he shifted his shoulders as the source around them gave a shudder.

"We'll work on alleviating that," Nea said softly. "He's right. It is a lot like my keen ... almost like Ambrose was trying to create his own child of Shadow. Fascinating, regardless of how perverse the reasoning behind it was."

Harvey got the sense she was talking to herself rather than him.

After a moment, the sensation of her keen stopped, and her fingers curled away from his.

"Right." She rubbed her hands together. "Mage lights are a visual extension of our keen."

"Like the green smoke that signals healing magic or the purple shimmer that sometimes runs over you when you are using your necromancy?"

"Yes and no. To create a mage light, you need to—" She rolled her hands in the air and chewed her lip. "It's like breaking off a tiny part of your keen and sending it out, then the source interacts with it and forms the light. You extinguish the light by pulling that piece of your keen back into yourself."

Footsteps crunched to their left, and Declan stepped out of the trees followed closely by Garret. The warden's shoulders relaxed as his grey gaze settled on Nea.

"There you are, my lovely. We were about ready to send out a search party," Declan said smoothly, but the quip lacked the usual jovialness, almost like he was trying to keep up appearances.

"I've been with Zephyr and Mateus. *I'm* not the one who disappeared when Warren asked if I had had a chance to read *that book*. Which book?"

Declan ran his fingers along his lip. "It's nothing, just an old dusty tome about reanimations and necromancy. He thought it might help me ..."

Nea gave a slow nod. "The one with the chapter on deathwalkers."

"You've heard of it?"

She nodded. "Have you read it?"

He shook his head. "I'm not sure I actually want to."

Her violet gaze softened at that. It might have been the hollow tone of Declan's voice or the defeated slump of his shoulders.

"Did you and Trenton figure out that new watch roster?" Harvey asked Garret, to change the subject, not because he actually wanted to know.

"We did. But it will likely change again soon. Leith is talking about moving the camp. Niall and Warren believe if the tear extends any farther, it will put the keen-folk here at too much risk."

Harvey nodded. "Is that where you and Declan have been? Checking out the tear?"

Garret's jaw tightened as he glanced at the technicoloured patch of sky. "No, but it should be a priority in the morning." He flicked a look at Nea. She and Declan had moved a short distance away and were discussing something in hushed tones. "Did we interrupt anything?"

"Just an impromptu lesson," Nea said, settling her gaze on them.

"A lesson?"

"Mage lights," Nea answered. "It seems as usual my father has chosen to skip over the basics and toss his student straight into the deep water."

"I never showed Garret how to create mage lights," Declan said. "And I don't recall you doing it either, my lovely. Though how the pair of you managed to get any—"

"Declan," Garret almost growled.

"Boundaries, I know," the storm mage said with a grin.

"Declan is right though—about the mage lights," Nea said, shutting down Declan's retort with a sharp shake of her head. "You could also benefit from this lesson." She snapped her fingers and extinguished the bobbing purple orb. "Now, pay attention to what the process *feels* like." Her eyes shone in the gloom, and then she lifted her hand and another ball of light formed above it.

Harvey didn't know what he was supposed to be feeling. Nea's keen had spiked cold for a moment then calmed again, and beside him Garret's keen changed from the steady throb of a warden to an almost ticklish prickle.

"I don't think it is as simple as you make it sound," Harvey said.

One of her grey brows arched, and the corner of her mouth drew in. "It is a skill most mages learn to master when they are just barely beyond infancy."

Garret toyed with his scar as he shared a look with Harvey.

"What Nea means is it is extremely simple magic, so try not to overthink it," Declan said. "Actually, that is a good way to approach most magic."

Nea had said he needed to break off a piece of keen and then what? He turned his focus inward, where his keen sat coiled at his core, waiting. Teasing a bit of it to the surface, he focused on the air above his fingers and willed a light to form. Nothing.

Beside him, a golden glow erupted.

"How did you do that so quickly?" Harvey asked as he studied the golden orb of light hovering around Garret.

The warden shrugged. "I've felt Nea do it often enough now … I just copied that feeling, or rather my keen did. One of the perks of being a brightling, I guess." He gave Nea a soft smile.

She folded her arms and leant against a tree. "Well done. Harvey?"

"Do you mind showing me again?"

Pushing away from the tree, she held her hand out and gave him a nod. "I think directly feeling it might help."

Harvey pressed his palm against hers.

"Ready?"

He nodded.

"Okay, focus." Skin to skin, her keen seemed to invade every inch of his body. It built briefly and then twisted. A small piece detached but was held close by a thin thread that anchored it to the rest of her keen. The source moved along that thread and smoothed around the separated piece, forming a kind of pocket. And then the lilac orb of her mage light burst to life beside them. She pulled it back into herself, extinguishing the light before going through the process again.

Harvey let his keen run along the thread that joined the second mage light to the rest of her keen.

"I know Nea's keen is intriguing, but are you going to spend all evening fondling it?" Declan quipped.

Harvey felt his cheeks colour. It wasn't the same as when his keen had mingled with Janey's when they kissed, but it was still— intimate. He flicked a guilty look at Garret, but the warden was just watching them with mild interest, his own multi-layered keen a warm throb.

"Sorry, I was just—" He started to pull his hand away.

"Declan is just being an arse. Take as long as you need," Nea said.

"I think I can do it now." Letting her hand go, he focused on his keen again and teased a piece to the surface. He pushed it forward, and the source latched onto it. A red orb of light laced with flickers of purple shimmered in the air in front of him. It bobbed there for a few seconds before snuffing out.

Nea clapped her hands. "Good job. Now you just need to practice."

"Was there a point to this exercise?" Harvey asked her.

"I told you—I wanted to get a measure of your keen. But also, you needed to learn that having a keen isn't just about learning how to control the big, frightening things it can do. It's about cultivating the small things as well, embracing all the parts that make you whole. Your keen is not a separate entity to your body or your soul—it is an intrinsic part of both."

Harvey rubbed the back of his neck.

"Which is why mages who are cut off from their keen often experience slow, painful deaths. Like plants starved of light."

Did she know he was considering permanent bind-shackles? That once this was done, he didn't want anything to do with his keen? But if he did, then he'd never feel what he had earlier when Janey kissed him. The way their keens had connected—"Mages can share keen, can't they?" The question was out before he could stop it.

The weight of three gazes fell on him, and he rubbed the back of his neck.

"Janey ... her keen and mine, they kind of melded together."

Declan's wolfish grin snapped into place, and he got that sparkle in his eye, ready to pounce.

"You can't share keen by accident," Nea said, cutting in before Declan got a chance. "It generally takes a fair amount of effort. However, magic is governed by emotions. So if there is a strong attachment then it is not uncommon for keens to brush up against one another, and that can create a sense of *melding*. It's not the actual sharing of keen though, and the feeling can be addictive, which is why mages often end up choosing sexual partners who are also keen-touched in some way." Her tone was academic, but the small look that she shot in Garret's direction was anything but.

"I am rather well versed on the subject if you have further questions." Declan grinned.

Garret gave a snort.

"What? I can't help it if women want to feel the brush of my keen against theirs." Declan's grin widened, and he settled a smouldering look on Nea. "Storm magic comes with a whole assortment of intimate applications, you know?"

"Well, there is a visual that I didn't need," Harvey said.

Nea shook her head. "Given the reactive nature of the source to your keen specifically, you may find that those moments are somewhat more intense than the norm. It's nothing to worry about, but it can be overwhelming." She chewed her lip as she studied him. "Have you ever noticed it before? I know your keen was under a block but that doesn't mean it was absent. There was still something there that the source could have reacted to."

"No. I haven't noticed it before."

She gave a nod and then glanced towards camp. "We should head back. I know my father wanted to run though the plan for tomorrow at least once more before bed. And I am starving."

"You're starting to sound like Molly," Garret said.

"We're both more alike than either of us wants to admit," she said with a ghost of a grin.

Harvey blew out a breath, falling into step beside Declan as they followed Garret and Nea across the field.

The lock-stone. The reason Niall had skipped over the basics of using his keen and jumped right to the impossible. Improbable, Niall would say to correct him. The mind mage didn't seem to believe anything was truly impossible. Now that Nea was back, surely they would use her magic to anchor the tear and not Harvey's. Knowing Niall, though, he would probably still get Harvey to do it. He'd call it character building or something like that.

CHAPTER TWENTY-EIGHT

NEA

Leon trailed his cold fingers across her chest then latched onto her chin, forcing her to meet his eye. "How long do you think Garret will be able to control himself when I make him watch as I defile this lovely body of yours?"

"Try it and I will kill you."

Leon's lip curled as his grip on her jaw tightened. "Maybe I should let Gwyn toy with Garret while you watch instead. She's quite enamoured with him, and I am sure she would jump at the chance to bend him to her will. Of course, I could just have her force you to submit yourself to me instead, but then that would take away the fun of breaking you."

"I will die before I give you the satisfaction."

"I have already proved you wrong," he whispered, loosening his hold and smoothing the pad of his thumb over the ache left in the wake of his fingers. "Your screams were such lovely music. Maybe I should skip the foreplay I have planned and jump straight to the main event. After all, I can't wait to hear you sing again." He held her jaw firmly again as he smashed his mouth against hers.

Nea sat up with a gasp. Just a dream—a nightmare that left her skin crawling and her heart pounding, but it wasn't real. Not any more at least. She touched her fingers to her scarred cheek—her punishment for biting Leon and tearing his lip. The skin pulled strangely now, making every expression feel foreign. She glanced around the dark tent. The dream wasn't the only thing that had woken her. Cold crept along her spine, the heat of Garret's body achingly absent. Panic closed sharply around her chest, and she sucked in a series of too fast breaths. What if—

"It's alright; you're safe." His voice soothed over the edge of her panic, though didn't abate it entirely.

She found him by the door of the tent, one hand holding the flap ajar. A voice rumbled outside, and Garret tore his gaze away from her. "It can wait."

"But, sir," the voice outside said, and she thought she heard Garret growl.

"I said it can wait. If you are so concerned, then go and rouse Trenton or Leith. If they feel it's urgent, then come back and get me." He let the flap fall shut and moved back to Nea. "Sorry. I didn't mean to wake you."

She tucked her knees to her chest and rested her chin on them. "I would have woken anyway." Her fingers shook as she ran them through her hair.

Garret was so close now, his warmth a beacon that was drawing her towards him. He settled in behind her, his arms forming a protective cage as his chin rested on her shoulder and his cheek pressed against her scarred one. "I'm sorry." It was barely a whisper, and she felt, rather than heard, the words.

"It's not your fault. I haven't slept properly since Kalhanna."

"I know what those nightmares sound like. This one was different," he said.

She twisted around until she was facing him, her back supported by his arms and her legs tucked over his thigh. "What did the messenger want?"

"Nothing that's important right now." His keen was stirring in a warm thrum against hers. After several weeks of being apart, it was comforting. Almost as much as the steady warmth of his solid presence.

She leant forward, waiting for him to meet her halfway. They hadn't kissed since escaping from Leon. They had touched, much like they were now, as though they both needed to be sure the other was actually there. But something still seemed to be holding them back.

Garret studied her mouth, one hand lifting to cup her undamaged cheek. "Are you sure? I don't want to push—"

She cut him off with the press of her lips against his.

He let out a soft groan, and his arms tightened around her, pulling her closer as her fingers laced into his hair.

Manoeuvring so she was sitting fully in his lap, she let her legs rest over his hips and swallowed as she lifted her shirt over her head. The scars weren't visible in the dark, but she could feel them. Garret could too because he traced his fingers along the lines that marked her back then skimmed them over one of the nastier brand marks on her chest.

"Make me forget," she whispered and brushed her lips against his again.

The hand inspecting her scars moved across the smooth swell of her breast, thumb ghosting over her nipple as he guided her back onto the bed roll.

His warmth left her briefly as he made short work of his clothes before pulling her into his lap once more. Hands cupping her backside, he lifted and repositioned her, so they fit snuggly together.

The source around them quivered, and a lump rose in Nea's throat, a hot sting coming to the corner of her eye. She ignored both and swept forward to claim Garret's lips again. He traced his tongue along hers, his strong hands holding her steady as the movement of their bodies chased all coherent thought away.

A heavy mist hung in the air as Nea emerged from the tent. The fields to her left were adorned with thick swathes of white where the fog had settled in the contours of the land. She rubbed her hands together and blew out a white breath as Garret left the tent behind her. Rubbing her arms to fend off the cold, she resisted the urge to drag him back to the warmth of the bed. There would be plenty of time for that later. Right now they had work to do.

Her father, Aveline, Donnic, Harvey, and Mateus stood around one of the fires, nursing steaming cups. Margot and Molly joined them, followed by Declan, Zephyr, and Bran.

A light touch at her elbow drew her attention back to Garret as he said, "Be careful."

He wasn't coming up to the college. Leith needed him to help organise the moving of the bulk of the camp.

The lock-stone would hopefully prevent the tear from expanding farther, but moving the camp was for the best. A small group of mages and wardens would be left behind to keep an eye on the tear. Everyone else was returning to the capital to deal with any remaining reanimations and aid the refugees left there. Aveline and her father would be heading to Loch Bastien. That was if the lock-stone worked. There was every chance that the magic required would react with the tear and cause a cataclysm the likes of the one that had sunk Port Brenna and created Mother's Deep.

"I'll try."

A wry smile twitched at the corner of his mouth. "I guess that's fair. Morning, Janey." He glanced towards the fire mage as she approached.

She waved and gave them a warm smile, which faded as she studied Nea.

"I'm—" Was all Nea managed to get out before Janey swamped her in a warm hug.

As the other woman pulled back, she patted Nea's shoulder and gave a nod before signing something.

"You're not fine, but you don't have to be. It's okay to admit that to yourself," Garret translated. "And Janey is correct as always."

"We're ready when you are, Nea," Zephyr said as she joined them. The dark circles under her eyes suggested she hadn't gotten enough sleep, and her skin had a slightly ashen hue to it.

"Are you okay, Zephyr? You look like you should be back in bed."

She waved Nea's concern away. "Just a little under the weather. I'll be fine."

"Have you seen Margot? If you're not feeling well, she can fix you something."

"It's not necessary. But if I start to feel worse, I certainly will."

"Did I hear my name?" Margot and Molly joined them. "Zephyr, are you—"

"I'm alright. Everyone needs to stop fussing. We have work to do," Zephyr snapped and rubbed her forehead.

Marot's mouth tightened into a thin line, and her keen stirred in a warm swell. Then her features softened, and she gave Nea a nod. "She's fine. But, Zephyr, you should come and see me later. I can fix you something to help with the headaches."

"Leith is waiting," Molly said to Garret and Janey. "If we don't go now, I think he'll start turning people out of their beds and tearing the camp down around them."

Janey's nose twitched as she studied Zephyr, then she smiled brightly at Nea and signed.

"Be careful, and take care of Harvey," Garret translated, then he pressed a kiss to Nea's hairline. "Alright, Molly, let's go and save Leith from himself. I swear he's trying to make up for years of shirking responsibility in one fell swoop."

As Garret and the others left, Nea turned to Zephyr. "I have a theory about how we can fix Rourke and Wade," she said as they started towards the fire where her father and Harvey were waiting.

"You do?" Zephyr brightened at that. "It would have been done already if I could just get the polymorph magic to work on this side of the barrier."

"The barrier is the problem. They came through the tear and the source reacted to their magic which transformed them, right?"

The other woman nodded.

"Maybe if I create a portal and send them back to the Between, their magic will right itself and they will switch back."

"It's plausible. But what if you get stuck in the Between or the crossing polymorphs you too?"

Nea chewed her lip. She had considered both those outcomes already. "I wouldn't be going with them, but I could keep the portal open long enough that they can come back across."

"I should probably go with them." She glanced at Declan, who was laughing about something with Harvey.

"Would you want that?"

"The Nundle need me."

Nea sighed. She could definitely relate to the need of the many outweighing personal need. It wasn't healthy, and once again she found herself considering running off with Wren and Gendry when all this was done. "As someone who has thrown away nearly half a decade doing what is best for the greater good, I ask that you at least consider what will make you happy before you let duty decide for you. It might save you some heartache."

They reached the fire. Mateus, Donnic, and Nea's father were there, along with Declan and Harvey.

"We're not taking a warden?" Nea asked and glanced over her shoulder, looking for Garret.

"Emil and Warren have gone on ahead," her father replied. "Are you ready?"

She nodded. "As ready as I can be."

"Good." He studied her for several heartbeats. His violet gaze held the same soul-reading weight that Nonna's did. "Let's get to it then."

The walk up to the college felt extremely short. The magic of the Between that radiated from the churning patch of sky seemed to twist the world around itself. Things were much worse than they had been even yesterday when they had come up to inspect the tear. Was the tear preparing itself for another expansion? It was definitely a possibility.

Warren and Emil stood in the middle of a pile of bodies—dark twisted shapes that vaguely resembled the devourers Nea had encountered in the Between.

"We need to act quickly," Warren said as they approached.

"Another expansion seems imminent. Perhaps we should wait for it to pass. If we time it wrong and the magic reacts, we could end up with another Port Brenna," Declan said, an edge to his voice as he shifted his shoulders.

"The threat of this whole thing exploding in our faces and blasting a crater halfway to Fengate is there regardless of if it is preparing to expand again or not. We can't delay any longer."

"Warren is right," Niall said. "Now everyone get in position." He handed a large rock to Donnic, who placed it in the centre of what had once been the courtyard.

Donnic's keen lifted in a bright flicker, plying at the hairs on the back of Nea's neck as he traced a series of runes in the dirt around the stone. They shimmered with the green-purple hue of oil on water before fading.

Mateus and Warren stepped forward, cold necromancy frosting across Nea's skin. Her own keen rose in response, but she pushed it away. It wasn't her turn yet.

Twin beacons of purple magic twisted down from the tear and touched the top of the stone. The source trembled, and Mateus let out a grunt, a sheen of sweat forming on his brow. Declan's storm magic built in a static prickle as he placed a hand on Mateus's shoulder and bolstered the necromancer's keen. Her father did the same to Warren, who was looking like he might keel over at any moment.

"Alright, Harvey." Nea took hold of the source and wove it with the threads Warren and Mateus had created. Harvey's keen joined hers in a hot-cold rush. "Easy does it," she whispered.

Her knees shook under the strain. The edges of the tear frayed farther with each beat of her heart. The push of magic from the other side of the barrier was like a tidal wave smashing and then withdrawing, again and again. It would not hold much longer. It couldn't hope to.

Her jaw ached from pressing her teeth together. "Now, Harvey," she ground out.

Time seemed to slow. Only she and Harvey were moving at normal speed. The sky above them flashed, then a deafening ripping sound started. The source jolted, and Harvey stared at her wild-eyed.

"Don't panic," Nea said to him as much as herself. They were holding onto the source, but it was wild a beast bent on consuming the entire world and them along with it. "Three ... two ..."

Boom.

An angry whine buzzed in Nea's ears, and the ground beneath her bucked, throwing her and Harvey into a tangle of limbs in the dust.

The flashing sky above them dimmed, the swirling colours slowing to a steady pulse that matched the ripples of magic twisting over the stone plinth that had appeared in the centre of the Kalhanna courtyard.

"Did it work?" Harvey shouted, rubbing at his ears.

"Looks like it," Nea shouted back as he helped her to her feet, and she got a good look at him. "You could pass as Bran's older brother," she shouted with a laugh.

"What?"

"Your hair—it's as white as fresh snow." She pointed to the unruly curls, which were now just like Bran's. If his eyes had been a darker blue, she would say the resemblance was uncanny.

Harvey ran his hand through his hair.

"You did it!" Zephyr suddenly swamped Nea in a hug.

"Is everyone else alright?" Nea asked as she extracted herself. Her ears were still ringing, and she shook her head, trying to clear them.

"Headaches, ringing ears, and a couple of cases of exhaustion, but no one was seriously hurt," Zephyr said as she moved over to Declan, who was looking fit to throw up. Warren and Mateus sat on the ground beside him. The younger necromancer had a cloth pressed to his nose. Donnic and her father were farther away with Emil, who was rubbing his temples.

"That look suits you," Declan said to Harvey, though his attempt at a grin was ruined by a wince.

"Do you think it's permanent?" Harvey asked.

"More than likely," Nea replied. "You did well, Harvey."

"You did all the work; I just supplied a little bit of keen."

"I don't think I could have done it without you," she said truthfully. Her insides felt like they had been jostled out of place and then rearranged, and yet she felt strangely invigorated. Like the source itself had permeated her entire being.

"I didn't expect it to be quite that easy," Donnic said.

"I think it was the combination of keens. If we didn't have Nea and Harvey, it is highly likely the tear would have exploded and killed us all," Niall said. "Lock-stones are notoriously unpredictable magic."

"Now you tell us," Emil quipped and held out a hand for Mateus. "Come on. Margot should have a tea that can put some colour back in your cheeks."

Mateus took Emil's hand, and Donnic helped Warren up. The old necromancer suddenly looked ancient, and Nea didn't like the way his breath was coming in shallow pants as though he couldn't quite fill his lungs. "I can create a portal to get us back."

"No, you've used too much keen. It's not that far. We can walk," her father said with that same tone he had used when she was younger and being particularly stubborn. He helped Donnic support Warren, and they ambled towards the gate.

Nea studied the lock-stone before falling into step beside Harvey. Now that the tear had been stabilised, there was nothing stopping her from going after the thrones. But going after them meant she would encounter Leon again, and she wasn't sure she was ready for that just yet.

CHAPTER TWENTY-NINE
MARGOT

A dull boom like distant thunder rumbled through Margot, and a flash of light blinded her as the source gave a heavy jolt. Penny shuddered, and Margot followed the line of her sight to the churning patch of sky that was the tear. Only the sky was still now, the colours within shifting slowly, undulating like the technicolour curves of a serpent.

"Do you think they succeeded?" Margot asked.

Penny's brow furrowed. "I don't know. That shockwave was intense. Imagine what it felt like at the epicentre."

"You don't think they ..." She glanced across the campsite and found Garret. His fingers were wrapped around his right wrist, and his jaw was set tight, but he was still standing, which would suggest Nea was alive as well. "Maybe we should go check on them."

"If something went wrong, they might need our help," Penny replied, brushing her hands on the front of her pants. "Come on."

Margot waved Molly over, and Janey came with her. "We're going up to check on them. That shockwave was concerning."

Janey pointed to herself and nodded.

"I'll let Garret and Leith know, then catch you up," Molly said, jogging away.

The mages and wardens they passed were all shifting their shoulders as though a weight had been lifted. The air definitely felt different, with the ever-shifting magic seeping from the tear absent. The source was still prickly, like it had been at the college in the wake of the purge, permanently scarred by the onslaught it was never meant to bear.

They hurried up the slope towards the college. Dark shapes emerged, but as they got closer, it was clear it was Niall and Donnic, supporting Warren between them, his head lolling to one side in a worrying manner. Behind them, Mateus was hobbling along supported by Emil.

"I'm fine really, Emil. It is nothing a strong drink and good nap can't fix. You don't need to fuss." But the necromancer's voice was shaky and his cheeks pale.

Declan and Zephyr were beside them, but there was no sign of—

"Where are Nea and Harvey?" Molly asked as she came jogging up with Bran and Garret in tow.

"We're here," Harvey said.

"Shadow's teeth, what the fuck happened to you?!" Molly exclaimed, and Harvey chuckled.

Janey moved to him and touched her fingertips to his hair. It was as white as Bran's, making his steel-blue eyes look brighter.

"Are you alright?" Garret asked as he stopped in front of Nea. She looked fine—better than fine, revitalised.

"Yes, I'm great actually," she replied.

"Margot," Niall said softly as he rested Warren against the trunk of a tree by the side of the road. "Zephyr had a look at him but—"

"My magic was affected by the lock-stone," she said, her honey-gold eyes apologetic.

Margot hurried over and crouched in front of Warren, letting her magic rise in a warm swell. His keen was weak and growing weaker by the moment.

"Just let me die in peace."

"You're not dying, old man. You're too stubborn for that," Niall said.

He was right. Warren was not dying, not yet anyway.

"You've overextended your keen. We'll need to get him back to the camp, so I can treat him properly." She said the last bit to Niall.

"I can create a portal," Nea said.

"No, travelling through a portal right now won't do him any good. Garret, you and Donnic can carry him. Molly, will you run ahead and get everything ready for my restorative? He'll need a dose." She studied Warren. "Add a finger of whiskey to it and make enough for four more. Niall, Declan, Donnic, and Mateus could do with a dose as well."

Molly nodded and took off at a run towards camp. Donnic and Garret bent and hoisted Warren between them then followed her.

"I hate that tea," Declan said, scrunching his nose up. "What about the others? Don't they need a dose as well? They all used a good chunk of their keen, too."

"Nea and Harvey are both fine. Their keens are energised rather than weakened. Emil is unaffected also."

"And Zephyr?"

"I'm fine. My keen isn't spent, just scrambled," the woman in question said in a light tone.

"Even if that wasn't the case, the restorative is inadvisable given her recent string of headaches."

"But I feel fine. Surely I don't need the worst tea in the world either."

Bran chuckled. "Oh, come on, Declan. Don't tell me you can survive death but can't handle a little restorative."

Declan frowned at his feet. "Fine."

As they walked back to the campsite, Zephyr fell into step beside Margot.

"You didn't overextend yourself, did you? It will only make the symptoms worse."

Zephyr shook her head, the sleek black locks shining blue as they caught the sunlight. "No, the others did the bulk of the work. I was just there for backup." She pulled her shawl tighter around her shoulders and studied Declan's back. "Nea is going to send Wade and Rourke back to the Between. Hopefully, it will fix them."

"Do you want to go too? The Between is your home, isn't it?"

Zephyr's mouth twitched, and she tore her gaze away from Declan. "The Nundle gave up their true home long ago. Now home is wherever we find ourselves. But I should go back."

Should was a weighted word. Margot *should* never have let Warren put the anchor in her. Nea *should* have asked for their help when she first suspected Evard's plan instead of trying to protect them all by handling things herself. Garret *should* never have gone running off after Leon on his own.

"But what do you want?"

Zephyr's golden gaze settled on Margot. "I don't want to go back. I want to stay here."

"Then stay."

"But—"

"Take a good look at Nea. Her entire life, she put the benefit of others before her own needs and what did she get in return? A past full of anguish and regret."

The other woman drew a long breath. "That's different."

"It's not." They had reached camp. "I'll fix you something for the headaches once I have seen to Warren. You should talk to Declan."

"Talk to me about what?" Declan asked as he joined them and slid his arm around Zephyr's waist. He pressed a kiss to her temple.

"Nea is going to send Wade and Rourke home through one of her portals. She thinks encountering the magic of the Between that way should reverse the effects of coming through the tear."

"It's plausible. We should go experiment with it now."

"You're not getting out of having the restorative." Margot shooed them both to the fire where Molly was pouring a dark liquid into cups.

Later, after she had seen to Warren, she joined Nea by the edge of the fire. The necromancer was cradling a cup of tea, a steady swirl of peppermint-scented steam rising from it. Garret and Leith were close by, discussing the next cause of action. The tear was still a threat, even with the lock-stone, so it made sense to leave some of the force behind. But they needed to figure out who would be staying here, who would go with Leith back to the capital, and who would be going with Nea and Garret to find the thrones. It seemed so strange to think that it would all be over possibly before the first buds of spring started to push their heads through the frost.

Nea sighed as Margot sat across from her.

"Something wrong with your tea?" Margot asked.

"No, the tea is fine. My memories are just heavy."

"Thinking about Kalhanna or something more recent?" Margot didn't want to mention Leon directly. Both Nea and Garret tensed when talk turned to him, and that was expected given he had tortured them both and most likely raped Nea. Margot hadn't asked her if he had. She wasn't sure she wanted the confirmation.

"Both."

Margot nodded and poured herself a cup. "Are you worried about facing Leon again?"

Nea's brow furrowed, and her violet gaze was sharp as it met Margot's. "No, that is one thing I am not worried about. I am actually looking forward to tearing the fucking bastard's soul from his body and banishing it to the farthest wastes of the Between where it will be slowly consumed by the devourers. Even though that is a kinder fate than he deserves."

"Did he ..." She still couldn't bring herself to say the words, but she gestured at Nea's body, hoping she would catch her meaning.

Nea frowned at her, then her amethyst eyes darkened, and her mouth tightened. "No, he didn't get that far. Though that didn't stop him threatening it."

Relief smoothed down Margot's spine. "Good. Not him threatening it—that's vile—but good that he didn't follow through on the threats."

"If he had, I doubt there would be any physical body left to tear his soul from."

"No there wouldn't have been. When Garret was done with him, I would have taken my turn with whatever was left and made sure of it," Emil said as he plonked himself down next to Nea.

"Shouldn't you be over discussing the plan with Garret and Leith?" Margot asked as Emil helped himself to a cup of tea.

"Nothing I can do there." He took a sip and stared into the flames. "If the world wasn't going to shit around us, you could almost think this was like old times. Margot playing the mother hen, Nea being all philosophical and contemplating her own navel—"

"And you needing to get patched up because you wouldn't stop running your mouth and ended up in a tavern brawl."

"That was one time, Margot."

"What about Fengate?"

"Dale started that one. It wasn't my fault."

Margot folded her arms. "I'll give you that one, and you are right—this is nice, despite the circumstances."

"You mean despite the fact that all of us have been irrevocably changed and the world is coming apart at the seams?" Nea's tone was droll, but a playful smile curved her lips.

"There you are, my lovely." Declan came over. "Zephyr tells me you have an idea about how to fix Rourke and Wade." He seemed more his usual self than he had for the past few weeks, as though a weight had shifted.

"I do," Nea said.

"Can we try right now?"

"I guess if the others are ready."

"They are on their way."

Nea threw back her tea and stood as Zephyr and the two dogs joined them. "You're sure you want to do this now?"

"Arf," Wade barked, and Rourke nodded.

"What about you, Zephyr? Are you going through as well?"

Zephyr shook her head and linked her arm with Declan's. "I don't want to risk getting stuck there."

"Alright." Nea's keen built, and a shimmering oval appeared in front of her. "Through you go. I'll keep it open for as long as I can."

The anchor ached at the proximity of Nea's magic. It was like it was yearning for a missing part of itself. Given they were both of the Shadow, it didn't surprise Margot. But the anchor hadn't reacted to Nea's keen that way before. Had something changed when she had created the lock-stone? The necromancer didn't feel all that different through the lens of Margot's healing keen, but the anchor was good at picking up on things far beneath the surface.

After a short while, Nea's keen began to wane, and she shared a look with Zephyr as the portal flickered.

"Do you think something happened to them?" Zephyr asked.

Then a short man with golden-blond hair and a monocle over one of his grey eyes stepped out of the portal, followed by another who was taller and broader than Garret. He had bronzed skin a similar shade to Mateus, and his black hair hung in a tight braid down his back. Even without the pair of hand axes at his belt and the swirls of tattoos that were just peeking above the collar of his shirt and on the backs of his hands, he would look formidable.

Nea let out a panting breath as the portal snapped shut, and Declan caught her as she staggered sideways. "Easy there, my lovely." He scanned her face, worry etched at the corners of his mouth.

"I'm fine." She waved him away and rubbed her temples.

"Wade!" Zephyr squealed and rushed forward, swamping the golden-haired man in a hug.

"We should have tried that weeks ago," he said as he chuckled and rubbed circles on her back.

"Moira says hello," Rourke said to Nea and Declan. His voice was a deep, velvety rumble. Molly would love it—she had a soft spot for what she referred to as bone-melting voices.

"Thank you, Nea," Wade said, holding out a hand. Something glimmered between his fingers, and Nea held her own hand out. He dropped what he was holding into her open palm. It was a silver chain with a delicate rose pendant on it. "You might be needing that. I can tell you how to use it when we get a moment."

Nea fingered the pendant as she examined it. "This is the one you tried to give me before."

"The same. As I said back then, it belongs to you. Now where is Garret?"

They spent the rest of the afternoon introducing Wade and Rourke to everyone else. Donnic insisted on seeing the rest of Rourke's tattoos. The two men then discussed magical tattooing for an hour. Niall spent equally as long discussing Nundle magic with Zephyr and Wade as though he hadn't already picked Zephyr's brain clean over the past few weeks. Even Catriona joined them for dinner. She looked better than she had when Micha had brought her to the camp. She also seemed more humble. It was fair to assume that her ordeal had changed her as much as the rest of them had been changed by their own challenges.

Nea was right; none of them were going to emerge from this unscathed.

With a full belly and Molly's citrus-scented warmth pressed against her side, it was almost easy to forget that they still had a long way to go before they were finished saving the world. But maybe they just needed this one night to pretend that Leon wasn't still at large, and the fate of the known realms wasn't at stake.

"We can't all go after the thrones. Some of us should stay behind with Leith."

"Penny is right," Nea said. "Really, the only ones who need to go after the thrones are Garret and I. The rest of you should stay here in case we've misjudged Leon and he decides to send a force to take the tear."

"Not going to happen, my lovely," Declan said. "If Leon was going to try and take the tear, he has had ample opportunity. And given that it is now effectively sealed, there is nothing for him to exploit."

"And we have no way of knowing what sort of force Leon might have with him while he searches for the thrones," Emil added.

"There is also Amelia to consider. She seemed to be working with Ambrose, and if he is with Leon, then we will likely have her to contend with as well," Harvey said, and Janey gave a nod.

"Leith is going to need some of you," Nea argued.

"He has Trenton, his soldiers, and close to half of the Order. Not to mention the mages. I think they can deal with whatever Leon throws at them—if he throws anything at them at all." Bran piped up.

"You are staying here with Leith, though you should have gone with Father, Aveline, and Warren to Loch Bastien." Nea folded her arms. "I still have half a mind to send you with Donnic to Wren's ship. You need to stay—"

"I'm old enough to make my own choices, and besides, Garret already told me I could come."

Garret let out a groan and rubbed a hand over his face. "Don't drag me into this. You told me you had spoken to Nea already."

"Yeah, and she told me to ask for your opinion on the matter."

"Bran—"

"*Nea.*" The right corner of his mouth tightened, and his eyebrow flicked up. It was a perfect match to the expression on Nea's face.

Emil laughed. "You are ridiculously good at that."

"Fine." Nea let out a huff. "But if you get yourself killed, don't come crying to me."

Garret rubbed his finger along his scar and turned back to the rest of them. "How about this? Declan, Zephyr, Harvey, Molly, Bran, and Rourke come with Nea and I. Janey, Emil, Penny, Margot, Wade, and Mateus stay here?"

"No," Margot said abruptly. "Zephyr should stay. She hasn't been well, and the mountains will be in thick snow by now. Not the best environment for her to recover in and I'd like her close, so I can keep an eye on her."

"I agree," Declan said quickly.

"I can take care of myself, and I am feeling much better. Though I do appreciate the concern."

Margot pressed her lips together. "But—"

"I'll be fine."

"Any other objections?" Garret asked.

"I have a few," Leith said as he stepped up beside Garret.

Now that Margot knew that they were half-brothers, it was easy to see the features they both shared with their father. Particularly those steel-grey eyes. Leith's were more like Evard's, being a touch closer to silver. While Garret's were more a storm-cloud grey, like Nea's hair when it wasn't dyed black as it currently was. But the resemblance was so strong it was hard to believe it had slipped her notice before.

"Just a few?"

Leith's smile didn't waver at Garret's tired tone. If anything, it deepened. "I think you should take as many people with you as you can. Emil is correct. We don't know how big a force Leon has with him; I am almost ready to insist we move the camp to the foot of the Spine just in case."

"I can't keep a portal open long enough to move that many people, and going over land will take too long," Nea said.

"Leith does have a point though," Margot said, and Leith gave her a wide smile.

Janey waved her hands to get Garret's attention then signed. "*What if we moved the camp in small groups?*"

"It's a good suggestion, Janey," Garret said with a nod. "She asked if we could move the camp in smaller groups."

"How many people can you move at one time?" Leith asked Nea.

"It's not the number of people passing through. It's the length of time I can keep the portal open. Even with Garret's help, we're only looking at a short window before I start to exhaust myself. And I would need to rest between. It's likely to take two days or even three to move the entire camp."

Leith scanned the camp before meeting Nea's gaze once more. "What if we were only moving half the camp?"

"It would still take a lot of time—"

"And you are asking Nea to risk over-extending her keen," Bran said, his tone suggesting that he hadn't forgotten over-extending his own.

Nea gave him a small smile. "There is also the fact that we don't know where along the Spine to start looking. We know that Ambrose has been scouring the mountains around Merston. However, the map that Margot and the others uncovered at Loch Bastien suggests the temple is closer to Del Harol. Moving the camp once might be doable, but we would be wasting time if we have to move it a second time."

"What if I leave the majority of my men here under Trenton's command and only take a handful of my personal guard? Even that will give you better odds against Leon."

"Absolutely not. You can't put yourself in that kind of danger."

"But you can?" Leith swept forward and grabbed hold of Nea's hands.

She tensed and pulled back. "I am not the leader that people will be looking to, to help them recover once this is done." She gently extracted her fingers from his and took a step away from him.

Leith studied his fingers then ran them through his hair before straightening. "As king, I do get final say, and going against my wishes would be considered treason."

"You're seriously going to play the *I'm the king, so do what I say or I'll toss you in the dungeons* card?" Emil asked, a hint of a grin evident in his tone.

"Well, no. But if Nea and Garret are going to be stubborn."

"I agree with them," Margot said, and Leith shot her a look of betrayal.

"Really, Margot?"

"Well, I agree with Leith," Penny said, and a chorus of sound broke out as the others all threw in their own opinions on the matter.

"Alright, everyone, that's enough!" Garret yelled, and they all quieted down. "If you want to come with us, I am not going to stop you, given you are the highest-ranking person here. However, I will not have you put Nea in danger of over-exhaustion moving troops about." Garret settled a hand on Nea's shoulder, and their keen stirred almost like a single entity. "And I still don't think it's wise. I agree with Nea that it is foolish to put yourself in danger when the people will need you—"

"I can't sit on my hands any longer. I—"

Garret cut him off with a gesture. "I *understand,* which is why I am not going to argue the point any further. Go and choose who you're bringing. The rest will stay here with Trenton in charge. I recommend leaving Micha behind as Trenton's second. I'll have Ryan and Haley take charge of the remaining wardens, and Jasper will stay as well in case they need the assistance of a healer."

"Right, I will go and see Trenton." Leith rubbed his hands together and strode away towards the row of tents his men were staying in.

"So, the rest of us are coming with you and Nea as well, I gather," Emil said, and Garret gave a nod as he cast a glance around the small group.

"Best go make yourselves ready."

"Bran, a word," Nea said, grabbing the boy's arm and dragging him away as the group started to disperse.

Once they were out of earshot, she said something and held out the silver pendant Wade had given her. Bran shook his head and took a step back.

"Garret?" Catriona asked, tentatively drawing Margot's attention away from Nea and Bran.

The princess traced the bands around her wrists and licked her lip as Garret studied her.

"Yes?"

"I heard that you can remove bind-shackles without a need for the key."

His jaw tightened. "It's an extremely painful and taxing process, especially for the mage."

"I want to help fix some of the damage I caused, but I can't do that without my powers. I am willing to endure whatever I have to, to get them back." Her voice was thick, anguished. Her keen had been shackled for weeks, and the effects of that were starting to show.

Margot had been where she was. She understood the pain of a body that missed its connection to the source. But Catriona was a mind mage, and she had been working with Leon.

"What do you think, Margot?"

"I think ..." She studied Catriona. If the woman really wanted to make amends for what she had done, then she deserved that chance. And she had tried to protect both Henry and Nora once she realised the full extent of Kieran and Leon's plans, hadn't she?

Unshed tears swam in Catriona's sapphire eyes as they met Margot's.

"I think she deserves a chance to prove herself."

Catriona's lip wobbled, and she let out a sigh that was half sob. "Thank you."

Garret rubbed his scar. "Alright, but the first sign of deceit and these shackles go back on."

"That's fair." Catriona nodded.

"Come on. You'll need to sit down." He guided her to a chair and then crouched in front of her. "I'll warn you one last time, this will be painful."

"I can endure it."

"Hold your wrists out."

Catriona did as she was told, and as Garret's warden keen rose in a steady numbness, Margot shifted her shoulders. Removing Nea's shackles had left a nasty ring of blistered and burned flesh, but Margot hadn't seen the whole process, only the aftermath. Catriona gasped as Garret's keen pressed down, and she bit into her lip but did not attempt to pull her hands away.

"Almost there," Garret said as the mind mage tilted forward as though she might fall out of the chair.

Margot caught her and held her steady. She met Garret's eye. His jaw was tight, but he gave her a nod and let his keen build again. One shackle fell away and then the second, and Garret released his hold.

Catriona let out a gasp and nearly fell forward as he stood, but Margot caught her.

"Easy does it. Let me see those wrists." Margot gently examined the burned flesh of Catriona's wrists and then let a coil of her healing magic smooth over them. The blisters disappeared, and the burned skin dulled to a soft pink before fading entirely.

"Thank you," Catriona said to both Garret and Margot. "Thank you," she repeated and pressed her face into her hands.

Margot knew what she was feeling—the soothing rush of her keen re-entering her body after so long being absent. The way all the keens around her would suddenly feel almost overwhelming.

Garret let out a breath and shared a look with Margot. She had known him long enough to know he was wondering if freeing

Catriona had been the right thing. She studied the other woman, not completely sure either, but the anchor gave a little throb. The spirit believed in second chances, and so did Margot.

CHAPTER THIRTY

NEA

"No." Bran shook his head violently.

"I don't know that I will survive what is coming, and the death ward means that if I perish then Garret does too. He doesn't deserve that fate."

"Have you discussed it with him?"

"I don't need to because this will work. It will make me a deathwalker like Declan."

He paced away from her, his knuckles white as he squeezed the silver rose-shaped pendant. "But not even Declan knows how he managed that; you can't be certain that it will be successful."

"It will be."

"You're the only family I have! What if you're wrong about this?"

Nea toyed with her lip. "That's not true. You have my father and Margot, Emil and Nonna, and everyone else at Hartswood."

"But you're the only one who really understands," he whispered, running the chain through his fingertips.

"If this is successful then Garret will survive, which means you'll be able to use the death ward to bring me back."

Declan had been wrong in the Between when he'd said they could use the death ward to resurrect her if she perished. The second her soul fled her body, the ward would take Garret's life—there would be no time to save them. But if she was right about being able to turn herself into a deathwalker, then her soul would enter a kind of limbo like Declan's had, which should mean that Garret would be spared. Whether they could then revive Nea or whether she would be stuck in that limbo for eternity was uncertain, but Bran needed to believe that he could bring her back. Otherwise, the plan would fail before it started.

"Why me? Why not Mateus?"

"Because our connection is stronger, which means your keen is less likely to reject mine."

Bran studied the pendant in his fingers before holding it out to her. "Alright."

Nea closed his fingers over it and pushed his hand back towards him. "Hang onto it for now."

They found Donnic chatting with Rourke. He folded his arms as Nea explained her theory, but a wide smile spread across Rourke's face. "That's a sound plan, Shadow Girl."

"I don't know. You want me to fuse a piece of your keen to Bran's? That sounds awfully complicated, and there's a lot that can go wrong," Donnic said.

"It's just a simple oathing, that's all."

"But won't your death cancel the oathing?"

"No, because Bran has a spirit anchor, and as long as he has both the anchor and the piece of my keen, he will be able to bring me back."

Donnic rubbed his hand over his face and sighed. "Why can't you ever come to me with a simple request? Something like, hey, Donnic, I want a mermaid tattooed on my arse. Can you do that?"

Bran laughed. "Can you do that?"

"You don't want a mermaid tattooed on your arse, Bran," Nea said. "Look, Donnic, all you're doing is setting the ward. Bran and I are doing the heavy lifting."

"I need my—"

Nea held up a small vial of iridescent ink.

"When did you pilfer that?"

"Before Molly and I crashed Vince's party."

He let out a huff. "Fine. But you are going to owe me. Alright, Bran, give me your arm."

Bran rolled back his sleeve and held his arm out. Rourke leant closer to watch as Donnic took a knife and opened a thin line along the skin of Bran's wrist. "Ink."

Nea unstoppered the vial and passed it to Donnic. He smeared the ink on his fingertips and then rubbed them into the cut. "Your turn." He nodded to Nea.

She copied Donnic's actions with the ink, pushing a small piece of her keen out and under Bran's skin. He winced, and his fingers tensed, but he didn't pull his arm away.

Donnic's keen stirred, and the cut pulled itself closed. Lilac magic twisted over the thin scar, slowly forming into an image.

Bran bit his lip as the magic started to darken and a red mark formed beneath it. Then with a flash of purple-green, the magic dissipated, leaving behind an indigo crescent moon on the inside of Bran's wrist.

"I'm not sure I ever want to go through that again," Bran said, scrunching his nose and working his hand as though his fingers were stiff and he was trying to get feeling back into them.

Donnic caught Bran's arm and inspected the mark, his keen building in that warm flicker. He nodded. "Looks good, though I am still not sure it will work as you intend."

"It will work," Rourke said. "Very clever, Shadow Girl. The Master was right to choose you."

"We should get on with it." Nea started towards the remnants of their camp but stopped. "Bran ... don't tell the others."

"What about Garret?"

She drew a long breath. "Garret doesn't need to know. It will just distract him."

"I think you should tell him," Bran said, folding his arms.

"You're probably right, but just keep it quiet for now. Please."

"Alright."

She should tell Garret. But if he knew she didn't think she would survive going after the thrones then he would worry. Right now, he needed to be focused—they all did—and worrying about Nea's welfare was a distraction none of them could afford.

✖

The next morning, Nea delivered Donnic back to The Azure Queen and then started sending the first of Leith's chosen men to the meadow outside Hartswood. They had decided it was the better option given that Del Harol was overcrowded with refugees. She held the portal open as they went through in groups of five, carrying supplies and other equipment. The going was slower than she would like, but once the small contingent of soldiers, mages, and wardens had all been sent, it was Leith and Catriona's turn.

Nea turned to the group that was left. "This is your last chance to stay here. I don't know what we are going to have to go through to find the thrones."

"Nice try, Nea, but you're not going to change anyone's mind now," Emil said. "Just open the portal and let's get on with it. We're all more than ready to take this fight to Leon."

There was a chorus of agreement, and a lump rose in Nea's throat. She swallowed it down. "Alright, but don't say I didn't try to warn any of you. Now I know some of you are not familiar with winter so close to the Spine. It will be bitterly cold, which is why we are heading to Hartswood to get properly kitted out before we head into the mountains. I have sent word to Nonna already, and she has organised everything we need to be delivered there. Leith is setting up camp in the fields at the front of the manor, but the rest of us will stay in the manor itself given that Nonna has taken everyone to Del Harol in the wake of Kieran's attack."

"We know the plan, Nea. Garret has already made sure of that," Molly said.

"I know. I'm just—"

"Stalling and hoping we'll change our minds about coming?" Molly quipped.

Yes. Even now it was hard to let them all help. The thought that any of them could get hurt because they had chosen to help her was a tough one to bear.

Janey squeezed her shoulder, the warmth of her keen soothing the tension in Nea's spine.

"Let's go then." She lifted her hands and created another portal. This one led to the garden at the back of the Hartswood manor.

No one hesitated to jump through, and finally it was just Garret and Nea standing there. He took hold of her chin, tracing the pad of his thumb along her lower lip before he brushed his lips against hers in the way that made her knees weaken. The portal flickered beside them, but Garret's keen twisted around Nea's, bolstering it.

"We shouldn't keep them waiting."

"You're right, but I've been waiting for a moment alone with you for the last two days. So, I am stealing one now. I doubt we'll get many more chances before this is finished." He slid his fingers into her hair and kissed her again. Her lips parted, allowing his tongue to explore her mouth, and the portal flickered again, dimming as it threatened to close.

"We really should ..." she said in a weak effort to protest, but she didn't want to go.

"You're right," he said softly before pressing another kiss against her mouth and then one to her hairline. "To be continued, once we've dealt with this mess."

"I don't think I can wait that long," she whispered, and he laughed, weaving his fingers with hers as he tugged her towards the portal.

When they stepped out on the other side, Declan gave Nea a knowing look and opened his mouth to speak, but Zephyr lightly punched his arm. "Bran and Margot are inside working out sleeping arrangements for the night and sorting through the things Abigail sent over from Del Harol. Molly and Janey are organising tonight's meal, and Harvey and the others have gone down to Leith's camp to see if he needs anything," she said.

The lightness of Garret's kiss had evaporated the second they stepped out of the portal. The air around Hartswood was heavy with sorrow. The source wasn't just tattered here; it had been obliterated.

She turned her gaze to the grove. Snow dusted the blackened branches of the trees, making them look ghostly in the afternoon light. "I'm just going to take a walk in the grove. I'll be back soon, and we can discuss the plan for tomorrow."

She dropped Garret's hand and wandered across the field. The cows were absent, probably taken to Del Harol by Angus. When she reached the gate in the hedge that led to the grove, she stopped and drew a halting breath before stepping through. Hartswood had always existed in a climate of its own created by the wards around the valley and the magic of the grove. The grove itself was always warm with life, and she normally wouldn't hesitate to slip out of her shoes and press her toes into the magic-soaked grass. But the grass was gone, hidden under a thin blanket of snow. She bent and pressed her palms to the ground. Nothing stirred. No wild zing of magic, no ghosts of necromancers from eons ago. Nothing. A sob caught in her throat, and Garret's keen burrowed under hers as his fingers splayed across her back. "If you want me to go—"

"No. Stay." She turned to him, and he traced his fingers along her scarred cheek, catching the tear that was rolling down it. "I wish you could have seen it before," she whispered.

"Abigail believes it can be mended, doesn't she?"

"It can, but it won't be the same. It will be forever scarred, like Kalhanna, like ... me."

His gaze softened, and he held out a hand to pull her to her feet. "Scars aren't always a bad thing."

She led him across the grove to the ancient hawthorn in the centre. It was dormant now, but it was hard to tell whether it was the destruction that had been wrought or the winter-induced sleep that hawthorns outside Hartswood would typically enter. She placed her hands against its trunk, and a quiver of magic ran up her arm.

"Time heals," an age-soaked voice said, and Agatha's ghost appeared next to her. It was beyond comforting to see her cloud of white hair and sparkling blue eyes, but the image of the woman was flickering in and out of focus. "It will heal faster when you defeat the Usurper and reset the lock-stone."

"I don't know that I can reset the lock-stone."

But Agatha just made an annoyed noise and waved her concern away. "Of course you can. Stop defeating yourself before you've even tried."

The magic under Nea's hands gave a weak flutter.

"Sorry I can't stay any longer. Be sure to bring tall, broody, and ridiculously handsome back with you when you return." With that, the ghost blinked out of existence again.

"Speaking of returning, have you given any thought to what is going to happen after we find the thrones and fix everything?" Garret asked.

She had given it some thought, hadn't she? Provided she managed to survive what was coming or Bran could put her back in her body if she didn't. "A little. I think I might disappear over the horizon with Wren and Gendry for a while. I would probably leave Henry with Leith; it will do them both good."

"Oh." He frowned and rubbed his fingers along his lip.

"Of course, it depends on what you had in mind."

"I hadn't really given it much thought. I did wonder if you would stay with Leith."

"He'll have more than enough people around to help him. I don't see why he would need me."

"I don't think it's a matter of needing your *help*."

Oh. She moved forward and slid her arms around him. "I will not be *staying* with Leith. I thought I had made that pretty clear already, but if you need a reminder." She shifted her hands to the back of his neck and rose on the tips of her toes to kiss his cheek. "Wherever you go, I go. But I need a break from everything, some time to just … *heal* … and I would really like it if you wanted to come with me. Would you join me on the Queen for a little while?"

He swallowed and licked his lip, his gaze dropping to her mouth. "Wherever you go, I go," he repeated her words in a whisper as he cupped her neck with one hand, the other dropping to her hip and pulling her closer.

His breath tickled across her lips as he hovered just out of her reach. She pulled herself against him, lifting on her toes as high as she could, trying to close that agonising distance. Her fingers laced in his hair, and he let out a groan, his lips dropping swiftly to claim hers. A tremor ran through the source, and beside her the hawthorn erupted in tight green buds, the air around it warming the way it had when the grove was whole.

Garret guided her back against the trunk of the closest apple tree, and she let out a gasp as his hands dropped to her hips and he lifted her, pinning her to the trunk and supporting her weight. The source trembled again, and a flicker of magic stirred across the ground, leaving a path of green in the thin coating of snow. He skimmed his fingertips along the edge of her throat and then laced them into her hair as his lips traced the place just below her ear, and she let out a soft, whimpering moan.

A noise caught Nea's attention, and she opened one eye to see Agatha perched in the branches nearby, watching them with a wide grin on her face and mischief in her sapphire gaze. The old ghost pointed to something, and Nea twisted then let out a startled yelp before pulling Garret's face away from the path of burning kisses he was placing across her collarbone.

"Sorry to interrupt, but I felt the grove," Bran said, clearing his throat and looking every which way but at the pair of them. The tips of his ears were slightly pink, and Nea didn't think it was from the cold.

Garret let out a soft groan that she didn't think Bran heard as he extracted his hand from beneath the opening of her tunic and set her neatly on her feet once more.

Nea straightened her clothes and ran a hand over her hair. She was certain her lips would be a delightful shade of kiss-chapped pink. But Bran wasn't looking at her.

Instead, he was studying the patch of lush green grass devoid of frost. It spanned out from where Nea and Garret stood in an eight-pointed star. Bran crouched and touched the point that ended just before his toes and closed his eyes. "The magic was *dead*. How did you revive it?" He looked up at Nea, and she shook her head.

"I wish I could tell you, but it just happened when"—she flicked a look at Garret—"when the source reacted to me."

Bran straightened and followed the path that led from the centre of the star to the hawthorn, which was budding like spring was imminent and there wasn't at least a good month of winter left.

Agatha was standing at the foot of it. She smiled widely at Bran. "Welcome home, little foundling."

"How is this possible?" Bran gestured to the healed section of the grove.

"They are of the divine blood; their keen reacts in seemingly impossible and unpredictable ways. It is a far cry from a completely healed grove, but it proves that what was whole once can be again."

Bran studied them. The look on his face at the prospect of revitalising the grove sent a pang through Nea's chest. She would be needed to heal the magic of Hartswood, and Agatha had already said that she could recreate the lock-stone. But to do so she would have to stay and disappearing with Wren and Gendry for some much-desired rest would become nothing more than a fantasy. She had an obligation like all Hartswood necromancers—perhaps more so because of the circumstances of her birth.

Garret's hand pressed against the small of her back, his fingers tracing soothing circles. "Once we are done dealing with Leon and thrones, we are all going to need to catch our breath before we set everything to rights again. The grove can wait just like everything else."

"But—"

"The brightling is right," Agatha said.

"His name is Garret."

One of Agatha's milky eyebrows flicked upwards as her sapphire gaze settled on Nea. "Well, how was I supposed to know? He's never been formally introduced to the grove."

Nea took hold of Garret's hand and tugged him towards the hawthorn. She pulled the dark-bladed knife out of her satchel. The hilt was cool against her skin, but instead of making her skin crawl like it had done when she retrieved it from Willem, it felt almost comforting.

"I just need a little bit of blood," she said, holding the knife out to him hilt-first.

He took it from her and pricked the tip of one finger. Nea pulled his hand towards the trunk of the hawthorn and smeared his blood on the bark. It shone for a moment then was sucked into the tree. Several flowers burst to life among the green buds.

"It's not just Nea's keen that effects the grove," Bran said as he wandered over to examine the flowers.

"The grove was a gift from the Bright," Agatha said as though it was obvious.

"So that's why the eight-pointed star formed. Garret and Nea's keens were reacting to each other, and the source was—if I hadn't interrupted you, half the grove would probably be green by now." He grinned in a very Declan-like manner. "I should go and leave you two to it. You'll have the grove back on its feet in no time."

Nea rolled her eyes and let out a huff. "We probably need to start getting ready for tomorrow." She turned to the ghost and dipped her head. "Agatha."

"Don't disappoint me, little death-bringer. You tear that bastard to pieces and send him our way. We'll take care of the rest." Then she disappeared from view.

"Death-bringer?" Garret asked.

Nea shrugged. "Just another title I've collected."

"Do you think the bastard she was referring to was Leon or Kieran?" Bran asked.

"The Usurper most likely. He is ultimately the one pulling the strings that led to the grove's destruction." Nea ushered Bran towards the manor. "Come on. I should check in with Margot, and I am sure Leith needs to go over the plan with Garret again."

"Most likely. I'll head over to his camp now." He caught Nea's arm and spun her around. Then, sliding his thumb along her scarred cheek, he cupped the back of her head and gently tipped her face up to press a kiss to her lips. He released her far too quickly, but Bran was watching them with an almost indulgent smile. Beneath their feet another patch of frost and ash had cleared, leaving soft warm grass in its wake.

Garret pressed a final kiss to her hairline before they ducked through the gate in the hedge, and he went striding off towards the front field.

Bran grinned at Nea as they crossed the snow-dusted meadow to the manor house.

The hearty scents coming from the kitchen and bustle of activity in the main room as Margot and Penny sorted through the supplies that had come from Del Harol made it almost possible to forget that the magic around Hartswood had been damaged. Nea might be entertaining thoughts of disappearing again, but Hartswood would always be her home, and she hoped that one day it would return to its former self. And based on the grove's reaction to her and Garret's keen, perhaps that particular hope wasn't in vain.

CHAPTER THIRTY-ONE

GARRET

Nea was curled facing him, her hand gripping his like he was a lifeline. It was too dark to see her face, but he was sure her eyelids would be flickering rapidly. She twitched, and her fingers flexed. He smoothed a hand over her hair and murmured a soft, calming, "You're safe."

Her body relaxed, and her grip on his fingers loosened. She was dreaming about Kalhanna, he was sure.

Her reactions and outbursts were familiar enough that he could tell the difference. The new nightmare, the one she had been having since they'd escaped from Leon, was like she was fighting for her life. So different from the Kalhanna dream in which she was reliving trying to save her friends. Not that she talked about the content of either openly, but he could assume enough from the names she called out during the latter.

His jaw ached as he pressed his back teeth together. He was an idiot for going after Leon. Everyone had tried to tell him that, but the corruption had been so deep under his skin, driving his impulses. His mistake had gotten Nea hurt, and the scars on her cheek and body would forever be a reminder of that. He rubbed a hand over his face and let out a long breath. "I'm so sorry," he whispered as he gently extracted his fingers from Nea's. Now that she had calmed, it was relatively easy. She rolled and muttered something in her sleep as she burrowed deeper under the blanket.

Garret shifted himself to the edge of the small bed they were sharing and let his bare toes meet the cool boards of the floor. He needed to clear his head. After quietly finding his clothes and pulling them on, he pressed a kiss to Nea's forehead before leaving the room.

The hallway was dark and silent. A glimmer of silver-blue light shone under the door to the room Declan and Zephyr were staying in. The murmured sounds of a quiet conversation drifted from that way as well. Garret turned and started to head for the stairs only to stop and whisper a curse as one of the boards creaked under his foot. He paused and listened hard, but no one seemed to stir.

Outside, his breath came in a white cloud as he tilted his head back to examine the star-studded sky. He rubbed his palms together and pulled his jacket tighter as he headed in the direction of the grove. Halfway across the field, he stopped. "You can go back to bed. I'm not in the mood for company."

"That's never stopped me before," Declan said as he joined him. The mage had always been sensitive to the cold, and he looked almost comical with a scarf wrapped several times around his neck and thick woollen tunic under his cloak. "Not exactly the best weather for a pre-dawn stroll, old boy," he said as he pulled his cloak tighter around himself and burrowed into it. "What's got you stomping around in the frosty dark rather than wrapped around that lovely necromancer of yours in a nice warm bed?"

"I'm an idiot."

Declan's breath plumed the air as he let out a soft chuckle. "Well, that's not exactly new. But what specifically makes you an idiot this time?"

"I should never have gone after Leon."

Declan rubbed a gloved hand through his hair. "No, you probably shouldn't have, but you weren't exactly acting under your own influence." He rested the same hand on Garret's shoulder and gave it a squeeze. "At least you didn't go and get yourself killed and then somehow jammed between worlds."

The attempt at humour was appreciated, but it fell flat. Not because of Garret's own mood, but because of the hollow tone of Declan's voice and the way the corner of his mouth had tucked in. Garret could count on one hand the number of times Declan's features had worn that look of anguish. It was the same one he had given Garret after his father, Hector, had lost his battle with corruption.

"Seems I'm not the only one who has a head full of regret."

Declan let out a bitter laugh. "It has been harder than expected to come to terms with my death. Everyone wants to talk about it, to pick the mechanics apart and discuss the theories of the magic involved, but it just reminds me that I threw all this"—he gestured at his body—"away to chase down a fairy story. And I am not certain that I am deserving of this second chance."

"I—"

"You all grieved me. I saw it while I was haunting Nea, saw the anguish that I could do nothing to absolve. And then I just waltzed back in like nothing had changed. All the hurt that my death put you and my mother and Margot and everyone else through was for naught."

Garret let out a sigh. "It wasn't for naught, but is that all that bothers you about it? Nea suggested that your brush with death might have made you more aware of the fragility of the human body."

The storm mage licked his lip. "She's correct as usual. It's not that I considered myself invincible, but when Harold ... Did Nea tell you he drugged me with mage bane so I couldn't use my keen."

She hadn't. Maybe to spare him the thought of how that must have felt for Declan or maybe because she felt it wasn't her right to tell him. "No, she didn't."

"He still didn't deserve what Evard made Nea do to him," Declan said as he ran his fingers along his lip. "She called herself a monster afterwards, and that nearly broke my heart." He whispered the words, breath barely stirring the night air. With a sniff, he seemed to shake off the melancholy that had taken over. He had always been infuriatingly good at doing that. "Still, there are more important matters to concern ourselves with at the moment. We can all contemplate our navels and beat ourselves up over our mistakes once this is through."

Garret almost laughed at that. "You're right of course. How is Zephyr doing?" It seemed like a good time to change the subject. "Margot said she hasn't been well."

"Zephyr?" A small, somewhat intimate smile touched Declan's mouth, and he bit down on his lip almost as though he was trying to hide it. "She's doing a little better."

"That's something then."

"It is." Declan's tone was tight like he was holding back. "Yes, it certainly is something."

"Are you alright?"

"I'm good. Just, you and Nea are being cautious, aren't you? I mean, surely Margot has fixed her the *tea*."

"Tea?" Then it suddenly dawned on him. A lot of Margot's regular patients were mostly women who were seeking preventative measures to avoid pregnancy. "Zephyr's sickness isn't a winter cold, is it?"

"Well, it is currently winter, so you could say it was seasonal. But, ah, no, it's not a cold."

Garret clapped him on the back. "Does anyone else know?"

"Only Margot. It's early days yet and regardless, we didn't want to say anything until after Leon has been dealt with."

"Fair enough." The sky had started to lighten.

Declan shivered. "I think it is high time we headed back to the manor. A nice cup of tea and some hot breakfast is in order, I believe."

Garret clapped him on the shoulder again as they turned towards the house.

By evening the following day, they had moved from Hartswood to the foot of the mountains just beyond Del Harol. Leith and his men had set up a new camp, and a small group of scouts had been sent out in search of any sign of Leon. Garret didn't expect them to find anything this far from Merston, but it paid to err on the side of caution, especially when dealing with Leon and the Usurper.

Dark came fast here at the foot of the mountains and brought with it a seething cold that reminded him of Nea's keen. He glanced to where she stood with Janey and Penny by one of the fires. Wade had been busy, and each of the women wore a woollen hat, in a different colour, adorned with small flourishes of embroidery, except Nea's, which was a simple deep indigo. Janey's was a dark emerald, dotted with small white flowers with sunny yellow centres, and Penny's bore a single swallow on a deep vermillion background that brought attention to her striking dark eyes. All three wore matching gloves, though Nea kept fidgeting with hers as though she were ready to take them off.

Catriona approached them slowly, and Nea's attention shifted from Penny to her.

"I owe you an apology," she said as she adjusted the front of her fur-lined coat.

Whatever Nea said in response was too soft for Garret to hear.

"I told Cat that Nea might not be receptive to her no matter how repentant she was," Leith said as he stopped beside Garret. "She really does seem remorseful though."

"For helping Kieran take Henry and Nora?"

"For *all* of it."

"And you forgive her?"

"I told her I need more time."

Garret nodded slowly. "The old you probably would have welcomed her back open-armed, without a second thought."

"Probably." He cast a glance at Catriona and Nea.

Nea had her arms folded and was rocking back on one foot, but her features weren't completely closed off. There was a chance she was going to accept the apology.

"We should discuss the plan for tomorrow," Leith said, turning back to Garret. "Who is going with you and Nea in search of the temple?"

"Molly, Rourke, Emil, and Declan. However, once we find signs of the temple or Leon's forces, we will come straight back and regroup. You don't have any intentions of moving the camp, do you?"

"Not straight away. If my scouts return with information about Leon's whereabouts, that may change. I brought a messenger with me though, so if I decide to move, we can get word to you quickly enough." He pointed to a boy sitting beside Bran. He had the grey cap of a messenger pulled down over his ginger curls and a scarf wrapped multiple times around his neck. A plump grey bird was nestled in his lap.

"Nea is going to use her portals to send back daily reports. Harvey and Margot have orders to follow if we miss one of those check-ins." He glanced back at Nea and Catriona. Penny was holding out a cup of tea to Catriona, who was settling down on a log next to Janey. Nea had disappeared, but he spotted her over with Margot, Molly, and Zephyr, who were all carrying two bowls of the stew Molly had thrown together. She pointed to Catriona, and Margot nodded.

"Are you going to fill me in on those orders?" Leith asked.

"Harvey will in the morning. Right now I think it's time we got something to eat and settled in for the night." He ushered Leith towards the cooking fires where people were milling around in small groups, tending a collection of pots. They joined Emil and Mateus, who were filling their bowls.

"If Margot isn't careful, I'm going to steal Molly," the necromancer said as he inhaled the fragrant steam rising from the pot. "She might not be a mage, but Bright preserve me, she is magic with food."

"You should try her spiced fruit bread. Nothing beats it hot out of the oven with a good lashing of butter." Emil grinned.

Garret and Leith filled their own bowls and followed Mateus and Emil to the fire where Declan and Harvey were sitting. The storm mage looked up as they approached and then shifted sideways to make room for Garret.

They spent the rest of the evening swapping stories about the stupid things they had done. Of course the story about Declan's run in with the sentry golem came out as it always did. Garret knew plenty of others—after all, in the pursuit of knowledge Declan had done some profoundly stupid things—but he kept them to himself.

It was different from the camp at Kalhanna. There the tear had been hanging over them like a heavy shadow reminding them constantly that they were trying to save the realms from catastrophe. But here in the quiet, cold shadow of the mountains, it was almost easy to forget they still had to hunt down the thrones and deal with Leon. Not for the first time, Garret wondered what they would do if the thrones weren't real, or worse, if Leon somehow beat them there.

By midday on the third day after leaving the new camp, they reached a place where the old road they had been following branched deeper into the mountains. The ground at the crossroads was churned into a mess of muddy ice; a reasonable-sized group of people had been through here recently.

"If we keep going straight, we'll hit Merston, right?" Garret asked Nea as she stopped beside him.

"After a few days, yes." Her keen stirred in a cool flurry. She turned in a slow circle before rushing to the side of the road and tearing into a thick bush growing there, scattering leaves and thin branches behind her.

"What are you doing, my lovely?" Declan asked as he joined her.

"I knew it!" she exclaimed, taking a step back and colliding with the storm mage.

"Wait, is that—didn't Vince have one of those in that ridiculous shrine of his?" Molly asked, bumping Declan with her hip as she pushed around him to examine the statue Nea had uncovered.

The statue had been carved from a dark stone littered with white pinpricks of glittering quartz. It was a large hound, his snout tilted towards the branching path and the ground between his paws littered with carved roses.

Nea removed her glove and lifted her hand towards the dog's cheek. The crescent moon on her palm lit up, and violet light shone out of the quartz freckles that covered his coat. He reminded Garret of the midnight-blue hound that had been the form of the Shadow Man in the labyrinth.

"There is another here." Rourke had moved to the other side of the road and uncovered a second statue. This one was carved from a buttery yellow stone with swirls of cream across it. It was a large cat sitting on an eight-pointed star. She had one paw pointing towards the same path the dog was indicating. The path that Leon's force had recently taken.

"We were going that way anyway, right?" Emil asked. "I mean, it's obvious that Leon has been through here and he has a considerable force with him. But if Merston lies that way"—he pointed at the road that they had been following—"then surely Leon would have found the temple already if it was anywhere between here and the college."

"Should we regroup with the others?" Molly asked, her palm resting on the shoulders of the dog statue.

Nea shook her head as Garret said, "Probably."

"I think we should keep going. If this is the beginning of a pilgrim's path, then that means the temple is close and Leon already has a head start."

"As Emil has already pointed out, he has a considerable group with him, most likely including Amelia and Gwyn." Garret wouldn't forget the way Gwyn's magic had stolen his control. It was nothing like the subtle compulsion of mind magic. It was a crushing command that turned your body into Gwyn's puppet.

Nea bit down on her lip and studied the path. "It will take too long to find a suitable place to move the camp to."

"If the temple is close then we don't need to move the camp, just the people," Declan said. "We don't have the luxury of time to set up the camp anyway."

Nea pulled her glove back on as she studied the path that wound away into the trees. Her keen was a soothing cool as it tested the air. Finally, she gave a nod. "Let's go back to that clearing we passed earlier, and I'll get the others. I have a feeling we are going to need all the help we can get."

CHAPTER THIRTY-TWO

Harvey

Harvey rolled his shoulders as the source bristled. The air to his left shimmered before splitting into an oval-shaped doorway and Nea stepped out. It was too early for her daily check-in, and she didn't usually step completely out of the portal. Had something happened?

"Harvey," she said by way of greeting.

"Did you find the temple? Or Leon? Where are the others?"

"Slow down." She lifted her hands. "We found the start of a pilgrim's path, which most likely leads to the temple, and we found evidence of Leon. At least we believe it's Leon. The others are fine but given that it appears Leon has a decent force with him, we thought it was best if the camp came to help us."

"The whole camp?" Leith asked as he reached them.

Nea nodded.

"We'll need time to break camp and reorganise."

"There's not enough time to fuss about breaking camp and hauling supplies through the portal. The temple is close, and Leon has a head start."

Leith rubbed a hand through his hair and let out a breath. "Alright, we'll batten everything down and be ready to go shortly." He strode off to gather his men.

"Where are Margot and the others?" Nea asked as she turned back to Harvey.

"We're here," Margot said. She was standing off to the side with Penny, Zephyr, Janey, Wade, Bran, and Mateus. "And we're ready to go."

"Good." Nea rubbed her hands together, and the source bristled again as the shimmering oval reopened. "Off you go then. Garret will fill you in on the plan." Once Mateus had stepped through the portal, she flicked a look at Harvey. "You too. I'll catch you all up as soon as Leith is ready to go."

Harvey didn't need telling twice. He stepped through the portal and nearly stumbled into Bran, who was rubbing his temples and groaning.

"I know portals are fast but once we are done saving the world, I am never taking one ever again," the boy said.

Harvey couldn't blame him. Passing through the portal had not been pleasant before the block had lifted from his keen, but now that he was affected by even the most minute fluctuations in the source, using portals made him feel like his entire being was turning inside out. It was a feeling that lingered long after the portal had closed. He clapped Bran on the back. "Apparently they get better."

"They really don't." This from Molly, who was standing with Janey. "You steady enough on your feet for a little recon, Harv?"

He nodded and immediately wished he hadn't as his head swam, and his stomach rolled.

"Alright, you're with me." She shouldered her crossbow. "Declan and Rourke will fill the rest of you in while you wait for Nea to get back with Leith and his men. Stay alert. We don't know exactly where Leon and his cronies are hiding out."

Harvey hadn't noticed that both Garret and Emil were missing until Molly had drawn his attention to it.

She led Harvey along a ruined road to a small crossroad. Two statues flanked a path that branched off into the trees. The ground here had been churned up as though many feet had passed by. They continued down the branching path in silence. Molly held her crossbow loosely, but Harvey knew that at the first sign of trouble she would snap it up and send a bolt flying with deadly accuracy. She was beyond skilled with a normal crossbow, but the enchanted bow Angus had found at Hartswood and given to her had enhanced that natural ability. It was like she and the bow were the same entity. Not that he would mention that to her directly though. Molly would shoot him if he so much as hinted that she might have hidden magical abilities. And she didn't. His keen-sense, though new to him, had never picked up on anything out of the ordinary around her.

Something ahead, however, was calling to him, dragging him forward. It was familiar, cool and soothing but edged with sharpness, almost like Nea's keen.

Movement in the trees to their right drew Molly's attention, and she lifted her bow. Harvey's keen-sense recognised the numb throb of a warden the same second Molly lowered the bow with a huff.

"You fucking fool, Emil. I nearly put a bolt through your chest," she hissed.

Garret stood behind him. "It looks like Leon has set up camp just beyond the next bend," he whispered and guided them off the path into the forest. "We couldn't get a good look from this side, but we're definitely going to need Leith's soldiers."

"Nea should have brought most of them over by now," Harvey said. "What do you want us to do?"

"See if you can scout around the western side of that ridge. Be careful, though. The drop on the other side is deadly. Emil and I will head around the east. I haven't seen signs of a temple, but Leon set up camp here for some reason."

"Mostly like to set a trap for us," Emil said.

"That is a given at this point. When do you want us back? Will we meet you here or head straight to the clearing where the others are waiting?" Molly asked.

"Without a camp we can't risk being out here at night. We need to move on Leon as soon as we can. I'd say we have another three hours of daylight at the most, and I told Rourke and Declan to move out as soon as Nea returns."

"So, speed is of the essence then," Molly said, and Garret nodded.

"Alright. Come on, Harvey." Molly led him to the ruined path again and then into the trees on the other side.

Garret wasn't kidding about the drop. To their left there was a steep ravine, a thin snake of glittering ice that looked like it might be a river in the warmer months, at the bottom. They stayed as far from the edge as they could as they crept along, following the sounds of Leon's camp, which were getting louder.

The air in front of them felt tight, the source throwing out a warning. Harvey grabbed Molly's jacket and yanked her backwards.

"There's something there," he said apologetically as she glared at him.

"I don't see anything."

"I think it's a magical barrier of some kind. I can feel it," he replied, and her blue eyes widened.

"Like a ward?"

"I guess." He didn't know much about wards. Then again, he didn't know much about magic in general.

"We should get back to the others. We can't risk tripping it. Nea said that wards can either alert the mage who created them to someone crossing them or they can explode on contact, like an invisible trap. Either option is not ideal."

Harvey nodded. "We must be close to the camp though if Leon has had one of his mages ward it."

"Definitely."

"What an astute observation," a silky voice said behind them, and Molly spun, letting a bolt fly.

It tore through Amelia's chest, and she staggered back a step, examining the gaping hole left behind. "Now that wasn't very nice. You've gone and ruined my new coat."

The source puckered and twisted as the hole in Amelia's chest drew shut once more. Harvey's fingers twitched, but Amelia moved faster than he could have imagined. She pinned Molly to one of the trees by her throat and snarled. "You're such a pretty little thing. It is a shame to kill you."

"I could say the same to you," Margot said, and the air around her grew tight with the familiar cold of necromancy, her normally brown eyes a soft rose gold.

Amelia's body jerked and she dropped Molly as the keen Margot was wielding latched onto her.

"You won't escape this time." The voice wasn't Margot's own, and the air around her was crackling with green and lilac flickers.

"You won't kill me," Amelia spat. "*You* would never do anything that would disappoint Father."

"You're wrong about that." Margot's keen flared, and Amelia's body writhed.

Harvey had seen this before when Nea had killed Harold. Amelia's body stilled, her limbs stretched at awkward angles.

"Let's see who disappoints Father now," the voice coming out of Margot's mouth whispered, then the healer slumped to the ground.

"Margot!" Molly rushed to her, tearing off her gloves to check Margot's pulse. "Oh, thank the Bright." She cradled Margot against her chest.

"I'll be alright," Margot whispered. "The anchor just overextended my keen. Go and help the others."

A loud yell broke through the trees followed by the sounds of booted feet charging and the clash of swords.

"Margot?" Bran emerged beside them flanked by Wade and Zephyr.

"She overextended her keen," Harvey said.

"You two go; the others will need you. We can take care of this," Wade said, gently extracting Margot from Molly's arms and waving them away as Zephyr's keen built in a warm throb that mimicked healing magic. Harvey had noticed that Zephyr didn't seem to have a keen of her own but rather she borrowed traits from several different schools of magic.

"Come on, Mol." He pushed Molly's crossbow into her hands and dragged her along behind him. Once they had gone a dozen or so steps, she shook herself free and her posture straightened.

Leon's campsite was a mess of fighting bodies. Mateus stood in the middle of a collection of collapsed reanimations, Janey by his side with flickers of fire running over her hands. Kieran and Emil were grappling nearby, Emil's warden keen a thick bubble around the pair of them. All the different keens mingling together was making Harvey's head ache, then an old man with grey streaking his sandy blond hair stepped into view. He looked vaguely familiar, but his keen was like nothing Harvey had ever felt before. It was twisted and seething, almost like the dark taint of corruption but not quite as volatile.

"Hello, Harvey," he said.

Molly lifted her crossbow, but he made a flicking gesture with his hand and her body went flying.

"Now that it is just the two of us." He opened his arms wide. "How about you be a good lad and greet your father properly."

His—*Ambrose*. This man was the one responsible for making Harvey what he was. He had performed experiments on Harvey's mother and then locked away Harvey's keen because he had deemed it not worthy. He was also the mage responsible for this entire mess—every life lost since this had all begun was blood on his hands. The source tightened, and Harvey fought the urge to fold it around himself.

"Oh. I did make a mistake with you, didn't I? So much raw power under your skin. You almost rival Nea and the brightling, don't you? Now I see I shouldn't have wasted my time with Jackson."

Jackson was the mage beneath Evard's palace. His brother—full brother, not like Lorie. Lorie's father had been an abusive drunk, but he wasn't this abomination who'd tortured and twisted one of his children until they lost all semblance of humanity and who'd cast the other aside when he was found wanting.

"Nothing to say to your father?"

Something snapped inside Harvey. The source twisted around him, and the world blurred. Then he slammed against a wall, his feet coming out from under him and his spine colliding hard with the ground.

"I created you, remember?" Ambrose said softly. "And I created her." He pointed his thumb at the woman standing above Harvey.

She had short dark grey hair and indigo eyes. "Oh, you do look like Jackson. That's going to make killing you harder, but I think I'll manage."

His body went rigid, his limbs refusing to answer any of his commands. His heart sounded too loud in his own ears, an ache overtaking his chest and extending into his jaw until his left side started to go numb. The woman let out a laugh that was cut as someone tackled her, and the tension in Harvey's body abruptly loosened.

"You fucking bitch! I should have killed you when I had the chance," the woman growled as she thrashed beneath Nea.

"Yeah, you should have." Nea's keen frosted the air, and the woman screamed.

"Please. No, please," she gasped. "I surrender."

Nea hesitated, her keen flickering.

The woman took the opening, driving the heel of her palm into the centre of Nea's chest and pushing her aside. She then lunged, knocking Nea to the ground again and straddling her. Harvey started forward to help, but Ambrose's seething keen stirred behind him.

"My money is on the actual daughter of Shadow," his oily voice said. "Gwyn is special, but she is no Nea. Then again, the latter's bleeding heart might just get the better of her."

Gwyn. Garret had mentioned that name, hadn't he?

"Now where were we?" Ambrose said smoothly. "Hopefully, you learned your lesson. No kin of mine can raise their hand against me. It's a nice little perk that I made sure to include in all my children, not just those of my blood."

"I don't need to use my keen to kill you." Harvey drew his sword.

"No." Ambrose's smile widened as Nea's keen spiked cold behind him, and Gwyn screamed again. "I suppose you don't. Go on then." He opened his arms and tilted his head back.

Harvey swallowed and took a step forward. The hilt grew hot under his fingers, too hot to hold, and the sword clattered to the ground.

"You cannot lay a single finger on me. Now how about you give up before—"

"Harvey!" Nea yelled, and a dark-handled knife thudded into the ground beside his feet.

Familiar magic clung to the knife, cold and swirling like Nea's keen. A voice whispered across the back of his mind, compelling him to take hold of the hilt. Without a second thought, he grasped it and pulled it free from the dirt. He would have preferred a sword—the moment the thought crossed his mind, the blade lengthened and the hilt shaped under his fingers as cold magic sang along his veins.

"Xaria's razor? That's impossible," Ambrose growled.

"*Improbable*," Harvey said, hefting the weight of the blade. It felt like it had been made for his hand. "Not impossible." He lunged forward, almost expecting to be brought up short again, but the magic of the sword throbbed through his core, and the tip drove soundly into Ambrose's chest.

He staggered back, his hands closing around the several inches of blade still free of his body. Blood welled from his palms as he tugged Harvey closer. "Tell me, how does patricide feel? Not even I had the gall to kill my own father." As the last word left his lips, he collapsed to his knees then keeled sideways.

Nea gently took the sword from Harvey. It shifted again, this time into a delicate rapier that hugged her hand as though it had been meant for her. She swallowed and pressed the base of her thumb to her nose, which was bleeding. Gwyn was nowhere to be seen.

"She got away," she said softly. "Are you alright?"

Was he alright? No. No, he was definitely not alright. "I'm—"

"Before you say fine, just know I am very familiar with that lie." Was that an attempt at humour? She wasn't smiling.

"No. I'm not alright. Are you?"

She shook her head. "But I didn't just kill my own father."

"He wasn't my father. I never had a real one of those, nor did I need one. He was simply my creator, and he needed to die."

"That doesn't mean you have to be okay with it. If I hadn't been distracted by Gwyn—"

"Don't pretend you would have been okay with it either. I know she didn't just *get away* from you."

"Harvey. Nea." Emil came jogging over. The sounds of fighting were starting to wane around them. "Who is that?" He stared at the body at their feet.

"Ambrose," they said together.

He gave a sharp nod. "There's no sign of Leon. Garret thinks he's gone on ahead to the temple."

"Then we need to move. Leith has this under control now." Nea took off towards the edge of the camp where Garret, Declan, and Bran stood, surrounded by a ring of bodies. Judging by the cold remnants of necromancy in the air and the drained look on Bran's face, they had been reanimations.

"Emil said Leon—"

"Are you alright, my lovely?" Declan asked, cutting Nea off.

She let out a huff. "I had a run in with Gwyn—I'm alright," she added the last quickly as Garret took a step towards her, his jaw tightening. "My keen has just been stretched to its limits today."

"We can rest and regroup," Garret said.

"There's no time. Leon has a head start and if he finds those thrones ..."

"He can't use them though, can he? Not without you and Garret anyway," Emil said.

"We don't know that for certain. Ambrose was extremely good at finding magical loopholes. I won't rest until we've seen this through to the end just to be safe."

"But you're practically dead on your feet." Emil was right, but Harvey wouldn't have said it out loud like that, especially given the scathing look Nea settled on the warden. He just shrugged it off though. "Don't look at me like that. What would Nonna say?"

"It doesn't matter what she would say because she's not here right now."

"But I am," Margot said. Her eyes were still a soft pink, and a second black streak had appeared in her hair. Molly, Penny, and Janey stood behind her, and Mateus, Rourke, Zephyr, and Wade were making their way over as well. Zephyr leant heavily on Wade, her face pale and drawn. Both Declan and Margot rushed to her, Nea's exhaustion seemingly forgotten.

"I'm fine," she said, waving them away. "I just need a rest."

"We're wasting time," Nea said, taking a step towards the path that led out of the camp.

Garret grabbed hold of her wrist, and his keen flared for a moment, sending a small tremor through the source. Nea's keen rose in response as though it had been revitalised. "Better?"

"Much. Thank you." She gave him a small smile and pressed a kiss to his cheek. "Let's go."

He nodded then turned back to the rest of them. "Ready?"

"I'll just see to Zephyr, and then we'll catch you up," Margot said.

The rest of them fell into step behind Nea and Garret. Janey slid her hand into Harvey's and gave his fingers a squeeze. He wasn't sure how this was going to end, but he was glad for the company marching along around him, especially Janey. With her warm presence by his side, he felt he could face down whatever else Leon had to throw at them.

CHAPTER THIRTY-THREE

NEA

The ever-shifting magic of the Between permeated the air around them, a siren song tugging at her core and dragging her feet forward. Garret's keen throbbed under her skin, bolstering her own and giving her exhausted body just enough energy to see this through.

The path steepened into a set of age-worn steps with crumbling archways rising above them, and that magic singing through her increased as the air warmed, making her fur-lined jacket uncomfortable. She slipped out of it as she picked up her pace, nearly breaking into a run. The trees that sided the road were lush and green, untouched by the snow that fell everywhere else on the mountain.

As she reached the top stair, a large stone plateau opened out before her, and she sucked in a series of deep breaths. A single archway stood a short distance away, flanked by two statues. One was a large hound with stars carved across his back, the other a depiction of the Bright Mother, her hair tumbling over her naked breasts. In front of the archway stood Leon, his head tilted back as he examined the statues.

"Ah, Nea, perfect timing as always," he said as he slowly turned. One side of his face was covered by the black webbing of corruption, the pupil of that same eye a dark violet. The source around him was twisted and thorny. "I should thank you for sparing Gwyn. Her keen was the last little boost I needed. Ambrose gave me a gift, you see." He stroked his blackened cheek.

Gwyn's body was slumped by the edge of the plateau, the tiniest flicker of keen clinging to it.

"Shall we proceed?" Leon asked, lifting his hand.

Molly's gasp drew Nea's attention to her. The keystone was floating in front of her, the chain pulling against the back of her neck. Molly gripped the stone as the chain snapped and it jolted towards Leon. Her feet dug into the ground, but the stone slipped through her fingers, whistling through the air before landing in Leon's open hand.

He traced his fingers over its quartz-studded surface before placing it in the outstretched hand of the Bright Mother statue.

Garret started forward, but the ground shuddered, knocking him back as a deafening scraping noise filled the air.

Technicoloured light formed a dome over the plateau. The sky split, a dark shape emerging from the twisting landscape beyond the tear to land with a heavy thump behind the archway. It was a gargantuan dog with large, branching antlers set between its ears and long whiskers that formed a kind of beard around its muzzle.

It turned its head to regard Leon with one amber eye before shifting its gaze to study Nea and Garret. "Only those of the divine blood may proceed beyond this gate," it said in a rumbling voice.

"I am the son of your Master. It is my right to claim the power you guard." The Usurper's voice twisted with Leon's as he spoke.

"The skin you wear is tainted. Are you certain you wish to risk losing your prize?"

"As the rightful heir of Shadow, I order you to open the gate," Leon said.

The dog sat back on his hind quarters and rested his paws on the top of the arch. The air within lit up with the shimmering miasma of a portal. Leon sneered at Nea over his shoulder and then leapt through.

"Only he who knows the mettle of his own soul will know the true treasure when he sees it." The deep rumbling voice of the dog reverberated through Nea. "You two may pass, but the rest must stay."

Nea cast a glance at the others. "Wish us luck then," she said and slipped her hand into Garret's, tugging him towards the gate.

This portal was different to the ones she created. It felt like walking through thick treacle with phantom fingers dragging over her skin and plying her hair. When she emerged on the other side, it was into a large circular room. Dozens of chairs of all different kinds littered the floor. Some of them had been knocked over and others smashed in a path that led across the centre of the space to the door at the other side.

"We should be care—" A violent shudder rattled the chairs, throwing some onto their sides and knocking Nea into Garret.

He steadied her on her feet. "What do you think the guardian meant?"

She worried her lip as they picked their way through the still-trembling chairs, pausing to brace themselves as another shudder rocked the room. "I am guessing that the thrones are not going to be out in plain sight, and there will be some kind of puzzle or challenge we must beat to find them. We are in a pocket of the Between, so I expect this place acts in a similar way to the labyrinth."

"I figured as much," he said, his voice weary.

The thought that this was the end, no matter what happened, kept Nea moving forward towards that door, but the fear that Leon would somehow manage to claim the thrones set a band around her chest.

The next room was the same size as the first, but the chairs here lined the walls like spectators around a ring. Leon stood in the centre of the clear patch of floor and behind him a stone golem, ribbons of black and purple magic twisting around it.

"This place is rather frustrating," the Usurper's voice drawled. "It's almost as ingenious as my labyrinth, but it lacks the same finesse." His dual-toned gaze settled on Nea as a calculating smile pulled across his mouth. "I have a proposition for you ... Or maybe your precious brightling might prefer my offer."

Garret put himself between Leon and Nea. "How many times do we have to reject your offer before you'll take the hint?"

"There's no need to take that tone with me. If you are subservient now, I will be more inclined to be compassionate with you once I have reclaimed my power." He licked his lip. "Make no mistake, you cannot win this fight. Mother and Father may have put all their remaining power into creating you both, but their effort *will* prove futile."

While the Usurper was focused on Garret, Nea scanned the chairs at the side of the room, then she turned her attention to the door behind the golem. Glowing runes ringed the arch around it. If only she could get closer.

"I wouldn't," the Usurper said as she edged towards the door. "It's a clever trap." He gestured to the golem. "Once triggered, he must have blood before the door will open. You see, one cannot claim ultimate power without giving something in return. My Father's rule, that one. He always was a selfish bastard. All magic must come at a price." He let out a sniggering laugh. "Of course, it did give me both the idea and the means to create my corruption. Mortals are so willing to give their souls to me for *just a little more power*."

"That's why two were needed. A child of Bright and a child of Shadow," Nea whispered as she eyed the golem. It had a long blade of obsidian in one hand. "That's why you were creating deathborn and you had Ambrose create Amelia. It was only partially about getting out of the Between. If you could inhabit a body, then you could face this trial and the mortal body would be shed in the process. That's the sacrifice you must make."

"You see that brilliant mind of yours is why you would have made the perfect consort. But we've wasted too much time talking, and I have a throne to claim."

"If the golem will kill Leon's body but leave you able to pass through the door, why haven't you?" Garret asked.

"Because he's afraid that it won't work," Nea said. "He has to trust that it will, and he can't because he lacks faith."

"Maybe I am not ready to give up this body. As wretched as the mind it housed was, the skin is ... comfortable. And I will admit, I love seeing that little glimmer of fear in your eyes when you look upon this face. You didn't look at me with the same trepidation when I wore my own skin."

Nea swallowed and took a step towards the door. The golem turned its focus to her. She closed her eyes and clenched her fists to stop her fingers shaking. Bran had a tiny piece of her soul safe. If she was right, then Garret would survive this. He had to. She turned back to face him. "Whatever happens, you need to beat him," she said, then spun and ran for the door.

"NO!" Garret's shout reverberated through her as her palms slammed against the wall of rock and she sent her magic out into it.

The golem turned, and the obsidian blade tore through her. She bit down on her lip as she fell to her hands and knees, scarlet splattering the stones between her palms. Each pound of her heart was agony as the world seemed to hold its breath then, with a loud scrape that reverberated through her soul, the door opened.

CHAPTER THIRTY-FOUR

GARRET

He'd known from the moment the Usurper started talking about sacrifices that Nea would throw her life away if it meant saving everyone. But it could have been him; it should have been. He stared after her, but her hands slammed against the wall in the centre of the archway, her keen washing out in a cold splash.

The golem moved at lightning speed, the obsidian blade flashing as it dove clean through Nea's torso, and she fell to the ground with a pained gasp.

"Such a waste," the Usurper muttered and stepped around Nea as the wall grated open to reveal a thin slice of the room beyond.

Garret didn't follow, though he probably should have. Nea herself had said whatever happened he had to beat the Usurper. But how could he when the one person who had come to matter most in the world was bleeding out in front of him? He expected it to feel different, given the death ward would take him too. Maybe there was a delay or maybe that pain slicing through his chest wasn't his heart breaking. He lunged forward, his keen flickering out of his control. Why hadn't he taken the time to learn to use healing magic? He might be able to save her if he had.

"Why?" He hovered, afraid to touch her in case it made the end come quicker.

"One of us had to, and I couldn't bear the thought of it being you." She coughed and winced.

It *should* have been him. He caught her as she started to slump sideways, her hands trailing through the puddle of blood beneath her.

"Go," she implored and pressed her palms against his chest, her violet gaze shining.

There was no point. The second she breathed her last, so would he. That was how the death ward worked, wasn't it? But her death would come slowly. He'd seen men with similar wounds take hours, sometimes days to die. Maybe he had time to beat the Usurper and then get Nea back to Margot. Margot would know what to do.

He moved her to the wall and rested her gently against it, then he touched a kiss to her lips and hoped it wouldn't be the last.

As he turned to follow the Usurper, she whispered, "Wait."

He looked back at her.

Her eyes were closed, her forehead furrowed and mouth tight with pain. "I love you."

This wasn't how he wanted to remember her, but if death claimed her, it would claim him too, so he wouldn't be left with that image for long. "I love you," he said, then stepped through the stone archway.

The room was empty save for Leon standing in the centre, his back to Garret. His shoulders were tight and his fists clenched by his sides. He spun around as Garret approached.

"She's not dead yet then," he said in a soft drawl that sounded something between Leon's voice and the Usurper's. "I wonder how she'll feel when she learns she threw her life away for nothing. Your life too, I suppose. It must be agony—"

Garret tackled him with a growl, and they both went tumbling to the ground. Leon kicked and thrashed, breaking free and rolling away. But Garret followed him, pulling his brightling keen to the surface. He ignored the prickling static of the storm magic that stirred with his anger and instead focused on the deep chill of Nea's keen. He drove the fingers of that twisted version of necromancy along the edge of the Usurper's soul and latched on, hauling it towards himself.

Leon's body jerked, and his mismatched eyes widened. "You can't kill me," the Usurper said, but his tone didn't sound so sure.

Garret tugged at the soul again, and Leon fell to his knees, a trickle of blood running from his nose.

"Now, now," the Usurper gasped. "You're wasting your time with me. You should be finding the thrones. After all, if you don't then Nea's sacrifice will be in vain."

"Killing you would still solve the problem."

"Except, I'm a god-kin who cannot be killed. Even if that were not the case, as long as the Sovereigns are in their weakened states, their powers are there for the taking and I am not the only being waiting for a chance at full godhood."

Garret twisted the soul and felt several of the strings holding it to the body snap. He might not be able to kill the Usurper, but he could tear him out of Leon's body and send him back to the Between. It would buy him time to find the thrones and return to Nea.

"It's entertaining watching that mind of yours work."

"Shut up." Garret yanked the soul again, and another thread tore.

The Usurper felt that one because all the colour drained from Leon's face. "What are you—"

Garret pulled again and forced as much keen as he could into the action. The scent of blood filled his nose, and his temples started to ache. Just one more burst and—he yanked savagely, and the threads tore. Leon staggered backwards, and the soul in the grip of Garret's keen thrashed. He had felt necromancers send souls before, and he'd learned enough about the barrier from Nea that he understood the process. He focused on the source and on the feeling of the Between then fed that feeling with the necromancy.

A massive stone wall appeared, emerald moss and silvery lichen adorning the grey stones. The section of stones directly in front of him folded back to reveal a twisted landscape. It wasn't the Between as he remembered it from being there physically, but Nea had said it appeared differently from this side of the barrier. He tightened his grip on the Usurper's soul and flung it across the barrier then slammed it closed.

Pain blossomed against his jaw, and sparks scattered across his eyes. He staggered away and drew his sword as Leon snarled and leapt for him.

Leon drew his own. "It's a shame Nea went and got herself killed; I was looking forward to delivering that blow myself."

Garret charged. Metal clashed and scraped, sending a shockwave down his arms.

"You should thank me. After all, this will be a mercy killing. Nea's death will be slow and agonising, but I will make yours quick." He lunged, and Garret dodged, twisting at the last second and sliding around Leon's defence to deliver a clean slice to his side.

Leon snarled. "Did Nea tell you that I was going to fu—"

Garret landed a bone-jolting punch to his jaw. He shook the ache from his hand, dodging backwards as Leon went on the offensive again.

"Touched a nerve, did I? I was going to make her—" His body jerked, eyes widening as they dropped to study the dark blade sticking through his heart. A dribble of red ran down his chin, and he staggered to his knees to reveal Nea standing on shaking legs behind him, the caged guard of a sword wrapped around her hand like a gauntlet of roses. She let out a ragged, panting breath and slumped to the floor, the blade clattering away from her limp fingers.

"There are no thrones," Garret said as he knelt beside her.

"Remember what the guardian said," she whispered and shut her eyes; her breath was coming in ragged gasps. She didn't have much longer.

What had the guardian said? *Only he who knows the mettle of his own soul will know the true treasure when he sees it.*

"The thrones aren't physical. But then how can we claim them?" He stood and turned in a slow circle, examining the floor. There was a tile that had a faded orange eight-pointed star and another with a purple rose. He walked to the star tile and brushed his fingers over its smooth surface. The lines lit up, and his keen warmed under his skin. Power was locked beneath the temple—bright, warm power that was holding the whole complex together. Something was twisted around that warmth. A deep chill full of unfathomable secrets. The sensations seemed contained behind a seething tangle of dark magic.

Was the entire temple the seat of the Sovereigns' power? Was that why there were no actual thrones?

Garret moved back to Nea and carefully scooped her up. She mumbled something too soft to hear and tried to lift her hand, but her arm just twitched at her side, her fingers flexing. He carried her to the rose tile and gently laid her upon it. Her keen flared in response, and a shudder went through the temple. Then he moved back to the star tile again and stood at its centre. His keen stirred, pulling into the ground beneath him, and another shudder rocked the temple, but nothing else happened. He studied Nea where she lay staring blankly at the ceiling, her chest barely stirring.

The dark cage of magic that contained the Sovereigns' power twisted, itchy fingers pulling at the edges of Garret's keen as though it would capture that too. It was almost like a stickier version of corruption. He traced the death ward; Nea's keen was a weak flutter beneath its surface. When she had cured his corruption, she had seemed to take it into herself and then send it out again. What if he did the same now with this magic?

He crouched and placed his hands against the floor, letting his brightling keen out. It wrapped around the seething darkness, and he pulled it towards himself. The silver scars of corruption on his side itched, but the braying voice of the Usurper didn't rise to scrape against his mind. He pulled more and more of the darkness into himself, and then Nea's keen burst in an icy spike, twisting around the corruption and forming it into something new.

The magic rolled in a wicked heat through his limbs, only to be replaced with a teeth-chattering cold. When he could no longer stand the sensation, he forced it out of his body and into the floor of the temple. A web of cracks fanned out through tiles around him, sending small chips of mosaic flying into the air. Another shuddering jolt ran through the temple, then the walls started to crumble, and Garret found himself hurtling through empty space.

He landed softly in a grassy meadow, two statues standing before him. One was a dark granite hound, the other a creamy yellow cat. Nea was spread out on the grass before the statues, her entire form deathly still. He dropped to his knees and pressed his head into his hands.

A gentle flutter stirred his hair, and he lifted his head again. A glowing bird was flitting around him. It let out a trill and then flew down to land on Nea's chest. Her keen stirred under the death ward, and the bird flitted to the statue of the dog and perched there.

"I don't know what else you want from me," he said. Nea would know what to do, but she—"We gave you everything we had."

The bird let out a sharp chirp and ruffled its feathers.

Weren't they supposed to claim the Sovereigns' power for themselves and send it back to them somehow? But he didn't want their power. He wanted Nea to sit up and give him one of those soft smiles. To chide him for being stubborn or tell him that everything was going to be fine and then slide her hand into his and lead him home. What good was all the power in the world if it couldn't fix what had been broken?

"I don't want to claim the thrones," he said, and the bird tilted its head. "I don't want power or godhood. I just want the world set to rights."

"Then you know the mettle of your soul," the voice of the Bright Mother said as she appeared in the place of the cat statue. Orbs of golden light drifted down from the sky. They twisted around her, and as each one entered her body, it seemed to glow brighter. "I wish that returning my power had not come at such a cost." She glanced at Nea.

The Shadow man had appeared in his human form as well. He was surrounded by similar orbs to the Mother's, but his were nearly every shade of purple imaginable. He bent and brushed Nea's hair back from her forehead and then met the Bright Mother's eye and shook his head.

"You can't save her? But you are gods—take my life and spare hers."

"It doesn't work that way, and even if we could, we wouldn't," the Mother said gently.

Garret nodded; it didn't matter—the ward would take him soon too.

"I don't think it will." The Shadow Man responded to Garret's unspoken thought. "Nea has done something to her ward mark. I expected her tenacity and cleverness when I chose her. Her bloodline has always produced exemplary rule breakers. It only stands to reason that she of all people would find a loophole to the death ward's life-stealing properties."

"If she tampered with the mark, does that mean—" He rushed to her and pressed his fingers against her neck. Nothing. His keen brushed over her, searching for that familiar soothing cool. But it had fled her body entirely. A lump tore through his chest and settled in throat as he pulled her into his lap. He pressed a kiss against her hairline then rested his forehead against hers.

"It appears I am late to the party," the Usurper said. "Sorry about Nea. It was a terrible waste but fear not, because the second I claim my parents' powers, I will send you to join her."

Garret gently placed Nea on the grass and stood to face the Usurper.

"You can't hope to beat me—not when you have rejected the Sovereigns' power."

"He's right," the Shadow Man said. "Take Nea and go." He moved his dark violet gaze to the Usurper. "We should have locked your soul away when we had the chance."

Locked his soul away. The Usurper had a collection of souls locked in jars in his Night Estate and one particularly ornate glass vessel that had been intended for Nea. Could the Usurper's soul be trapped within that glass? If Garret could make a portal, he could go to the Night Estate and retrieve the phylactery. He could use all the other functions of Nea's keen—there seemed to be no reason he *couldn't* create portals as well. Pulling the familiar cool of Nea's necromancy to the surface, he studied his hand, and a flicker of lilac ran over his fingers.

Without a second thought, he charged and focused on the source directly behind the Usurper as he tackled him. An oval doorway opened, accompanied by the sound of ripping fabric, and the momentum of Garret's charge carried them both right through it. They rolled across the floor of the Usurper's private chambers. The glass phylacteries contained in one of the shelves at the side of the room rattled against each other as Garret slammed the Usurper against their shelf.

"Oh, you think you're clever, do you?" The Usurper snarled and drove his fist into Garret's gut. "What do you hope to accomplish here? I'll just end you and hop back to my parents. Until their powers fully return, they will be vulnerable."

Garret had staggered backwards and bumped into the pedestal holding the ornate vessel within its robrillium cage. He gripped the neck of the bottle and lurched forward, slamming the open mouth into the centre of the Usurper's chest. He didn't know how it was supposed to work, but he used Nea's keen to grab the edge of the Usurper's soul and drag it towards the opening.

"No!" The Usurper snarled and punched Garret's jaw. He grabbed the phylactery and tried to pull it away from himself, but his form was starting to fade. A dark purple mist swirled in the bottom of the vial; it was laced with flickers of black.

With a last snarl, the Usurper disappeared completely, and a robrillium stopper formed over the neck of the bottle. Garret drew a long breath and summoned another portal. It was easier than he was expecting, as though the source was just waiting to spring open for him. He stepped back into the meadow where the Bright Mother and the Shadow Man sat beside Nea's still form. They both stood as he approached and held the phylactery out.

The Shadow Man took it with a sardonic twist of his mouth. "Impaled on his own sword, was he?" He placed the vessel on the ground, and a new statue appeared; a large black boar. "Yes, that seems appropriate. Now." He turned to Garret. "I imagine you will want to be getting back to your realm."

Garret didn't want to go back, not without Nea. But she would want to go home and be laid to rest in the Hartswood grove. He rubbed his hands over his face then bent and scooped her up.

"You have both our deepest sympathies and our heartfelt gratitude," the Bright Mother said.

It was hard to be angry with her. And even if he could, Nea wouldn't have wanted him to be angry with either of the deities that stood before him now.

"Not that either sentiment means anything to you at this time, we are sure." She waved her hand, and a portal opened in front of him.

"Don't forget this." The Shadow Man held out the sword Nea had used to kill Leon. It shimmered with magic then shortened into a dark knife that Garret recognised. The one Nea had given him with the dark metal blade and the roses carved around the handle. "I'll just—" The Shadow Man slipped the knife into Nea's satchel and balanced it on top of her. "I am truly sorry." His violet gaze bored through Garret and seemed to scrape against his soul in the way Nea's always had.

With a nod, Garret stepped through the portal and back onto the stone plateau. The guardian was gone, but all his and Nea's friends were standing there waiting. Janey noticed him first, her green eyes widening as she took in Nea's limp form, and then tapped Harvey on the shoulder to get his attention.

As Harvey's questioning gaze met his, Garret swallowed down the lump that rose and laid Nea carefully on the ground.

"No. No, no, no." Bran dodged around Harvey and rushed to Garret. "She's not—is she?" He dropped to his knees and pressed his fingers against her neck the way Garret had done.

Garret was sure his face had shown the same look of anguish.

"No. You promised me!" He clenched his fists and punched the ground beside Nea. "You *promised*!" His sapphire gaze met Garret's. "She promised," he whispered in a defeated voice.

"Nea!" Margot's broken tone tore through Garret's chest, and he had to swallow the sob that threatened to rise. She slid in beside Bran, her healing keen flaring in a deep warmth.

A hand fell on Garret's shoulder, and he met Declan's green eyes, which were swimming with tears. "I'm so sorry, Garret. I ..." One brow flicked up, and his mouth twisted curiously. "*How?*"

"How?" Garret blinked and gestured to the wound in her stomach. How did he think?

"Not that. How are you still standing when she's ...?" He gestured to Nea's prone form, seemingly unable to finish the sentence.

Oh. He toyed with his scar. "She did something to her death ward." Then what Bran had been saying hit him. "Bran?"

The boy stood to make room for Penny and Emil, who had come running. Penny made a strangled noise and dropped beside Margot, but Emil just sucked in a deep gasping breath and met Garret's gaze, his hands shaking.

"Bran, what did Nea promise?" Garret asked slowly.

"She thought she might not survive, so she ..." He rolled his sleeve back to reveal an indigo mark in the shape of a crescent moon.

"Is that an oathing?" Declan asked.

"Donnic said it was like an oathing. Nea told me if she locked a piece of herself in here, then the death ward wouldn't kill you if she died. She said she got the idea from what Declan did."

"What I did?" His green eyes widened, and he grabbed Bran's arm to run his fingers over the mark. "Is she here in spirit form, like I was?"

"I can't see her or feel her," Bran replied.

"Nea couldn't see or hear you until she performed the re-enactment, remember?" Garret said to Declan. He couldn't feel Nea either, but the tiny piece of her keen trapped under Bran's skin was calling to him in a way that made his death ward ache. "May I see that mark, Bran?"

Bran pulled his arm free of Declan's fingers and placed his wrist on Garret's open palm.

"Did Nea explain how it was supposed to work?"

Bran shook his head. "She said I would be able to bring her back. I think she meant make her a deathwalker like Declan. But I have no idea where to start."

"Do you have the anchor?" Wade asked, seeming to materialise beside Bran.

Bran fished inside his shirt and pulled out a long silver chain on which a rose-shaped pendant hung.

Wade nodded and held his hand out. When Bran dropped the pendant into his waiting palm, he examined it then gave a nod and moved to Nea. He gently slipped the chain over her head before settling the rose at the centre of her chest. "Rourke," he said softly. "Show the lad what needs to be done."

Rourke guided Bran to Nea's side. He rolled her sleeve back and examined her death ward, which was currently a milky apricot colour.

Garret edged closer to watch.

"Arm," Rourke said to Bran and snapped his fingers.

Bran held his arm out for Rourke.

Rourke nodded and pulled a knife from his belt. "Sorry, it's going to sting." He drew the blade across the crescent-shaped mark and then did the same to Nea's death ward. Then he pressed the two marks together. "It's up to you now. You need to separate the piece of her keen from under your skin and send it back to her. It should revive her."

Bran licked his lip. "What about that?" He pointed at the stab wound.

"It won't be a problem."

The cool kiss of necromancy built as Bran's keen stirred. All necromancy felt similar, but each individual necromancer had a slightly different *essence* to their keen. Bran's was as close to Nea's as Garret had ever felt. It was deep and steady, almost soothing, and it was easy to imagine it taking on the same breath-stealing cold that Nea's did at times. The rose pendant shone with purple magic, which rippled out over Nea's form before fading. A snag formed in the source, and Garret glanced around. It felt like Declan had when he was in spirit form, haunting Nea. Something brushed against his shoulder, and the scent of peppermint clouded his senses, then both the scent and the snag were gone.

After a while, Bran's keen died down, and he sat back on his heels. He examined Nea's face then flicked a look at Margot and Emil before settling his gaze on Garret. "It didn't work ... I'm sorry." He collapsed forward, burying his face against Nea's chest as a deep sob broke from him and his shoulders shook.

Garret crouched and placed a hand on the boy's back. The stab wound had drawn into a thin scar visible through the tear in Nea's shirt. It seemed to glint with magic as Bran shifted and the light hit it.

"She promised me it would work. She trusted me, and I let her down." Bran's voice wavered as sobs rattled through him.

This close, the piece of Nea's keen inside Bran's body was strong. It invaded every inch of Garret and seared along the lines of the death ward.

"Bran, it's alright." Nea's bloodstained fingers contrasted against the snow-white hair of the boy.

"I failed. I—Nea! You're alive." He engulfed her in a tight hug.

"I won't be if you keep crushing me." She smiled weakly at Garret over Bran's shoulder.

"Sorry. Sorry I should—" Bran dropped her and stepped away, but she caught herself on her elbows.

Garret started to stand.

"Where do you think you're going?" She grabbed him and pulled him back to her, pressing her lips against his.

He collapsed onto his backside and lifted her into his lap, not letting his mouth leave hers for a second.

CHAPTER THIRTY-FIVE

MARGOT

Margot pressed her hands over her mouth as Bran tried to revive Nea. Molly trembled against her side, tears cutting a path down her cheeks. They had won, but the victory felt hollow without Nea there to celebrate it.

"It didn't work ... I'm sorry." Bran's voice broke, and he fell across Nea, sobs tearing through him.

Garret crouched to soothe him. The tightness in the warden's jaw and the sorrow in his gaze broke Margot's heart all over. She couldn't imagine losing Molly ... twice. Garret had watched Nea die and then had the hope at Bran's revelation about bringing Nea back shattered.

"She promised me it would work. She trusted me, and I let her down," Bran said, his voice trembling.

Poor Bran. Margot should be furious at Nea for putting him through this. But she was too tired and heartsore to be angry.

"Bran, it's alright." That was Nea's voice.

She must be delirious with grief and hearing things. Nea was dead. Margot's keen had confirmed it, but Nea's hand was stroking the back of Bran's head. Margot blinked.

"I failed. I—Nea! You're alive." The relief in Bran's voice brought tears tumbling down Margot's cheeks.

Alive. Nea was alive!

"I won't be if you keep crushing me."

"Sorry. Sorry, I should ..." He flicked a look at Garret, who was staring at Nea as though all his deepest wishes had been granted. Bran let go of Nea and hopped to his feet, a beaming smile on his face as he clapped Rourke on the shoulder.

"Where do you think you're going?"

Garret had started to stand as well, and Margot took a step forward, but then Nea grabbed hold of Garret and dragged him down for a kiss. He sat and pulled her into his lap, kissing her in a way that made Molly whistle.

"Now that's what I call a kiss," Molly said with a grin.

"Jealous?" Margot asked, a delirious laugh bubbling up from nowhere.

"Of who? Nea or Garret?" Molly wrapped her arms around the back of Margot's neck. "The answer—if you're wondering—is neither." She pressed a light, slightly salty kiss to Margot's lips. "But I am happy. After everything Nea's been through, she didn't deserve to die like that."

"Don't tell me you've—"

Molly silenced her with another kiss. "I will deny it until my last breath," she whispered against Margot's lips. "But yes, I might have changed my mind about Nea."

"I won't tell a soul."

"Margot?" Nea asked.

Margot let go of Molly and turned to the woman who had always been her sister, even though they weren't bound by blood. Her normally pale skin was almost as white as Bran's hair, her clothes covered in blood. "Nea."

"I'm sorry I made you worry." Nea let out a sob on the last word and threw her arms around Margot's neck. Margot staggered back a step.

"Margot? What about me?" Emil said, and Nea threw out her arm, tugging him into the hug.

As Penny and Mateus took their turn to welcome Nea back, Margot moved to stand with Garret and Harvey.

"I don't know about you two, but I have certainly had enough adventure for several lifetimes," Harvey said.

Garret nodded.

"So, what now?" Harvey asked.

What now indeed? They needed to get back to the capital and help Leith fix things there, then they needed to rebuild Loch Bastien, and someone would need to check on Merston. And there were the wraiths at the Crossroads to contend with ... and—

Someone cleared their throat, and they all turned. A man was standing there. He had bronze skin hinting at Osmarian heritage, and the keen clinging to his form had the warm throb of healing magic.

He met Garret's eye and gave a nod. "I came for Gwyn," he said.

Garret pointed to the woman laid out at the edge of their small group.

Whatever Leon, or rather the Usurper, had done had exhausted her keen beyond anything Margot had ever seen. That she was still breathing at all was a sheer miracle, or perhaps it was something to do with the experiments that Ambrose had used to create her.

The man frowned and moved to crouch by Gwyn's side. "What a mess you've gotten yourself into this time." His tone was the same one that Emil used with Nea and Margot—intimate but in a brotherly way.

"I tried to help her, but ..." Margot said as she joined him. "Leon drained all but the tiniest thread of her keen. I don't think she will recover." The anchor throbbed, and Margot rubbed her palm. "By the way, I'm Margot."

"Hugh," he said, automatically taking her offered hand.

His keen was soft and steady, the warmth of healing magic accompanied by something bright and flickering that reminded Margot of Arcarnius Greffon.

"I warned her that Leon would turn on her, that like Ambrose, he considered us disposable." He spat the last word.

"I can end it now if you want. It would be kinder—"

"I can help her," Nea said. "She hasn't died yet because her soul is still tethered to her physical form. Most likely due to what Ambrose did to her to alter her keen. I can put her back inside her body and it might help. Or she might die ... She will still suffer the symptoms of exhausting her keen."

"You would help her? But she—"

"If she does survive, then she will need to be held accountable for her actions in assisting Leon. I cannot save her from that, and frankly, even if I could, I wouldn't." She touched the scar on her cheek. "But this death will be slow and wasting, and she doesn't deserve that. Alternatively, I can sever the threads binding her to this body. It will be over quickly which, as Margot has already mentioned, would be kinder."

Hugh licked his lip as he studied Nea. "I'm sorry I couldn't prevent some of the scars."

Nea waved his apology away. "What do you want done with Gwyn?"

"If she survives, is there a chance she will be executed for assisting Leon?"

Margot and Nea shared a look.

"Leith is nothing like his father. He is more inclined to be lenient, but I imagine he will have her powers bound indefinitely," Margot said. "I am sure I don't need to tell you what sort of effect that might have on her."

"There is also a chance that Leon has permanently damaged her keen, and even if he hasn't, it will take some time for her to get back to full strength," Nea said.

Hugh drew a long breath. "Heal her if you can. Please."

Nea nodded, and her keen frosted the air. She placed her fingertips on the centre of Gwyn's forehead, and a ripple of lilac magic shimmered over her body. As Nea removed her fingers, Gwyn drew a ragged breath and opened her sea-green eyes. Her lip rolled, and she made a lunge for Nea, but her body didn't respond the way she was expecting, and she collapsed onto the ground again.

"What have you done to me?" Gwyn panted, glaring daggers at Nea.

"She saved you," Hugh said. "After the pain you have caused her, she certainly didn't have to, but she did anyway."

"She stole my keen!" Gwyn drew a halting gasp and pressed her fingers to her temples.

"You have me confused with the Usurper. He stole your keen. I, if you remember correctly, spared you when I didn't have to, and I have saved you from a slow, wasting death as a favour to Hugh." The tone was familiar; it was the same one Nonna sometimes used when explaining something that she expected you to already be aware of.

"I would suggest you calm down, Gwyn. Your keen has been exhausted, and your body needs time to recover," Hugh said with the practiced manner of a healer who was used to his patients arguing with him.

"Well, I don't know about the rest of you, but I am more than ready to get off this rock and back home so we can celebrate. I mean, we just kicked some major arse and saved the world," Emil said.

Penny grinned as she threw an arm over his shoulders. "For once I am going to agree with Emil.

BRAN

It had taken the better part of three years to set everything back to rights, but it was good to finally see the bustle of activity returning to the capital. It probably would have happened sooner if Nea hadn't insisted on running off to join Wren and Gendry on The Azure Queen. She and Garret had spent about six months away at sea, recovering from the aftermath of the fight with the Usurper. Not that Bran could really blame them. Nea had sacrificed everything to save them all—if anyone deserved a good break it was her and Garret.

When they had returned, they had set about repairing the magic around Hartswood, starting with the lock-stone, which they replaced with Donnic and Harvey's help. The grove was almost back to the way it had been before Kieran destroyed it, but both Nonna and Nea seemed to think it would always bear the scars of the attack. Much like Kalhanna, he supposed.

The sky above college was still marked by the remnants of the tear in the form of a great shimmering line, like a seam in cloth, that was more visible at night. The lock-stone they had created to anchor the tear still stood proud in the centre of the old courtyard, but the magic that had roved in coloured ripples over it had died down as the source had restabilised itself over the past few years. People had flocked there to pay their respects, and it was now a shrine—not only to those who had lost their lives in the purge but also those who had been taken in the war against the Usurper. Given the increase in traffic to the site, Niall thought it best to have the relics and books removed from the Kalhanna repository and redistributed between Del Harol and Loch Bastien. Bran had assisted him and Declan in the task.

Leith had offered Garret his old position as Warden Commander of the capital garrison, but the warden had turned it down and suggested Emil be promoted instead. It was weird to see Emil in charge, but he had taken to the position like a duck to water. As had Declan to his new role as High Mage of Loch Bastien. He and Zephyr had also welcomed their son, Hector, into the world the autumn following the final fight against Leon. He was loud and curious like his father but had the same honey-coloured stare as his mother. And they weren't the only ones welcoming fresh blood into what Bran had come to think of as his found family. Janey was due any day now. That was one of the reasons Nea had brought Bran, Henry, and Garret back to the capital. That, and because Leith had summoned her. Bran had no idea what the reason for the summons was, but if some arsehole was threatening the world again, it was likely that Nea and Garret would just tell Leith to find someone else to deal with it. And Bran wouldn't blame them—he hadn't been central to *everything* that had occurred between the purge at Kalhanna and that final fight against Leon, but even he felt that he'd seen enough action to last him several lifetimes.

"Bran, were you listening?" Henry tugged at the side of Bran's shirt. He had the same silver-grey eyes as Leith, but his head was covered in an unruly mop of iron-grey curls, which marked him as a necromancer like his mother. But like Nea, Henry wasn't your run-of-the-mill necromancer. His keen had the same uncanniness that seers often possessed, and at times he spoke with a wisdom far beyond his years.

"Sorry, Henry, you have my full attention now." He bent slightly to meet Henry's stare. Not that he had far to bend. Henry seemed to have inherited his father's height, as well as his eyes, and he towered above most other seven-year-olds.

"I asked if you think Molly would like one of those chimes." He pointed to the brightly painted wind chimes hanging at a nearby stall.

"I think Margot would," Bran replied. Molly would probably prefer something she could stab someone with.

Henry tilted his head. "But it's not Margot's birthday next. It's Molly's. Garret?" He turned to face Nea and Garret, who were following them.

The warden had Nea tucked against his side as he pressed his lips to her forehead, but he glanced up as Henry called his name. "Yes, Henry?"

"Do you think you can help me carve one of those?" He pointed to the chimes again.

"Maybe," Garret answered with an indulgent grin. "Provided you sit still long enough."

"I will. But we'll need to make two—one for Molly and one for ... Adelyn."

"Adelyn?" Bran asked, flicking a look to Nea.

She shrugged. "No idea."

Henry just grinned. "Can we start tonight?" he asked Garret.

"Not tonight, but how about tomorrow afternoon?"

The boy nodded. "Tomorrow afternoon. By the way, Bran, that pretty girl is watching you."

Bran turned. A girl was indeed watching them. She stood farther down the market, partially concealed by the bulk of a stall. She had a head of dark curls through which beads and ribbons had been braided. Her skin was a warm brown that contrasted against the gold jewellery that adorned her wrists and throat. The sunset-coloured fabric of her shirt hugged her arms and chest but left her torso mostly bare. Bran had seen a similar outfit on Nea when she had returned from Quel'sapar several years ago.

As Bran's gaze met hers she hastily ducked out of sight.

"She's probably with the delegation from the Isles," Nea said. "And on that note, we shouldn't keep Leith waiting much longer."

"Do Bran and I have to go?" Henry asked. "I want to find that girl. Did you feel her keen? It was so strange—wait, don't tell Nora I felt that girl's keen without asking first. She'll lecture me about being impolite again."

Nea chuckled. "Yes, you and Bran have to come. But as soon as we are finished, we'll go and visit Margot and Molly at the clinic."

Henry made a face, but he grabbed Bran's hand and dragged him towards the palace.

Leith was waiting for them in the throne room. He had removed the heavy green and gold drapery that had been his father's colours and replaced everything with indigo and silver. He stood talking with a large man with skin a shade or two darker than the girl from the market.

"Ah, here they are now. Nea, Garret, I would like you to meet— oof." Henry had gone flying across the room and crashed into his father to deliver a hug. "Hello, Henry, it is good to see you, too."

Henry turned his silver gaze to the stranger. "Hello."

"Hello," the man said in a deep voice that reminded Bran of Rourke.

"Henry," Nea reprimanded.

"It's fine," Leith said, grinning at the boy. "How about you run up to the library. I am sure Cat would love to see you. She received a package of Osmarian sweets this morning."

Henry was gone nearly before Leith finished speaking.

"Sorry about that," Leith said to the stranger. "Now, Nea, Garret, and Bran, this is Idir from the Faridean Guild of Singers."

"A pleasure to meet you, Idir," Nea said, holding out her hand.

Idir studied the swirling grey marks that covered her skin with a strange smile before taking the hand. "Mateus said you were *different* ... Shadow-kin?"

Nea nodded. "I am guessing that this isn't a social visit," she said as Idir shook Garret's hand and then Bran's.

The Faridean mage's keen seem to sing along Bran's veins, and at first he couldn't quite make out just what kind of mage he actually was. Then a soft fingered touch at the edge of his mind alerted him. Mind mage.

"I see you are not the only unique mage in this city." He studied Garret and then Bran.

Ever since Bran had housed a piece of Nea's magic inside himself, his own keen had been different, as though it had taken on some of the properties of Nea's. He hadn't tested that theory; he wasn't sure he wanted to do even half the things Nea could.

"Idir is here because Chief Soma's son has been exhibiting some strange behaviours, and Mateus suggested you would be the best mage to help him," Leith said to Nea.

"His song has changed," Idir said, turning his warm gaze on Nea. "It is not something we have encountered before. The new song is discordant and has granted him the ability to move souls from one body to another. Not the souls of the dead but the souls of the living."

Nea shared a look with Garret.

"Mateus assured me that you have an extensive understanding of soul magic. Would you come and inspect the boy? Then you might be able to help us find a way to fix his song."

She chewed her lower lip, her hand dropping to briefly touch her stomach. "I would be happy to assess the boy for you, but the isles are some distance away, and—" She flicked a look at Leith.

"We would happily compensate you," Idir said.

"What about Niall?" Garret asked. "He has a deep understanding of the way magic works. And whilst he is not a necromancer himself, he does have extensive knowledge of soul magic. Alternatively, could the boy be brought here instead?"

"Is it possible to speak with Niall?"

"Yes, of course. I can—"

"I'll go get him," Garret said, cutting Nea off and heading for the door.

"I am sorry that I can't be of much help at the moment, but my father, Niall, will be more than happy to assist. And I think you should go, too," Nea said to Bran. "A necromancer's insight will be helpful."

Idir sized Bran up. "Our soul singers have already studied the boy, and they have not been able to understand his song."

"Bran is different from normal necromancers. Between him and my father, you probably won't need my opinion on the boy," Nea said.

The Fardiean mage nodded slowly as his keen brushed against Bran's and that same strange smile touched the edge of his mouth. "Very well."

The door opened, and Garret returned with Niall in tow. Both had that unsteady, *just-been through a portal* look about them, but Niall smiled warmly at Idir. "I believe my particular skills are required."

"If you'll excuse me, I shall leave you in my father's capable hands," Nea said.

"It was a pleasure to meet you, Shadow-kin," Idir said with a dip of his head.

"Likewise," Nea replied before she ducked out the door, followed by Garret.

Bran frowned as he watched her leave. Why was she going out of her way to avoid travelling to the isles to study a previously unknown form of magic? Usually, she would be chomping at the bit for the opportunity. Unless— "Excuse me," he said over the top of Niall discussing the boy with Idir. He rushed out of the room and caught sight of Nea rounding the corner. "Nea, wait."

She and Garret had stopped in the next hall, and they both gave him a bemused smile as he reached them.

"Why didn't you tell me?" he blurted out.

"Tell him what?" Margot asked as she and Molly entered the hall from the other end. Her keen swelled in a thick warmth, and she grabbed hold of Molly's arm, drawing her to a stop as a wide grin split across her face. "*No.*" Her gaze dropped to scan Nea's body before flicking back to her face again. "When did this happen?"

"The month before last, but I didn't want to tell you in a letter."

"You're not?" Molly suddenly said.

"Bit slow on the uptake there, Mol." Margot chuckled.
"You do have an unfair advantage in this regard, Margot," Bran quipped. "Not all of us have a magical ability to sense these things, you know?" he added, his grin mirroring Margot's.

THANK YOU FOR READING SOVEREIGNS

If you enjoyed this thrilling conclusion to *Sovereigns of Bright and Shadow*, I would love it if you left me a review either at your favourite online store or on Goodreads.

Nea and Garret's story might be over but there are definitely more adventures to be had in the realms of Bright and Shadow. Starting with an upcoming series tentatively titled, *Isles of Bright and Shadow*. This new series will take us to the Faridean Isles. An archipelago full of strange magic the like of which we haven't seen before. Can our new cast of characters unravel the secrets of an ancient curse before the sleeping gods wake and drag the isles and all their inhabitants into the deep?

Book one due late 2022.

GLOSSARY

Bind-shackles: Bands of robrillium that prevent a mage from using their keen by blocking their connection to the source. Each pair is struck with its own key. If this key is lost, that pair can only be unlocked by a warden's keen.

Brightling: Extremely rare keen-folk who have the ability to absorb and use the keen of others or turn a mage's own keen against them, even though they seem to have no keen of their own.

Corruption: A type of possession / magical disease that primarily affects mages. The afflicted become increasingly violent as they slowly lose control of their minds and their keen.

Creationist: A type of mage who doesn't manipulate an element but can alter a certain type of matter. Wade is a creationist whose talent lies with cloth and tread, and Donnic's affinity is ink.

Deathborn: A mage who appears to be stillborn but reanimates within the hour following its birth. Only found among healers, mind mages, and necromancers, and even then, reasonably rare.

Death ward: (sometimes called deathbond) A type of oathing that permanently fuses the souls of two mages together. This bond is unbreakable and continues even after death. Because the souls are connected in this way, if one of the pair dies, so does the other.

Deera solvec: In the old language, it means Daughter of Shadow. Though Shadow-touched children could be any gender. Deera solvec possess the ability to tear holes in the barrier and create portals between worlds. Like brightling, they are extremely rare. However, unlike brightling, they are almost always born mages.

Devourer: A construct of thought and memory that dwells in the Between. They usually exist in nests, which consist of a Queen and her drones. They have no true shape of their own but can take on any shape they please. Usually they prefer to appear human in an effort to trick their prey.

High Mage: The head of each college of mages. There used to be an arch mage who was the head of all mages, but the position was dissolved long ago.

Keen: The soul essence of an individual or the 'flavour' of their magic. Interchangeable with the word magic, however, *keen* generally refers to the feeling of the life force of an individual and how that part of them interacts with the source as a whole. Magic is more so the direct effect they have on the world through channelling the source.

Keen-folk: A general term that covers all types of magic-users, not just mages and wardens, but seers and other gifted.

Keen-less: Those without magic.

Keen-sense: The ability to sense magic. Something all keen-folk innately have but also something that certain keen-less can possess (though this is rare).

Keen-touched: Sometimes interchangeable with keen-folk but generally used to refer to those keen-folk who are not mages or wardens. Seers and those gifted with 'low-magic' i.e. savants and prodigies who cannot control the source but have uncanny abilities regardless.

Lock-stone: A trans-dimensional construct that can be used as an anchor for magic. The lock-stone outside Hartswood solidifies the wards around the estate and protects it.

Mage: Keen-folk who have complete control of the source in one element E.g. weather (storm mages), fire, earth, water, healing, mind, death and the spirit world (necromancers) etc. There are certain nuances among the generic types of mages. For example: Sophia is a water mage, but she is particularly skilled with frost and ice magic. Declan is a storm mage who has an affinity for lightning, something not all weather mages are comfortable with.

Oathing: A kind of soul marriage between two mages. The bond dissolves after death. Often used for shorter-term pacts between individuals.

Oathbond: (sometimes called an oath ward) Refers to the connection created by an oathing.

Reanimation: Undead given 'life' by a necromancer. They are created by forcing a spirit, whether once human or not, into a corpse. They are generally mindless puppets controlled by the necromancer who resurrected them.

Robrillium: The enchanted metal used to create bind-shackles. It ranges in colour from light-pinkish gold through to a deep-rose gold.

Shadow-kin: What the Faridean's call those that possess the blood of the Shadow.

Shadow-touched: Those that have been somehow touched or tainted by the Shadow. They could be divine blooded or cursed. Those that are possessed or corrupted are sometimes also referred to as Shadow-touched.

Spirit-glass: Enchanted mirrors, usually made of obsidian or black glass, through which necromancers use to communicate. They can become corrupted and slowly steal the lifeforce of those using them; functioning ones are rare as a result of this.

The barrier: The veil between realms as seen by necromancers. It can appear in a range of different ways depending on the individual interacting with it. E.g. Nea's barrier is a hedge of pale-pink and grey roses, and Nonna's is a bramble of blackberries.

The Between: A magical spirit realm that the souls of the dead are believed to pass through on their way to the grove of the ancestors.

The maelstrom: An enchanted storm that exists in the stretch of ocean between Beldaren and Osmar, known as the Fathoms. It is a direct result of the actions of a group of mages several centuries ago, actions which also led to the sinking of the city of Port Brenna (now called Mother's Deep). Not much is known about the storm. Its movements are unpredictable, and any ship that passes through it either completely disappears or is washed up as a wreck miles away from the Fathoms.

The Order: The term used to refer to the wardens as a whole. Has a specific hierarchy of splinter cells and commanders.

The Source: The fabric of the universe from where keen-touched get their powers.

Thrones of Eternity: The mythological seat of the gods and the root of their power.

Warden: Keen-folk who can suppress the keen or connection to the source in other keen-folk. Theorised to be a type of mage even though they don't channel the source. Originally called ward mages.

ABOUT THE AUTHOR

C. E. Page has been dreaming up stories of faraway places and strange magics for as long as she can remember. She lives on the east coast of Australia with her partner, Evan, two balls of pure energy in the shape of young boys, and a honey badger masquerading as dog.

An avid reader and gamer, she loves devouring a good story in whatever form it takes.

You can find out more about her and her upcoming works at: www.cepageauthor.com